AF557808

A WONDERLAND *of* WORDS

Also by Shashi Tharoor

NON-FICTION

The Less You Preach the More You Learn: Aphorisms for Our Age (with Joseph Zacharias)

Ambedkar: A Life

Pride, Prejudice, and Punditry: The Essential Shashi Tharoor

The Battle of Belonging: On Nationalism, Patriotism, and What It Means to Be Indian

Tharoorosaurus

The New World Disorder and the Indian Imperative (with Samir Saran)

The Hindu Way: An Introduction to Hinduism

The Paradoxical Prime Minister: Narendra Modi and His India

Why I Am a Hindu

An Era of Darkness: The British Empire in India

India Shastra: Reflections on the Nation in Our Time

India: The Future Is Now (ed.)

Pax Indica: India and the World of the 21st Century

Shadows Across the Playing Field: 60 Years of India-Pakistan Cricket (with Shahryar Khan)

India (with Ferrante Ferranti)

The Elephant, the Tiger, and the Cell Phone: Reflections on India in the 21st Century

Bookless in Baghdad

Nehru: The Invention of India

Kerala: God's Own Country (with M. F. Husain)

India: From Midnight to the Millennium and Beyond

Reasons of State

FICTION

Riot

The Five Dollar Smile and Other Stories

Show Business

The Great Indian Novel

A WONDERLAND *of* WORDS

Around the Word in 101 Essays

SHASHI THAROOR

Illustrations by Priya Kuriyan

ALEPH

ALEPH BOOK COMPANY
An independent publishing firm
promoted by ***Rupa Publications India***

First published in India in 2024
by Aleph Book Company
161-B/4, Gulmohar House,
Yusuf Sarai Community Centre,
New Delhi 110049

ISBN: 978-81-19635-53-5

9 10 8

Printed in India.

In memory of my father
Chandran Tharoor
(17 December 1929–23 October 1993)
the author's author

'The true alchemists do not change lead into gold; they change the world into words.'

—William H. Gass

'I run after certain words... I catch them in mid-flight, as they buzz past, I trap them, clean them, peel them, I set myself in front of the dish, they have a crystalline texture to me, vibrant, ivory, vegetable, oily, like fruit, like algae, like agates, like olives... And then I stir them, I shake them, I drink them, I gulp them down, I mash them, I garnish them... I leave them in my poem like stalactites, like slivers of polished wood, like coals, like pickings from a shipwreck, gifts from the waves... Everything exists in the word.'

—Pablo Neruda

'Raise your words, not your voice. It is rain that grows flowers, not thunder.'

—Rumi

CONTENTS

Introduction: My World of Words xv

SECTION ONE
BORROWED PLUMES

1. British Versus American 3
2. Australian English 9
3. Irish Words in English 12
4. Words Borrowed from German 15
5. Indianisms 18
6. English Words of French Origin 23
7. Words from Japanese 26
8. Loanwords from Various Languages 29
9. Ukraine-related Words 32
10. Words That Don't Exist in English 36
11. Foreign Words You Must Know 41

SECTION TWO
THE POINT OF PUNCTUATION

12. Punctuation 45
13. Apostrophes 52
14. Hilarious Hyphens 57

SECTION THREE
SPELLING BUGS

15. Absurdities of Spelling 63
16. Silent Letters 69
17. The Rule of Ablautreduplication 74
18. Vowel Rules 77

SECTION FOUR
TYPOS, SUPERFLUITIES, MISPRINTS, AND OTHER ERRORS

19. Crash Blossoms 83
20. Misprints 86
21. Needless Words 89
22. Pleonasms 92
23. Ghost Words 96
24. Disputed Word Origins 99

SECTION FIVE
LINGUISTIC REGISTERS

25. Diplo-speak 105
26. The Language of Love 108
27. Language and the Environment 111
28. Words in the News 114
29. Idioms Using Places and Nationalities 117
30. Linguistic Afflictions 120
31. Phobias 123
32. Words About Money 126
33. Wartime Words 128
34. Nautical Jargon 131
35. Words from Aviation 134
36. The Language of Elections 137
37. The Language of Colonization 139
38. Computer Terms 142
39. Body Parts 147
40. Physically Active Words 149
41. Fabric(ating) Words 151

SECTION SIX
IN[APPROPRIATE] WORDS AND CARDINAL GUIDELINES

42. Appropriate Inappropriate Words 161
43. Literary Insults 164
44. Words About Nonsense 167
45. Most Hated Words 170
46. Forbidden Words 173
47. The Significance of Slang 176
48. Dysphemism 179

SECTION SEVEN
LITERARY TOOLS

49. It's OK! (Not Okay) 185
50. Acronyms 189
51. Alliteration 193
52. Anagrams 198
53. Aptagrams 201
54. Anaphora 204
55. Bacronyms 207
56. Contronyms 210
57. Eponyms 212
58. Homonyms 217
59. Oxymorons 220

SECTION EIGHT
LITERARY ACROBATICS

60. Eggcorns 225
61. Malapropisms 228
62. Paraprosdokians 231
63. Puns 234
64. Hyperbole 240
65. Red Herrings and Wild Geese 245

66. Spoonerisms 248
67. Ambiguous Sentences 251
68. Misnomers 254

SECTION NINE
BEER AND SKITTLES

69. English Quirks 259
70. Kangaroo Words 263
71. Kennings 267
72. Limericks 270
73. Palindromes 273
74. Mixed Metaphors 278
75. Zeugma 286

SECTION TEN
LEXICAL EVOLUTION

76. Food for Thought 291
77. Country Names 294
78. Long Words 299
79. Unpaired Words 302
80. Talking 'Turkey' 305
81. The Watergate Legacy 308
82. Words for Things You Couldn't Name 311
83. The Anecdoche Anecdote 313
84. Trademarks in Language 317
85. Can You Un-invent Words? 322
86. Idioms from Great Stories 325
87. Newspeak or Genocide 328
88. Plastic Words 331
89. Inkhorn Terms 334
90. Fossil Words 337

SECTION ELEVEN
LANGUAGE OF INCLUSION

91. Euphemisms 343
92. Words You Can't Use at Stanford 346
93. The Oxfam Language Rules 350
94. The Language of Equity 353
95. Sexist Language 356

SECTION TWELVE
MASTERS OF MIRTH

96. Captain Haddock's Expletives 361
97. Wodehousian Words 364
98. Books and Reading 369

SECTION THIRTEEN
BELLWETHERS

99. When Meanings Change 375
100. New Words for New Years 380
101. Words of the Year, 2021-23 383

Conclusion: The Linguistic Legacy 395
Acknowledgements 405
Notes 406
Bibliography 425

Introduction

MY WORLD OF WORDS

When my publishers at Aleph invited me to put together a book on words and language, I hesitated for a brief moment. A book on words (following on the heels of the successful *Tharoorosaurus*) was all very well, but did a serious politician really want to reinforce the image that had grown up of himself as an etymological egghead? As one journalist rather breathlessly asked me, 'Your vocabulary has become the subject of memes, comedy shows and now a book! Did you ever think things would take such a turn?'

Well, no, I didn't. I fell in love with language as a child, and used the words I came across quite unselfconsciously, as a beachcomber might blow into the shells he's picked up on a stroll along the seaside. But in the process, I found I had inadvertently acquired a rather inflated reputation as a vocabularist. Such reputations tend to build gradually, but mine reached escape velocity with a specific tweet. Incensed by a libellous TV programme about me, I had tweeted that it was 'a farrago of distortions, misrepresentations and outright lies broadcast by an unprincipled showman masquerading as a journalist'. These were all words I had flung about with abandon in my debating days at St. Stephen's College, Delhi, but for some reason this sentence did not just strike a chord but triggered an almighty wave of enthusiastic curiosity on the internet. The *Oxford English Dictionary* even recorded in some puzzlement an unprecedented spike on its search engines, with over a million people, mostly in India, looking up the meaning of the word 'farrago' within the span of a few hours. My notoriety was established—I was India's Mr Difficult Words.

From there it was a short step to being caricatured. Memes rolled off the versatile keyboards of those who seem to spend their creative juices entirely on web parody. Desi wits translated Diwali greetings and descriptions of bhelpuri into logorrheic English and attributed them to me. A clever meme-maker put my tweet into the mouth of Captain Haddock, replacing his usual 'billions of blue blistering barnacles', while a taken aback Tintin responds, 'Captain, I told you to stay away from that Shashi Tharoor fella!' Photographs of my meeting the then home minister, Rajnath Singh, were modified to add a speech bubble above his head, saying 'And I don't even have a dictionary!' While many of these were formulaic even if good-natured, the best was probably a rueful meme that stated, 'I used to think I was poor. Now I've met Shashi Tharoor and I realize I'm impecunious.'

There are only two things you can do when a tidal wave of caricature descends upon you like this—either sulk crossly and reject any attempt to slot you into the jokers' stereotypes, or embrace the caricature and try to turn it to your advantage. I preferred the latter course. I accepted an invitation to author a weekly column on words for the Dubai-based *Khaleej Times*. Many of these found wide circulation online, and the demand arose for a book. So here I am.

Yes, words have always mattered to me. My father, Chandran Tharoor, was an immense influence on my life. After a village and small-town education in rural Malabar, he had moved to the UK in 1948 and relearned English from scratch. He was my teacher, guide, research adviser, imparter of values, my source of faith, energy, and self-belief. My enthusiastic approaches to life and learning are inherited from him; so is my work ethic—and my love for words.

My father was a word-game addict, from Scrabble to Boggle and acrostics in newspapers. Of these, Scrabble was his favourite; Daddy was a Scrabble fanatic. He picked up the game as a young man in England, played it obsessively, and when he returned to India in 1958, organized a small group of equally dedicated Scrabble addicts in Mumbai for a weekly joust around the board. As soon as his children became old enough, we were roped in to play with him too. It's since become a family habit, and I know Daddy would have been proud that one of his grandsons has become a formidable conqueror of the board, scattering seven-letter words every time he plays.

Scrabble, for the uninitiated, is a word game designed for two to four players. The objective of the game is to arrange lettered tiles on a square board to create words that connect with others already played. Each tile carries a point value, which may be doubled or tripled if placed on specific marked squares on the board. The idea is to score more points than the other players with the words you play. Using all the seven tiles you're allowed to play per turn gives you a 50-point bonus. Luck enters into it too, since you may draw tiles that don't combine well together, or have low point value, or don't connect with the words already played on the board.

The earliest recorded usage of the word 'scrabble' is in a 1537 translation of the Bible (1 Samuel 21:13): 'And he...scrabbled on the doors of the gate.' Almost four centuries later, in 1931, Alfred Mosher Butts, an unemployed American architect, created a game called 'Criss-Cross words', based on the crossword puzzle. The rights to the game were acquired from Butts by James Brunot, who in 1948 changed the game's name to 'Scrabble' to better reflect players scrambling for tiles and forming coherent words with them. It was an instant hit, and continues to be universally popular, in multiple languages and even Braille.

Scrabble isn't just a clever word-game; it both reflects and expands the changing usage patterns of the English language. The quest for creating viable words out of seemingly unsuitable tiles has led people to revive and sanctify some unusual words. There are 'official Scrabble dictionaries', listing every word permitted in the game (over 276,000), published by Merriam-Webster in the US and Collins in the UK (and they sometimes differ!). Inclusion in the authorized dictionary gives words legitimacy that other dictionary-makers notice. The US dictionary's most recent update incorporated an additional 500 new words and variations, including 'inspo' (for the generationally-challenged, acceptable shorthand for 'an inspiring influence'), 'vibed', and 'vibing'.

Scrabble teaches me new words every time I play with really dedicated Scrabblers, who have mastered rare combinations of letters—the word 'ixnay', for instance, meaning 'to reject or put a stop to'. (It's also been elevated to verb status, permitting variations like 'ixnayed', 'ixnaying', and 'ixnays'.) Scrabble has even transformed the word 'verb' into a verb, allowing players to use terms such as 'verbed' and 'verbing'. It has accommodated twenty-first century vocabulary by accepting compound words now in popular usage, such as 'pageview', 'fintech', and 'retweet', along with new words beginning with 'un' such as 'unfollow' and 'unmute'. The term 'faux-hawk', describing a Mohawk-style haircut, makes the cut; so do two rare words using the high-scoring letter 'z', 'zonkey' (an animal born from a male zebra and a female donkey), and 'zedonk' (whose parentage is the other way around). The latest Scrabble dictionary also resurrects the term 'yeehaw', a popular cry in cowboy movies but not often seen in writing.

It has, however, removed over 200 words containing racial, ethnic, or offensive content. Even though some of them exist in other dictionaries, you can't play them in Scrabble. Should the meaning of the words you play matter, or is it enough that they exist? Scrabble purists objected that all they're trying to do is score points, not insult anyone. But the Scrabble dictionary decrees otherwise. Some consolation—foreign words used often enough in English have made it to the dictionary—recent inclusions include 'iftar', for the post-fasting meal during Ramadan, 'kharif', for the autumn harvest in India, 'yaar' (Hindi for friend)—and (appropriately enough) the South Indian exclamation 'aiyo'. I wish my father had lived long enough to play 'aiyo' on a Scrabble board.

Daddy would invent games for my sisters and me, seeing how many words with four letters or more we could make up from the letters in a nine-or-ten letter word. Another game we played on long car journeys was when one passenger had to imagine a five-letter word, and the others guessed at it for twenty attempts by trying out five-letter words and being told only how many letters matched. Yes, you guessed it—my father had invented an early version of the game that has since become a worldwide phenomenon, Wordle. A word game played on your phone or computer that involves five-letter words, the popping up of green, yellow, and grey boxes, and globally-shared bragging rights, Wordle has been the word-game phenomenon of the decade.

Wordle, invented by software engineer Josh Wardle (its name is a pun on his surname) for his word-game fan girlfriend Palak Shah, is simple in concept: the programme issues a five-letter word of the day online, and players have to guess it within six tries. When you log on to the website hosting the game (initially https://www.powerlanguage.co.uk/wordle, since acquired and hosted by the *New York Times*) the rules of the game are explained—if, when you guess a word, a letter you guess is in the word and is in the right place, the box turns green; if the letter occurs in the secret word, but is in the wrong place, the box turns yellow; and if the letter isn't in the word at all, that box will turn grey. The keyboard beneath helpfully replicates those colours, so you can quickly see which letters are left. That's the only clue that you're given; you have to use your vocabulary and your smarts to guess what the secret word is from the remaining valid letters. You get six tries, and most of the time that's more than enough.

Sounds ingenious, and it is. But for my family, the Wordle experience has caused a particular pang of nostalgia, because as I have said, our father, a passionate wordsmith and crossword, acrostic, and Scrabble enthusiast, had invented this very game before the internet era. It never got named for Chandran Tharoor, but for us it was the game he invented in the late 1960s for family car journeys, to keep his three obstreperous kids occupied. Wordle's major contribution is the use of technology: my father, sisters, and I used to play it in our heads and it was much harder, especially he never told us if our letters were in the right place or not, but then Daddy gave us twenty chances. Because we had so many chances, though, we wasted a lot of turns. Our family soon evolved a formula of beginning our guesses with 'stick', 'stack', and 'stock'—three turns gone just to eliminate one or two vowels. You wouldn't do that with Wordle. Part of the art is to take stock of the letters that have been eliminated with each guess and come up with words using only the remaining letters.

My sisters and I have been nostalgically musing about how much our father would have enjoyed this game. His grandchildren today, and their spouses, are constantly exchanging the outcomes of each day's game on the family WhatsApp group, showing off how many (or ideally, how few) attempts they needed to guess the word of the day.

This 'share' option has also increased the game's popularity, since players can now display the results without giving the game away. The Covid pandemic and associated lockdowns also enhanced the game's appeal—it was an ideal activity for those involuntary indoor hours that many didn't know how to fill. When a killjoy using the handle @wordlinator started spoiling people's fun by hacking the source-code of the game and revealing the next day's word to players, the collective outrage led X (formerly Twitter) to ban @wordlinator altogether.

But if you get hooked, as I did, and impatient with the fact that there's only one puzzle a day, the killjoys at the *New York Times* won't help you play games you've missed. I used to go to https://www.devangthakkar.com/wordle_archive/ to find a storehouse of past puzzles made by a fan, where you could find an archive of all the Wordle puzzles thus far (at that time there were more than 200; today it is nearing 1,000). The *New York Times* put paid to that. But another site, mywordle.me, lets you set your own Wordle challenges.

For me, it's a rare thrill to relive those games with my father and sisters more than half a century ago. One tip, though: 'stare' and 'store' are better starting guess than 'stack' and 'stock'. The letters they use simply recur more often in English words than c and k....

Daddy taught us that too. This great love of words and language, and the inventive ways my father put it to practise, inevitably rubbed off on his eldest child: me.

But it was never just words for their own sake. My father instilled in me the conviction that words are what shape ideas and reflect thought, and the more words you know, the more precisely and effectively are you able to express your thoughts. Hence a book on the wonderland of words, often a source of fascination—and indispensable for communication—seemed not such a bad idea after all.

From the era of Renaissance explorations to the time when the British empire extended its influence worldwide, and continuing into the present, a constant influx of fresh vocabulary has entered the English language. These new words and phrases serve as linguistic bridges, and enable English-speakers to navigate and label the complexities of life.

In some ways words are like families. Just as there are different relationships among members of the same family, there are similar relationships among words and also among those who love words.

My father was probably my 'milver', though I don't think he knew the word: an individual who shares a strong interest in words with another person, particularly an interest related to usage and wordplay. This term was coined by the American essayist and critic Logan Pearsall Smith (1865–1946) as a response to a friend's complaint about the lack of a suitable English word to describe 'a person who is enthusiastic about the same thing you are enthusiastic about'. Smith found expressions like 'fellow fan' or 'co-enthusiast' too cumbersome, leading him to invent the term 'milver'. As he elucidated in his 1936 book *Reperusals and Recollections*, 'Language being never adequate to describe all the relationships of people to each other, I have invented the word milver to describe those who share a fad in common.' (It is not clear what the etymology of the word is, but it does have the merit of providing poets with the only possible rhyme for 'silver'!)

'Milver' epitomizes our ongoing exploration of the boundless possibilities of language—playfully exploring it and creating new words is fun. When we delve into the realm of words and wordplay, whether we're coining new terms or unearthing existing linguistic gems, it's a vivid reminder of our capacity to invent and adapt words and our innate ability to craft and modify language. Often, scepticism towards unfamiliar words and an aversion to linguistic innovation are ingrained in children from a very early age by uninspiring parents and teachers. Fortunately, I was blessed to have a father and teachers who taught me the exact opposite—always uncover the most appropriate word, even if it wasn't widely used.

As Barbara Chatton, professor of elementary education at the University of Wyoming, suggests in her book *Using Poetry Across the Curriculum: Learning to Love Language*,

> A love of words comes from the work of playing around with language. We learn words by hearing them, rolling them around on our tongues and in our minds like a small child does as she learns language. A person who loves language plays with it—hears words and links them with other sounds, other meanings, and other words. The patterns and sounds of language are fascinating to the lover of words.

This deep and enduring love of words, which I acquired in childhood and have not ceased to nurture, has been with me throughout my life. Blessed with a keen ear for words and a capacious memory, a robust lexicon of exceptional and highly specific words has found a place in my mind. There exists a term for people like me who have a deep affection for words—a logophile. Despite the presence of many members of the tribe, the word logophile is yet to be widely used, though it is included in most dictionaries. Logophile has its origins in two Greek roots: *logos*, which signifies 'speech, word, and reason', and *philos*, which means 'dear one or friend'. Their condition is 'logophilia', the love of words. These roots have also contributed to the formation of more commonly used English words. *Logos* has historical ties to words like 'analogous', 'apology', and 'logic', while *philos* has given rise to the noun combining form '-phile', denoting 'someone who greatly enjoys something'. A Francophile, for instance, likes all things French.

A 'logophile' is someone who has a deep affection for words; a 'milver' is one who exhibits a significant enthusiasm, especially for language and wordplay, with people of similar interests. When we converse with others, our words possess the power to inspire, connect, and influence. This book is a testament to my intellectual curiosity and my desire to share a strong interest, particularly one related to words and wordplay, with others. But is there a 'milver' out there among my readers, another devoted word enthusiast like me who shares the same enthusiasms? I'd love to hear from them!

Whenever I am asked by someone to teach audiences a 'new word', I respond to this perennial (and frankly tiresome) request by replying with an old word: 'read!' Read enough books and you will come across new words—and usually figure out not just what they mean, but their usage and nuance. I don't think today's young are doing enough of it.

If one stands up to decry the evident decline in reading, the defence comes back: 'oh, the younger generation are reading all the time—it's just that they're reading on their mobile phones and not in books.' But that's precisely the problem—many in the younger generation seem to believe that books are only for schoolrooms and homework, and that when you're not studying them in order to pass examinations, they have no appeal or value in their lives. It is true that they *are* reading: text messages, WhatsApp forwards, and the like, and in that sense, the reading they do digitally may cover as many words and as much text as my generation read in our analogue era. But even if the young are, in that sense, reading more than ever, they are also reading rapidly, carelessly, and superficially—and that's dangerous for our society and our democracy.

The alarm bells have been sounded in a new scholarly article on the internet (in a journal called *First Monday,* 27(5)), entitled 'Why Higher-level reading is important', which laments the global decline in serious reading and of readers interested in and capable of complex interpretative interactions with texts. The short attention-span required and perpetuated by the digital era has led, the scholar-authors say, to a significant decline of critical and conscious reading, immersive and slow reading, literary reading, non-strategic or non-goal-oriented reading, and long-form reading. Even audiobooks, the authors point out, are not the equivalent of reading but a poor substitute for it, for 'listening does not train the higher-level abilities' that reading promotes.

The scholars identify many psychological processes involved in reading, including motivation and frustration, pleasure and leisure, emotional responses, therapeutic and meditative effects, imagination and mental imagery, creativity and inspiration. In my own asthmatic childhood, reading was my escape, my education, and my entertainment; I read essentially for pleasure but grew in the process, widened my mental horizons, and enhanced my vocabulary. That sense, of reading being an enjoyable activity which you can still benefit from, is sadly missing among many of today's young.

Ironically, the higher-level reading skills that are now out of fashion are all the more essential to negotiate the complexities of the twenty-first century information society. We live in an era of fake news, conspiracy theories, distortions and disinformation, simplifications and outright lies, assiduously spread by our rulers to compromise society's capacity for informed democratic decision-making. We need all the more to be able to critically interrogate what's around us, and that comes with experience in engaging with the content and language of texts we read. Those who read very little are the ones vulnerable to manipulation by false and motivated WhatsApp forwards.

The scholar–authors conclude that reading skills and practices are 'the foundation for full participation in the economic, political, communal and cultural life of contemporary society', including 'social, cultural and political engagement' as much as 'personal liberation, emancipation and empowerment'. A healthy democratic society that requires 'the informed consensus of a multi-stakeholder and multi-cultural society' also needs resilient readers, they argue; 'reading is our culture's central training technique for cognitive and social behaviour and a precondition for a properly functioning democracy.'

They therefore call for 'concerted policies' to ensure that future reading education will promote reading habits and 'practices to match the pivotal role of reading'. They want policymakers to invest in further reading research, including especially of higher-level reading and how to teach it. Poetically and rather dramatically, they quote the line: 'War is what happens when language fails.'

This scholarly 'white paper' has prompted something called the Ljubljana Reading Manifesto, signed by a variety of writers, publishers, and readers (including myself). The manifesto is a global appeal to promote reading—something I've been doing anyway. It really does matter. The manifesto ends with Margaret Atwood's much quoted warning, 'If there are no young readers and writers, there will shortly be no older ones. Literacy will be dead, and democracy…will be dead as well.' If you want to save democracy, encourage the next generation to read!

That seems to me to offer possibly the best justification for this book. If it helps readers acquire some of the passion for language that my father imparted to me—indeed, if it prompts them to read at all—it will have well served its purpose.

I am besotted with words; it's fair to say that I love them. But even I could not have expressed my love for words as well as a young job-seeker called Robert Pirosh did in 1934, when he headed to Hollywood looking for a new career as a screenwriter. Pirosh was working in advertising in New York and had no connections in the American film industry. But he collected the names and addresses of as many directors, producers, and studio executives as he could find, and sent them this brilliant letter:

> Dear Sir,
>
> I like words. I like fat buttery words, such as ooze, turpitude, glutinous, toady. I like solemn, angular, creaky words, such as straitlaced, cantankerous, pecunious, valedictory. I like spurious, black-is-white words, such as mortician, liquidate, tonsorial, demi-monde. I like suave 'v' words, such as Svengali, svelte, bravura, verve. I like crunchy, brittle, crackly words, such as splinter, grapple, jostle, crusty. I like sullen, crabbed, scowling words, such as skulk, glower, scabby, churl. I like Oh-Heavens, my gracious, land's sake words, such as tricksy, tucker, genteel, horrid. I like elegant, flowery words, such as estivate, peregrinate, elysium, halcyon. I like wormy, squirmy, mealy words, such as crawl, blubber, squeal, drip. I like sniggly, chuckling words, such as cowlick, gurgle, bubble and burp.
>
> I like the word screenwriter better than copywriter, so I decided to quit my job in a New York advertising agency and try my luck in Hollywood, but before taking the plunge I went to Europe for a year of study, contemplation and horsing around.
>
> I have just returned and I still like words. May I have a few with you?

Many would concede that no better job application has ever been written in the English language, and I would add, no better paean to the marvels and joys of words either. The letter worked. Pirosh landed three job interviews, one of which led to a job as a junior writer at Metro Goldwyn Mayer studios, the fabled MGM. His career soared; in 1949, screenwriter Robert Pirosh won an Academy Award for Best Original Screenplay for his work on the war film, *Battleground*. A few months after the Oscar, he also won a Golden Globe Award from the Hollywood Foreign Press Association. These were opportunities he might never have landed if he had not loved words enough to craft such a brilliant letter.

But what about the words he used in his letter? Many of them might escape comprehension, so in tribute to Pirosh, here's a cheat sheet to the several unusual or difficult words he cited, just in case you fall in love with them too! (I am omitting those words I expect most readers to be familiar with already.)

In order of appearance: 'turpitude' describes wicked or depraved behaviour or character; it is common to speak of someone being guilty of moral turpitude. Glutinous simply means 'sticky' and pecunious is a fancy way of saying 'wealthy'; there's no good reason to use either when such easy alternatives exist. On the other hand, 'tonsorial' is an unusual word for the work of a barber: it means 'giving shaves and haircuts'. The 'demi-monde' refers to a group of people on the fringes of respectable society; prostitutes, for instance, though the term is also used these days for anyone whose activities you don't particularly approve of, like arms merchants or moneylenders. A Svengali, based on a fictional character, is a person who exercises a controlling or mesmeric and usually sinister influence on another. A person or thing is described as 'scabby' when it is very unpleasant or unappealing. A churl is a rude and mean-spirited person; someone who's tricksy is playful or mischievous. To estivate is to spend a hot or dry period in a prolonged state of torpor or dormancy; to peregrinate is to travel or wander from place to place. Elysium is paradise, the abode of the blessed. Your halcyon days were a period in the past that was idyllically happy and peaceful.

And then Pirosh threw in a curveball: a word that doesn't

exist, 'sniggly'. To sniggle is to fish for eels by thrusting a baited hook into their hiding places, but he simply made up 'sniggly'. Word-lovers do that: they invent some too!

Read on!

SECTION ONE

BORROWED PLUMES

In the old Wild West, a .45 cartridge for a 'six-gun' (revolver) cost 12 cents—so that was the price of a 'shot'. But a glass of whiskey at a Wild West saloon also cost 12 cents—so it was easy to conflate the two. If a patron was low on cash, he would instead offer the bartender a cartridge in exchange for a drink. This became known as a 'shot' of whiskey.

1

BRITISH VERSUS AMERICAN

As an Indian schooled in the English language, I have long been fascinated by its different variants in use around the world—from the Singaporean 'la' suffixed to every sentence to the Australian 'G'day' prefixed to every greeting. But most compelling, for me, are the multiple differences between British and American English, the two languages fighting for dominance in the Anglophone world.

In my first week on a US university campus, I asked an American where I could post a letter to my parents. 'There's a bulletin board at the Student Center,' he replied, 'but are you sure you want to post something so personal?' I soon learned that I needed to 'mail' letters, not 'post' them (even though in the United States you mail them at the 'post office'). To 'post' something, in American English, is to publish it, such as by putting up a 'poster' on a bulletin board or (these days) issuing a 'post' on social media.

In Britain, one concludes a restaurant meal by asking for the bill, and conceivably paying by cheque; in America, one asks for the check and pays with bills. What the Brits call chips are fries in America; what the Yanks call chips are crisps in Britain.

An English friend of mine says that he nearly had a heart attack on a flight in the United States when the American pilot announced that the plane would be airborne 'momentarily'. In British English, 'momentarily' means 'for a moment', and he says he thought the pilot was suggesting an imminent crash soon after take-off. In American English, however, 'momentarily' means 'in a moment', and the pilot was merely appeasing the impatient passengers. The plane took off, stayed aloft, my friend's heart stopped thudding, and he lived to tell the tale. But he understood better than ever before the old adage that Britain and the United

States are two countries divided by a common language.

Anecdotes abound about the misunderstandings that arise when foreigners come to the United States thinking that they know the language. In one anecdote, a young man, in the course of a passionate courtship, tells his American girlfriend, 'I'll give you a ring tomorrow.' All he meant was that he would call her by telephone. But she understood him to have offered betrothal, and the relationship didn't survive the misunderstanding.

Then there's the hotel that failed to understand an English guest who called to say he had left his 'trousers in the wardrobe'. Translators had to be summoned before the hotel staff finally cottoned on: 'Oh, you've left your pants in the closet. Why didn't you say so in the first place?'

Sometimes you can get the right word but the wrong concept. Our former foreign minister, M. C. Chagla, once ruefully recounted the time he wanted to order a modest bite from room service in a New York hotel and requested sandwiches.

'How many do you want?' Chagla was asked. Imagining delicate little triangles of thinly sliced bread, he replied: 'Oh, half-a-dozen should be enough.' Six sandwiches duly arrived, each about a foot long and four inches high.

The language of politics is also not exempt from the politics of language. When a member of parliament in Britain 'tables' a resolution, he puts it forward for debate and passage; when an American Congressman tables a resolution, he kills it off. A 'moot' point is one the Englishman wants to argue; but if it's moot, the American considers it null and void.

Such differences in usage reveal something of the nature of American society. It is no wonder, after all, that while the British 'stand' for election, Americans 'run' for office. A British linguist once told a New York audience that whereas a double negative could make a positive, there was no language in the world in which a double positive made a negative. A heckler put paid to his thesis in forthright American: 'Yeah, right.'

Yeah, right, indeed. With the universality of English largely a result of US global dominance, it's time for other English speakers to accept the American usage is winning worldwide. Even Indians are saying 'elevator' and 'apartment' rather than 'lift' and 'flat'. 'Cookies' are supplanting 'biscuits'.

And as the Americans have taught the rest of us to say: that's OK. Though not even they can tell us (without reading Chapter 49 of this book) what those two initials are meant to represent!

◆

Historically, British English was the version of the language that initially prevailed in the Gulf and South Asia, thanks to the impact of British colonialism, but American English has been gaining ground around the world, as US dominance of world communications, social media networks, movies, and satellite and cable television, has meant that most English speakers hear a lot more 'American' than 'British' English spoken these days. As I have mentioned earlier, Indians have started saying 'apartment' rather than 'flat' (though 'lift' still prevails over 'elevator'). This trend is all to the good, since it multiplies the possibilities of language, and has enhanced global familiarity with a number of distinctively American expressions that have added colour to the English language, despite having originated well outside England.

Take, for instance, the expression 'the whole nine yards'. 'Do you want walnut toppings on your sundae, bananas, cherries, whipped cream?' asks the ice-cream saleswoman. 'Yes, the whole nine yards,' you reply. Or, 'Did you hear that Ahmed has sold his tea shop?' a friend asks, and another replies, 'Yeah, the whole nine yards.' You might be puzzled since neither the sundae nor the tea shop measures nine yards, but the meaning is clear—to have or do something to the fullest extent possible is to go the full nine yards. But why? American fighter planes in World War II used machine guns fed by a belt of cartridges. The average plane held cartridge belts that were 27 feet (9 yards) long. If the pilot used up all his ammunition, he was said to have given it the whole nine yards!

While we are on World Wars, have you come across the American expression 'buying the farm', which goes even farther back to World War I? 'I have bad news—Joe, the boy next door who enlisted in the army, has bought the farm.' In other words, the poor chap has died or been killed. The reason for this turn of phrase is that during World War I, soldiers were given life insurance policies worth $5,000, which was also the price of an average farm in America in those days. A soldier who died 'bought the farm' for his survivors, when they collected the insurance claim.

American soldiers are not the only ones of that nationality to ask for and enjoy a 'shot of whiskey'. What has alcohol got to do with shooting? Again, history and old prices come into the story. In the old Wild West, a .45 cartridge for a 'six-gun' (revolver) cost 12 cents—so that was the price of a 'shot'. But a glass of whiskey at a Wild West saloon also cost 12 cents—so it was easy to conflate the two. If a patron was low on cash, he would instead offer the bartender a cartridge in exchange for a drink. This became known as a 'shot' of whiskey. The West is no longer quite so wild, but the expression endures!

Perhaps the most famous Americanism—and certainly the most widely used—is that of 'passing the buck', often modified colourfully into President Harry Truman's famous desktop sign, 'the buck stops here'. 'Passing the buck' means giving responsibility to someone else, usually hierarchically above you; the 'buck' stopped with the president, since there was no one above him to pass it to. But what is the buck in the first place? Most men in the old American Frontier carried a jackknife made by the Buck Knives company. When these rough and ready folks, many of them cowhands and gunslingers, played cards, usually poker, it was the practice to place a Buck knife in front of the dealer so that everyone knew who he was. When it was time for a new dealer to take on this responsibility, the deck of cards and the Buck knife were passed on to that player. If this player didn't want to deal, he would 'pass the buck' to the next person to deal instead of him. That was how the expression 'passing the buck' came into the language. It has also acquired the connotation of shirking responsibility—one who does not want to take on a burden 'passes the buck' to someone else so he would not be held responsible if anything goes wrong.

If someone speaks of an 'iron-clad contract' or an agreement that cannot be broken, he's using a term that goes all the way back to the US Civil War of the 1860s, when iron-clad ships plied the waters, armoured against the artillery of the other side. 'Iron-clad' came to mean something so strong that it could not be destroyed, a perfect analogy for an agreement so unshakeable that it could not be broken.

Many Americanisms that are in common usage wherever English is spoken originate, for the most part, in America's great rivers, especially the Mississippi. It is common, for instance, for people of a certain age to dismiss low-class, ill-bred persons as 'riff-raff'. The expression comes from travelling in the nineteenth century on the Mississippi River, which flows north to south in the US. Riverboats carried well-off passengers and freight, but they were too expensive for ordinary people, who instead used rafts to travel more cheaply. Rafts were steered using oars called 'riffs' and so the rafts themselves were called riff-rafts. Riff-raft soon got transmuted into riff-raff, meaning cheap or low-class.

Also, in the late nineteenth century, when travelling by steamboat was the preferred means of transportation for the affluent who wished to travel in comfort, their equivalent of First Class was the ship's 'state rooms'. The expression came from the fact that these elite passenger cabins were not numbered, which would have seemed too *déclassé*. Instead, they were named after American states—so your room was in the 'Ohio State Room' or the 'Connecticut State Room'. To this day, luxury cabins on ships are called staterooms, even though the names of the states are no longer used and—horror of horrors—they may even be numbered!

Riverboats were not only used for transport but also for entertainment. 'Showboats' were floating theatres constructed on top of barges that were pushed by a steamboat, offering entertainment at each stop, usually small riverside towns along the Mississippi. Since they existed to attract attention from potential paying patrons, they were rather gaudily done up and everyone noticed them when they steamed in. People who similarly deck themselves up and who try to grab attention by their behaviour are often described in America as 'showboating'.

Theatres were not the only river traffic using barges. Heavy freight also travelled along the Mississippi in large barges pushed by steamboats that plied the river. These were often hard to control and the barges would sometimes be pushed by the waves into piers or bang into other boats. Thus was born the expression 'to barge in'. Today it applies to people, not boats, who intrude into other people's conversations or social occasions without an invitation—'barging in' just like those old freight barges on the Mississippi.

In those days, steamboats were used to carry both people and animals, including hogs or pigs. Since these creatures gave off a rather powerful smell, they would be washed before being brought on board. The mud and other odorous filth that was washed off the pigs was considered 'hogwash'. The expression soon became synonymous with anything absolutely useless or unacceptably false or exaggerated—'that Spokesman's explanation was a load of hogwash!'

Once in a while, of course, a boat would capsize, and some sailors and passengers might even drown in the river. When drowning people were rescued alive from the water, the technique of CPR had not been invented in those days, so a victim would be placed face down over a barrel, and the barrel would be rolled back and forth in an effort to empty the lungs of water. It worked sometimes, but more often did not. So it began to be said, in grim tones, that the person was 'over a barrel', meaning that he was drowning in deep trouble which he might not survive. The technique has mercifully been long abandoned, but the expression survives!

2

AUSTRALIAN ENGLISH

In the course of the preceding chapter, we have examined American influence on the English language. But what about the longer-lasting British colony, the place where for decades convicted criminals were deported with no hope of return—Australia?

The Australians have understandably bristled at centuries of British disregard, and the British in turn have enjoyed joking about the Australians. A favourite topic is their accent, which is pretty distinctive. 'What is a bison?' one riddle runs. Before you reply that it's a bovine animal, kin to buffalo, often featured in stories about the American Wild West, the answer comes: 'It's what an Australian washes his face in.' For indeed, most Australians pronounce 'basin' as 'bison', with the 'ay' sound commonly rendered as 'eye'. Another common joke is about the tourist injured in a bad accident who wakes up from a coma and melodramatically asks the Australian nurse, 'Have I come here to die?' to which she replies cheerfully, 'No, you came here yester-die.'

But pronunciations apart, Australia has a rich variety of distinctive expressions, some 7,000 of which—both words and idioms—are currently being considered for the next edition of the Australian National Dictionary. As a fascinating article in the *New York Times* describes it, Australian English is full of colourful terms that other varieties of English don't use. 'Few bricks short of a pallet', for instance, refers to someone not quite all right in the head. An angry friend is said to be 'mad as a cut snake'. A pug-ugly person might be described as having a 'face like a bucket of smashed crabs'. Someone else, perhaps a person with a sour and drooping countenance, might have a 'face like a half-sucked mango'. (Another variant: 'face like a twisted sandshoe', assuming you know what a sandshoe is—a light canvas shoe with a rubber sole). All of these reflect the unique culture of a country very different from the 'Mother Country' in which its language was born.

Those are delightful idioms, but Australian English also has a number of uniquely Australian expressions that, though not as colourful, belong exclusively to their country. Thus hard work, to an Australian, is 'hard yakka' in the local language. The country's criminal antecedents show up in expressions like 'never dob in your mates' (for 'never betray your friends by informing on them') or 'don't rort the system' (don't cheat or engage in fraud). Former prime minister Scott Morrison described his rival (and now successor) Anthony Albanese as a 'loose unit', a term uniquely Australian to describe someone as unreliable, uncouth, unpredictable (or all three). Another word for an uncouth person is 'bogan', though a bogan is now seen as an authentic Australian and a 'fogan', or 'faux bogan', is a bigger insult, while finding your 'inner bogan' is an honourable objective. The indigenous aboriginal languages of the country have also given rise to words like 'boomerang' and 'kangaroo', as well as the less widely known 'billabong' (an Australian name for a stagnant pool or a dead-end water channel), 'dingo' (a local species of wild dog) or 'yabby' (an undefinable edible item). In turn, immigration into Australia has also impacted the language, as new communities of Australians have required new vocabularies to describe them—like 'ABC' for Australian-born Chinese.

The Times tells us that the first edition of the Australian National Dictionary—a partnership between the Oxford English Dictionary and the Australian National University—came out in 1988, including only words and phrases that originated in Australia, or have a greater currency or special significance there. The first edition of the dictionary had 10,000 entries. That went up to 16,000 in the second, and now they are working on the third, which will have much to add. Might it include 'selfie' which the Oxford English Dictionary says first appeared in an

Australian newsgroup online? There's a debate raging: given how widespread the term has become, can it truly be considered uniquely Australian? We'll have to wait for the new edition of the dictionary to find out.

3

IRISH WORDS IN ENGLISH

My occasional excursions into the French, German, and even Japanese origins of words we use in English (in essays that follow) prompted an Irish friend to object that I had left out the most important language English had borrowed from, his own. The Celts of Ireland may have used a language which, when written down, seems impossible to pronounce (their prime minister, for instance, is called the taoiseach, which sounds something like 'TEE-shock' in English!). But their claim to have infiltrated their words across the Irish Sea is well-founded.

The most obvious evidence of Irish influence is the word 'whiskey', an Anglicization of the wonderfully named 'uisge beatha' (pronounced *ish-ce bah-ha*)—the water of life. And if you are partial to those single malt whiskies which have a smoky smell and taste, you would know that comes from the peat bogs in Scotland and Ireland, whose water gives off that distinctive aroma. That may be associated in your mind with Scotland—but the word 'bog' itself is the Irish word for 'soft', and was applied to the peaty wetlands of Ireland where the land was soft and yielding to walk on.

One of the few English words that is widely known to be Irish is 'shamrock', the country's national symbol, a direct English version of the Irish 'seamróg' which means young clover. But there's also 'banshee', from 'bean an sídhe' (woman of the burial mound), for those ghostly female creatures who haunt stories of the supernatural, wailing and shrieking. If you say a movie about banshees has horrors 'galore', you're using another Irish word, which comes from the Irish 'go leor' meaning plenty. And if you are of a certain vintage, you'll understand that the expression 'Hey man, do you dig it?' means 'do you understand?' in the 1970s 'cool cat' lingo. 'Dig' in the sense of 'do you get me?'

comes straight from the Irish 'an dtuigeanntú' (pronounced *on dig-in too*).

If you're a football fan, you're surely aware of the tribe of English football 'hooligans', whose bibulous depredations during matches once caused their compatriots to be banned from the European continent. The word is a twist on the Irish surname Hoolihan. A nineteenth century English comic strip featured an Irish family called the Hooligans, who in those racist times were depicted in a stereotypically negative fashion, and the name stuck.

Irish words have travelled extensively. In Australia, it's common, and not offensive, to refer to women as 'sheilas'. This Australian slang for members of the female sex comes from the Irish name Síle. Or you can travel to South Africa and discover the Irish word 'shebeen', for an illicit drinking tavern. The word descends from the Irish 'síbín', which in turn derives from 'séibín' (small mug), but then became synonymous with the mug's contents (home-brewed whiskey) and eventually to the premises where the drink was sold. It is said that during the bad years of the apartheid system in South Africa, shebeens were the only bars available to blacks in that country who felt like a drink.

So we have much to be thankful to the Irish for in terms of words, but what's really special are the expressions in English that reflect a uniquely Irish sensibility. An Irishman wishing you a 'grand soft day' is celebrating a very particular kind of rainy day—'when you can't see or feel the rain but you get wet anyway', as the *Irish Times* puts it. Someone who is really, truly stupid is described as being 'as thick as two double ditches'. And if he is also useless or worthless, you could say he's only 'fit to mind mice at a crossroads'. The profligate Irish habit of spending your money before having it in your hands is called 'eating the calf in the cow's belly'. And if you did something wrong while pretending you had a good reason to do so, you're guilty of 'blindfolding the devil in the dark'. After all, the devil can see what you're up to!

But then you'd merely have been 'chancing your arm', an expression originating in fifteenth century Dublin where two feuding families, the Butlers and the Fitzgeralds, needed to end hostilities. The Fitzgeralds asked the Butlers, who were holed up in St. Patrick's Cathedral, to come outside and make peace, but the Butlers were unwilling to risk it. The Fitzgeralds then suggested cutting a hole in the door so that they could offer a handshake through it—in effect, 'chancing their arms'. The Butlers agreed, and thus was born the Door of Reconciliation, and a lovely Irish phrase. The door is still there today.

4

WORDS BORROWED FROM GERMAN

In a tweet criticizing the media attacks on actor Shah Rukh Khan's twenty-three-year-old son, I decried the 'ghoulish epicaricacy' that animated this all-out assault on the young man. My use of the word epicaricacy, meaning deriving pleasure from the misfortunes of others, sent many scurrying to the dictionary. Amusingly enough several objected that I need not have employed such an obscure English word when there was a perfectly adequate substitute available from German—*schadenfreude*, a word far more commonly used in English to describe the malicious satisfaction that some people gain from seeing others suffer!

This is true—*schadenfreude* is more often used than epicaricacy—and it points to the remarkable capacity of the English language to absorb infusions from elsewhere. Where a foreign language has a word that precisely connotes something, English is happy to embrace it. And a surprising number of these borrowed words come from German, a language more commonly associated with long, polysyllabic formulations that are usually considered hard to pronounce and harder to spell!

One of those sesquipedalian German words that has found a place in many people's vocabulary is *Weltanschauung*, translated most simply as 'worldview' but embracing a comprehensive personal philosophy or conception of the universe and of human life than the simple 'worldview' suggests. A writer's *Weltanschauung* is often the subject of literary scholars' attention. These would not necessarily be the same scholars who would write learned theses on the *Bildungsroman*, an untranslatable term for a novel that details the psychological development of the principal character. (There are many novels like that—and where one English word couldn't be found to describe them, German came in handy!)

Amongst German words I find myself using, a favourite in my college days was *zeitgeist*, a term coined by the German philosopher Hegel in the late eighteenth century to refer to the spirit of an age. Thus one might say that 'globalization was the zeitgeist of the post-Cold War era'. The word embraces the overall trend of thought and feeling in a historical period.

More commonly used and therefore familiar to readers of English-language newspapers would be words like angst, ersatz, kitsch, hinterland, leitmotiv, realpolitik, and wanderlust—words that are so common they are not even italicized in English and many don't even realize they were borrowed from German. Kitsch describes cheap, often gaudy art or tourist trinkets, and is used with a sneer to refer to items purchased by people with poor taste. Some of those items might be ersatz, a German word meaning 'replacement' that's used in English to refer to a cheap, inferior substitute for something. ('That ersatz plastic statuette was such a piece of kitsch! why did she buy it?') Hinterland is the inland trade region or district behind a port and served by it, often bordering a coast or river and claimed by the state that owns the coast. Realpolitik, which may gradually be falling into disuse in English, refers to the practice of hard-nosed power politics to pursue a country's national interests without heed to moral or ethical considerations. (It was first devised in German to describe the policies of the Prussian statesman Otto von Bismarck in the second half of the nineteenth century, and the term stuck.) Realpolitik was the leitmotiv of his foreign policy (leitmotiv being another German term, this time used in music, for a dominant and recurring theme).

Wanderlust animates many inveterate travellers—it's a wonderful word for a deep-seated longing to travel, or an urge to go for long walks or hikes, or to impulsively head out without a planned destination, just to get away from it all. That's how the Germans use it, and we do too. But *angst* is special, because its English usage actually goes beyond the German original. In German, I am told, angst describes fear of any kind of fear, but in English it has acquired more profound connotations, denoting a combination of fear and anguish defined by one dictionary as 'a gloomy, often neurotic feeling of generalized anxiety and depression'. I hope reading this chapter doesn't generate any angst in purist users of the English language!

5

INDIANISMS

Many of the readers of the *Khaleej Times* (and of this book) are Indians, and will understand if I admit that I have long immodestly considered myself the inventor of the term 'prepone'. I came up with it at St. Stephen's in 1972, used it extensively in conversation, and employed it in an article in *JS* magazine soon after. 'Prepone', as a back construction from 'postpone', seemed so much simpler, to a teenage collegian, than clunkily saying 'Could you move that appointment earlier?' or 'I would like to advance that deadline' or 'Please bring it forward to an earlier date.' Over the years, I was gratified to see how extensively its use had spread in India.

But I was wrong. In keeping with the longstanding wisdom that there is nothing new under the sun, I was told by Catherine Henstridge of the *Oxford English Dictionary* (OED), no less, that they have an example of the use of the word 'prepone' from 1913 in the *New York Times*. It didn't catch on much in the West, but the proceedings of the 1952 Indian Science Congress reveal that other Indians thought along the same lines: 'In Indian villages... demand for power can be preponed or postponed not only by hours but even by days.' Clearly, the origin of 'prepone' has been preponed from 1972 to 1913, and I duly withdraw my claim to its origination. Mind you, I can still make a case, through frequent usage, for being somewhat involved in its popularization!

Still, the persistence and survival of what is called Indian English (often with a sneer, as if to differentiate it from the Queen's 'propah' English) deserves to be taken seriously. Our English, spoken without the shadow of Englishmen looming over us, is a vigorous and local language, which draws strength from local roots. If Americans can say 'fall' for autumn and 'gotten' for 'have got', though both are archaisms in England itself, why can't Indians say 'furlong', 'fortnight', and 'do the needful', even if these have fallen out of use centuries ago in London? So many words in Indian English, including 'prepone', have stood up to the only test that matters—the test of time and usage. If enough people find a word or phrase useful, it is, to my mind, legitimate.

Indian English is a living, practical language, used by millions every day for practical purposes. I am not referring to expressions like satyagraha, namaste, or yogi, that have passed into the English language and are used exactly as they are in India. I am referring to the usage of English words differently in India from the Anglophone West. Many phrases we take for granted in ordinary conversation are actually quite unusual abroad—calling elders 'auntie' or 'uncle', for instance, or using the expression 'non-veg' to convey a willingness to eat meat. That doesn't make them wrong, or even quaint. It just makes them Indian.

Some Indian English was created by our media and passed into regular usage—'airdash' ('the chief minister airdashed to Delhi') and 'history sheeter' ('the police explained that habitual criminal X was a history sheeter', i.e. that he had a long criminal record). Some, like my 'prepone', came from school and college campuses: 'mugging' (cramming hard for an exam, with much rote learning and memorization involved) uses a word that means two very different things to Americans or Brits abroad (a criminal assault by a robber, as in 'She was the victim of a mugging in a dark alley' or an elaborate and often comically exaggerated expression, as in 'he was mugging for the camera'). When an Indian student tells a foreigner he was 'mugging for an exam', bewilderment is guaranteed. Yet it's a vivid word that conveys exactly what is intended for every user of Indian English.

So the way Indians speak the English language is often distinctive but not necessarily incorrect. Some Indian Englishisms are merely translated from an Indian language: 'What is your good name?' is the classic, since all Bengalis, for instance, have a 'daak naam' that they are called by, and a 'bhalo naam' (or 'good name') for the record. But 'what is your good name?' is still the most polite form, in any Indian version of the English language, for finding out the identity of your interlocutor. 'Is he your real brother?' someone asks, not to accuse you of having imaginary siblings, but to differentiate this brother from a cousin, who is also referred to as a 'brother' by affectionate Indians.

Such cultural assumptions inevitably influence language. The widespread preference for—or at least acceptability of—vegetarianism in India makes Indian English the only language that uses the expression 'non-veg' for meat, fish, and those who consume them. The Indian arranged-marriage culture has also had its impact on our local English. Our matrimonial ads have created their own cultural tropes with expressions that only mean something in Indian English—'wheatish complexion', of course, and better still, 'traditional with modern outlook'. Many ads require a prospective bride in India to be 'homely' (that is, home-loving and a good housekeeper) and to have 'passed out'—not fainted or lost consciousness, as a Brit or American might assume, but graduated—from a 'convent school', in other words a school established by a missionary order, where the medium of instruction is English.

Some Indianisms are creative uses of an ordinary English word or phrase to reflect a particularly Indian sensibility—such as 'kindly adjust', said apologetically by the seventh person slipping into a bench meant for four. We have nothing to apologize about: we should defiantly celebrate their use as integral parts of our Indian English vocabulary. After all, 'we are like that only'. And if you don't like it, kindly adjust....

But acknowledging the legitimacy of Indian English and many of its formulations doesn't mean that 'anything goes'. Some things are simply wrong. The Indian habit of saying 'I will return back' is an unnecessary redundancy: if you return, you are coming back. I am more neutral about 'revert' as an Indianism for 'get back'—a correspondent saying 'I will revert to you by next week' does not mean that he will convert himself into what you used to be, merely that he will issue a reply. Since the meaning is clear, objections to its use are unwarranted. But the desi practice of using 'till' to mean 'as long as' is simply incorrect English; it is wrong to say 'I will miss you till you are away' when you really mean is 'I will miss you till you come back'! 'I am staying Bandra side' is not an acceptable equivalent of 'I am living in the Bandra area'. And 'back side' for 'rear' causes much unwitting hilarity, as in signs proclaiming, 'entry through back side only'. These can't be justified under the rubric of Indian English. They are just bad English.

Indians are excessively fond of euphemisms: we would rather use a roundabout way of conveying an interest in a delicate topic rather than the direct word that foreign English speakers might. Thus we use 'reduced' as a synonym for losing weight ('you've reduced?'). Your 'intended' spouse is your 'would-be' in India. A 'loose character' has dubious morals. Women speak of 'chums' for menstrual periods—'chum' is old English slang for 'pal' and must have been applied since these 'chums' are monthly visitors! Asking about 'good news' is a polite way of enquiring about pregnancy, and we speak of 'issues' when we mean 'children' ('you've been married for ten years? Any issues?' doesn't mean 'do you have problems in your marriage?' but 'do you have any children?')

Cultural practices and assumptions are inevitably reflected in Indian English. You 'belong to' your 'native place' rather than simply being 'from' there, and your native place might be a 'mofussil town', that is in a rural or provincial area. If you're not in town, you're 'out of station'. If you meet a lady who is elder to you, she is usually 'auntie' even if there is no blood relationship. Relationships matter in India and so terms are invented for which there is no English equivalent: thus your 'co-brother' is your wife's sister's spouse. There is even a term, going back to the days when travel beyond our shores was a rare and inordinately expensive privilege, for someone who'd come back after sojourning abroad: they were 'foreign-returned'. And a unique Indian cultural practice gave us the expression 'give me a missed call', meaning 'ring me briefly and hang up so your number shows up on my device and I will call you back at my expense when I am free'. The caller might be an impecunious relative who can't afford to pay for the call, or merely a junior who would be seen as presumptuous otherwise: the 'missed call' addresses both these handicaps.

Then there are Indian formulations that have nothing to do with cultural sensitivities but simply reflect the way we apply certain words: you are sometimes required to 'do the needful'; if you do it perfectly, you've achieved 'cent per cent', and your friend's 'thanks' is met with 'mention not', rather than 'don't mention it'. We have a noun, 'timepass', for activities to while away one's idle moments; we 'take lunch' rather than 'have lunch', see a 'picture' rather than a 'movie', and 'put up' somewhere rather than 'stay' there. What foreigners call sunglasses are 'cooling-glasses', 'goggles', or 'glares' in India. We ask for a 'cold drink' when we want what Americans call 'soda' (and the pompous refer to as an 'aerated beverage'), though the drink may not in fact be cold.

Some Indian English expressions emerge from translating phrases in local languages, like 'eating my head' for 'bothering me', 'sit on her head' for 'pressure her', 'I took his class', or 'I scolded him'. Others are more modern: an unfamiliar problem is 'out of syllabus', a good experience is 'first-class'. Then there's 'rubber' as a synonym for 'eraser'. In the US a 'rubber' is what you use (in bed) to *prevent* a mistake; in India, you use it (in the classroom) *after* you make one.

Of course, some Indianisms are just awkward and arguably wrong, like 'God promise' and 'mother promise', to swear upon the divine or your mother, or saying 'years back' rather than 'years ago'. The telephone has brought about other solecisms: 'Hello, Ramu this side' when you mean 'Ramu here', or the stranger on the line who says 'Myself Salman, yourself?' I'm tempted to reply 'myself gone', and 'cut the call'—that is, hang up!

6

ENGLISH WORDS OF FRENCH ORIGIN

It is said that somewhere between one-third and two-thirds of all the words in the English language are actually of French origin. Most of the French vocabulary in English entered the language after the Norman Conquest of England in 1066, when William the Conqueror trounced King Harold II at the Battle of Hastings. William's followers became a new French ruling class (called Norman because they hailed from a part of France called Normandy) and, like colonizers everywhere, imposed their language on the society they now ruled.

French was, of course, spoken by the new elite. While the upper echelons of society spoke Norman French, the local plebeians spoke the Anglo-Saxon dialects that had prevailed earlier. But the Norman language (strictly speaking, Old French, specifically the Old Norman dialect) supplanted Anglo-Saxon English in the royal court and the government, among the upper crust, the judiciary, and the Church. Since the Norman settlers used their native language in their daily lives, it seeped into the quotidian English of the locals, forming a hybrid that took on the syntactical structure of English and used words from both sources. English itself became 'Frenchified', while the French spoken in England took on English influences.

The political separation of England and France in the early thirteenth century, marked by increasing hostility (culminating in the Hundred Years' War between the two), inevitably led to the decline of French as the preferred language in England. In 1349, English became the language of instruction at the University of Oxford, which had previously taught its courses in French or Latin. King Henry IV (1367–1413) was the first English king whose principal language was English, and his successor Henry V (1387–1422) became the first to use English in official documents.

English as we would know it came into its own just over 600 years ago.

Today few are even aware of the French origins of many words taken for granted as English. These include words reflecting the feudal practices of the Normans (ranging from chivalry, homage, and vassal to liege, suzerain, and even villain) to words connected to warfare (armour, dungeon, rampart). Royalty and governance naturally required words from the French overlords; thus came baron, count, dame, duke, and marquis, 'heir apparent' and Prince Regent. So too, 'minister' and 'parliament' and even the word 'government' itself, all came from French, as did 'sovereignty', and the ABCs: 'administration', 'bureaucracy', and 'constitution'. Justice, judge, jury, and even court, were gifts of the French as well.

The vocabulary of politics and economics is understandably dominated by French: you can't talk about 'money', the 'treasury', or the 'exchequer', or commerce, finance, and even tax, without using words that were originally French. Political concepts from liberalism and capitalism, to materialism and nationalism, and for that matter the somewhat more obvious 'coup d'état', came from French.

French was for long the premier language of global diplomacy, some would argue right up to the twentieth century. The words used in English for most diplomatic activities unsurprisingly derive from French. While the use of the accent mark in attaché, chargé d'affaires, démarche, communiqué, aide-mémoire, and détente betray the French origins of these words, other basic terms in diplomacy, from 'envoy' to 'accord', 'alliance' to 'passport', and for that matter 'protocol' itself, are also French—as is the very word diplomacy. Some diplomatic concepts take French words even in regular English, notably entente and rapprochement.

If language is the vehicle of culture—and France prides itself on both—it's not surprising to see how many terms from cuisine, art, and architecture are owed to French. Almost everything on a menu seems to be in French, so that's not a theme that need detain us here. But art is more Francophone than many realize. From the words 'art', music, dance, and theatre, to specific terms like paint, canvas, gallery, portrait, brush, pallet, montage, surrealism, impressionism, fauvism, cubism, symbolism, art nouveau, gouache, collage, and frieze, you cannot describe art without using French terms. When a musician 'performs' in 'harmony' or plays a 'melody' with 'rhythm', she is using French terms. In the theatre, the words 'director', 'author', and 'stage' all come from French as well.

And architecture would be impossible without borrowing words from French. A short list would include: aisle, arcade, arch, vault, voussoir, belfry, arc-boutant, buttress, bay, lintel, estrade, facade, balustrade, terrace, lunette, niche, pavilion, pilaster, and porte-cochère, before, like budget-strapped architects, we run out of space....

7

WORDS FROM JAPANESE

The remarkable capacity of the English language to borrow and absorb, in regular usage, words from other languages—with words that originated in French and German before coming into common use in English—is rather widely known. But an even more unlikely contender for loaning words to the English is Japanese.

A word many booklovers have learned is *tsundoku*, which refers to the growing pile of unread books one acquires or buys, without finding the time to read them. Most people know tycoon, to refer to an opulently wealthy business magnate, and *honcho*, for chief, are derived from Japanese, as (of course) is karaoke. Kids will tell you about the Japanese terms *manga* (comic books and graphic novels) and *anime* (a reverse usage from the English 'animation'); elegant homemakers will know *bonsai*, *ikebana*, and *origami* from their décor. Even more people speak of *ramen* noodles and sleep on a *futon* without realizing these words came from Japanese too. But there are several other Japanese words which—though not as widely understood as 'rendezvous' (from French) or *zeitgeist* (from German)—are nonetheless finding increasing acceptance in English, as words that describe something better than any existing words in our dictionaries.

My favourite Japanese loanword is probably *wabi-sabi*, a marvellous term that means accepting imperfection as a natural part of life. The Japanese are actually perfectionists—spotlessly clean, neat, and well-organized—so it may surprise you that they have developed a philosophical acceptance of the idea that not everything is perfect, permanent, or immutable; things and people eventually decay and die. An attitude of wabi-sabi also extends to aesthetics, like admiring an object because of a natural flaw in it rather than demanding that it be blemish-free.

Better known is perhaps *ikigai*, a term that summarizes your sense of purpose in life. More and more I find New Age friends referring to some source of motivation as ikigai—the sense of purpose that drives them on to taking on demanding new challenges. Someone whose ikigai hasn't yet been ignited might be *boketto*, unfocused and daydreaming, staring vacantly into space, aimless and unpurposeful.

Japanese culture not only gives us such words as *geisha*, *haiku*, *kimono*, *wasabi*, and *zen*, as well as several terms from Japanese martial arts, such as *judo*, *ju-jitsu*, *karate*, and *ninja*, but also *dojo* (a room or padded mat for judo). Japanese also has some lovely terms for people and relationships that English culture did not generate. A friend you can always rely upon in times of need, someone who will always be there for you, is *majime*, a word which encapsulates a number of qualities—reliability, sincerity, willingness to put in the hard yards. It's unlikely that a majime can be an *ozappa*, a person who is totally relaxed, unfazed by adversity and, by and large, couldn't care less about anything at all. A very different kind of relationship is conjured up by *Koi No Yokan*, the feeling you get when you meet a stranger and are so taken by her or him that you are sure you will fall in love with them—even if you have just met them.

Just as the Eskimo language is said to have seventeen different words for different types of snow and ice to distinguish them (whereas Hindi, for instance, just has 'baraf' to cover both snow *and* ice, since Hindi speakers see so little of either), so also Japanese has very precise words for weather. The word *kogarashi*, literally 'leaf wilting wind', has made its way into English usage to refer to the first cold winds of the late autumn season that alert you that winter is around the corner.

American English has become fond of the word *skosh*, a synonym of 'tad' or 'smidgen'—such as in 'could you turn the air-conditioning up a skosh'? It comes from the Japanese word *sukoshu* which means the same thing—a spot, a dash. (You could ask an Indian waiter for a skosh of milk in your tea, but I wouldn't be optimistic about the results.) Indians assume that the English word *rickshaw,* pronounced *raksha* in Hindi, originated in the subcontinent, but in fact it comes from the Japanese *jinrikisha—jin* means 'man', *riki* means 'strength' or 'power,' and *sha* means 'carriage'.

But why worry about words at all, you might well ask, when the Japanese have given us *emojis*, those clever little pictures that serve increasingly as a substitute for text? Perhaps we should just say *sayonara* to the whole subject?

8

LOANWORDS FROM VARIOUS LANGUAGES

The last few chapters, highlighting words of French, German, Irish, Indian, and even Japanese origin in the English language, might prompt an enthusiastic reader to wonder if there is any language spoken around the world that English has not borrowed words from. There may well be a few—no one can pretend to know all the 6,000 languages on our planet but it is remarkable to note how many languages have contributed to the English lexicon, brought in over many centuries of trade, colonization, imperialism, and migration.

To proceed alphabetically, using only words in common usage, *apartheid* comes from Afrikaans, a language spoken in South Africa. Arabic, of course, gave English words like *algebra*, a form of mathematics that Europe learned from the Arabs (and the Arabs learned from India). Bengali is credited for *jalfrezi*, a kind of meat, fish, or vegetable dish cooked with fresh chillies, tomatoes, and onions. When you say you are enthusiastically *gung-ho* for something, you are borrowing from the Chinese words for 'working together'. The English words *landscape* and *easel* were introduced by Dutch painters in the seventeenth century, as was *bumpkin (*as in 'country bumpkin', an unsophisticated rural figure) and *quack* in the sense of a fake doctor. Finnish most famously gives English the *sauna*. French is the subject of a separate chapter in this volume.

The word *jukebox* is from Gullah, a creole language spoken in the Sea Islands off the coast of Georgia in the United States. So, it seems, is *mojo* (originally meaning 'magical power' and now often used for the spark you possess to achieve something, as in 'he's got his mojo back'). Greek features in the roots of too many English words to list: *antique*, *ido*l, *dialogue*, *geography*, *grammar*, *architect*, *economy*, *encyclopaedia*, *telephone*, and *microscope* are just a handful of the thousands of words Greek gave English.

Hindi, as we have noted before, provides English with *shampoo*, *loot*, and *thug*, among many other words. Hungarian gave us *goulash* and *paprika*. The Inuit language of Greenland and the Arctic lands offers *kayak*, a canoe, and *anorak*, the weatherproof jacket. From Japanese, as we have seen in the preceding chapter, comes many words commonly used these days, including *karaoke*, *bonsai*, *futon*, *geisha*, *haiku*, and *zen*. Korean words in English have not crossed over from Korean culture: there are only the martial art, *tae kwon do*, and the food *kimchi* in English. Latin outdoes Greek in its contributions to English and, as the root language, requires no list.

Malay gives us *amok* in the expression 'run amok', which has come to mean 'going crazy' in English. Malayalam gives English *pariah*, the name of someone from an 'untouchable' caste, which in English refers to someone to be avoided, as in 'don't treat me like a pariah, talk to me!' Portuguese has blessed English with *monsoon*, *marmalade*, *molasses*, and *flamingo*, as well as the Indian English word *brinjal* for aubergine or eggplant. When you call someone a *czar*, you are, of course, borrowing from Russian, but so are you when you use the words *mammoth* and *steppe*. Spanish is the source of *alligator*, *vigilante*, *guitar*, *hurricane*, *plaza*, and *cafeteria*. Tagalog from the Philippines gives English *boondock* (which means 'mountain' in Tagalog but 'the back of beyond' or an 'isolated region' in English); 'he's from the boondocks' is an unkind way of referring to a country cousin freshly arrived from a remote area.

Urdu gave English *pyjamas* and *pashmina*, as well as *khaki*. Jewish migrants to the United States introduced Yiddish words into American English, which in turn flowed into the language through their use by Jewish–American writers: *chutzpah* ('audacity'), *kibitz* ('to offer unasked-for advice'), *kvetch* ('complain'), *maven* ('expert, know-it-all'), *meshuga* ('crazy'), *mensch* ('a good, upright man'), *nebbish* ('insignificant person'), and, of course, the ubiquitous *schmooze*.

Most of these words no longer feel as if they are 'borrowed' from other languages, so thoroughly have they infiltrated English. This is the strength of English, which makes it such a prime contender for the status of a global language. In an era where travel and the internet have brought the world much closer, pretty much everyone is learning English as a second (or third, or fourth) language. Whether its increasing acceptance worldwide is because it's a repository for words from other languages, or the other way around, English is evolving into the Esperanto of our times.

9

UKRAINE-RELATED WORDS

The scale of the suffering and destruction of the Russian invasion of Ukraine in 2022 have got every section of the commentariat exercised. Even the linguists, at least the amateur ones, are frothing at the mouth over a number of Ukraine-specific usage issues we need to be aware of.

For example, beware of lazily referring, as so many have done, to 'the Ukraine'. The use of the definite article ('the') unwittingly lends credence to the Russian proposition that Ukraine is not a country but a territory, a part of Russia for ages, when it was referred to as 'the Ukraine'—in the way that Lebanon used to be called 'the Levant' when it was part of Syria. The name 'Ukraine' actually means 'borderland', so calling it 'the Ukraine' in English implies it's just a territory that serves as Russia's borderland, whereas calling it simply 'Ukraine' is politically correct, since it honours the name as that of an independent entity. (In India, too, the British used to refer to 'the Punjab' and 'the Carnatic', but we have dropped the article since each are now states of the Indian Union as Punjab and Karnataka.)

Similarly, using the spelling 'Kiev' for the capital city is to give in to the Russian version of the name, which was in use from the days of the tsars to that of the USSR. The Ukrainians spell it 'Kyiv' in their language, and that's the version we should honour. That may be a problem for restaurant menus that still sell 'Chicken Kiev', a popular dish around the world. But at least it can keep its name while spelling it differently. Other food items were not so lucky in wartime. During World War I, the popular dish called *sauerkraut* suffered a huge drop in sales in the US because, with a name like that, it was obviously a German dish, prompting restaurant owners in New York to rename it 'liberty cabbage' (the old name resurfaced once hostilities had subsided).

The same war saw calls in America to rename hamburgers (named after the German port city of Hamburg) as 'liberty steaks', which flopped, though re-baptizing another popular food named for a German city, frankfurters, as 'hot dogs' was more successful. When I served at the UN in New York during the Iraq war, Americans angry at France's opposition to the war against Saddam Hussein's Iraq clamoured to rechristen the ubiquitous French fries as 'freedom fries'. They even did this on the menu of the Senate restaurant, but the silliness did not last. (No one pointed out that the French themselves took no national credit for the greasy food item, which in French is called *pomme frites* or simply *frites*, meaning 'fries', and not French at all.)

What next? Would bartenders start renaming the popular 'Moscow Mule' as 'Kyiv Mule'? What about 'Russian salad', which is not even Russian but a Belgian chef's concoction? It would make no sense to call it a 'Ukrainian salad,' since it has even less connection to Ukraine than it does to Russia. But the passions of war do strange things to otherwise sensible people.

One dish that is already in trouble is Canada's popular *poutine*, which many consider Canada's truly national dish (move over, maple syrup!). It's a preparation of potato fries, cheese curds, and gravy that's guaranteed to clog your arteries and send your cholesterol numbers shooting up. But the Ukraine war has affected many restaurant-goers' blood pressure first, and some are objecting to celebrating a dish whose name sounds distressingly similar to that of the reviled Russian president who ordered the invasion. What to do? One Canadian café thought it was being clever when it renamed the poutine dish on its menu 'Vladimir' instead. That raised even more objections, and the café was abashed enough to change the name to its Ukrainian version, spelling it 'Volodymyr', in honour of the Ukrainian president, Volodymyr Zelensky. But does that make any sense either, since poutine has nothing to do with either Russia or Ukraine anyway? Ironically, it turns out that the word 'poutine' is derived from a Quebecois French slang word meaning 'a mess'. That, I'm afraid, is exactly what the eponymous Russian president has created by initiating this war.

The war has also placed other expressions into circulation that may not have been familiar to everyone, at least judging by queries I received. What, one might ask, is 'Finlandization'? This is the term many are suggesting could appease Russian anger at Ukraine's alleged desire to join NATO. It refers to the policies followed by Finland, which managed to preserve its independence despite the proximity of the powerful Soviet Union by pledging neutrality in foreign policy, refusing to join NATO or any alliance that could have been seen as hostile to the USSR, and taking care to defer to Moscow on any issue that mattered enough to its superpower neighbour. As a result, it never provoked Russia into the kind of belligerent action that has now been inflicted on Ukraine. What Kyiv should do, some pundits say, is to learn from how Finland conducted itself during the Cold War. Thus, they suggest, its 'Finlandization' would ensure that Ukraine could live in peace. (Ironically, however, even Finland has given up its neutrality in response to the Russian invasion of Ukraine; it has now joined NATO, for fear that otherwise it might be next.)

'Why are the Ukrainians hurling javelins at the Russians?' another reader asked me. 'I thought they would have more sophisticated weaponry?' The Javelin is, in fact, a pretty sophisticated weapon. It's not the spear-tipped rod hurled by Olympians but the nickname of an American anti-tank weapon. You're reading a lot of references to Javelins because with the Russians moving in with tanks, the Javelin has become a potent symbol of Ukrainian resistance.

Who or what is the 'siloviki', and is it edible? asks one. Siloviki's a Russian word referring to the Russian president's 'inner circle'. The siloviki are his most trusted advisers and, at least according to Western media, are mainly people who served, as President Putin once did, in the dreaded secret service, the KGB.

And the 'oligarchs'? That's an English word applied very deliberately to a handful of very privileged Russians. The word oligarchy translates as 'government by a small group of people' but in regard to Russia, the term has a very specific connotation. When the formerly communist Soviet Union, in which all businesses were owned by the government, divested itself of its major holdings, the fruits of this privatization went to a handful of businessmen, many of them cronies of the new rulers of Russia. Market liberalization created a group of new businessmen who got their starts running what used to be state enterprises. Though they subsequently built them up into legitimate private sector behemoths, their association with the government continued, since their prosperity depended on not crossing the authorities. They were dubbed the 'oligarchs'.

So do oligarchs participate in 'friend-shoring'? No, they don't—they're not those kinds of friends! 'Friend-shoring', also called 'ally-shoring', is an American term defined as a commitment by Washington to work with countries that have a strong adherence to a set of norms and values that the US upholds, about how to operate in the global economy and about how to run the global economic system. The Ukraine war has led to calls on the US to promote the 'decoupling' of Western, and in particular European, economies from Russia, by helping these economies or 'shoring' them up. For instance, the US is attempting to wean European countries off their dependence on Russian oil and gas by finding them alternative supplies, or increasing American shipments of the same commodities. That's 'friend-shoring'.

And finally, what's with all the references to the letter 'z'? The innocuous final letter of our alphabet has been transmuted into a symbol of support for the Russian invasion. A large white Z has been seen painted on a number of Russian military vehicles and even tanks. Those wishing to express support and sympathy for the Russians have followed suit, painting a Z on their vehicles or waving flags with a big Z on them. Don't make the mistake, as one innocent did, of assuming that Z stands for Zelensky, the Ukrainian president who is the leader of his country's resistance to the Russian invasion. It stands for his enemies.

10

WORDS THAT DON'T EXIST IN ENGLISH

Most English speakers think of English as an extraordinarily well-endowed language, equipped with words for every occasion and situation, if only one knew them. After all, English has an exhaustive vocabulary of more than 750,000 words. Yet there are numerous words in other languages to express ideas, concepts, and emotions for which there is no English equivalent.

As a speaker of Malayalam, the language of India's Kerala state, I have been struck by some Malayalam terms for which there is no equivalent in English. Of these my favourite is 'ethramathe'. Malayalis are hardly reputed as mathematical geniuses, but the coinage of this numerate word was an act of genius. Imagine you have to identify a person, an item, or an object by their position in a long line of similar people, items, or objects. You go to pick up a rental car, for instance, and are told you can collect it from a row of cars in a parking lot. In English you would have to ask 'in which [number] position is my car parked?' to elicit the answer 'it's the ninth car in that row'. In Malayalam one word covers the idea—'ethramathe'. '*Ethramathe vandiaane*?' you ask, and your car is identified for you by its exact spot in numerical order.

Numbering doesn't always call for such precision, however. In Swedish, 'lagom' refers to when something is just the right amount; you don't specify the number, but you convey its exactitude. In Sweden, 'lagom' also represents the idea of living a balanced life. 'Enough' in English doesn't measure up to 'lagom'. Maybe 'just right' comes closer, but it still doesn't convey everything the word connotes—'just enough to satisfy my needs and leave me contented'. The Swedes' Scandinavian neighbours, the Danes, have gone farther with the word 'hygge'. It seems 'hygge', pronounced 'hue-guh', combines cosiness, comfort, well-being, and contentment in one word. It's meant to connote a strong feeling of comfort, security, reassurance, familiarity, and even kinship if you're among loved ones.

But when things are not right, and you can't properly express it, you have to turn to Russian, for 'toska'. As the famous novelist Vladimir Nabokov explained it: 'No single word in English renders all the shades of toska. At its deepest and most painful, it is a sensation of great spiritual anguish, often without any specific cause. At less morbid levels it is a dull ache of the soul, a longing with nothing to long for, a sick pining....' In English you could try melancholia, but Russians swear that doesn't go far enough, because toska is an inexplicable sadness, undirected at anyone or anything in particular, and implies a feeling of deep longing or wistful sadness without any coherent reason.

The Portuguese have a term that comes closer than any in English: 'saudade'. It's a sombre term with many definitions in English, but no equivalent, conveying as it does a beautiful, bittersweet longing for something absent in your life, maybe something you have never even experienced—or have experienced once, loved and lost, and may never experience again. There are many tinges of nuance to saudade that Portuguese-speaking people tell you cannot be rendered in English. A feeling of saudade is more than nostalgia, not just bitter-sweetness; it has elements of love, happiness, sadness, hope, emptiness, and desire. The writer Manuel de Melo describes it as 'a pleasure you suffer, an ailment you enjoy'. In other words, there isn't another word for it. It is just saudade.

I suppose the truth is that English just isn't as good at conveying emotions as some other languages are! We've already encountered, earlier in the book, 'schadenfreude' (the German word for the malicious pleasure you enjoy at another person's suffering). It's so much better than the English equivalent 'epicaricacy' that practically no one uses. But the most untranslatable emotion of all must be 'Mamihlapinatapai'—a word in the Yaghan language of Tierra del Fuego at the southern tip of Latin America. According to *Atlas Obscura*, 'Mamihlapinatapai' describes 'a look shared by two people, each wishing that the other would initiate something that they both desire, but which neither wants to begin.' Try expressing that in one English word!

One of the common features of some of the words from other languages for which there is no equivalent in English was that they conveyed emotions for which English just doesn't have the vocabulary. This is obviously a reflection of culture; with the famous English 'stiff-upper-lip' repressing all unseemly expressions of emotion, the English probably felt no need to devise those terms, since they were not permitted to experience them!

If you look around the world, there are several more emotions captured in other languages which describe feelings that cannot be expressed so easily in English. Love generates many of them. The Tagalog language of the Philippines has *kilig* for the 'feeling of butterflies in your stomach, especially when something romantic takes place'. (They also have *gigil* for the sense of happiness that comes from being around something or someone so irresistibly cute that you want to hug it!) The Norwegians speak of *forelsket* to describe the 'euphoria experienced as you begin to fall in love.' It's more than 'infatuation'; it's a heady emotion but not a superficial one, less transient than *kilig or gigil*. Readers in the UAE may be familiar with the Arabic word *ya'aburnee*, defined as 'a declaration of your hope that you will die before another person because of how unbearable it would be to live without them'. Can there be a more sincere expression of love?

Some terms are so culturally specific that they can't really exist anywhere else. Like *cafune*, which is not just Portuguese but specifically used only in the Portuguese spoken in Brazil. It means 'tenderly caressing or running your hands through your lover's hair'. As mentioned earlier, the Japanese phrase '*Koi No Yokan*' captures the feeling you experience when you meet someone for the first time and know you're going to fall in love. That sense of inevitability is also captured in the Mandarin Chinese term *yuanfen*, which relates to the fateful predestination or serendipity that draws one person to love another person. And when things don't work out, as sometimes happens in love, you have to turn to Russian for *razbliuto*, which describes 'the empty feeling you have for someone you once loved'.

Of course, love is not the only emotion that English words can sometimes fail to capture as succinctly as foreign ones. *Waldeinsamkeit* (in German) captures 'the feeling of solitude and connectedness to nature when being alone in the woods.' As we have seen, *wabi-sabi* is Japanese for 'finding beauty in imperfections'. In Spanish, *duende* conveys a sense of art's mysterious power to deeply move a person through the emotions aroused by the beauty of an artistic performance. Similarly, the Italians speak of *commuovere* to describe a heart-warming story that moves you to tears.

Some terms for emotions are startlingly precise: the Spanish have the word *estrenar* to describe the feelings you get when wearing something for the very first time! In Thai, *greng-jai* is the term for needing to ask someone for help or directions but feeling awkward or embarrassed to do so because it's an imposition, or you're afraid to hurt their feelings. On the other side of the coin, have you found yourself feeling helplessly flustered because someone is either watching, instructing, or nagging you and you just aren't able to do what they're expecting you to? The Germans even have a word for that feeling—*fisselig*, which is particularly used when that sense of being out of your depth to the point of incompetence is heightened by an important person watching you mess things up. Maybe you can take refuge in Yiddish and tell him you're just a *schlemiel*, an inept or clumsy person, or a *schlimazel*, a very unlucky person. In that case, there's nothing to do but shrug and say in Japanese, *shouganai* or *shikata ga nai*—terms to convey a resigned sense of 'what can I do, it just can't be helped?'

And if all these words make you feel overwhelmed by the unfamiliarity and confusion of trying to speak in a foreign language, don't worry, the Japanese have a word for it: *yoko-meshi*. And there's an easy solution for readers afflicted by *yoko-meshi*—just stick to English!

11

FOREIGN WORDS YOU MUST KNOW

In the preceding chapters, I have delved into the foreign origins of English words, but in this chapter, I'd like to discuss foreign words that are commonly used in English, but remain in their original languages and have not undergone transmutations of spelling or usage. Yet you need to know them because they are, in fact, commonly used in English, while remaining recognisably foreign.

One arena where a number of such phrases is used is the judiciary; judges are inordinately fond of them, often using phrases taken straight from Latin or French for ideas that could be easily expressed in English. Thus an 'amicus curiae' is a 'friend of the court'—someone appointed by the judges to delve into an issue in greater detail than the judges have time for, to advise the court. The Supreme Court of India prides itself on being 'a sentinel on the qui vive', which simply means it's 'on the alert', qui vive translating to 'who lives?' in French. Judges also like to use phrases like 'de jure' (according to the law), 'quid pro quo' (to refer to one thing given in exchange for another) 'sub rosa' (for secretly), 'in toto' (the whole thing), and 'status quo' for the existing state of affairs. A particular favourite is 'suo moto', sometimes wrongly spelled 'suo motu', relating to an action taken by a court of its own accord, without any request by the parties involved. The phrase 'suo moto' is Latin for 'on its own motion'; thus, 'the Supreme Court had taken suo moto notice of the case'.

Just in case anyone reading this is a budding lawyer (or if you just like reading news reports about court cases!), here's more judicial Latin you need to know: ad locum (at the place), ad interim (in the meantime or temporarily), ad valorem (in proportion to its value), ipso facto (by the fact itself), modus operandi (the method of doing something), modus vivendi (a way of living together), nota bene (note carefully or mark well), ex officio (by virtue of the office a person holds), persona non grata (a person no longer welcome), pro tem (temporarily, used for an acting office-holder, such as a president pro tem), pari passu (side by side, at the same rate, or equally), and sine anno (without a specific date).

For those of us who are happy to steer clear of the courts, there's still a few expressions we need to know that aren't, strictly speaking, English but are still used widely by native speakers. You might be invited to dine alfresco (outdoors) by an inamorata (a female romantic companion); and if you had hoped you were going incognito (with your identity concealed) and you don't behave, you could be caught up in an imbroglio (a difficult situation, a complicated mess). She might be a prima donna (a vain woman) who, for a divertissement (entertainment), wants to be taken to an expensive concert, where she can applaud a maestro (a master conductor or composer) of whom she is an aficionado (a fan or devotee), giving a virtuoso (highly skilled) performance that's a tour de force (literally a 'tower of strength', but meaning an exceptional achievement). You might have approached the ingénue (innocent young woman) with éclat (flair) and élan (vivacity), but since you don't enjoy music, be reduced to ennui (boredom). As soon as it's over, you decide to carpe diem (seize the day, or grab an opportunity), but you are caught in flagrante delicto (in blazing offence, or in the course of a transgression) by her father, who demands to know what you think you are doing. Unable to come up with a riposte (a quick reply), and with no great talent for repartee (a quick and witty response), you are struggling for the mot juste (the right word, the perfect expression) for your act of dolce far niente (sweet idleness). No longer attired comme il faut (properly), your amour proper (self-esteem) in tatters, you flee in dedecus (disgrace). Bonne chance! (Good luck).

As you might have surmised, all these expressions are from a melange (mixture) of European languages, mostly French, Italian, Spanish, and Latin. Unsurprising—such things usually happen only in Europe!

SECTION TWO

THE POINT OF PUNCTUATION

'Let's eat grandma'. Unpunctuated, it suggests a cannibal family deciding to consume the grandmother for dinner; with a simple comma—'Let's eat, grandma'—it's a friendly invitation!

12

PUNCTUATION

Punctuation is something no wielder of words can do without. One of the more delightful stories about the misuse of punctuation comes from the popular grammarian and author of the delightful book on punctuation, *Eats, Shoots & Leaves*, Lynne Truss:

> A panda walks into a cafe. He orders a sandwich, eats it, then draws a gun and fires two shots in the air.
> 'Why?' asks the confused waiter, as the panda makes towards the exit. The panda produces a badly punctuated wildlife manual and tosses it over his shoulder.
> 'I'm a panda,' he says, at the door. 'Look it up.'
> The waiter turns to the relevant entry and, sure enough, finds an explanation.
> 'Panda. Large black-and-white bear-like mammal, native to China. Eats, shoots and leaves.'

That comma carelessly placed after the word 'Eats' completely altered the meaning of the sentence—and the behaviour of this fictional panda. Instead of 'eats shoots and leaves' (pandas consume bamboo shoots and foliage) a single comma made this panda consume food, discharge a revolver, and depart!

The story is instructive, but it's not the only example of how punctuation marks can completely alter the meaning of a phrase or sentence. A simple comma could have transformed the unfortunate magazine headline that informed us 'Rachael Ray finds pleasure in cooking her family and her dog'.

A similar story has a computer class teacher announcing 'Let's learn to cut and paste kids!' Panicky parents had to be calmed down by the headmaster inserting the missing comma after 'paste'.

Worse is this true story: a man unfortunately sought to publicize his wife's recipe blog by announcing 'All those who like to cook and eat my wife just made a new blog at [URL provided]. Tell everyone.' I have no idea what 'everyone' was told, but I am sure he never heard the end of it from his wife. A colon [:] after 'eat' could have saved him (and her) endless amounts of grief from trolls.

One of the earliest (and arguably sexist) jokes I remember hearing in English class at school related to punctuation. The teacher told us of a mixed group of schoolchildren at a co-educational institution who were asked to punctuate the sentence: 'Woman without her man is useless.' The boys in the class duly punctuated it as 'Woman, without her man, is useless.' The girls, on the other hand, punctuated it this way: 'Woman! Without her, man is useless.'

A similar story in Truss' book concerns an unpunctuated letter which goes like this: 'Dear Jack I want a man who knows what love is all about you are generous, kind and thoughtful people who are not like you admit to being useless kind and inferior you have ruined me for other men I yearn for you I have no feelings whatsoever when we're apart I can be forever happy—will you let me be yours Jill.'

The question is, was it a love letter or a note of dismissal? All depends on how you punctuate it, without changing a single word. Here is the loving version first:

> Dear Jack, I want a man who knows what love is all about. You are generous, kind and thoughtful. People who are not like you admit to being useless, kind and inferior. You have ruined me for other men. I yearn for you. I have no feelings whatsoever when we're apart. I can be forever happy—will you let me be yours? Jill.

Now here is the same, identical text, but punctuated in a way that gives the totally opposite meaning to its contents:

> Dear Jack, I want a man who knows what love is. All about you are generous, kind and thoughtful people who are not like you. Admit to being useless, kind and inferior. You have ruined me. For other men, I yearn. For you, I have no feelings whatsoever. When we're apart, I can be forever happy—will you let me be? Yours, Jill.

If that hasn't convinced you that punctuation is king, then consider the simple sentence 'Let's eat grandma'. Unpunctuated, it suggests a cannibal family deciding to consume the grandmother for dinner; with a simple comma—'Let's eat, grandma'—it's a friendly invitation! As the poster on which I saw this example says: 'Punctuation can save a person's life!'

◆

It's not often that you derive an essay from an X (formerly Twitter) thread. But though it's a first for me, I wish to acknowledge my indebtedness to a tweeter who calls himself (or herself) 'The Cultural Tutor' for much of what follows—a disquisition on the origins of punctuation marks.

One of the most essential punctuation marks is the full stop. Without it, sentences would run on into each other and be difficult to tell apart, impeding our understanding. Just as spaces separated words, sentences were demarcated by the full stop, invented in the third century BCE by the Alexandrian scholar Aristophanes, who was the chief librarian of the famous library in that Egyptian port city.

The colon is also said to have originated with Aristophanes as a single middot (·) until it assumed the more familiar double form (:) used to indicate a medium-length pause. The colon has been around in English for centuries, but its modern usage is more extensive: for instance, it serves to provide examples like this, and it is so much easier to introduce lists with a colon. The semicolon is used as an intermediary between the full stop and the colon to connect two thoughts related by meaning but not syntax.

The idea of the comma (,) as a pause in speech, originates, like the colon, with Aristophanes' middot. But the Cultural Tutor tells us that the comma itself took the form of a slash (/) known as the *virgula suspensiva* during the Middle Ages. That '/' was reshaped into the ',' by the seventeenth century.

And then we have the parentheses () throughout this chapter. Their name refers to the Ancient Greek rhetorical concept to describe the inclusion of supplementary information in the middle of a speech. They serve to provide additional explanatory material that supplements the main information in a sentence (like this).

Does this raise some questions in your mind? No one really knows where the question mark (?) came from, but we are all familiar with the exclamation mark (!). It was probably derived from the Latin phrase 'io', which was an expression of joy that medieval writers placed at the end of sentences for emphasis. Eventually the 'I' was placed above the 'O' and it became an! So enjoy!

The hyphen (-) was first used like this (‿) by the grammarian Dionysius Thrax in 100 BCE, before proper letter spacing, to indicate that two words should be read together. Its purpose was the formation of compound words. Then, during the medieval era, with the formal introduction of letter spacing, it was used to connect words in handwritten manuscripts that had been incorrectly spaced. At this point it was still written as ‿ or sometimes as ⸗. But when Gutenberg invented the printing press in the fifteenth century, those forms became untenable, since printing type had to be set in a straight line and the ‿ was 'sublinear' (i.e., it appeared below the line of letters). This is why Gutenberg moved the connection sign to the middle of the line and the hyphen (-) as we know it today was born.

The dash is not exactly the same as the hyphen, though the two are often confused. A hyphen is really a short dash (-) to link two words but a dash is longer (– versus -) and serves to separate words; it is often seen as serving a similar purpose to the parenthesis. The dash has a different origin from the hyphen—it may have originated as a sentence terminator, like a full stop, and acquired its present use later—but there is no doubt about its usefulness. Printers differentiate between the 'em dash' and the 'en dash': the shorter 'en dash' is approximately the length of the letter N, and the longer 'em dash' the length of the letter M. The shorter en dash (–) is used to mark ranges and has the meaning 'to' in phrases like 'the Dubai–Sharjah highway,' while the longer em dash (—) is used to separate extra information and usually takes a space on either side.

One of the most ubiquitous punctuation marks in the age of the internet is the slash (/ or \): you can't type a URL without it. As noted, the / symbol started off in the medieval age as a comma. Once replaced by ',' it became known as an oblique stroke, modernized in the informal Swinging Sixties into the term 'slash'. Who could have known this centuries-old obsolete punctuation mark would have found a new lease of life in the computer era?

An amusing sidelight: at one time the slash did serve a useful purpose in British English, before the internet found a new use for it. Before decimalization of the currency, the British had to deal in pounds, shillings, and pence. The symbol '/' was used in the United Kingdom to separate shillings from pence when writing out sums of money: thus '2/6' meant two shillings and sixpence, whereas '5/-' meant five shillings exactly. Once the British decided life would be easier with a hundred pence in a pound, the slash fell into disuse, until the internet era came to its rescue!

Another punctuation mark that has found a new lease of life in the internet era, and more specifically on Twitter, is the ampersand (&). The symbol is a morph of the Latin word 'et', meaning 'and'. Since, as Twitterati know, one is limited by the number of characters one can use in a message, '&' has become a useful way of reducing three characters to one. The history of the name is also curious: apparently the '&' was often added to the end of the alphabet, read aloud as 'and per se &' which was abbreviated into 'ampersand'. A long term for a space-saving mark!

The most famous revival though, without which we couldn't send email, is the '@' in our email IDs. Oddly it's a very old symbol from the medieval era: in Bulgaria it stood for the 'A' in 'amen', it was an abbreviation for 'arroba' (a weight) in Spain, and for 'amphora' (a unit of volume) in Venice. By the seventeenth century @ was being used as short for 'at' in France—and that's where we're @!

For those who believe there's nothing new under the sun, the hashtag (#) is also antique—it was morphed from the letters 'lb', short for the Latin 'libra pondo' or 'pound weight'. From a symbol for pound weight the hash was widely used in business accounts, and then as a general number sign, before its social media reinvention.

The asterisk (*) has also found an extra use in social media, since placing one on either side of a word on WhatsApp types the word in bold. But its origins go back to the second century BCE when Aristarchus of Samothrace used them to correct mistakes in Homer. The Cultural Tutor tells us that the asterisk is 'perhaps the oldest unchanged punctuation mark'.

The apostrophe (') was borrowed from fifteenth century Italy as an 'elision marker', to stand for a missing letter ('loved' could be rendered by poets as 'lov'd'). The possessive apostrophe followed: apparently before its invention, a 'King's throne' had to be written as 'Kinges throne', until the apostrophe made it 'King's'.

We've used a lot of quotation marks in this chapter. 'These started as notations in the margins of medieval manuscripts,' says the Cultural Tutor, 'either to indicate emphasis or to indicate that somebody else had [first] said it.' (Like this!)

As the Tutor points out, these punctuation marks are in English, but can be used differently in other languages, and some languages have different marks altogether that are rarely used in English. But what's remarkable is that these symbols, invented by scholarly monks and medieval librarians, have survived through the ages to be essential in printing, then adapted in computing, and are now finding new uses on our smart phones!

13

APOSTROPHES

The closing of the Apostrophe Protection Society—because, it says, of the 'ignorance and laziness' of the general public—strikes a body blow against those fighting for correct English. After eighteen years of existence, the British Apostrophe Protection Society was disbanded by its founder and chairman, retired journalist John Richards, because, in his words, 'the ignorance and laziness present in modern times have won!' Despite his best efforts, he told the media, he lost the battle for proper usage of the 'much abused' apostrophe.

Derived from the Late Latin *apostrophus* and the Greek *apostrophos*, signifying 'turning away', the word 'apostrophe' first referred to an orator turning aside in the course of a speech to address someone briefly before returning to his audience. We also *apostrophize* when we address or appeal to someone who is not present—'Oh Mahatma Gandhi, where are you now when we really need you?' That too is called an apostrophe. But unless you are given to such overly dramatic flourishes, this form of apostrophe need not detain us much in this chapter.

The society was focusing instead on the apostrophe as a punctuation mark (') standing for a sign showing where a letter has been omitted in a word. In this role, the apostrophe helps clarify meaning, permits contraction, and helps with disambiguation.

The apostrophe (') was introduced into English in the sixteenth century in imitation of French practice; but just as English has dropped the various accent marks that still abound in French, some feel the apostrophe should be dispensed with as superfluous and unnecessary. According to Richards, they're winning.

This humble punctuation mark is more often misunderstood and misused than any other. It stands for a mark showing where a letter has been omitted in a word. In English, the mark often stands in for 'i', as in 'it's' for 'it is', or indicates possession ('Modi's government'), or marks contractions ('I'll', rather than 'I will', or ''twas' for 'it was'). Sometimes, more disputably, it's used for abbreviations, as in T'puram for Thiruvananthapuram, or to indicate the plurals of numbers ('three 7's'), letters ('there are four s's and two p's in Mississippi'), symbols ('too many &'s and #'s'), acronyms ('mind your p's and q's') or decadal dates ('he was stoned through most of the '70's').

The apostrophe as a punctuation mark poses ordinary users of English a number of problems. The most common is people's tendency to use 'it's' when they mean 'its'—a confusion arising, no doubt, from the assumption that the apostrophe is needed to indicate possession (but 'its' is that curse of all grammar students, an exception). 'It's an exception' is correct, since 'it's' stands for 'it is' in that sentence. But if you said 'The problem with grammar is it's exceptions' you'd be wrong, since here 'its' is sufficient to relate to the exceptions.

Also on the list of challenges would be when the possessive use of the apostrophe involves a double 's', as in 'Jesus's disciples'. Many prefer to leave the second s out altogether, and let the apostrophe do double duty in standing for both a possessive and an omitted letter, writing 'Jesus' disciples'. Other exceptions are generally made for familiar phrases like *whys and wherefores, oohs and ahs, ins and outs*.

Life gets really complicated when you're dealing with a phrase like 'do's and don'ts'. The *Oxford Style Guide* suggests spelling it as '*dos and don'ts*', which looks odd and inconsistent—and Lynne Truss argues for '*do's and don't's*'. So there's no unanimity on the do's and don'ts of apostrophizing.

A simple trick is to remember the exceptions: it's is always 'it is', 'who's' is always 'who is', and the possessive forms are 'its' and 'whose'. Another is 'won't', which is not a contraction of 'will not' (then it would have to be 'wi'n't') but of the archaic 'woll not', which means the same thing.

One clear rule of thumb could be to use apostrophes when not using them would obscure your meaning or even confuse your reader. This is because a function of the apostrophe is disambiguation (to make your meaning clear). For example, the phrase 'dot your i's and cross your t's'. If you left out the apostrophe, it would become 'dot your is and cross your ts'. Since 'is' is a different word altogether, omitting the apostrophe would require your reader to pause and re-read the sentence to get the intended meaning. The rule of disambiguation makes it clear that if an apostrophe will avoid confusion, you should use it.

The usefulness of the apostrophe was made clear when the British novelist Kingsley Amis, challenged to produce a sentence whose meaning depended on a possessive apostrophe, came up with three versions of the same sentence:

> Those things over there are my husband's. (*Those things over there belong to my husband*.)
> Those things over there are my husbands'. (*Those things over there belong to several husbands of mine*.)
> Those things over there are my husbands. (*I'm married to those men over there*.)

In addition to Amis's clever example, writers can use the apostrophe to represent a particular style of speech. They might write somethin' to convey the speech of people who don't pronounce the final 'g' of the word 'something'. And in places like the American South or the Bombay in which I grew up, the apostrophe does duty in the local patois, 'y'all' (a contraction of 'you all'). My Anglo-Indian friends in that city were much given to asking 'How're y'all, men?'—which charming expression simply cannot be rendered without the apostrophe!

However, as grammarians and rhetoricians will tell you, that is not all. The apostrophe comes in handy to make your meaning precise. For instance, if you wrote 'Abdul and Ismail's restaurants', the placing of the apostrophe makes it clear that Abdul and Ismail own several restaurants together; but if you wrote 'Abdul's and Ismail's restaurants', it means you are speaking about restaurants that Abdul and Ismail own separately. Thus the apostrophe is one of the more indispensable elements of language, since its absence can provide a wholly different meaning to what you intended to say.

On the other hand, when it's not needed, don't use it. The British speak ruefully of the 'greengrocer's apostrophe', an error made particularly in signs on grocery stores saying 'banana's by the dozen', 'carrot's for sale', and so unnecessarily on. But what can one do about the retail trade when chains have inflicted such howlers on the world as 'Toys 'R' Us' and other examples of punctuation as decoration, rather than conveying any meaning?

Similarly, apostrophes should not be used for the plurals of letters referring to examination grades—'She scored all As', *not* 'She scored all A's'. Nor is there any need for an apostrophe when you wish to convey the plurals of abbreviations containing capital letters: 'This job vacancy attracted a lot of applicants with MAs and PhDs' is correct, not 'MA's and PhD's'.

Opponents of the apostrophe have pointed to the maddening inconsistency of its use in everyday life. Take just one common name found in many British cities. While Newcastle United play football at a stadium called St James' Park, Exeter City play at St James Park (no apostrophe), and London has a St James's Park (apostrophe plus second s), though it really is a park and not a football stadium!

Many have suggested that apostrophes ought to be abandoned altogether, as the department store Harrods has done but the grocery chain Sainsbury's has refused to. The argument is that they are superfluous, and the meaning is evident to most people with or without it. This 'apostrophe apostasy' is not new: George Bernard Shaw called them 'uncouth bacilli', and many linguists have argued that apostrophes are unnecessary. But in my own view, *this little-noticed but often-misused mark is an asset to the language*.

Apostrophes may have begun to go out of fashion, as the Apostrophe Society has concluded, but let's still use them for the sake of clarity—at least till the world exclaims: 'it's time's up for the apostrophe!'

14

HILARIOUS HYPHENS

A hyphen, as we all know, is a brief horizontal line employed to link two words together or to unite syllables within a word that have been split by the line break in a printed text. It indicates which word belongs to which, and saves readers from wasting time in figuring that out. The term originates from the Greek word 'huphen', which signifies 'together'. The ancient Greeks proposed a sublinear hyphen (‿) positioned beneath the words to establish a connection. Modern writing simplified that into -.

Shakespeare, or Shak-speare as some spelled it during his time, stands out as the pre-eminent practitioner of hyphenation, thanks to his prolific creation of novel compound words in English. Among his innovative hyphenated compounds were 'sea-change', 'leap-frog', 'bare-faced', and 'fancy-free'. Another prominent literary figure, Milton, also embraced hyphenation in his writings, employing it in words like 'dew-drops', 'man-slaughter', and 'eye-sight'. Donne, too, exhibited a penchant for hyphenated compounds, as seen in expressions like 'death-bed' and 'passing-bell', a reminder of his unique ability to connect dissimilar ideas. Many of these terms have become so common that they've shed their hyphens over the centuries. There is unquestionably a clear trend indicating that the hyphen is becoming less prominent, even though assertions of its extinction are premature.

And yet the common hyphen is often essential to make sense of a text; its presence or absence can dramatically alter the meaning of a phrase. How would you react if you saw a 'man-eating chicken' instead of a 'man eating chicken'? An 'anti-animal cruelty charity' probably doesn't adore puppies as much as you might assume an 'anti-animal-cruelty charity' would. Someone who has recently acquired a century-old house is indeed a 'new homeowner', and not a 'new-home owner'. Individuals who advocate 'hate-free speech' are distinctly more liberal than those who 'hate free speech'. A 'slippery-eel salesman' sells slippery eels, while a 'slippery eel salesman' takes your money and slinks away. And, not to forget, a 'little used car' is not necessarily the same as a 'little-used car'.

According to linguist Angus Stevenson, there were 16,000 hyphenation changes in the sixth edition of the Shorter Oxford English Dictionary. Certain compound nouns, such as 'ice cream', 'fig leaf', 'hobby horse', and 'water bed', have been separated into two distinct words. Meanwhile, others like 'bumblebee', 'crybaby', and 'pigeonhole' have been amalgamated into single words. Shakespeare's 'leap-frog' is often rendered as 'leapfrog', Milton's 'man-slaughter' has lost its hyphen in court, and 'dewdrops' aren't seen as needing a hyphen any more.

The reason, Stevenson suggests, is that people are not confident about using hyphens any more. Printed writing in advertisements and web sites is very much design-led these days, and designers feel that hyphens mess up the look of a nice bit of typography. However, scholars admit that there are places where a hyphen is necessary to avoid ambiguity.

The misplaced hyphen that frequently occurs in newspapers, the narrowness of whose columns often require non-hyphenated words to be printed over two lines and therefore hyphenated for clarity, can be an irritant to readers. A prominent London newspaper once published a series of irate letters to its editor expressing strong dislike for the resultant irrational hyphenations. Among the more hilarious hyphenated words from newspapers and online sources were these treasures (some of which were actual mistakes, while others were fabricated): 'pronoun-cement', 'brains-canner', 'bed-raggled', 'the-rapist', 'prose-cute', 'surge-on', 'not-ables', 'cart-ridge', 'pa-rent', 'off-end', 'diver-gent', 'generations', 'man-aging', 'past-oral', 'pro-state', and 'fat-her'.

Additionally, there was a series of hyphenated words related to the different stages of life: 'ad-age', 'plum-age', 'mess-age', 'front-age', and 'pass-age', with 'dot-age' being the culmination. These were akin to 'broke-rage' and 'stop-page'. 'Rampage' lent itself to double hyphenation hilarity. It could be misprinted as either 'ram-page' or 'ramp-age'.

Thanks to the advancements in computer technology which have ended the role of typesetters and compositors, modern newspapers and magazines space the words automatically to fit column widths, and so seldom need to hyphenate printed words awkwardly any more. Consequently, situations that used to result in typographical mishaps like 'mans-laughter' and legendary errors like 'leg-ends' are now almost non-existent. The notorious yet frequently deployed 'comical hyphen' that loved hanging out at the end of lines of newspaper print may finally fade into oblivion.

SECTION THREE

SPELLING BUGS

Let's face it, English spelling is ridiculous, as the linguist and author Arika Okrent bluntly explains: 'Sew and new don't rhyme. Kernel and colonel do.'

15

ABSURDITIES OF SPELLING

Years ago, the popular sitcom *I Love Lucy*, starring Lucille Ball, featured a hilarious scene of her correcting her Cuban–American husband Desi Arnaz's English pronunciation. He reads aloud the word 'cough', and is told the 'ough' rhymes with 'off'. Then he reads 'bough' as 'boff', and is told it should be 'bow'. Then he pronounces 'through' as 'throw' and is told the 'ough' is pronounced 'oo'. He goes through the same confusion with the words 'thought' (where 'ough' is pronounced 'aw'), 'tough', where it's pronounced 'uff', and 'though' where it's supposed to come out as an 'oh'. And this is the same four letters, 'ough', that's pronounced six different ways! Arnaz gives up in frustration—and many an unwary learner of the English language might do so too. Even before encountering more complicated discoveries like the fact that 'drought' does not rhyme with 'thought'!

Let's face it, English spelling is ridiculous, as the linguist and author Arika Okrent bluntly explains: 'Sew and new don't rhyme. Kernel and colonel do.' So similar spellings involve completely different pronunciations, while words that sound alike can be spelled very differently. Thus the vowels 'ea' often come together in many words, but can be pronounced three different ways: as 'ee' (in teak, please, deal, or beach) or as 'eh', as in bread, head, instead, dealt, or wealth, and even as 'ay', if you're saying aloud the words break, steak, or great. If you find that exasperating, it is—there are no really absolute rules and you just have to know how the words are spelt.

In most languages around the world words are mainly pronounced as they are written, so when you learn one of these languages, your accent might be off but your pronunciation should be largely right. Languages like French have silent letters and other quirks, but the rules governing them are largely predictable. You certainly can't say the same about English. The letter 'l' is silent in English words like 'could' and 'should', but pronounced clearly in 'mould'.

Even vowels by themselves are not reliable indicators of pronunciation. The simple letter 'a' is not pronounced the same in all words. It sounds completely different in 'father' (the 'ah' sound) than in 'bather' (the 'ay' sound), just as *dame* is not pronounced with the same 'a' as *dart*. The same is true of 'e' in 'bed' (the short sound) and in 'eh' (the longer 'ay' sound); of 'i' (which in 'different' is not the same as in 'diverge'); of 'o' ('o' from 'host' is not pronounced like the 'o' in 'cost'); and of 'u' ('cut' versus 'cute' or 'but' versus 'duty'). You don't have to be an American sitcom character to realize such differences aren't absorbed in a day, but require years of reading and hearing the spoken language to correlate the two.

Two of the vowels also reinforce themselves in words where they are repeated, but even when you double up the vowels they don't sound alike: 'oo' in 'moon' or 'boot' is a long sound whereas 'oo' in 'book', 'cook', or 'foot' is a short one. (It gets even more complicated with 'roof', which some native English speakers pronounce with the long 'oo' while others render the same word with a short sound.) The long and the short of it is that such pronunciation inconsistencies recur elsewhere: the 'u' in 'push' is a short sound while the 'u' in 'June' is a long one.

Very many of those for whom English is a second language have given up trying to master these intricacies and simply rely on the 'spell checker' embedded in their word-processing software to correct their spellings for them. But these aren't perfect either, as Karan Thapar wrote hilariously a couple of years ago: 'Eye halve a spelling chequer, it came with my pea sea, it plainly marques four my revue Miss steaks eye kin knot sea. Eye strike a key and type a word, and weight four it two say weather eye am wrong oar write, it shows me strait a weigh. As soon as a mist ache is maid, it nose bee fore two long, and eye can put the error rite, its rare lea ever wrong. Eye have run this poem threw it, I am shore your pleased two no, it's letter perfect awl the weigh—My chequer tolled me sew.'

◆

Earlier in this book, I discussed some of the differences between British and American English, but did not discuss the most visible difference for literate Anglophones—spellings. I was reminded of this omission recently when a kerfuffle broke out in Australia over a letter written by King Charles III to the Governor of Victoria, commiserating with her about the floods in her state. It began: 'Whilst I realize that this emergency is not over….'

'Whilst' passed muster with Australians as one of the acceptable eccentricities of royal usage, but 'realize' left many Australians shocked. One purist erupted in print. 'Realize?! I had to read the letter more than once,' she wrote. 'To zee, or not to zee?' quipped another. For generations of schoolchildren trained by British teachers have been taught to write 'realise', while Americans 'realized' otherwise. (And whilst we are at it, 'zee' is not the King's English either; the Brits, and those they colonised, not colonized, are taught to say 'zed'.)

Ironically, the King's letter was suitably accurate in traditional terms, since 'realize' was the common spelling in Elizabethan England. Much of the preference for 's' comes from the French origins of many English words—the verb 'realiser' in French (meaning 'to realise') is at the root of the English spelling. But the Americans went for the z-option, just as they preferred the Elizabethan 'fall' to the later-English 'autumn' now used in modern Britain. Dr Samuel Johnson's Dictionary supported the s-spelling, while Noah Webster's in America chose the z, and the two versions have existed ever since.

Many English users around the world use the two spellings interchangeably, often depending on which version their word-processing spell checker favours (or favors, if your default language is 'English (US)' rather than 'English (India)' which this colonized columnist favours.) Webster, seeking to standardize spellings in American English when preparing his famous dictionary during the 1780s, not only turned every -ise into -ize, he also transformed 'gaol' into 'jail', 'plough' into 'plow', and 'labour' into 'labor'. Any English teacher scrutinizing your text in Britain would dock you points for using any of the latter spellings.

The British are much more old-fashioned in staying true to word origins in determining spellings—thus 'mediaeval' in English, whereas America goes for 'medieval' without its additional Greek 'a', and 'manoeuvre' in English rather than the American 'maneuver', which is less faithful to the French root word 'oeuvre'. Americans with an upset stomach have diarrhea; Brits suffer from diarrhoea. As an American remarked sourly: 'Yeah, that spelling makes sense, since it looks like you've really lost control of your vowels!'

In 1906, the philanthropist Andrew Carnegie, who had given away much of his fortune endowing public libraries, created a Simplified Spelling Board to 'rationalize' American spellings. Carnegie and his supporters argued that the only thing preventing English from becoming a 'world language' and an instrument of global peace was its 'contradictory and difficult spelling'. They were careful not to speak of reform but of 'simplification by omission'. This would be achieved by dropping unnecessary letters, which were not pronounced anyway, like the superfluous 'a' and 'o' in 'mediaeval' and 'manoeuvre'. Thus 'anemia', 'anesthesia', 'archeology', 'encyclopedia', and 'orthopedic' replaced their British versions, whose spellings still reflected fealty to their word origins in classical Greek or Latin. The Simplified Spelling Board also changed the British -re endings to -er, as in 'caliber' for 'calibre' and 'fiber' for 'fibre', and dropped the Frenchified spellings of 'catalogue to 'catalog' and 'programme' to 'program'. (All these changed spellings have caught on and become the American standard.)

But the Simplified Spelling Board went even farther. Why

should the letter 'i' be present in the word 'believe', they asked, and also changed 'through' to 'thru' and 'surprise' to 'surprize'. These and others were a step too far, and a backlash began. When President Theodore Roosevelt endorsed the recommendations and vowed to use the new spellings in his own communications, the press had a field day. The *Louisville Courier-Journal* mocked him: 'Nuthing escapes Mr. Rucevelt. No subject is tu hi fr him to takl, nor tu lo for him to notis. He makes tretis without the consent of the Senit.' Nothing works as well as ridicule. The president rescinded his order, and American English is still recognizably English, give or take an extra zed!

Many of the differences between American and British spellings are attributable to the British remaining more traditionalist in reflecting fealty to the original roots of the words (often derived from French, Greek, or Latin) while the Americans sought to rationalize their spellings in the interests of practical contemporary usage. Roosevelt's endorsement of the most radical attempts at this drew more attention and scrutiny than some of the new spellings could withstand, and in the face of a widespread backlash and much ridicule, the president backed off. The Simplified Spelling Board collapsed in 1920 upon Carnegie's death, which ended its sole source of funding.

But some of its rejected ideas have continued to find favour with reformists. Those of its changes that stuck and have survived in American usage to this day include 'program' for 'programme', 'fiber' for 'fibre', and 'maneuver' rather than 'manoeuvre'. Other proposals did not fare as well, because while they indeed simplified spellings of commonly used words, they made the user seem semi-literate. The proposal, for instance, to eliminate superfluous letters that are not pronounced was acceptable in 'catalog' or 'analog', but not if you converted 'have' to 'hav' or 'are' to 'ar'. These just didn't look right, and people shrank from adopting them.

Since the Simplified Spelling Board's proposals were all based on rational principles, it's interesting to examine some of them today. One suggestion was to eliminate silent letters, not just at the end of words, but also within them, so 'debt' would be spelled 'det', and 'island' as 'iland'. 'Ghost' and 'paradigm' would lose the unpronounced 'h' and 'g' respectively. Double consonants before a silent 'e' would be trimmed, so cigarette would be cigaret, giraffe 'giraf', and (one change that did work) gramme became gram, including in 'telegramme'. Most double-consonant word-endings would be reduced to single ones, so 'add' would become 'ad', 'bill' would become 'bil', and sure enough, 'spell' would henceforth be 'spel'. If that seemed to many to be a loss—pardon me, a 'los'—there was an exception for 'short vowels', so the double consonant was retained in 'all', 'roll', or 'needless'. The exception, of course, immediately nullified the value of the change.

Another rule rendered less simple by insistence upon an exception was to drop the silent h in words like 'character', except before E, I, or Y—so 'school' would become 'scool' but chemist, architect, and monarchy would be unchanged. Similarly, the unnecessary 'ue' endings would go in 'prologue' (prolog) and 'tongue' (tung), but not in 'vague' or 'rogue'. Confused? Sensibly enough, the superfluous 'ough' would be eliminated in 'although', borough, and doughnut—and thorough, through, and though would become thoro, thru, and tho. But exceptions rose again: 'For plough write plow, but not bow for bough.' Go figure—or should that be figger?

There were, however, entirely reasonable propositions like dropping the 'ea' in words like 'head' or 'heart' and rendering them 'hed' and 'hart' respectively. Eccentricities like 'hiccough' would be replaced by a no-nonsense 'hiccup'. The French 'eau' ending would be dispensed with, so 'bureau' would become 'buro'; scissors and scenery would lose their 'c's', and 'guard', 'guess', and 'guide' their misleading 'u's'. 'Young' would shed its 'o' and 'rhetoric' and 'haemorrhage' their extra h's. And 'gh' would not be allowed to be pronounced 'f', so that cough would be spelled 'cof' and laugh become 'laf'. Had enuf?

16

SILENT LETTERS

English may well be the world's most popular language, but spelling its words properly can be a nightmare. Amongst the biggest challenges is the curse of 'silent letters'—the letters that pop up in words but are not pronounced, like the 'k' in 'know' or the 'w' in 'wrong', the 'b' in 'subtle', the 'a' in 'bread', and the 'h' in 'ghost'—leading the foreign student of the language to tear their hair out in despair, wondering what on earth these letters are doing there in the first place.

And they're everywhere. According to the author of *The Word Snoop: A Wild and Witty Tour of the English Language!* Ursula Dubosarsky, about 60 per cent of English words contain silent letters, and they can be consonants as well as silent vowels. Worse still, they can be found at the beginning, middle, or end of a word. There is no simple rule to explain when to use a silent letter. You just have to know the spelling of the word.

How did this awkward phenomenon come about? In many cases, it's because the English word originated in a foreign language and retained elements of the original spelling in that language, like 'psychology' with the silent 'p', which testifies to its Ancient Greek origins. Fans of the immortal English humourist P. G. Wodehouse will recall his memorable character Psmith telling people the 'p' in his name was silent, 'as in Phthisis and ptarmigan'. Tsunami, similarly, is a Japanese word, and though the 't' is silent in English, it helps indicate the foreign origin of the term.

These are 'dummy silent letters', which are written but produce no sound. There are also 'auxiliary silent letters', letters that work with other letters to form a distinct sound, such as silent letters in exocentric combinations (two letters that produce a new sound, like 'ch') or endocentric combinations (two letters that produce the sound of one of the letters in the pair, like the 'ff' in different).

That's all very well, you might say, if you're a linguist or an etymologist. But for ordinary folk, do these silent letters serve any useful purpose? Well, arguably they do. Different spellings help you tell similar sounding words (or homophones) apart, like 'our' and 'hour', which takes a silent 'h'. Silent letters help you distinguish among the different meanings of the words know, now, and no.

But for the most part, silent letters just *are,* and you simply have to know them to get your spellings right. Attempts to spell out rules are so complicated that no normal person will remember them, such as:

- B is silent before 't' and after 'm'.
- C is silent after 's' and before 'i', 'e', or 'y'. C is also silent in the combination 'ck'.
- E is silent at the end of a word and makes the internal vowel a long vowel.
- GH is silent at the middle or end of a word, and when preceded by an 'i' the 'i' is long.
- H is silent after most consonants and between two vowels. An initial 'h' may be silent or pronounced.
- K is silent in the combination 'kn' at a word's beginning.
- N is silent in the digraph 'mn'.
- P is silent in the combination 'ps' at the beginning of a word.
- S is only pronounced once in the combination 'ss', and is sometimes silent after an 'i'.
- T may be silent in the pair 'st', after 'f', and in the combination 'tch'.
- U is silent in the pair 'ui' and when it follows 'g' in the combinations 'gui' and 'gue'.
- W is silent in words beginning with 'wr' as well as in some other words.

And to make matters worse, there are exceptions to almost all these rules. So I tend to sympathize with the brilliant anonymous poet who wrote this verse that a friend forwarded to me recently:

The Sound of Silenced Letters

We know the letter B doesn't belong in subtle
But what has the letter C got to do in a muscle?
The role of the D in Wednesday we can't define
Why should G be present in a gnat or in a sign?

To be honest, does the H in rhyme ring a bell?
And can the J in marijuana anybody smell?
Who knows why the K in knee won't knock
And why the L in walk or in calf would not talk

The first M in mnemonic is hard to understand
Would the damned N in the column ever stand?
We can't say the P in psalm or in psychology
And S alone gets tossed out from the debris

Is the T heard when you listen to a whistle?
W is not write, it's wrong, don't try to wrestle
X is the mistake in a faux pas, get the clue?
Hush, no rendezvous with Z, goodbye, adieu!

There's no doubt that English spellings are irrational. It was George Bernard Shaw who suggested that following English rules, 'fish' could be spelled 'ghoti': 'gh' as in 'rough', 'o' as in 'women', and 'ti' as in 'motion'! But the interesting thing about language is that irrationality is part of its charm. It's absurd, but it's English, most people thought, and we love it the way it is. That's why, however rational the Simplified Spelling Board's ideas might have seemed, most people preferred to leave most words spelled the way they traditionally are—even when those spellings don't really make any sense.

If English didn't have silent letters, just imagine how this paragraph would sound if read aloud exactly as written, pronouncing every consonant: 'The rogue knight doubted that the asthmatic knave in knickers could climb the castle columns, but when their wrangle wrought chaos on the couple, the knight resigned with the knowledge that their tight-knit friendship wouldn't succumb to dumb disputes.' In reality, almost every word contains silent letters that save them from sounding absurd.

Silent letters serve different types of purposes in the language. Take, for example, the silent letter 'e' at the end of words like lapse, bee, pile, ride, and cattle: each serves different purposes. The [-e] of 'lapse' shows the word is different from the plural 'laps'. Since 'be' and 'bee' are homophones (words that sound alike), they must use different spellings to aid understanding. The 'e' at the end of 'pile' is essential to distinguish it from 'pill' and similarly 'ride' from a word with an entirely different meaning, 'ride'. The word 'cattle' cannot be spelt without the 'e' because it would look odd—and as the grammarians tell us, syllabic consonants are always spelt with a vowel letter and a consonant letter. (Of course, that rule overlooks the 'sm' in sarcasm or prism). The same would apply to words like giraffe, cassette, largesse, or gazelle. Basically 'e' serves as a diacritic letter, one that is not pronounced but changes the pronunciation of another syllable next to it.

But then how do you defend words like pterodactyl and tsunami, which begin with letters that are not pronounced? The answer lies in etymology—these words originated in other languages, Greek and Japanese respectively. The Greek-origin 'mnemonic' loses the sound of its first 'm', though when 'mn' also come together in 'solemn' or 'hymn', it's the 'n' that's not pronounced. The 'th' in 'asthma' are silent; their only purpose is to advertise the word's classical Greek and Latin origins. Many words borrowed from French end with silent letters, like apropos, rendezvous, and faux. Occasionally a silent 'p' comes before the end of the word, as in 'receipt'; but the 'p' is pronounced in 'concept'. There are silent 'b's' in subtle and debt, and also at the ends of words like bomb, climb, comb, crumb, dumb, lamb, numb, and thumb.

It gets more maddening: the 'g' is silent in the word 'phlegm' but pronounced in the word 'phlegmatic'. When the letters 'sc' come together, the 'c' is pronounced in 'school', but silent in 'scent'. There are differences between British and American pronunciations of 'schedule': the 'c' is silent for the former, who say 'schedule', while the 'h' is silent for the latter, who say 'sked-yule'. The practice is repeated for 'herb', where the 'h' is silent for the Americans, while 'erb' sounds uneducated to the British ear. Mercifully, neither pronounces the silent 'k' in 'knight', which is essential to distinguish it from the English word 'night', just as 'write' needs a different spelling from 'rite' and 'right' to avoid confusion. Similarly, 'w' is silent in wrist, wrack, wrangle, wrap, wreath, wrench, wrestle, wrinkle, writ, and wrong—and also in answer, sword, two, and who!

The letter 'u' and 'ue' are silent in words like build, catalogue, dialogue, colleague, guard, guess, laugh, league, and tongue. (Though the Americans have already accepted 'catalog' and 'dialog' as valid spellings, British English frowns upon taking such liberties). Growing up in India, I enjoyed a childhood joke about the silent letters 'ue'. A man wishing to travel to the Netherlands goes to a travel agent, and asks for a ticket to the Hague, which he pronounces 'Haig-you'. The travel agent corrects him: 'You mean the Hague.' The belligerent client responds: 'Do what I tell you, and hold your tung-you.' The agent laughs: 'It is not "tung-you". It is "tongue".' The exasperated client shouts: 'Just sell me the ticket, you cheeky fellow. I am not here to arg.'

17

THE RULE OF ABLAUTREDUPLICATION

'Because without our language, we have lost ourselves,' the Australian writer Melina Marchetta wrote in *Finnikin of the Rock*. 'Who are we without our words?' Indeed, our words are fundamental to who we are, and the way we use our words includes things we think about before saying, and things that come to native speakers of a language instinctively, without thinking. One of these is the rule of ablautreduplication.

The rule of what? I hear you saying. Never heard of it! Ablautreduplication? What are you talking about? Is it even English? Bear with me, and I will explain.

Have you ever wondered why, in English, we say that a clock goes 'tick-tock', not 'tock-tick', or if it's a grandfather clock, why it chimes the hours with a 'ding-dong', not a 'dong-ding'? Why is a weak leader given to making feeble statements considered 'wishy-washy' rather than 'washy-wishy', or the pattern on his tie described as 'criss-cross' rather than 'cross-criss'? Why does the giant ape in the horror movie 'King Kong' sound just right while 'Kong King' somehow doesn't work?

There is a good reason for all this—and that is the rule of ablautreduplication. It is one of the unwritten rules of the English language that native speakers of English know instinctively without having to learn it formally. Ablautreduplication (usually merged as one word) is the pattern by which vowels change in an expression consisting of two repeated words to form a new word or phrase with a specific meaning, like tick-tock, ding-dong, wishy-washy, or criss-cross. The rule states that if there are more than two such words, then the order of the words has to correspond to vowel sounds I, A, and O, in that order. If there are only two words, then the first is I and the second is either A or O.

The reason for this (and even instinctive rules have reasons) is that the vowel sounds in these words move from the front to the back of your mouth. This is why English has the expressions mish-mash (confused mess), chit-chat (idle conversation), dilly-dally (delay), tip-top (spiffy), hip-hop (music), flip-flop (reversal of positions), tic-tac (the game or the mint), sing-song (to describe a high-pitched voice), tick-tock, ding-dong, wishy-washy, and criss-cross—and for that matter even proper nouns like ping-pong (table tennis) or even King Kong. If you reverse the order of the words in any of these expressions, it just doesn't sound right. To the English speaker, even though all four of a horse's hooves make exactly the same sound on a cobble-stoned street, the horses always go 'clip-clop', never 'clop-clip'. What about vowels other than A, I, or O? Follow the front-of-your-mouth-to-the-back rule, and you understand why donkeys bray 'hee-haw' and not 'haw-hee'.

English is full of such unwritten rules, just as England itself is home to an unwritten Constitution. There's another similar rule in the name 'Little Red Riding Hood' from the famous fairy tale: in any phrase or expression that uses multiple adjectives, a specific order must be followed. Adjectival order in English absolutely must follow this sequence: Opinion - Size - Age - Shape - Colour - Origin - Material - Purpose. That's why the English always describe fantasy Martians as 'little green men', not 'green little men'. This means that you can have a 'lovely enormous old circular brown Indian teak picture frame', but if you mix up that word order in the slightest particular, you'll sound like you don't know the language.

That seems clear enough, especially if you can even remember the mnemonic for the rule, which is OSASCOMP. (When in doubt, conjure up OSASCOMP, and like 'Open Sesame', it will resolve any confusion for you.) But hold on, you might say: this is English—aren't there exceptions? After all, the expression 'Big Bad Wolf', from the same fairy tale as Little Red Riding Hood, violates this rule; following the strict order of 'opinion - size

- noun' from OSASCOMP, shouldn't it be 'Bad Big Wolf'? No, because when there's a clash, the rule of ablautreduplication prevails. Remember the basic rule about the I-A-O order? That's ablautreduplication, and the rule of ablautreduplication is infallible—and inviolable.

18

VOWEL RULES

When we discussed the rule of ablautreduplication, we talked about inviolable vowel order in compound words—I-A-O, as in mish-mash or King Kong. Some of you may have noticed that the letter 'e' was missing from that rule, whereas it is often considered the most indispensable vowel in languages derived from Latin, like English and French. The brilliant if somewhat eccentric French writer Georges Perec took up the issue of the indispensability of the letter 'e' by writing an entire novel without using that letter. His lipogrammatic novel titled *La Disparition* in French, was the literary sensation of 1969. Translating it wasn't easy, since even the title means 'The Disappearance', which contains two 'e's', but Gilbert Adair pulled it off, and you can read Perec's book in English, also without the letter 'e' in it, under the title *A Void*. But it then turned out not to be an unprecedented feat, since the American author Ernest Vincent Wright had written a 1939 novel called *Gadsby* also without using the letter 'e'—and what's more, his book was 50,000 words long. (His feat fell short of Perec's, however, because he allowed three 'e's' to creep in, accidentally using the word 'the' twice and 'officers' once.)

Neither novel works terribly well as a story, because there is something contrived about the attempt to construct a narrative without the letter 'e'. But the feat is not easy to accomplish, precisely because the letter 'e' is so ubiquitous (in the 239 words in this column so far, there are several dozen 'e's' already!) The issue came up in the internet era when someone issued a challenge on Quora, 'can you make a sentence without using a single "E"?' The best answer came from Marcus Geduld, described as a 'published author, lifelong reader' who wrote:

> I doubt I can. It's a major part of many, many words. Omitting it is as hard as making muffins without flour. It's as hard as spitting without saliva, napping without a pillow, driving a train without tracks, sailing to Russia without a boat, washing your hands without soap, or shitting without a butt. And, anyway, what would I gain? An award? A cash bonus? Bragging rights? Why should I strain my brain? It's not worth doing. Now, a grammatical paragraph without commas: that would wow most folks on Quora, don't you think? Could you do it? If so, I tip my hat to you—or I would if I had a hat. Or, how about a paragraph without punctuation? Or a paragraph without nouns? If you can do that, you'll win my admiration. Go on. Try! I'm waiting…

But Geduld's paragraph, and Wright's and Perec's novels, serve to provoke some reflection on how truly vital vowels are to construct words, the building blocks of language. In his Introduction (which, not being part of the novel itself, does contain the letter 'e'), Wright says his primary problem in writing it was in expressing the past tense, which so often in English ends with the suffix '-ed'. Wright had to use verbs that do not take the -ed suffix and construct convoluted verb forms with the word 'do' (like 'did walk' instead of 'walked'). Because he did not use the letter 'e', he could not use a lot of common words like 'fed', 'bed', or 'red', pronouns like 'he', 'she', and 'they', or many basic words describing quantity (every number between six and thirty uses the letter 'e'!).

It's not just the vowel 'e' that's the challenge—doing this exercise without any one of the other vowels would be just as difficult. To those familiar with English, words without vowels, or using very few of them, seem odd: there was a wonderful joke once about an emergency humanitarian airlift of vowels to Poland, whose language seems startlingly starved of them! And yet there are some English words that manage not to use vowels at all: aside from three-letter words like shy, thy, and wry, a handful—crypt, cyst, hymn, myrrh, myth, pygmy, shyly, and sylph—are the only ones that I can think of. Let's hope the Wordle puzzle doesn't use too many of these: we rely so much on vowels we'd never guess words without them!

SECTION FOUR

TYPOS, SUPERFLUITIES, MISPRINTS, AND OTHER ERRORS

Newspaper headlines are an unfailing source of pleasure for language mavens, because of the howlers they commit in their desire for brevity. Consider 'Whale Watching Boat Carrying 27 Sinks'. Why was the whale watching a boat, and why was the boat carrying twenty-seven sinks rather than other bathroom appliances also? A 'crash blossom' could have been avoided by introducing a hyphen between 'whale' and 'watching' and replacing 'sinks' with 'capsizes'.

19

CRASH BLOSSOMS

Newspaper headlines are an unfailing source of pleasure for language mavens, because of the howlers they commit in their desire for brevity. An assortment of amusing ambiguities result from headline-writers omitting crucial verbs and punctuation marks to save space. Among the most famous of these was the *Japan Today* headline 'Violinist Linked to JAL Crash Blossoms'—for an article about how a musician, whose father died in a Japan Airlines plane crash, was now flourishing. But the phrasing of the headline led a testy copy editor to wonder, 'what's a crash blossom?' The phrase caught on in the esoteric world of copy editors, till 'crash blossoms' stuck as the term of art for all headlines that could be misread.

Legendary headlines from the colourful history of newspaper disasters include 'Squad Helps Dog Bite Victim' (a hyphen between dog and bite might have helped!), 'Red Tape Holds Up New Bridge' ('delays' instead of 'holds up' would have worked better) and 'MacArthur Flies Back to Front' (the general was returning by plane to the war front—perhaps less economical phrasing could have prevented the hilarity that greeted this headline). I'll let you readers figure out what the headline-writers of these actual newspaper stories presumably meant with the following (all true headlines, believe me!): 'Giant Waves Down Queen Mary's Funnel', 'Eighth Army Push Bottles Up Germans', 'Missing Woman Remains Found', and 'Whale Watching Boat Carrying 27 Sinks'.

That last one raises the obvious questions, why was the whale watching a boat, and why was the boat carrying twenty-seven sinks rather than other bathroom appliances also? A 'crash blossom' could have been avoided by introducing a hyphen between 'whale' and 'watching' and replacing 'sinks' with 'capsizes'. Even the famous BBC News is not exempt from such errors as 'St John Ambulance to teach teens to help stab victims'. Is the ambulance company seeking to drum up business by teaching teenagers to stab people, one might ask—or performing a humanitarian service by instructing young people how to assist victims of knife-attacks?

Such headlines reflect the haste with which newspapers work, because many of them could have been avoided if the writer had re-read before submitting the headline. Thus the headline 'McDonald's Fries the Holy Grail for Potato Farmers' made the elementary mistake of forgetting that 'fries' is a verb as well as a noun. The writer obviously meant to convey that 'McDonald's French-Fries *Are* the Holy Grail for Potato Farmers'. Instead, his slapdash headline left many readers wondering why a fast-food chain was cooking the most mythical sacred object in Christian legend. 'Gator Attacks Puzzle Experts' suffered from 'puzzle' being both noun and verb, so 'puzzle experts'—people very good at solving puzzles—must have feared that alligators were especially targeting them!

Similarly, the headline 'Google Fans Phone Expectations by Scheduling Android Event' could be read as admirers of Google telephoning their hopes. Wouldn't it have been better to say 'Google Raises Expectations of New Phone by Scheduling Android Event'? Nouns that can be misconstrued as verbs (and vice-versa) are often the hallmarks of crash blossoms. A classic example is *The Guardian* headline 'British Left Waffles on Falklands'. The newspaper clearly meant that the left-wing political parties in Britain were unable to articulate a coherent position on the Falklands crisis (in other words they intended the word 'Left' to be read as a noun and 'Waffles' as a verb), but many readers thought their compatriots abandoned their breakfast food on these Atlantic islands!

The Guardian headline-writers were guilty again of 'Supreme Court Plans an Attack on Independent Judiciary, says Labour'. Most readers thought this meant the Labour Party was accusing the Supreme Court of planning an attack on the judiciary. You had to read the first line of the article beneath the headline to understand that it actually meant the opposite: 'Government-backed plans to reduce the size of the Supreme Court and rename it have been condemned by Labour as an assault on the independence of the judiciary'.

The desire to summarize is often the newspaper editor's biggest bugbear. But as long as newspapers exist and headlines have to be written, we can expect crash blossoms continuing to bloom.

20

MISPRINTS

No one who reads the printed word can escape the experience, and often the pleasure, of coming across misprints. Human beings are often hasty when they type or proofread, and if I had a rupee for every time, during my UN career, I came across my organization being referred to as the 'Untied Nations', I could probably buy myself a fancy computer.

There are four types of misprints that tend to evoke hilarity. 'Untied' for 'United' represents the commonest kind of misprint, that results from the transposition of adjoining letters. The most famous of those tend to border on the risqué, such as the time the *South London Press* reported that 'The strike leaders had called a meeting that was to have been held in a bra near the factory, but it was too small to hold them all.' This kind of transposition of letters can create other problems. An American newspaper carried a notice for a festive Christmas Day event that was meant to feature a 'special appearance by Santa at 3 p.m.'. Unfortunately, it ran the announcement of a 'special appearance by Satan at 3 p.m.'.

The second kind of misprint involves the omission of a letter, as when the *Bristol Gazette* informed its readers after a fire, 'One man was admitted to hospital suffering from buns'. Various Indian newspapers have announced leaders taking a 'plan' to Delhi rather than a 'plane', and one captioned a museum photograph as being of the 'goddess Venu'.

The third kind of misprint involves the typing of the wrong letter altogether, as when a local newspaper in England in 1897 solemnly announced that 'to commemorate the Queen's Diamond Jubilee, the Parish Council intends to place a commemorative plague on the village green'. (Of course, what was intended was a 'plaque'.) Or the *Surrey Advertiser* story saying that 'Arthur

Kitchener was seriously burned Saturday afternoon when he came in contact with a high-voltage wife'. (wire!)

The most notorious example of this type of misprint among journalists involved a nineteenth century British newspaper, in whose intended, innocuous headline 'Queen Passes Over Bridge' (prompted by Queen Victoria inaugurating a new bridge), the first vowel in the second word was inadvertently (or maybe maliciously!) replaced by another—an 'i'! The consequences were calamitous for the newspaper—every printed copy had to be recalled and pulped, and that paper was not circulated that day. But enough readers had spotted the headline for the misprint to enter the annals of legend.

The fourth kind features an unintentional error that seems startlingly appropriate, such as the repetition of a phrase in the *Irish Press* story: 'The Irish Stammerers' Association will hold a seminar will hold a seminar entitled 'Aids for Stammerers' tonight.' Or the *South Wales Evening Post* headline that announced a 'Cash plea to aid dyslexic cildren'.

But the prize for the most misprints undoubtedly goes to *The Guardian* in England, whose misprints were so frequent and so notorious that in 1998 it began running a daily corrections and clarifications column, necessary for a newspaper which its rivals affectionately dubbed the '*Grauniad*' for the large number and hilarity of its misprints. In August 1998, its finance pages reported the payment of a record £250,000 advance for Vikram Seth's novel, '*A Suitable Buy*'. *Guardian* readers were also famously informed that the 2003 spring season at the Royal Shakespeare Theatre in Stratford-upon-Avon would feature 'The Taming of the Screw'. The Scottish band 'Frightened Rabbit' was referred to as 'Frightened Rabbi' and a women's *a cappella* group as 'Foul Purpose' instead of 'Soul Purpose'. In an interview, the chairman of Wolverhampton Wanderers was quoted as saying 'Our team was the worst in the First Division and I'm sure it'll be the worst in the Premier League'. He had actually just declined the offer of a *tea* as being the worst tea, not his *team*!

To cap it all, in 2007 *The Guardian* once had the humiliation of admitting: 'We misspelled the word misspelled twice, as mispelled, in the Corrections and clarifications column on September 26.' No wonder the paper actually published a note on 26 January 1999: 'The absence of corrections yesterday was due to a technical hitch rather than any sudden onset of accuracy.'

21

NEEDLESS WORDS

For a lover of language, can there be such a thing as 'needless words'? I would have thought not—I am one of those who often tends to enjoy multiple words, the more the merrier—but no less an eminence than William Strunk Jr., author of the classic *The Elements of Style*, disagrees with me. Strunk says there are needless words—words with no purpose—and his advice is simple: delete them.

Several examples that the stylists give of such 'needless words' comes in this sentence: 'I really don't care for flying in aeroplanes all that much, so I came in on the train because of that.' It's full of what some refer to as 'sticky' words that 'glue' up a sentence. Experts like Strunk would prefer the speaker of that sentence to revise it by saying simply: 'I hate flying, so I took the train instead.'

Lawyers are particularly guilty of such 'stickiness'—no lawyer would use a simple, declaratory sentence or word when a florid one full of multiple subordinate clauses can be found. One of my favourite examples of unnecessary legalese is the standard formula: 'In witness whereof, the parties hereunto have set their hands to these presents as a deed on the day month and year hereinbefore mentioned.' What does it mean? In one word: 'date'. Just write today's date in the legal document and you don't need that entire pointless sentence!

Language maven Richard Wydick, who objected to unnecessary legal jargon in his deservedly famous *Plain English for Lawyers*, writes: 'In every English sentence are two kinds of words: working words and glue words. The working words carry the meaning of the sentence. In the preceding sentence, the working words are these: working, words, carry, meaning, and sentence. The others are glue words: the, the, of, and the. The glue words do perform a vital service. They hold the working words together to form a proper, grammatical sentence. Without them, the sentence would read like a telegram. But if the proportion of glue words is too high, that is a symptom of a badly constructed sentence. A well-constructed sentence is like fine cabinetwork. The pieces are cut and shaped to fit together with scarcely any glue. When you find too many glue words in a sentence, take it apart and reshape the pieces to fit together tighter.'

Wydick's advice makes sense: you can't eliminate 'sticky words' altogether from your writing, but if you can use as few of them as possible, your sentences will read better and be easier to understand. You need some glue to hold your sentences together and ensure they make sense, just as your cabinetwork fits together, but you don't need so much glue that it flows out of the joints of your furniture and makes holding it together a sticky experience.

In addition to 'glue words', there are also 'lazy words', words which mean so little that they are rarely appropriate. A classic example of a lazy word is 'nice'. 'Nice' is so imprecise that it always conveys less than you intend it to. If you say a dress is 'nice', do you mean it is pretty, elegant, formal, casual, colourful, well-cut, well-designed, shapely, or hides the wearer's flaws? All of those could be appropriate responses to a dress, but 'nice' is too lazy a term to convey any of them. Other lazy words used both in speech and writing that should be drastically reduced, if not eliminated, include 'basically', 'actually', 'certainly', 'literally', 'totally', and 'virtually', which people throw into their sentences—and often their conversation—because they don't know what to say.

I could, of course, end this chapter with the advice: 'If you were to really make the effort to take a close look at the content of your writing and further take the trouble to weed out any of those unnecessary connecting words that you might have used, you should be able to reduce the sticky sentences and make your narrative much more readable without losing the meaning of what you are trying to convey.' But if I had taken my own advice, I could instead simply end this chapter this way: 'By reviewing content and removing needless words, you can improve readability without sacrificing meaning.' Got it?

22

PLEONASMS

The previous chapter discussed 'unnecessary' words, taking a swipe at legalese in particular for piling word upon phrase to say the simplest things. There's a particular term for the use of superfluous words: pleonasm, a term derived from a Greek word that means 'excess'. A pleonasm uses two or more words, of which one is redundant, to express an idea. The classic example of a two-word pleonasm is 'burning fire' (after all, a fire, by definition, burns) and that of a whole pleonastic phrase is 'I saw it with my own eyes.' If you saw it you had to have used your own eyes, right? The same holds true for 'heard with my own ears' and 'touched with my own hands'—you can't touch with someone else's hands or hear with someone else's ears!

Whereas an oxymoron (like 'open secret' or 'act naturally') combines two contradictory terms, a pleonasm uses synonymous ones, like 'armed gunman' (if he's a gunman, he's armed) or 'tuna fish' (if it's tuna, it's a fish). A pleonasm isn't the same as a tautology, which is a repetition of the same idea in different words. A pleonasm uses redundant, superfluous words you don't really need—which is what I just did in this sentence to make my point!

What are the most common pleonasms you need to be conscious of and avoid? 'Advance planning' and 'advance warning' are widespread: if you plan or warn, you always do so in advance, so why add the word? The same with 'mix together'—once you mix something it obviously gets the elements together; you can't mix something apart! Similarly, 'close proximity', 'empty hole', 'exact replica', and 'young child'—the noun contains the meaning that the adjective seeks to add, so why not drop the adjective? My fellow Indians are often guilty of saying they will 'return back'—an Indianism and a pleonasm all in one!

One of the best examples of a sentence combining three or four pleonasms in one is: 'It was an unexpected surprise when a pair of baby twins was born at 12 midnight.' A surprise, after all, can hardly be expected; twins always come in pairs; midnight can only come at 12—so none of those extra words were necessary. And the fourth pleonasm? Can anyone be born who is not a baby? All four pleonasms could have been avoided by simply saying, 'They were surprised when twins were born at midnight.'

Our daily lives are full of pleonasms—shops trying to tempt us with 'free gifts' (if it's a gift it had better be free!), advertisements for 'hot water heaters' (if your water is already hot, why does it need heating?), travel agencies asking us to make 'advance reservations' (reservations have to be in advance of your going anywhere), mechanics breaking your things down to their 'component parts' (a component is a part), friends telling you they did something on a 'sudden impulse' (acting impulsively is always sudden), and even English teachers telling you to avoid 'overused clichés' (a cliché is, by definition, a term rendered trite by overuse). Every one of these phrases could have benefitted from deleting the first word in them.

It is, however, true that pleonasms are not always to be avoided. Orators love them as a rhetorical device to drive their point home: politicians will declaim their promises that they will deliver you services 'free, gratis, and you will pay nothing at all'. Indeed, pleonasms are also an accepted literary device used for emphasis by some authors and not just speakers. They were rendered respectable by no less an eminence than William Shakespeare, in whose *Julius Caesar* there appears the famous pleonastic phrase 'This was the most unkindest cut of all.... ' If it was the 'unkindest', it was already the 'most unkind', and if you wrote this in a high school essay your teacher would be expected to put a big red circle around the phrase 'most unkindest'. But Shakespeare is, well, Shakespeare, and he got away with this horrific pleonasm—which is not to say you would.

Many of these pleonasms are self-evident, but some can be more complicated. When I was at the United Nations dealing with the civil war in the former Yugoslavia, the Security Council chose to declare some towns in Bosnia-Herzegovina as 'safe havens'. Quite apart from the military feasibility of UN peacekeepers ensuring their safety, some grammarians thought the very term 'safe haven' was a pleonasm—as one put it, 'if it ain't safe, it ain't a haven'. In other words, a haven is by definition a safe place. But the diplomats who came up with the term could well have argued that they needed to call it a 'safe haven' to remove any ambiguity about what they intended. Similarly, when lawyers use pleonasms like 'cease and desist' and 'null and void', they are not impressed by grammarians telling them to delete the words 'and desist' and 'null and', since 'cease' and 'void' are sufficient to convey the intended meaning; lawyers insist they need the full phrase to make its meaning absolutely clear.

Word maven Charles Harrington Elster identifies a number of familiar locutions (like 'safe haven') that might, on balance, pass muster even though they are pleonasms: 'lag behind', 'personal opinion', 'protest against', 'filled to capacity', 'major breakthrough', 'best ever', 'brief summary', 'pick and choose', 'ultimate goal', 'root cause', and 'during the course of'. And some have justifiable rhetorical value in imparting emphasis, like the teacher or parent telling you, 'never ever do that again'. But he is less forgiving of 'future plans' (plans are always for the future), 'past history' (history is always past), please RSVP' (RSVP is a French acronym for 'please reply'), 'added bonus' (bonuses are always additional), and 'the reason is because' (since the word 'because' already means 'for the reason that').

There is another kind of pleonasm that has emerged in recent years—it comes from our contemporary fondness for acronyms. We all tend to add a redundant word to an acronym when we use it, like saying 'PIN number' when we talk about our postal code in India. PIN is an acronym for Personal Identification Number, so the word 'number' is already contained in the acronym itself.

In other words, saying 'PIN number' is like saying 'Personal Identification Number number'—a pleonasm if there ever was one!

Among the most common of these acronym-related pleonasms is saying 'ATM machine' (ATM is an Automated Teller Machine) and 'LCD display' (LCD is an acronym for Liquid Crystal Display). People who do this are wittily described as suffering from RAS syndrome (Redundant Acronym Syndrome syndrome)! They include old-fashioned folks who say they possess a 'PC computer'—a PC *is* a personal computer; strategists who solemnly warn of 'ICBM missiles' (ICBM stands for Intercontinental Ballistic Missile); doctors who talk about patients having the 'HIV virus'—that would mean 'Human Immuno deficiency Virus virus'—and even all of us who routinely say we watched the CNN news network : CNN is already Cable News Network, so we are committing a double pleonasm, saying in effect that we've tuned in to the 'Cable News Network news network'.

But it's a 'true fact' that you don't need to be an RAS sufferer to make other common pleonastic errors—as this sentence has done: sorry, there's no such thing as a 'true fact' or a false one, a fact is by definition true. Journalists have often asked me if I would write an 'autobiography of my life'. An autobiography can only be of my own life (if I wrote about someone else, as I've done about Nehru and Ambedkar, that would be a biography).

In short, as the grammarian Arthur Quinn explains in *Figures of Speech: 60 Ways to Turn a Phrase*, 'We know we have a pleonasm when we can eliminate words without changing meanings.' So here's my simple advice for avoiding pleonasms: don't use words whose omission would leave your meaning intact.

23

GHOST WORDS

One of the most fascinating phenomena I have come across in reading about words and language is that of 'ghost words'. Do you know what they are? Nor did I, till quite recently. They are words defined by the Oxford Dictionary as 'words recorded in a dictionary or other reference work which are not actually used.' Why would a word be in a dictionary, one might well ask, if it is not actually used? Remarkably, there are several examples of ghost words.

The term was coined by British philologist Walter William Skeat in 1886, in an address to the London Philological Society, describing words that had been erroneously recorded by dictionary-makers and had never featured in actual usage. He mentioned several, including 'abacot', the misspelling of 'a bycoket' (a type of headwear); 'kimes', which came about as the misspelling of 'knives'; and 'morse'—no, not the code, which required a capital M anyway, but a misspelling of 'nurse'. Skeat was alluding to an existing phenomenon, since such errors were rife. The word 'phantomnation' appeared in the 1864 Webster's Dictionary, defined as 'appearance of a phantom, illusion', and it was attributed to the poet Alexander Pope. But what Pope had written in his translation of Homer's *Odyssey* was the line 'all the phantom nations of the dead', and the words 'phantom' and 'nation' had been run together—by an eccentric philologist, Richard Paul Jodrell, who believed in compound words—to make a word no one actually ever used.

Webster's have much to answer for in the ghost words department, since their Second New International Dictionary of 1934 carried the word 'dord' as a synonym for 'density', after misreading a note written by Austin M. Paterson, Webster's chemistry editor at the time. The note said 'D or d, cont./density', and it referred to the uppercase letter D (or lowercase d) being used as an abbreviation for density. 'D or d' got conflated into 'dord', creating a ghost word—a word that, in fact, isn't a word at all. Ghost words were usually the result of such transcription errors or typos. The error was discovered by a Merriam-Webster editor, and 'dord' was dropped from the dictionary in 1947. But it was a ghost word for thirteen years!

Webster's is not singularly at fault. The 1755 Johnson's Dictionary defined the word 'foupe' as 'to drive with a sudden impetuosity' and noted that the word was out of use. No wonder, because it never really existed—it misread the word 'soupe', itself a rare word meaning 'swoop'. The same dictionary had 'adventine', a misprint of a Francis Bacon word, 'adventive' (which also no one uses). And 'cairbow', a misreading of the deer-like 'caribou'.

Sometimes, ghost words appear in dictionaries on purpose, just to protect copyright. Thus the New Oxford American Dictionary included in 2001 the ghost word 'esquivalence', defined as 'the willful avoidance of one's official responsibilities', to help the company track copyright violators who were lifting entries from them; if it appeared in another dictionary it would have had to have been stolen from them. (The fake did appear in Dictionary.com, from which it has now disappeared). The Americans call such deliberate fake words 'mountweazels', and the Germans have a term for them too: 'nihilartikel', meaning 'no article'—which originated in a false entry in the German-language Wikipedia!

Occasionally, though, ghost words can become real, when people, not realizing the error, start using them anyway. Thus 'syllabus' is a transcription error of the word 'sittybas' used by the Roman philosopher Cicero in the first century BCE in his 'Letters to Atticus' to mean 'a label for a book or parchment' or 'title-slip.' If you enjoy cherries, they come from the Old North French word 'cherise' which English speakers assumed was plural, giving birth to 'cherry'. As did 'orange', which came from the

Arabic 'naaranj'; when people spoke of 'a naaranj' it sounded to English ears like 'an orange'! And 'gravy' only became a word after a fourteenth century translator misread a French cookbook that used 'grane' to mean 'anything used in cooking' at the time. But the English translation used a V by mistake, leading to the word 'gravy' that is so commonly used, and consumed, today!

24

DISPUTED WORD ORIGINS

It's widely believed that the word 'sandwich' was invented because of the behaviour of eighteenth-century aristocrat John Montagu, the fourth Earl of Sandwich, reputedly an inveterate gambler who didn't like to leave the card table for an activity as mundane as dinner. Accordingly, it is said, he asked for meat to be placed between two slices of bread so that he could eat without interrupting his gambling. (The bread served the additional purpose of not getting his hands greasy from the meat, which would have rubbed off on the cards.) Soon enough, his fellow gamblers began to ask the servants for 'the same as Sandwich' and, later, just for 'a sandwich'. Disappointingly, however, this story is most likely a myth. The word 'sandwich' was actually in use before Montagu's time, and he probably did not invent the concept of putting meat between two slices of bread, which was in fact a common practice before the Earl demanded it from his valet. But it's a good story, and remains the best-known example of a word-origin story that may, in fact, be untrue—but is too interesting to give up.

A more recent example comes from the world of computing. On 9 September 1947, or so the story goes, the Mark II computer located at Harvard University in the United States experienced a malfunction. After a thorough examination, engineers determined that the root cause of the issue was a moth that had infiltrated the machine, possibly attracted by its light and heat. This insect had inadvertently caused a short circuit. The technical team documented this unusual incident in their logbook where they affixed the moth to the page using adhesive tape and made a notation: 'First actual case of bug being found.'

It is widely acknowledged that the incident played a significant role in promoting the adoption of the term 'bug' in the context of computers, a usage that has now become its primary application. The credit for this goes to Grace Murray Hopper, a mathematician born in New York in 1906, who held the rank of admiral in the US Navy. Hopper served as the programmer for the Mark II computer and also headed the group that discovered the moth. Her frequent retelling of the moth episode left a lasting impact on an assortment of individuals associated with the computer industry, resulting in the term becoming linked with her.

Alas, however, despite the immense popularity of this story, it's not actually the origin of the terms 'bug' for computer errors and 'debugging' for their correction. The reality is that well before this event, these expressions were commonly employed to describe machine malfunctions, as can be seen in the records of inventor Thomas Edison from the 1870s. London's *Pall Mall Gazette* in 1889 described how Edison spent two consecutive nights trying to identify 'a bug in his phonograph'—'an expression,' the article explained, 'for solving a difficulty, and implying that some imaginary insect has secreted itself inside and is causing all the trouble.' So these terms existed six decades before Harvard's Mark II computer encountered its bug. But the moth in the machine is so much more fun!

I'm rather fond of orange marmalade, complete with lots of peel, and have idly wondered where the term came from. The version I believed, as a French speaker myself, was that when Mary I of Scotland fell ill on a visit to France in the mid-1500s, she was served a sweet jam-like concoction made from stewed fruit and wanted to know what it was called. During this time, in her fevered state, she overheard the French maids and nurses who were caring for her muttering 'Madame est malade' (madam is unwell), and in her confusion she thought that was the answer to her question! Thus was 'marmalade' born. Or so I believed—until I discovered the wonderful tale is completely untrue. Apparently marmalade couldn't have gained its name from Mary's addled state, because scholars have found earlier references to marmalade in English, with one dating back to six decades before Mary was even born.

I love these stories, though; they are so much more enjoyable than the prosaic truth!

SECTION FIVE

LINGUISTIC REGISTERS

Physically active words: it's not easy *ploughing* through my inbox and *wading* across the accumulated paperwork. After all, it's me who has to be *picking up* the pieces afterwards.

25

DIPLO-SPEAK

After spending twenty-nine years at the United Nations, starting at an impressionable age, I became quite accustomed to diplomatic language. Diplomats, of course, think twice before saying—nothing. But when they have to speak, they are trained to be polite and placatory in their choice of words even when they are expressing the harshest ideas.

An unqualified person, confronted with a lady who, to put it politely, would not win the Miss India contest, might say, 'Look at that woman! She has a face that would stop a clock.' A diplomat would say, 'Ah, that lady! She has a face that would make time stand still.' The consistent desire to avoid giving offence once prompted me to twist an old sexist joke into one about diplomacy: 'If he says yes, he means maybe. If he says maybe, he means no. If he says no, he's no diplomat.'

Rudeness is always avoided. You never say: 'The two prime ministers disagreed bitterly over an issue.' You say 'there was a candid exchange of views'. Instead of saying 'the minister intends to do absolutely nothing about a particular problem', you say 'the minister is deeply concerned'. The fact that she is concerned does not, of course, oblige her to actually do anything about this problem, but you leave that unsaid. That's diplo-speak.

Inevitably, diplomacy acquires its own vocabulary, which might baffle people with a literal familiarity with the English language. One term I discovered at the UN was 'non-paper'. This was particularly confusing because it always involved a sheet or more of paper. So what was the 'non' doing there? The answer is that the paper existed physically but not officially; a diplomat who submitted a non-paper was putting down his government's ideas for discussion, and writing them on a paper for clarity and ease of comprehension, but the proposal had no official status until the other side (or sides) agreed to it. By calling it a 'non-paper' the official submitting it preserved full deniability—the right to disown its contents—until it became politically feasible to acknowledge them.

Of course, if the non-paper misfired and either caused offence or was rejected for its contents, the fact that it was a non-paper could help avoid a loss of face on the proposer's side. In fact, both parties could agree that the non-paper had been deemed 'not to have been received' at all, so that the proposal and its rejection did not become an issue between the parties.

My friend and colleague Alvaro de Soto, an elegant and perfectly trilingual Peruvian diplomat who served as political adviser to UN Secretary-General Perez de Cuellar in the 1980s, recounted a few expressions that were in vogue among diplomats at that time. 'That's an *empty pool* issue', for instance, was shorthand for 'let's not get involved in that problem because there just aren't enough elements available to help us solve it—it would be like diving into an empty pool'. The legendary UN peacekeeper, the late Sir Brian Urquhart, amplified the meaning of the phrase: 'Don't dive into an empty pool. It will create a temporary sensation, but will leave you stunned and incapable of further action.' Wise advice indeed! 'It is equally advisable,' Sir Brian added, 'to avoid diving into a pool of boiling water.' That refers to a situation in which a conflict is still freshly being fought and an attempt at a peace-making intervention will only scald the would-be peacemaker, rather than solve the problem.

When I was under-secretary general for Communications and Public Information at the United Nations at the beginning of the century, it was my pleasant duty to chair the press conferences of heads of state and government visiting UN headquarters. On occasion, Pakistani President Pervez Musharraf, then at the peak of his peace-offensive with India, remarked to the press that he wanted peace with India in the interests of the smaller countries of the subcontinent: 'When elephants fight,' he quoted a proverb, 'the grass gets trampled.' As we stepped off the podium to a private room behind the stage, I mischievously pointed out, 'Mr President, when elephants make love, also, the grass gets trampled.' To his credit, the president responded with a hearty laugh—and didn't tell me I wasn't very diplomatic!

26

THE LANGUAGE OF LOVE

What does the concept of the word 'love' truly entail? This perennial enquiry has captivated the minds of poets, dramatists, philosophers, as well as countless heartsick adolescents, and grown-ups, throughout the ages. It is said that Arabic has at least eleven words for love and each of them conveys a different emotion. English is not so fortunate.

Yet the word 'love' is a multifaceted gem in the realm of language. It assumes the role of a noun, embodying a spectrum of emotions and sentiments, ranging from profound attachment to tender affection, benevolent fondness to passionate romance. It can also transcend into intense affinity, a profound abstraction, an ardent passion, an unwavering devotion, a consuming preoccupation, a fiery desire. Love, as a noun ('my love'), can refer to a person or a cherished object. As a verb, 'love' encapsulates the act of experiencing any of these emotions. To 'love' something signifies everything from cherishing its bonds and feeling intense devotion, to being enveloped by flames of sensual longing, or simply deriving joy and gratification from something, whether a person, a sport, or a food!

Words have meaning in relation to each other; so how does 'love' fare in comparison to 'adore', 'like', 'care for', and 'be fond of'? Although love is a powerful emotion, the word 'adore' is even more potent, since adoration carries with it a sense of reverence. Initially, when 'adore' first came into English from French, it was used to denote a form of worship. However, by the time of Shakespeare, it had evolved to be used interchangeably with 'love' in contexts unrelated to religion.

The verb 'like' provides us considerable flexibility, given its ability to encompass a wide spectrum of emotions, ranging from mild to almost profound. Though you 'like' something or someone that gives you pleasure, which might involve lukewarm feelings or more intense ones, 'like' is undeniably less potent than 'love'. While 'love' is based on trust, and may take time to develop, 'like' is an instant feeling. You can 'like' anything, or lots of things, but you 'love' only a few. Of course, Facebook has diluted the significance of the word 'like', as one can express liking for virtually anything or anyone with a simple click. The meaning of the word 'like' still implies you approvingly take pleasure in something, but perhaps just fleetingly, only to the extent of passing it on to other people.

On the other hand, 'care for' typically steers us away from the romantic, into situations involving nurturing. Caring implies providing for or looking after another person, and carries connotations of sympathy or benevolence. You can care for someone without loving them. The same with 'being fond of', which also signifies a milder form of affection compared to love. It is certainly characterized by warmth and affection, and it may even involve indulgence. However, fondness lacks the passionate intensity associated with love.

These nuances of meaning are hard to define; they also contribute to the difficulty in discovering genuine substitutes for the word 'love.' You always lose yourself in love. You can 'fall in love', 'stumble across love', 'be struck by love', or 'be crossed in love'. All the other emotions we've discussed imply no loss of control.

People in love sometimes infantilize the object of their feelings; calling a loved one 'baby' is common. Indeed, there is often an overlap between the terms employed to describe or address children and the terms applied to romantic partners. Terms like 'honey', 'darling', 'sweetie', and even 'munchkin' can be used for both. At one time, men were careless enough to allow such language to slip into their conversations with women even in professional contexts, where they were grossly inappropriate. In recent years, after being called out, men have learned to keep such endearments out of the workplace.

'Love' conveys emotions, moulds relationships, and potentially influences our thought processes. It's difficult not to sympathize with (maybe even 'care for') the poor lexicographer who has the challenging job of explaining this complex term, including all its intricate nuances and variations. Fortunately, book publishers don't have a 'like' button to click at the end of this chapter!

27

LANGUAGE AND THE ENVIRONMENT

Environmental consciousness has been on the increase globally, and inevitably has infiltrated our language as well with new terms to give us a vocabulary to cope with new ecological challenges.

It's only in the last couple of decades that we have come to realize that we are all living in the Anthropocene, defined as a geological epoch marked by significant human impact on Earth's geology and ecosystems, including climate change. Terms like 'ecology', 'biodiversity', and 'greenhouse gas emissions' are, of course, better known and have been widely in use for a bit longer, but even they were largely unheard of before the 1960s.

Some of the basic environmental vocabulary we all need to have would feature these terms:

- *Climate change*: the long-term alteration of temperature and typical weather patterns.
- *Pollution*: the introduction of contaminants into the natural environment that cause adverse change.
- *Ecosystem*: all the plants and animals in a particular area, together with their surrounding environment. The destruction of habitat in a particular area can be termed ecosystem destruction.
- *Environmental degradation*: the deterioration of the environment through the depletion of resources such as air, water, and soil and the extinction of wildlife.
- *Resource depletion*: the consumption of natural resources faster than they can be replenished.
- *Biodiversity loss*: The reduction in the variety and variability of life forms on Earth.

But we have moved beyond the basics to more exotic terms than these. As far back as the 1940s, the author J. R. R. Tolkien, creator of the famous *The Lord of the Rings*, invented the term 'eucatastrophe', which he suggested was a 'good' catastrophe. Environmentalists know all about bad catastrophes that can threaten the very survival of the human race—supervolcanoes, nuclear winter, uncontrolled global warming, pandemics, a meteor colliding with the Earth. But what about those environmental disasters that led to a happy development? For example, some environmental catastrophe hundreds of millions of years ago wiped out dinosaurs from the earth. But their extinction led to the survival of mammals and the eventual evolution of human beings. That's an eucatastrophe.

An intriguing pair, Heidi Quante and Alicia Escott, artists who specialize in environmental vocabulary, have spent a decade collecting and creating new words on the environment in the name of what they call the Bureau of Linguistical Reality. But their neologisms are a bit too exotic to catch on easily—terms like 'nonnapaura' (derived from Italian, to describe the combination of hope and fear many feel for the future because of the global environmental crisis), 'chucosol' (of El Salvadorian and Korean origin, to describe the 'dirty sun' effect of sunsets viewed through polluted air) or 'shellaqua' (derived from 'shellac' and 'aqua', or water, for the act of covering a once-permeable surface like sand with human-made materials like tar or macadam, increasing the risk of floods). This last word may have the best prospects of catching on, because it can also be used metaphorically: an individual can, after all, shellaqua themselves, becoming impermeable and resistant to new ideas and thinking.

While the Bureau of Linguistical Reality is receiving serious attention, I am not too confident that all their words will enter popular usage. For instance, they have combined *pre* + *euphoria* + *eau* (the French word for water) to come up with 'preuphoreau', for the bodily feeling of sensing a change in the atmosphere because rain is coming. (Again, it can also describe a moment of hopeful anticipation of imminent change). It's clever, no doubt, but can most people pronounce it?

In the 'not-yet-popular' category of neologisms the pair have also coined terms like 'sandulate', a verb which means to understand that the coastline is alive, so we can't just build solid structures on it but must respect it. The attitude of some people that if the world is destroyed by environmental catastrophe, Mars could one day offer Earthlings a refuge from climate change, is termed 'marsification'.

Even if these terms remain obscure, arguably, the phenomenon of environmental neologisms is far from new. As far back as 1909, changes in our environment gave English a new word: in reaction to widespread air pollution, a word was coined that combined smoke and fog into 'smog'. So there's nothing new under the sun, except where (as in Delhi's National Capital Region) the pollution is so bad that you can't see it.

28

WORDS IN THE NEWS

Every newspaper reader has had the mortification of reading articles that use terms which the journalist seems to assume everyone knows the meaning of—but she, the reader, doesn't. This is particularly true of economic terms: many of us haven't studied basic economics in school or college, though reading a newspaper these days often seems to require it. If you feel that keeping up with the news these days makes you feel deficient in some way because you can't tell your supply curve from your demand graph, here's a short primer on some of the most commonly-used terms that have popped up in our newspapers in recent weeks when they covered economic news.

Inflation is all about rising prices. It is calculated by measuring how the prices of goods and services have risen, as calculated over a specific period of time, usually a calendar year. Thus if an item costs Rs 100 in September 2023 and costs Rs 110 in September 2024, the inflation rate for that item is 10 per cent. Of course, to understand the overall impact of inflation on an economy, you have to take into account the changing prices of a number of different items. That's why a useful benchmark is the Consumer Price Index, which measures the percentage change in the price of a basket of goods and services typically consumed by households in a country. Most prices tend to go up with time, increasing salaries and costs, so *moderate inflation* is considered normal. After all, all of us remember when things like cinema tickets or even a cup of tea cost much less than they do today. But high inflation occurs when prices increase significantly or sharply—and that's when they make the news.

Inflation is always comparative with the past, and is usually expressed as an annual figure, though in really unfortunate economies, prices can shoot up so fast that monthly inflation rates are talked about. Countries like Argentina and Zimbabwe have, in the recent past, experienced such *high inflation* that supermarket staff would change price stickers on items not just daily, but between the time you entered the shop and before you left it.

So *inflation* is clear enough to most readers. But what, then, is *stagflation*? It's a compound of 'stagnation' and 'inflation', and as the name suggests, it means high inflation and economic stagnation at the same time, usually accompanied by high unemployment. Stop me if this gets too technical, but stagflation occurs if economic activity slows down while prices are still rising—in other words, if there is a *recession* before the rate of inflation has subsided. (Before you ask: a *recession* is defined by two successive quarters of reduced or negative gross domestic product [GDP] growth.) Economists tell you that the cure for stagflation is to raise interest rates to curb inflation, but there's a downside to that too: when interest rates are high, people are happy to put their money in the bank rather than invest it or spend it on the market, and businesses find that borrowing money to invest is more expensive, meaning economic activity could slow down even further. Managing all this is the task of astute central banks and adroit finance ministers, and when we have neither, we all suffer.

OK, you say, but then what's *shrinkflation*? That's the term applied to a clever strategy to disguise inflation by not changing the sticker-price of an item but reducing its quantity: your cup of tea still costs the same, but the restaurant serves it in a smaller cup. Swiss chocolate addicts will recall when Toblerone in 2016 cost the same as in 2015 but seemed to suddenly have fewer triangles with bigger gaps between them. The price of the chocolate bar was unchanged, but its weight had shrunk from a net weight of 170 grams to 150 grams. The logic behind 'shrinkflation' is evident: consumers are price-sensitive, so it's easier to retain their loyalty if you don't change the price, even if you reduce the quantity of your product they are getting.

There's much more, of course, but this should help most readers keep up with the basics. The rest should just skip the finance pages!

29

IDIOMS USING PLACES AND NATIONALITIES

The English language is full of idioms, many of which refer to countries and nationalities—and often involve assumptions and biases that non-native English speakers may not share. Why, for instance, is unauthorized absence 'French leave' in English and '*filer à l'Anglaise*' in French? Because for many centuries the two nationalities didn't much like each other, and each was only too happy to attribute unattractive behaviour to the other. Similarly, colourful language, full of expletives, is often preceded by a request to 'excuse my French'. The words used are blunt Anglo-Saxon, but the intent is to apologize for using swear words and other inappropriate language, which the Englishman implies only the French would do.

Similar cultural prejudices are involved in the expression 'going Dutch' for sharing the bill or 'Dutch treat' for a meal at which the guest discovers he has to pay his own share. (The English clearly thought the Dutch weren't very generous, which is, of course, untrue.) There's also 'Dutch courage' for the false bravado expressed by someone who has had too much alcohol to drink. The expression goes back to the days when English and Dutch soldiers were fighting each other in the Thirty Years' War (1618–48) and the Anglo-Dutch Wars (1652–74), when Dutch soldiers allegedly fortified themselves with gin before going to battle. The result of those hostilities is a number of English terms which had 'Dutch' added to them as an insult: a 'Dutch bargain' is a contract made by someone drunk, a 'Dutch feast' a social occasion where the host gets drunk before the guests, a 'Dutch concert' is one where several tunes are played at the same time, and if something is 'Double Dutch', that means it's nonsense. Though the English and the Dutch are the best of friends now, many of these expressions linger in the language as popular idioms, often used by people without any intention to offend.

Mere unfamiliarity lies behind some idioms—'it's all Greek to me', for instance, means you can't understand something at all (the unstated assumption is that there are not many English speakers of Greek). Similarly, something complicated or difficult to comprehend is said to be 'like Chinese arithmetic'. One can understand why an unsound or incomplete argument or theory is said to have 'more holes than Swiss cheese'—since there *is* a Swiss cheese made with holes in it. Or that a period of unusually warm weather during a Northern Hemisphere autumn is called an 'Indian summer'. But why a disagreement or confrontation during which no agreement can be reached is called a 'Mexican standoff', I have no idea.

Some idioms are, of course, free of prejudice and easy enough to understand—if you refuse to do something and say 'not for all the tea in China', it's obvious that nothing could induce you do it, not even a vast quantity of something. However, it's not clear to me why China gets the blame for 'Chinese whispers', the process by which a message or piece of information (especially gossip or rumours) is distorted when passed on from one person to another, so that the final version is often very different from the original. As a children's game it's a lot of fun—but why do the poor Chinese have to bear the burden of having their name attached to it?

Countries are not the only places that feature in English idioms—many cities do, too. None more so than Rome, now the capital of Italy. The expression 'all roads lead to Rome' means that multiple methods can be used to achieve the same goal, but is also an allusion to the glory days of imperial Rome, when all its far-flung citizens desired to reach the great city. That greatness is implicit in saying that 'Rome was not built in a day', to convey that major achievements cannot be accomplished in a short period of time. The Roman emperor Nero, who was said to have played the fiddle while his city burned to the ground, prompted the expression 'fiddling while Rome burns'—which means that someone is doing trivial or irrelevant things instead of attending to extremely serious problems or crises. Time to get back to work!

30

LINGUISTIC AFFLICTIONS

Language is usually a delight, but not always: it is subject to afflictions too. The most familiar is *lethologica*, the condition you suffer when you can't remember the right word for the thought you are trying to express.

Lethologica happens to everyone—yes, including me! How many of us have gone through that awful feeling when you think of something you know well and wish to convey precisely to the person you are speaking to, but the word for it escapes you? Lethologica is not the same as simply mixing up similar-sounding words, as when people say 'reticence' when they mean 'reluctance', a common error. It's when the word you want is trembling at the tip of your tongue but your mind is simply unable to dredge it up from all the many times you have heard or used it before. This too is pretty common: according to the American Psychiatry Association, nine out of ten people will suffer from some form of lethologica during their lifetimes.

Lethologica is derived from the Ancient Greek word *lethe*, 'forgetfulness' and another Greek term, *logikos*, which means 'of or relating to thought or reason' (some also relate it to *logos*, or 'word'). There's a great story about the first part of the word lethologica. The Lethe, known as the River of Oblivion, was one of the rivers that flowed through the realm of Hades, the hellish underworld to which, in Greek mythology, you were banished in death. In these tales, the dead were forced to drink from the waters of the Lethe River in order to forget their past lives on earth.

The affliction of an inability to remember the proper word was first identified as a disorder by the famous Swiss psychiatrist Carl Jung in a 1913 study. But it's really far too common a problem to be elevated to the medical textbooks. It's also not incurable—though usually you struggle to remember the right word, and the harder you try, the more elusive it gets. (In the worst cases, that can lead to *loganamnosis*—when the sufferer from lethologica is so obsessed with trying to remember the word that she couldn't recall, to the point where she's unable to pay attention to the rest of the conversation.)

With so much to watch on television these days, especially a wide choice of entertainment on streaming platforms like Netflix and Prime Video, many also suffer from *lethonomia*, the inability to recall the right name. It's a harmless enough failing—unless, of course, you happen to be a politician, in which case forgetting the name of a party worker or a constituent is tantamount to ensuring the loss of his or her support.

There are other linguistic afflictions, too. One that the Western media have made us aware of is *Tourette's syndrome*, a nervous system disorder involving repetitive movements or unwanted sounds. Tourette's syndrome involves 'tics', uncontrollable repetitive movements or unwanted sounds, causing the sufferer to repeatedly blurt out obscene and offensive words. It's an affliction that usually starts in childhood and the bad news is that it cannot be cured. Tourette's sufferers are often accused of *lalochezia*, using profanity to gain emotional relief. But in truth, they cannot help it. Using offensive words is, for them, an ailment, not a linguistic choice.

Children can suffer from other types of language disorders too. The two most common are *receptive language disorder*, in which a child has trouble understanding words that she hears and reads, and *expressive language disorder*, when she has trouble speaking with others and expressing her thoughts and feelings. Both these, mercifully, can be treated, and often overcome.

But going back to adults, I suspect most of my readers will have had an experience of lethologica. You're talking about someone or something, a situation or a problem, and you are just about to use the word to describe it—and then suddenly you hit a blank. But just when you have parted from the friend you were speaking to—that's when the word pops up, miraculously and frustratingly. Or worse, just when you are falling asleep, the mind goes, 'Eureka! That's it! The word for not remembering the right word—it's lethologica!'

31

PHOBIAS

It's a pretty safe bet that there won't be too many readers of the original version of this piece, which appeared in a Gulf newspaper, who suffer from xerophobia—an abnormal fear of dryness and dry places, such as deserts. If you were xerophobic in the UAE, you're in the wrong country; India in the monsoon is probably the place for you! Provided, of course, you don't suffer from ochlophobia, a fear of crowds—then India surely wouldn't suit you either.

But the very idea of xerophobia and ochlophobia is a reminder that phobias—commonly defined as *excessive, intense, and usually irrational fears that cause people to avoid specific situations, objects, activities or creatures*—come in various shapes and sizes. Among the better-known ones are claustrophobia, a fear of closed spaces; and its opposite, agoraphobia, an aversion to wide, open spaces. But there's also acrophobia, a fear of heights (from the same root that gives us the word 'acrobat' for a high-flying trapeze artist or tightrope-walker), and the condition mentioned least often but widely suffered from, triskaidekaphobia (fear of the number 13), a widespread affliction of the superstitious. As a child I lived in a building in Calcutta, as it then was, that had a 12th floor and then a 14th, for fear people would deem a 13th storey unlucky and refuse to live there.

Most common of all is xenophobia, an aversion to strangers, and a widespread affliction in the Western world these days, as well as increasingly seen, sadly, in my own country. Again, the UAE, with perhaps as many as 89 per cent of its population as of 2018 qualifying as expatriates from elsewhere, clearly rejects xenophobia, and what's more, it has a minister of tolerance to ensure the country stays that way.

But these well-known phobias are far from exhausting the list.

Less common as a word, but not as a condition, is aerophobia, the fear of flying. This is a far more widespread affliction than most people realize, and it disproportionately affects women. I was seated on a flight once next to a very pretty young actress who suffered from aerophobia and asked me to hold her hand tightly during take-off, landing, and every time the plane hit turbulence, which got me some arch looks from the stewardesses! Aerophobia reminds us that many phobias relate to fear of death and the unknown. There's haematophobia, a fear of blood (which puts many students off biology when they first have to perform a dissection); and nyctophobia, a fear of the dark (how many children do you know who don't suffer from nyctophobia?).

Then there are the really rare and obscure conditions for which words nonetheless exist, like erythrophobia, the fear of blushing; emetophobia, a fear of vomiting (pity the poor emetophobe who becomes pregnant); amathophobia, an aversion to dust (in my case this manifests itself in itchy eyes and allergic sneezes); and arachnophobia (a fear of spiders, also a surprisingly common phobia among women). Spiders are not the only creatures who generate phobias—check out ornithophobia, the fear of birds, and its cousin zoophobia, an aversion to animals in general!

Some terms are quixotic: as a member of parliament from Kerala, I was struck by the term keraunophobia, which sounds like an aversion to the chief minister of Kerala (the Kera Uno!) but is actually the word for a fear of thunder, which we hear a lot of in Kerala, particularly preceding pre-monsoon showers. Kerala, incidentally, is no place for anyone suffering from astraphobia, a fear of thunder and lightning.

There are words you imagine should be in more common use than they are, like pyrophobia (the fear of fire); hydrophobia, the fear of water (which is also the name of the malady you get if you develop rabies, when you become unable to drink water); and autophobia, the fear of being alone, which particularly seems to hit people as they grow older. There's even phobophobia, the fear of fears. Go figure!

The one condition no reader of this piece need ever admit to is hippopotomonstrosesquipedaliophobia—the fear of long words. Appropriately enough, the word for this phobia is thirty-five letters long, but it can be broken down to be remembered. Unless, of course, the person suffering from it breaks down first!

32

WORDS ABOUT MONEY

Money has more different words to describe it, depending on how and where it's used, than almost anything else you can think of. They say that the Inuit dialect spoken in Canada's Nunavik region has at least fifty-three words for 'snow', because the Eskimos live with so much of it. I wonder what it says about the English language that it has so many different words for money!

In school it's called a *fee*, when you pay the government it's a *tax*, if they give some of it back it's a *rebate*, to the police or in court it's a *fine*, and when you owe someone it's a *debt*. Many who marry off a child pay a *dowry*, and if it doesn't work out and ends in divorce, it becomes *alimony,* with *maintenance* paid to support children living with a former spouse. A parent who gives some money to teenage children to allow them to buy things for themselves is handing out an *allowance*. Give money in church and it's an *offering*, to a charity or political party it's a *donation,* at a restaurant it's a *tip* (and if the establishment already includes it on your bill, it's a *service charge)*. Pay your manual labour for the work done and it's their *wages*, pay an employee and it's a *salary,* and when she retires it's a *pension*. Pay a writer for an article and it's *remuneration*; a speaker often expects an *honorarium*; an agent demands a *commission*. A wronged party must be paid *compensatio*n and you usually settle a deal for a *consideration*. When you borrow from a bank you take a *loan*, when you start paying it back it's an *instalmen*t. If you buy *shares* in a company, it's a *stake*; so also is a *bet* in a card game! Even criminals require different terms for their money: corrupt officials demand *bribes,* kidnappers ask for *ransom*. Every single one of these italicized words actually essentially means *money*.

Money also takes different forms. There's paper money, referred to in British English as *notes* and in American English as *bills*. Metal money from a mint is called *coins*, and notes (or bills) and coins together are *cash*. When you write a *cheque (*in English) or a *check* (in American) you authorize your bank to pay a specified amount to a certain recipient. When you don't have sufficient cash to fulfil a financial obligation, you can (if the other party trusts you enough) write the creditor a note committing yourself to pay later; this is called an *IOU*. A pre-paid coupon that can be exchanged for goods at a store is a *voucher.*

As tax accountants will tell you, there are other forms money takes. Your *income* is your money from all sources; your *funds* are the amount of money held by you; your *reserves* are the money you put aside for future use; and your *capital* is the amount of your total assets. *Deposits* are the money held by banks on behalf of their customers. Your *budget,* and the government's, are both formal projections of income and spending. *Subsidies* are financial assistance given by governments to help some industries or support some kinds of otherwise uneconomic activity. Money given to foreign countries in the form of assistance for their development is *aid. Currencies* are the medium of exchange between countries.

The English language is so fond of money that there are dozens of idioms relating to spending lots of it. A very expensive item may be said to 'cost an arm and a leg' and if it's more than you can easily afford, you are 'paying through your nose' for it. If someone is charging far too much money for something, the Brits call it 'daylight robbery', and the Yanks 'highway robbery'. If you pay a good deal more than you should for something, simply because you can afford it, you 'have more money than sense'. Behind your back you may be described disapprovingly as 'spending money like water' or even 'throwing your money around'. And if you waste money by continuing to spend it on a project that seems doomed, your friends will advise you 'not to throw good money after bad'....

33

WARTIME WORDS

As headlines speak of war and carnage in Gaza and Ukraine, a book about language must, unavoidably, turn to the vocabulary of war. Many of the terms go back to an earlier era of conflict, World War II—a time of immense upheaval, marked not only by physical destruction and killing but also by the birth of new words and phrases responding to the unique experiences of the era.

One of the earliest and most poignant wartime expressions was 'blackout'. It referred to the practice of turning off lights during air-raid alarms to prevent enemy aircraft from spotting targets. Some questioned the appropriateness of the term, suggesting alternatives like 'lights-out' or even 'black-in'. However, 'blackout' captured the essence of the practice, which involved plunging cities into darkness, emphasizing the urgency and sombre nature of the times.

The German term 'blitzkrieg', meaning 'lightning war', became naturalized in English during World War II. It described the swift and overwhelming style of warfare employed by the Nazis, particularly when they moved into Poland. The term demonstrated the rapid, devastating nature of the Nazi military advance. 'U-boat' was another term that found its way permanently into the English language; short for 'undersea-boat', it referred to German submarines. Among German techniques of war, 'blockbuster' was an aerial bomb of such magnitude that it could obliterate an entire city block, a chilling reminder of the destructive power of warfare and of the massive impact of aerial bombardments on civilian populations.

'Bomphleteer', meanwhile, referred to the brave airmen tasked with dropping propaganda materials in enemy territory. These individuals played a crucial role in psychological warfare, attempting to influence enemy morale through printed words rather than bombs. The term itself carried a certain irony, blending 'bomb' and 'pamphleteer' to describe a mission where words were used as weapons.

Civilians did not escape being labelled by war terminology. The British politician and diplomat Harold Nicolson invented 'chatterbug' for civilians who spread information or rumours. It was used in the context of efforts to combat the spread of misinformation during the war, highlighting the importance of maintaining secrecy and security. A 'roof spotter' was a lookout for enemy aircraft, stationed on rooftops to identify incoming threats. These individuals played a vital role in civilian defence, helping to protect communities during air raids. A frightened civilian was referred to as a 'shiver-sister'. This term underscored the need for national resilience and the need to maintain courage and solidarity in the face of fear during wartime.

The affectionate slang for air-raid shelters—'skelter'—emphasized the urgency of running helter-skelter to find shelter during air raids. The 'siren-suit' was a practical piece of clothing designed for use during air raids—the fusion of fashion and necessity in times of crisis. The colourful nicknames 'Moaning Minnie' and 'Howling Horace' for air-raid sirens reflected the eerie and unsettling nature of the sounds they emitted. They humanized these inanimate wails, to capture the anxiety and fear they instilled. 'Guinea pig' described both evacuees and soldiers billeted in local homes. The nickname drew a parallel with the small, defenceless rodents used for experiments, reflecting the mass movement and upheaval experienced by many during the war. A poignant term, 'warphan', was a shortened version of 'war orphan'. It described the heartbreaking condition of millions of children worldwide who lost their parents during the war.

Occasionally a proper noun makes its way into the language. The term 'quisling', for a traitor and collaborator, comes from the actual surname of Major Vidkun Quisling, a Norwegian officer who collaborated with the Nazis and betrayed his own people. The word 'quisling', derived from his name, embodied the profound contempt and distrust reserved for collaborators and traitors, reflecting the moral outrage that war so often evokes. Similarly, a British propagandist on Radio Berlin was dubbed 'Lord Haw-Haw' for his upper-class accent.

These words and phrases emerged to capture the unique challenges, emotions, and innovations of a world at war. Each term reflects the complex interplay of language and history during a defining period of twentieth century history. They serve as linguistic artifacts, providing a glimpse into the experiences and perceptions of people who lived through those turbulent times. No doubt Gaza and Ukraine will, in due course, produce their share of new words.

34

NAUTICAL JARGON

Many commonplace expressions in English are relics from the days of sailing ships, but have passed into common usage in ways that cause us to forget their origins.

For instance, when someone says 'I can't fathom what she's speaking about', we understand that he's saying he can't gauge her meaning. The expression derives from nautical days of yore, where 'fathom' is utilized as a maritime measurement equivalent to six feet. The term 'to fathom' started on sailing ships to signify 'measuring using a sounding line'. You drop a line from the side of the ship to estimate the distance it goes, and gauge the depth of the sea. In other words, to 'fathom' something was to get to the bottom of something, and that's why it was extended figuratively to come to mean 'understanding something in depth'.

Amusingly enough, the term is rooted in Old English, from the root words faedm or faethm, signifying 'embracing arms or outstretched arms'. To fathom someone originally meant to embrace or encircle the individual with your arms. That was because 'fathom' initially represented the distance from the middle fingertip of one hand to the middle fingertip of the other hand of a tall individual with arms fully extended. So its historical definition was 'the length of a man's arms around the object of his affections'. Why the sailors chose to convert this charming word into a nautical measurement one will never know—but I can't fathom why we can't fathom a loved one in the old sense any more!

When a superior is angry with you and takes stern disciplinary action, whether a tongue-lashing or worse, he is said to have 'keelhauled' you. That's another sailing term. 'Keelhauling', a disciplinary measure once employed by the Dutch and English navies in the seventeenth century, constituted a severe form of punishment for sailors found guilty of grave violations of the ship's code of conduct. The term 'keelhaul' is derived from the Dutch word kielhalen. In this punishment, crew members were thrown overboard from one side of the ship, often with attached lead or iron weights on their legs, and then drawn beneath the ship's keel either across its width or along its entire length. This perilous practice, which was not just horrible to endure but posed a significant threat to the sailor's life, was officially abolished in 1853.

The word 'scuttlebutt' is synonymous with 'gossip'—'the scuttlebutt is that the boss is going to resign'. Fresh water for immediate consumption on a sailing vessel was traditionally kept in a scuttled butt—a barrel or cask with a hole to facilitate drawing water. Sailors would gather at the scuttlebutt for a drink and chat; over time, the term 'scuttlebutt' evolved into slang for exchanging rumours or gossip. As technology advanced, steam replaced sails, and pipes replaced wooden casks, rendering the literal scuttlebutt obsolete. However, the term persisted, now referring to the conversations and rumours that had originally occurred around the sailors' water source.

Why does someone wanting you to shut up tell you to 'pipe down'? It goes back to sailing ships too. The tasks of setting sails, heaving lines, and raising anchors demanded a well-coordinated group effort, and boatswains, who led the deck teams, employed whistle signals to command these synchronized actions. Onboard a vessel, the boatswain's pipe was used to assemble the crew or convey orders. When it was time to dismiss the crew, the boatswain's pipe was again sounded, accompanied by the command 'pipe down'. As the noise level decreased significantly after the dismissal, the phrase became associated with quieting down, reducing noise—or shutting up!

Sailors onboard ships frequently found themselves occupied in mending ropes which held the sails up. This laborious activity included intertwining fibres, a process commonly known as 'spinning yarn'. It required only the use of hands, enabling sailors to gather and engage in storytelling or gossip while working. Consequently, narratives, jokes, and anecdotes derived from this practice came to be referred to as 'yarns'.

Now it's time for me to stop 'spinning yarns' and 'swallow the anchor'—which means to retire from life at sea and adopt a normal lifestyle on land!

35

WORDS FROM AVIATION

In the previous chapter, we looked at words derived from the days of sailing ships, but the English language has also been altered by a more recent phenomenon, aviation.

'Mayday!' is a familiar word from action films. Derived from the French phrase 'm'aider', which translates to 'help me', it was introduced into the English language in 1923 for use in maritime and aviation communication. Assigned the task of devising a clear distress signal for voice radio, ships, and individuals facing severe trouble at sea, Frederick Stanley Mockford, a senior radio officer at Croydon Airport in London, chose 'Mayday'. The term gained official international recognition in 1948 as a universally understood emergency distress signal.

When someone boasts he is 'ahead of the curve', in other words performing better, earlier or faster than the others in the competition, that expression also has its roots in flying. The phrase derives from the mathematics of flight, and refers to the way the aircraft gains power after take-off, which is why in aviation it is sometimes referred to as 'ahead of the power curve'. Similarly, someone who takes a bold or experimental step these days is said to be 'pushing the envelope'. This refers to the 'flight envelope', defined as the particular combination of speed, height, stress, and other aeronautical factors within which a plane can be safely operated. To go beyond that, or to push that envelope, is risky and dangerous in aviation, but in its figurative sense, it means 'to go beyond established limits' or 'to pioneer', and is used in admiration rather than admonition.

When someone says 'she took a lot of flak' or 'caught a lot of flak' for something she has said or done, we understand she came in for a great deal of severe criticism. 'Flak' originally referred to anti-aircraft artillery, and the term entered popular usage around the time of World War II. It came into English from the German flak, which was itself condensed from flieger abwehr kanonen, meaning aircraft defense gun. By the late 1960s, the literal usage soon morphed into the figurative, meaning 'excessive or abusive criticism' or 'fierce dissension or opposition'. By our own century even this figurative meaning has been further extended. In the realm of public relations, a 'flak catcher' is 'a slick spokesperson who can turn any criticism to the advantage of their employer'. This is principally an American colloquialism, but then American usage tends to spread around the world!

The word 'gremlin' has come to mean a bug that disrupts something and is commonly used to explain computer malfunctions these days, but it originated as Royal Air Force slang, and has been in use since at least 1941. Apparently British pilots facing inexplicable aircraft mishaps in those tense wartime days jokingly attributed them to this mischievous sprite, a gremlin—a word combining the Old English gremman, 'to anger, vex', and the ending of goblin, (though some say it may have come from the Irish gruaimin, a 'bad-tempered little fellow'.) The word later came to embody any type of mischief—including, in the early 1960s, of 'a troublemaker who frequents the beaches to ogle bathers but does not surf'!

Advertising pros are fond of the phrase 'lighter than air' to describe everything from clothes to laptops. But it originally referred to lighter-than-air aircraft, which 'flies because it weighs less than the air it displaces', a definition which goes back to the 1880s, according to the Oxford English Dictionary.

One often hears, in the context of a looming disaster (usually on the sports field), that 'it's too soon to push the panic-button'. The expression, which connotes a hasty emotional response to an emergency, originated as 1950s US Air Force slang, in which 'panic-button' described a 'state of emergency when the pilot mentally pushes buttons and switches in all directions'. The origin of the panic-button may have been an emergency bell system in World War II bombers used for bailout and ditching. During the

Korean War, for instance, pilots who 'bailed out at the first sign of action' were disparagingly referred to 'as panic-button boys'.

Don't press the panic-button—we're done for this chapter!

36

THE LANGUAGE OF ELECTIONS

'Elections belong to the people. It's their decision. If they decide to turn their back on the fire and burn their behinds, then they will just have to sit on their blisters.' So said Abraham Lincoln, in one of the more colourful comments made on elections. In India, the election season arrives with a deluge of political advertisements and news articles inundated with terms related to voting. Here are some of them.

The word 'election' comes from the Latin meaning 'to choose; to select from among a number of possibilities'. 'Electorate', the term for those eligible to vote, was first used in 1879 for a group of individuals who possess the right to participate in an electoral process. A 'candidate' or 'nominee' is an individual actively seeking a political position. The word 'candidate' is derived from the Latin word 'candidatus', meaning 'clothed in white': it was the custom in Rome for persons to wear a white toga when standing for election to the senate. To 'nominate' someone is to designate or choose a person as a potential candidate for a public office. (Nomination, of course, does not guarantee victory in the election, unless the preferences of the electorate are known in advance.)

A 'campaign' seeks to place a candidate in office. In the past, military forces often spent the winter in their encampments and ventured into the open field during the summer months to engage in battles. Over time, this concept evolved into a broader interpretation denoting 'continued or sustained aggressive operations for the accomplishment of some purpose'. That purpose is usually spelled out in a 'manifesto', which comes from Italian. Originally, 'manifesto' merely meant 'proof' and gradually evolved to the present meaning of 'a public statement of political objectives or intentions, especially immediately before an election'.

Next comes voting. The 'poll' in which one casts one's vote is derived from an old Germanic word meaning 'head', since from the late sixteenth century candidates began to demand a 'head count' of those voting. A 'booth' is a temporary table, tent, or area. A voting booth is a confined space, typically enclosed by partitions or curtains on three sides, within a polling location, where you cast your vote secretly. The 'ballot' is a record containing the available options in an electoral event. When a person seeks a political position, their initial objective is to secure a place on the ballot. The 'ballot' comes to us from the Italian word 'balotta' for a little ball, since such balls were used for secret voting, by placing them in the appropriate urn or box. The meaning now encompasses tools utilized for recording votes, from early forms like clay or paper to modern digital interfaces. Regardless of the medium, any instrument that presents the candidate choices and permits voting can be termed a 'ballot'. Of course, you can always 'abstain' or refrain from casting a vote. The term's origins can be traced back to fourteenth century French.

A 'recount' typically signifies the process of tallying votes for the second, third, or subsequent time, often conducted when an election is closely contested. The term 'count' itself has its origins in the old French word 'conter', which conveys the idea of 'summing up' or 'adding together'. The earliest recorded use of the noun 'recount' can be traced back to late fifteenth Middle English. Once elected, a victor is accountable to his 'constituents'. The word just denotes a component or element of a larger entity, like the constituent parts of a machine, deriving from the Latin term 'constituentem', meaning 'to compose', constituting a part within a greater whole. In political contexts, 'constituents' are the people politicians have been elected to represent.

'Suffrage' refers to the entitlement to participate in public elections by casting a vote. 'Universal suffrage' signifies that every eligible individual is granted the privilege to vote, regardless of gender, race, education, or income levels. 'Suffrage' and 'suffering' are like distant cousins—they're not exactly related, but if an unsuitable candidate is elected, suffering is guaranteed!

37

THE LANGUAGE OF COLONIZATION

One of the principal attributes of colonization was the transmission of language—mainly the conquered subjects learning the language of their imperial oppressors, though occasionally it also went the other way. Since language is an instrument of self-advancement, it was embraced quite enthusiastically, as this account by Charles Trevelyan in his book *On the Education of the People of India* (1838) suggests:

> The passion for English knowledge has penetrated the most obscure, and extended to the most remote parts of India. The steam boats, passing up and down the Ganges, are boarded by native boys, begging, not for money, but for books.... Some gentlemen coming to Calcutta were astonished at the eagerness with which they were pressed for books by a troop of boys, who boarded the steamer from an obscure place, called Comercolly. A Plato was lying on the table, and one of the party asked a boy whether that would serve his purpose. 'Oh yes,' he exclaimed, 'give me any book; all I want is a book.' The gentleman at last hit upon the expedient of cutting up an old *Quarterly Review*, and distributing the articles among them.

Trevelyan's account of the 'native boys' and their yearning for the English language is, unsurprisingly, portrayed in a way that illustrates and legitimizes their conformity and submission to the narratives of colonialism and colonial authority. Even the term 'native' carries a particular connotation: its root in the Latin word 'nasci', meaning 'born', originally denoted not only 'an original inhabitant, distinguished from outsiders or foreigners' in a non-European context, but was also inaccurately associated with 'a person of colour'. Indians, Arabs, and Africans were 'natives'. Newspaper advertisements often sought 'native servants' who had previously lived in London and 'spoke English'.

The imperatives and incentives which propelled colonization also influenced the transmission of language in a distinct manner. The term 'safari', a Swahili word derived from Arabic, denoting 'a journey', was employed in a colonial context to describe a tourist excursion through regions teeming with exotic wildlife, an adventure in which the natives played purely subordinate roles as servants and guides. 'Going on a safari' implicitly dismissed the inhabitants of the land as though the territory was devoid of human presence.

The use of the term 'tribe' also forms part of colonial vocabulary that advanced imperial policies of 'divide and rule'. The word helped divide the subject populace, accentuated tribal loyalties rather than troublesome national ones and categorized the colonized into 'superior' and 'inferior' tribal groups. 'Nation' was juxtaposed with 'tribe', and the English could justify their conquest by asserting their intention as a 'civilized nation' to bring 'civilization' to the 'uncivilized tribes'.

It is no accident that the English language assigns certain moral connotations to the terms 'black' and 'white', 'darkness' and 'light', 'evil' and 'good', and has also contributed to shaping a perception of Africa as a place in dire need of salvation. Of course, individuals who have been marginalized by such terminology have in turn responded by reversing the associated interpretations, adopting slogans such as 'black is beautiful' to affirm their worth and self-esteem.

Words such as 'wilderness', 'backcountry', 'settler', 'New World', and 'savage' were coined by those who sought dominance in their quest to control America. American English didn't transplant discernible characteristics from British dialects; instead, it homogenized the variations within the English language. People from all social classes in America used linguistic forms that were considered coarse by higher-status Britons. Pronunciations seen in Britain as indicative of lower social standing were accepted in America across diverse ranks and regions. Meanwhile the language diverged over time. Words that went out of fashion in England, like 'fall' for 'autumn', or 'gotten' for 'have got', thrived in the former colony but began to sound strange and even uneducated to metropolitan British ears.

Language was an indispensable instrument in the hands of the empire. The colonizers didn't stop at conquering nations; they also subjugated foreign words and relocated them into their dictionaries. As Canadian freelance game and speculative fiction reviewer James Nicoll wrote, 'English has pursued other languages down alleyways to beat them unconscious and rifle their pockets for new vocabulary.' A perfect metaphor, the Hindustani word 'loot', which the British in India added to their dictionaries as well as their habits!

38

COMPUTER TERMS

Language evolves over time, with new words emerging and the meanings of existing ones undergoing alterations. Neologisms can be invented, old words that have fallen out of use can be resurrected, existing words can be imbued with new connotations, and loanwords can be employed to denote new items. And so it is with the ever-progressing realms of computer and information technology, which have brought with them their own terminology.

The term 'computer' denotes 'a programmable digital electronic device that performs mathematical or logical operations'. Its origin can be traced back to the Latin word 'computare', which means 'to calculate, count, sum up, or think together'. The English language has incorporated the word 'compute', in the sense of 'to calculate', into its lexicon for centuries. The earliest documented use of the term 'computer' goes as far back as 1613, when English poet Richard Brathwaite published *The Yong Mans Gleanings*, using 'computer' to refer to an individual engaged in professional calculations. This usage endured until the mid-twentieth century until British polymath and inventor Charles Babbage conceived the idea of a programmable computing device.

Similar to many newly-coined words that gain wide recognition, the term 'digerati'—denoting 'people highly skilled in the processing and manipulation of digital information; scholarly techno-nerds'—made its initial debut without any detailed explanation, in the business section of the *New York Times*. The word itself possesses components that link it to both the realm of computers and that of elite expertise. The initial syllable of 'digerati' aligns with the first syllable of 'digital', a versatile term used to describe computer technology, while its concluding portion is a play on 'literati', a dignified Latin term adopted in English since 1621 to signify 'scholars' or 'individuals with a deep proficiency in literature'.

A computer web 'browser' assists us in exploring information across a network. In the era before the internet, we used to peruse libraries and physical stores to find information or specific items. Alternatively, we'd visit such places simply to pass the time while contemplating our desires, much like our current activity of internet surfing. Centuries ago, people engaged in the act of browsing amidst the open countryside and woodlands, seeking out shoots, leaves, and twigs to provide sustenance for animals during the winter season. The term 'browser' is derived from the verb 'browse', which itself originated from the Anglo-French term 'brouts', signifying 'young shoots, twigs'.

Originally, the term 'browse' referred only to foraging until the nineteenth century. Soon enough, though, the verb 'browse' started being used in contexts involving different forms of wandering and searching, such as the exploration of a library or bookstore in search of intellectual nourishment. The act of 'browsing' then became a common occurrence in the marketplace, where individuals casually explore items without a serious intention to make purchases. This shift in meaning likely played a role in using 'browse' to describe the action of viewing information on a computer, leading to the naming of the tool that facilitates this activity as the 'browser'.

The unassuming computer 'mouse' began its journey from 1970. It consisted of a wooden shell housing two metal wheels and was created through collaboration between two computer engineers, Douglas Engelbart and Bill English. Engelbart thought it resembled a mouse, particularly due to the cord coming out from its back. However, the design was soon altered to have the cord emerge from the front, for user convenience. An alternative theory suggests that, since in those days the on-screen cursor was referred to as a 'CAT', the mouse was so named since it was chasing the 'cat' around the screen.

A computer 'file' is 'a compilation of data treated as a single unit'. The term can be traced back to the era of handwritten documents, where it signified 'an assemblage of papers arranged on a file'. The expression 'on a file' denoted the use of a wire or cord for stringing together documents for safekeeping—an age-old practice dating back to the early sixteenth century. The word 'file' was adopted from the French word 'fil', which translates to 'thread', and this French term, in turn, derived from the Latin word 'filum', conveying the same meaning. Fortunately, modern computer files don't have threads or strings attached—except metaphorically!

Our increasing reliance on digital devices for daily tasks has affected the language. The terminology used to delineate these activities often resembles words we use for regular human interactions.

Instead of saying 'send me a message', a friend might tell you to 'ping me'. A 'ping', short for Packet Internet (or Inter-Network) Groper, serves as a fundamental tool in the realm of computer network administration, denoting the transmission of a message from one computer to another. Mike Muuss, the American scientist who wrote the ping code in 1983, was 'inspired by the whole principle of echo-location' and coined the term while alluding to the sound of sonar. 'Ping' refers to generating a high-pitched noise akin to the impact of a bullet striking a metal surface, analogous to the sonar technique employed in submarine navigation, using sound waves. When a submarine emits a sound signal towards another submarine, the latter responds with a corresponding acoustic signal. Consequently, both computers and submarine sonar systems emit a 'ping', whether in the form of a software programme or a brief burst of sound.

A computer 'host', rather like a human one, serves as the foundational structure for delivering computer-based services. A 'server', in the realm of computers, functions as a machine or software that offers a specific service. It facilitates client devices in connecting to shared resources within a network. It's worth noting that the term 'server' extends beyond the digital world and can also refer to an individual employed to attend to diners at a restaurant. In computing, the clients are the users receiving the service. The 'client' in computing is a software program that operates on a personal computer or workstation and depends on a server to carry out specific tasks. An email client, for instance, is a software application facilitating the sending and receiving of emails. In addition, the term 'client' can also denote an individual or entity that makes payments in exchange for products or services. Both computer clients and clients as individuals share a common characteristic—they rely on another party to perform specific actions for them.

'Memory' in the context of computers pertains to the internal storage compartments, typically in the form of chips, used for data storage. 'Memory', in the broader human sense, denotes the cognitive ability to preserve and recall information, events, impressions, or the recollection and recognition of past encounters. Both interpretations emphasize memory's role in storing and retrieving experiences, whether human or digital.

A 'directory' serves as a repository for arranging folders and files in a structured order. In the context of computing, a directory acts as an alphabetical catalogue of individuals' names and addresses within a city, district, organization, or a specific group. Analogously, it resembles a filing cabinet comprising 'folders' housing files.

The 'clipboard' in desktop publishing serves as a transient repository for text or graphics following the execution of a 'cut' or 'copy' command. In essence, it functions akin to a compact writing surface with an attached clip designed to secure documents. In the realm of computer applications, the clipboard serves a comparable purpose to the physical clipboard used for fastening papers.

Typically, a 'package' refers to a collection of items that have been assembled, enclosed, or boxed together. In the context of computer terminology, the concept of a computer package pertains to a grouping of software programs packed as one. A 'firewall' is a security mechanism comprising both hardware and software elements, intended to thwart unauthorized access by malicious individuals, such as computer hackers, to a system, thus safeguarding it from potential harm or corruption. In a broader context, the term 'firewall' can be likened to a fire-resistant partition.

In the realm of database management systems, a 'key' is a specific field utilized for organizing and arranging data. But the concept of a key in the realm of computers shares similarities with a physical key used to access a door. When you require a particular keyword or password to gain access to a computer system or retrieve specific information, the process of deciphering data through a key resembles the act of unlocking a secured door. I hope this chapter has deciphered some useful terms for you!

39

BODY PARTS

Have you noticed how many of our body parts double up and do figurative duty in English usage?

This is not totally unreasonable: English words, after all, constantly evolve, not only in the sense of what they mean, but *how* they mean what they mean. English language usage can, and does, transform its parts of speech from one sense to another without changing even a syllable. Thus, in golf, speaking of 'the green' is a common way of referring to a golf course; the noun comes from the adjective *green,* as in '*green grass*', whose meaning got adapted to describe the golf course itself, since its predominant feature is the green grass. English is flexible that way, creating a noun out of a descriptive adjective.

It turns out that human body parts lend themselves particularly well to this kind of adaptation. Making metaphors out of your biology, and applying them to situations that have nothing to do with your physical shape, is easy. Let me illustrate what I mean with this slightly discursive foray into *how*.

Assuming you, the reader works for a company, let's start at the top—you can *head* your firm, and it's quite possible that the announcement of your appointment will give you a *heady* feeling, especially if you have been promoted. Perhaps you always had a *nose* for sensing trouble and *heading* it off, which is why you were appointed *ahead* of your peers. Or maybe you were *blood*ed early in the company? You might be the kind of *head* who always *backs* his employees, and you've known early on when to *toe* the line laid down by the management. Or perhaps you *muscled* your way into the job, using strong-*arm* tactics to *elbow* out your rivals. (Or maybe you even *kneecapped* some of them!)

But never forget that, as every head knows, it's lonely at the top. You have to have the *heart* for it. It's clear the *neck-to-*

neck competition with business rivals can be a challenge, and a ruthlessly determined competitor can *skin* you. You might *eye* your rivals' business practices suspiciously, but still be unable to put a *finger* on what they're doing that makes them better than you. You may be a good *pupil* of the textbooks' best business practices, but it's not enough to *knuckle* down to your work—you need to have a *gut* feeling about how things need to be. A bit of research and you might be able to *nail* it! And they'll just have to *hand* it to you. But if things go wrong with some of your decisions, you'll have to *face* the consequences and *shoulder* the blame. Even worse, if you're held responsible for major losses, you'd have to don the *hair*-shirt and your *head* may be on the chopping block!

If the worst comes to the worst, you might be fired and the company car taken away from you. Then you would have to *thumb* a ride or *leg* it home. And if you take a cab, you'll have to *foot* the bill. I know it's not easy to *stomach* the thought. You'll need the *guts* to deal with adversity. And, of course, you must have the *spine* to face down your detractors in the *teeth* of their hostility. Failure brings out the *bile* in some people. Their comments won't be *palatable*. The nicer ones will *rib* you; the nastier ones will *skin* you alive. In any case you can be sure that in bad times, *tongues* will wag in *throat*y whispers and people you used to trust will start bad-*mouthing* you. You can try to *palm* off your mistakes on others, but that won't always work. There are always people trying to poke their *nose* into your business, even if you tell them to *butt* out! You've got to *hand* it to them—they do persist. The best thing is to turn a deaf *ear* to their comments.

I'm sorry to have told you such a depressing story. But don't let it upset you too much. Have a *heart*: life is always worth living...but that depends on the *liver*. (Yes, that has a double meaning too!) Don't worry; I was just pulling your *leg*....

40

PHYSICALLY ACTIVE WORDS

I am, I must confess, not the most physically energetic of men: I am much happier banging away on my keyboard than in pounding the pavement in a quest for physical exercise. Since this puts me at odds with the rest of the human race, particularly all the many members of my family who, out of genuine concern for my well-being, insist I must stir my increasingly well-padded frame out of my chair and onto a treadmill, I have a big problem. I have tried to overcome it by assuring my nearest and dearest that I am not as idle as they seem to think I am. There are, I tell them, a list of seriously strenuous activities that I undertake, albeit at my desk. The catch—and this I do not mention—is that they do not require much physical effort. But verbal callisthenics should not be sneezed at.

If there are any readers in need of similar excuses, I would be happy to share my justifications with them. It's said that there is safety in numbers, after all, and the more of you who use the same ones, the greater the chance that some of us can get away with them! So here goes.

When I have to do some work, I tend to start *dragging* my heels before *setting the ball rolling*. When I am required to explain something, I often *beat* around the bush. (I know the cynics amongst you will ask, how many calories do dragging and beating burn? Depends on the weight you drag and how heavily you beat.) When I argue, I'm good at *hitting* the nail on the head, and I do like to *jump* to conclusions. Mind you, if the other person argues back, you can often see me *climbing* up the wall in exasperation. I am often *going over the edge* because of other people's inadequacies.

I'm occasionally guilty of *throwing* my weight around. Sometimes, though, I *swallow* my pride and *bend over backwards* to accommodate them. Sometimes it's true that I just *pass* the buck to someone else. Of course, I realize that amounts to *pushing* my luck, and it might not work. Sometimes what I do amounts to *opening* a can of worms or *adding fuel* to the fire. And I have to admit to *putting my foot in my mouth* (though that's quite a *stretch*!) and *piling* on the problems in the process. But these people who blame it all on me don't realize how much effort it takes me to *make mountains* out of molehills. It's not easy *ploughing* through my inbox and *wading* across the accumulated paperwork. After all, it's me who has to be *picking up* the pieces afterwards.

I tend to *walk* my own path in life, though sometimes, if I see a good thing, I don't hesitate to *jump* on the bandwagon. It's not always easy *balancing* the books, and in the effort to do so I find I am often *running* around in circles. But I don't spare any effort and can be seen *pulling out all the stops* in doing what needs to be done. When I finally manage to *climb* the ladder of success, though, I am not averse to *blowing* my own trumpet.

So there's the list of my strenuous desktop activities: dragging my heels, setting the ball rolling, beating around the bush, hitting the nail on the head, jumping to conclusions, climbing up the wall, going over the edge, throwing my weight around, swallowing my pride, bending over backwards, passing the buck, pushing my luck, opening a can of worms, adding fuel to the fire, putting my foot in my mouth, stretching a point, piling on the problems, making mountains out of molehills, ploughing through my inbox, wading across paperwork, picking up the pieces, walking my own path, jumping on the bandwagon, balancing the books, running around in circles, pulling out all the stops, climbing the ladder of success, and blowing my own trumpet.

This may not have been the kind of workout the more tireless amongst my well-wishers want me to do, but it's hard work and I'd urge you all to *exercise* caution when undertaking them!

41

FABRIC(ATING) WORDS

Many of the words used in the English language for various kinds of cloth and fabric have fascinating Indian origins. Fabric production dates back to ancient civilizations, where early societies utilized flax fibres, which were separated into strands and woven into basic textiles, which were then dyed using plant extracts. However, the term 'fabric', defined as 'textile, woven, or felted cloth', only came into existence in the eighteenth century.

As early as the twelfth century, 'Madras' referred to a type of handmade fabric worn by peasants in India's Madraspatnam, now Chennai. Local weavers used soft fibres from the native trees' tip-skin to create a 36-inch-wide square cloth. Initially, they block-printed this cloth with vibrant check patterns. Over time, the Indian weavers shifted from block printing to dyeing the yarns with vegetable dyes, giving rise to the distinctive handwoven Madras check patterns. The British colonists exported the Madras fabric to their African colonies, where it was referred to as 'Injri' (Real India) and became an integral part of African customs. In the twentieth century, when Madras cloth was exported to America, buyers were concerned to discover that the dyed colours 'bled' into each other in their washing-machines. The Indian exporters, guided by advertising giant David Ogilvy, cleverly advertised that was an unusual quality of their product, rather than a liability. A 1966 catalogue advertisement announced: 'Authentic Indian Madras is entirely handwoven from yarns dyed with native vegetable colorings. Home-spun by native weavers, no two plaids are the same. When washed with mild soap in warm water, they are guaranteed to bleed and blend into distinctively muted and subdued colorings.'

'Bleeding Madras' became all the rage!

'Paisley', a decorative textile pattern featuring the Persian boteh motif, is teardrop-shaped with a curved upper end. This design was traditionally woven onto silk garments using silver and gold materials. While the motif itself has Persian origins, the intricate patterns are originally Indian. Paisley patterns gained popularity when the British East India Company imported the design from India during the eighteenth and nineteenth centuries. The term 'paisley' came from the town of Paisley, in western Scotland, a leading textile producer that was the first to adopt and reproduce this distinctive design, but the product originated in India.

'Seersucker', a lightweight linen material, derives its name from the Hindi term sirsakar, an Indian adaptation of the Persian expression shir-o-shakhar, which translates to 'milk and sugar' and reflects the alternating textures of the fabric. The striped and crinkled textile found its way to the European market by the seventeenth century. English and French textile producers promptly embraced both the term and the fabric for their domestic manufacturing. Seersucker, with its various patterns and colours, remained popular well into the twentieth century.

'Chintz' initially referred to a type of cloth adorned with flowers or vibrant patterns, crafted through woodblock printing, painting, or staining. This remarkable luxury textile was termed 'chintz' in English, derived from the Hindi term 'chhint'. Interestingly, the plural form of the word underwent a transformation, with the 's' changing to 'z', and it eventually came to be treated as a singular noun. This unique fabric, originating from the Coromandel Coast in south-east India, made its way to Europe in the seventeenth and eighteenth centuries aboard the ships of the East India Company, and made waves worldwide. In a letter to her sister in 1851, the author George Eliot wrote, 'The quality of the spotted cloth is best, but the effect is chintzy.' Eliot, who is credited with the earliest usage of the term 'chintzy', was probably criticizing not genuine chintz but rather an inexpensive imitation of it. British factories had inundated global markets with countless copies of chintz, rendering it easily accessible to the general public and stripping away any initial association with luxury.

Fabrics were often generically referred to as 'calico', a synonym for exotic cloth. 'Calico' has its origins in Calicut, the name of the seaport on the Malabar Coast in India, where Europeans initially acquired 'kalyko', or white cotton cloth, during the seventeenth and eighteenth centuries. You can credit India—the world's leading cloth exporter for centuries before the Industrial Revolution—for most of the key English words for textiles!

◆

The French are not far behind the Indians when it comes to contributing words relating to cloth in the English language. The Jacquard loom, an extraordinary innovation that revolutionized textile production, holds a significant place in history. It was named for Joseph-Marie Jacquard of Lyons, who invented a groundbreaking loom around 1800. Jacquard introduced an automated system utilizing a chain of punched cards to create a sequence, resulting in intricate and luxurious craftsmanship. For the first time, weavers gained the ability to produce patterns of seemingly boundless complexity on a large scale. Additionally, Jacquard's punched-card method served as a significant inspiration for Charles Babbage, who pioneered the first mechanical computer in the 1820s.

'Chambray' shares a significant connection with denim, particularly in its defining feature—the incorporation of a white horizontal thread in the fabric's weave. The true elegance of this technique becomes evident as the fabrics mature, with the white weft gradually becoming more prominent over time. The roots of the term 'chambray' trace back to 1801 and are associated with the French town of Cambrai, which in turn gave us the term 'cambric'. Cambrai town was a hub for the production of early plain-weave workwear fabrics.

The term 'chevron', derived from the Old French word

'chevron', meaning rafter, refers to a V-shaped symbol. This symbol is formed by two diagonal lines meeting at an angle, presenting either an inverted or upright V shape. Chevron made its way into the English language in the fourteenth century, though evidence of the design dates back to 1800 BCE. The chevron pattern was initially a single V shape but it evolved over time. Textile designs featuring the chevron pattern emerged in 1962 with the production of the first fabric incorporating this design. Modern chevron fabrics consist of multiple V shapes arranged closely, resulting in a pattern resembling a zigzag.

'Moiré' has its roots in the French language and can be traced back to the seventeenth century. In its adjectival form, moiré means shimmering and refers to a textile, typically crafted from silk, that exhibits a distinctive rippled or 'watered' appearance. The distinctive wood grain look was first attained by compressing and steaming two layers of horizontally textured fabric along their length. The irregular and closely spaced threads give rise to a unique undulating design, known as the moiré effect, which persists even after the fabric has dried.

The origins of the 'poplin' fabric lie in the medieval French city of Avignon, where some popes resided. The term 'poplin' is believed to have its roots in the fabric known as papeline, a term that translates to 'of the pope' or 'papal fabric'. Avignon served as a hub for silk production during that period. Initially, poplin was crafted by blending silk and wool, yielding a sumptuous and sturdy fabric. As time passed, the term 'poplin' expanded to include a diverse array of fabrics produced from various fibres. In general, poplin has maintained its enduring status as a lightweight, airy, and glossy material, solidifying its position as a 'timeless classic' in the realm of textiles.

'Tartan' is believed to have its roots in the thirteenth century, originating from the French word 'tiretaine', which denotes a robust, coarse fabric. The term tartan, referring to a kind of woolen fabric, emerged in the fifteenth century. Tartan is a distinctive recurring design featuring intersecting bands, stripes, or lines of various colours, arranged in a specific width and sequence. This pattern, known as a 'sett', is woven into woollen fabric, occasionally incorporating silk. While similar designs have been present across various cultures for centuries, Tartan has become particularly associated with Scotland, often serving as a characteristic feature of Scottish kilts.

'Camouflage' originates from the French word 'camoufler', which translates to disguise. Numerous prominent fashion designers have embraced the style and symbolism of camouflage, incorporating it into their designs. Military-inspired clothing or replicas thereof have found use not only as streetwear but also as a symbol of political protest. The term camouflage, deriving from French slang, gained widespread use in English during World War I. So let's not camouflage France's role in bringing these fabric-related words into English!

◆

The contributions of India and France have been substantial but the rest of the world has also contributed to the English language's storehouse of textile-related terms.

'Harlequin' originating from the Commedia dell'arte, a theatrical movement in sixteenth-century Italy widely embraced across Europe, was associated with humorous and playful figures like court jesters. Harlequins sported costumes crafted by stitching together fabric scraps, forming elongated diamond patterns. Textile designers employ the term 'harlequin' to depict a diamond motif characterized by elongated shapes positioned in a vertical arrangement. The diamonds typically feature high-contrast colours. Harlequin prints frequently grace the fashion runways as various designers incorporate this timeless aesthetic into their collections.

'Argyle' rose to popularity in the United Kingdom and subsequently in the United States after World War I. The distinctive argyle design, characterized by a diamond-shaped pattern featuring two or more colours on fabric, has its origins in the Clan Campbell of Argyll in western Scotland. This pattern, initially employed for kilts and plaids, as well as patterned socks worn by Scottish Highlanders, gained prominence as early as the seventeenth century. Argyle, sometimes spelled as 'argyll', features a diamond-shaped design. In general, argyle patterns exhibit layers of intersecting motifs, contributing to a sense of three-dimensional motion and texture.

The 'herringbone' pattern has its roots in the Roman Empire, where it was employed in the construction of roads. This unique fabric pattern also found its place in the historical textiles of Ireland, frequently appearing in traditional tweed suits. The zigzag elements on the cloth are interrupted by alternating colours in both directions. The design known as 'herringbone' gets its name from its resemblance to the skeletal pattern of a herring fish. Although herringbone fabrics traditionally utilize wool, they are now crafted from a variety of fibre combinations, including cotton, thick wool, and linen.

'Gingham', also known as 'Vichy check', is a type of cotton fabric that emerged in the 1610s. It is crafted by weaving plain dyed yarns together. The term 'gingham' is believed to have its roots in the Dutch word 'gingang', which is a trader's interpretation of the Malay (Austronesian) term 'genggang', signifying striped. Another theory suggests that the fabric we now recognize as gingham might have been produced in Guingamp, a town located in Brittany, France. It is speculated that the fabric could have taken its name from this particular town. In the seventeenth century, gingham, initially arriving in Europe, featured stripes; however, its current identity is defined by a checkered design.

'Batik', originating from Java, Indonesia, is a time-honoured practice of dyeing fabric using wax-resistant techniques. The term 'batik' finds its roots in the Javanese language, with 'bathikan' also signifying 'drawing' or 'writing' in Javanese. The earliest English documentation of the term batik dates back to 1880 in the *Encyclopaedia Britannica*, where it was spelled as 'battik'. This art form has historical significance in the Indonesian Archipelago, with variations like mbatik, mbatek, batik, and batek emerging during the Dutch colonial era.

'Brocade', originating in the 1560s, refers to a luxurious intricately ornamented shuttle-woven fabric, commonly crafted from coloured silks and occasionally incorporating threads of gold and silver. The term is derived from the Spanish 'brocado', which aligns with the Italian 'broccato', meaning embossed cloth. Brocade is commonly crafted using a draw loom. This involves a supplementary weft method, where decorative brocading is achieved through an extra, non-structural weft alongside the regular weft responsible for securing the warp threads—a technique that aims to create the illusion that the weave appears to have been embroidered.

'Damask', derived from the ancient Syrian city of Damascus, refers to an expensive textile fabric characterized by intricate patterns. Historically, the fabric goes back to the Tang Dynasty in China, where it adorned luxurious textiles such as silk and was exclusively reserved for royalty and nobility; but it was traders from Damascus that introduced this fabric to Europe during the eleventh century. Damask fabric is reversible, often incorporating a satin weave, and adorned with symmetrical motifs inspired by the natural world.

And that's enough of fabric-related terms. Onwards.

SECTION SIX

IN[APPROPRIATE] WORDS AND CARDINAL GUIDELINES

An even more dismissive term for nonsense was 'codswallop'—which remains one of the most colourful words for describing nonsense. When words or language were dismissed as meaningless or conveying no comprehensible or intelligible ideas, they were called 'codswallop'.

42

APPROPRIATE INAPPROPRIATE WORDS

I have always prided myself on using the right word for the thought or idea I wish to convey, but sometimes the word that strikes me as perfectly appropriate in a specific context might turn out to be the wrong choice simply because no one understands it. After all, if the purpose of communication is to get your point across, using words that are incomprehensible to most people rather defeats the purpose. The word I wish to use might well be the most apposite one, but if it's too difficult for the listener or reader, then it's actually inappropriate to use it.

Still, there are many words I actually think should be in greater use and would therefore be more widely understood. '*Apposite*' is one of them—how many of you thought it was a typing mistake in the last paragraph? It actually is a synonym for 'apt'—or specifically, apt in the circumstances, or apt in relation to something. This chapter italicizes a few useful words that I tend to use sparingly, or type and then discard with a sigh, knowing they would not be understood.

In the course of a *mundivagant* life (one spent 'wandering all over the world'), I have come across many cultural differences. The most glaring involves people from countries where it is considered polite to refuse the offer of a drink, a meal, or a second helping until the host insists (and then you politely give in). As an Indian in the US for the first time, half a century ago, I practised this *accismus* (or 'the pretended refusal of something one keenly desires'), only to be taken literally by my hosts, with the result that I would constantly go hungry!

This kind of self-defeating behaviour has deep cultural roots, but it also occurs in political conduct as *akratic* action—voting behaviour, for instance, that is manifestly not in the voters' self-interest. *Akrasia* comes from the Greek for 'lacking control of oneself', and it means 'to act against one's better judgement'. So akratic conduct is something you shouldn't do, and wouldn't if you thought a little more about its consequences: for instance, most public health specialists will tell you that smoking is an *akratic* action. Yet despite the widespread prevalence of the behaviour it describes, *akrasia* and *akratic* are hardly used in everyday conversation or reportage.

There's a word I can understand us not using much, even though it describes a common emotion: *antipelargy,* defined by the lexicographer Thomas Blount in 1656 as 'the reciprocal love of children to their parents, or (more generally) any requital or mutual kindness'. *Antipelargy* just doesn't sound pleasant enough for such a beautiful feeling. But there are other feelings that also get short-changed. Take a pair of words we really ought to use more often -- uxoriousness, 'the state of being excessively fond of or submissive to a wife,' and its counterpart, *maritality*, 'excessive fondness of a wife for her husband'. How many *uxorious* husbands have we all encountered, and how many wives totally immersed in *maritality*? And yet not many use those words to describe them.

People around us are constantly searching for that elusive target, happiness. And yet life is full of *infelicific* things (those that are 'productive of unhappiness'). For many, of course, a good pint of ice-cream or a stiff drink might be the only things they find *felicific (*productive of happiness), since they haven't found anything else to *averruncate*—to take away hurtful things. None of those words, though, is in common use.

I should stop, for fear of being *ultracrepidarian*, 'giving opinions on matters beyond one's knowledge.' As I grow older and hit my *peracme* ('the point at which the prime or highest vigour is past'), I am increasingly afraid of indulging in *anecdotage*. The word is a portmanteau of *anecdote* (defined by the Merriam-Webster dictionary as 'a usually short narrative of an interesting, amusing, or biographical incident') and *dotage* ('a state or period of senile decay marked by the decline of mental poise and alertness'). As venerable seniors enter our dotage, we tend to tell too many anecdotes—and that could lull the reader into *consopition*, or in other words, put you to sleep!

43

LITERARY INSULTS

Those of us who love words have to admit, occasionally, that the best words are the ones writers use to insult people. Shakespeare's *King Lear* has the most elaborate insult in the great man's oeuvre: 'Thou art a base, proud, shallow, beggarly, three-suited, hundred-pound, filthy worsted-stocking knave; a lily-liver'd, action-taking, whoreson, glass-gazing, superserviceable, finical rogue; one-trunk-inheriting slave; one that wouldst be a bawd in way of good service, and art nothing but the composition of a knave, beggar, coward, pandar, and the son and heir of a mungril bitch.'

As early as 1652, the Scottish writer Thomas Urquhart, in his *Ekskybalauron*, inveighed against 'quomodocunquizing clusterfists and rapacious varlets'. These words, alas, never quite survived into contemporary usage, but the Oxford English Dictionary informs us that someone who is quomodocunquizing 'makes money in any possible way', while a 'clusterfist' is a 'close-fisted fellow; a clown, boor, lout'. The seventeenth century also gave us 'cockwomble', another word sadly fallen into disuse, meaning a man who is prone to making idiotic statements and/or behaving inappropriately while thinking himself superior and being convinced of his own importance. Four centuries later the world seems even more full of cockwombles than ever before.

But the fading away of these fabulously insulting terms did not cramp the style of the famous twentieth century English novelist Virginia Woolf, whose diaries revealed a rare talent for insults. 'Pale, marmoreal [T. S.] Eliot was there last week, like a chapped office boy on a high stool, with a cold in his head', reads one diary entry in 1921. As for Sigmund Freud, he was 'a screwed up shrunk very old man: with a monkey's light eyes, paralysed spasmodic movements, inarticulate: but alert.'

Other authors brought out the worst in Ms Woolf. E. M. Forster 'is limp and damp and milder than the breath of a cow.' The writings of others rarely impressed her. 'I am reading *Point Counter Point* [by Aldous Huxley]. Not a good novel. All raw, uncooked, protesting.' Legendary reputations meant little: '[F]ate has not been kind to [Elizabeth Barrett] Browning as a writer. Nobody reads her, nobody discusses her, nobody troubles to put her in her place.'

Of Katherine Mansfield, she wrote: 'her mind is a very thin soil, laid an inch or two deep upon very barren rock. For *Bliss* is long enough to give her a chance of going deeper. Instead she is content with superficial smartness; and the whole conception is poor, cheap, not the vision, however imperfect, of an interesting mind. She writes badly too.' Her personal appearance did not make up for her literary deficiencies: 'one's first impression of [Mansfield] was not that she stinks like civet cat that had taken to street walking. In truth I'm a little shocked by her commonness at first sight; lines so hard and cheap.'

Nor did she think very highly of James Joyce's masterwork *Ulysses*: 'I have read 200 pages so far—not a third; and have been amused, stimulated, charmed, interested, by the first 2 or 3 chapters—to the end of the cemetery scene; and then puzzled, bored, irritated, and disillusioned by a queasy undergraduate scratching his pimples. And Tom, great Tom, thinks this is on par with *War and Peace*! An illiterate, under-bred book it seems to me; the book of a self-taught working man, and we all know how distressing they are, how egotistic, insistent, raw, striking, and ultimately nauseating. When one can have the cooked flesh, why have the raw?'

Virginia Woolf could dish it out, but she couldn't take it. A bad review in the *Granta that said she was 'defunct' as a writer prompted her to dismiss it as* 'a snub some little pimpled undergraduate likes to administer, just as he would put a frog in one's bed'.

Writers, of course, should never be crossed, since they can

skewer you with words. 'Gratiano speaks an infinite deal of nothing,' a Shakespeare character memorably told another. Charles Dickens wrote of a character, 'He would make a lovely corpse.' George Orwell dismissed another: 'He is simply a hole in the air.' An Ernest Hemingway character says: 'I misjudged you… You're not a moron. You're only a case of arrested development.' Agatha Christie is the politest of the lot: 'If you will forgive me for being personal, I do not like your face.'

But the prize still goes to Shakespeare: 'I desire that we be better strangers.' So much better than 'unfriending' an ex today.

44

WORDS ABOUT NONSENSE

Considering that 'nonsense' literally means something that makes no sense, it seems paradoxical that English offers so many ways of saying 'nonsense'. Some of them have amusing origins as well, including in other languages. One of the words commonly used in England for foolish ideas, talk, or activities was 'bosh', as in 'that entire theory is utter bosh'. Bosh, it turns out, comes from *bos*, a Turkish word meaning 'empty; useless'. In similar vein, I would have expected British colonials in India to create 'buckwash' out of the Hindustani *bakwaaas*, but they never got beyond 'eyewash'. Or you could tell someone to 'stop talking rot', and it amounted to the same thing; something that was rotten could not be consumed, just as an idea that was 'bosh' could not be ingested.

An even more dismissive term for nonsense was 'codswallop'—which remains one of the most colourful words for describing nonsense. When words or language were dismissed as meaningless or conveying no comprehensible or intelligible ideas, they were called 'codswallop'. So 'his explanations for not turning in his work on time were codswallop' could mean they were unbelievable, foolish, or nonsensical. The etymology of the term is shrouded in controversy. The most interesting explanation is that 'wallop' once meant a kind of beer and a nineteenth century manufacturer of soft drinks, Hiram Codd, made such undrinkable beer that 'codswallop' became a derogatory term for a drink you couldn't swallow—hence, by extension, for an explanation or argument you couldn't swallow either. A more prosaic theory suggests that hearing codswallop was the equivalent of being whacked (or 'walloped') with a dead fish (a 'cod'), and codswallop was nonsense so insulting that it was like being assaulted with a fish. Take your pick—either theory might turn out to be codswallop too!

If Hiram Codd's beer was undrinkable, so too was 'balderdash', which also referred to an odd and usually disagreeable mixture of unsuitable drinks (such as a cocktail of beer and milk or beer and wine). No one is able to pinpoint the incompetent bartender who came up with such 'balderdash', though. A more straightforward etymology can be found for 'folderol', since the French term *fol-de-rol* referred to a nonsense refrain in songs, usually in the theatre. And the even more evocative 'poppycock' comes from a Dutch dialect word 'pappekak', or 'soft dung'.

American equivalents of codswallop—words to describe foolish, empty, specious, or nonsensical talk, ideas, or opinions—range from 'bunkum' to 'claptrap' by way of 'flapdoodle' and 'hogwash', taking in 'garbage', 'bull', and its unprintable longer form, as well as 'bellywash' and 'mumbo jumbo'. The British could counter with 'twaddle', 'gibberish', 'tommyrot', 'phooey', 'piffle', 'tripe', 'tosh', and 'double Dutch'. If a Brit considers something to be 'cobblers', an American is more likely to call it 'baloney'. A Brit might say something is 'blah' while a Yank might suggest it's 'waffle'. (And thanks to infusions of Yiddish from Jewish immigrants, a New Yorker might prefer 'meshuggas'.)

All in all, there are many ways to describe something that old-fashioned people used to dismiss as 'stuff and nonsense'. Some of these terms were born in very specific circumstances. 'Bunkum' came from American politics in 1820, when the American politician Felix Walker delivered a particularly lengthy and tiresome peroration of limited substance, claiming he was speaking for the people of Buncombe County, North Carolina. 'Buncombe' was pronounced 'bunkum', and the hapless county soon found itself, thanks to its political representative, a synonym for pointless speech—mercifully spelled differently. 'Blatherskite', on the other hand, is of Scottish origin, and meant a blustering and often contemptible person given to voluble and inconsequential talk. But it was popularized in America by the immortal Walt Disney, whose character Scrooge McDuck liked to exclaim, 'blathering blatherskite!'

Of course, if all these terms are too exotic for you, there is a simple synonym for 'nonsense' that is perfectly respectable English: 'drivel'. If you want to be rude, you could dismiss something as 'rubbish', or metaphorically urge someone not to release 'hot air'. But if you wished to react to nonsense in more memorable language, the terms in this essay should be more than enough to settle multiple scores!

45

MOST HATED WORDS

As an omnivorous consumer of words, whether good, bad, or ugly, I tend not to discriminate among them, embracing them all as grist to the mill of my somewhat eclectic vocabulary. So it came as a surprise to me to discover that, when it comes to words in the English language, there are several that people actually dislike so much that they win contests for 'the most hated words'.

Some feature regularly in lists of people's least favourite words in English: 'vomit' is a perennial peeve, but some dislikes are more irrational, like people's visceral dislike of 'gushing' or 'renal'. One can understand 'vomit', because of the images and feelings the word conjures because of its meaning. There's similar hate for 'pus' and 'phlegm', and all of us can empathize with those who can't stand the words because of the thoughts they inspire. But the word that regularly tops the charts for the most hated word in the English language, surprisingly, is 'moist'.

Why 'moist', one may well ask? It's not a disgusting word like the others; it has associations with soft, sentimental tears ('she looked at her departing son with moist eyes'), with descriptions of weather ('the moist air of this humid clime') and of a gentle state between dryness and wetness that suggests neither extreme. And yet 'moist' has become a much-hated word. There's an entire article you can google from the *Los Angeles Times*, by June Casagrande—the author of a book called *The Joy of Syntax: A Simple Guide to All the Grammar You Know You Should Know*—on why people dislike 'moist'.

According to her, the use of the word 'has been in steady decline for over a century but took a big dip around 2010'. Around the middle of the first decade of the century, says Casagrande, 'countless thousands of people decided they hate the word 'moist'. Some had probably hated it all along. Others were clearly jumping on a bandwagon....' The result is that writers are actively trying to avoid using the word. 'It's unclear whether writers are avoiding the word 'moist' because they dislike it or because they know readers do, but either way there's a lesson here: When writing, choose your words carefully.'

I am clearly out of sync with the global mood, because I like the word, but I have since discovered, to my chagrin, that when the prestigious *New Yorker* magazine conducted a survey in 2012 on 'the most disliked words', poor old 'moist' had topped the list. Apparently, researchers at two American colleges, Oberlin and Trinity, even conducted a study on why people hated this inoffensive word and found that people who didn't like the word 'moist' also didn't like words such as 'phlegm,' 'vomit,' and 'diarrhoea'—'suggesting that a big part of why people hate the word so much is its connotations to bodily fluids'. This was confirmed by another survey conducted by the online language platform Preply, which concluded that the majority of the words that make people squirm are related to the human body (including 'foetus' and 'mucus') and bodily fluids. But the dislike also extends beyond the words already mentioned in this column, to more innocent terms like 'seepage', 'ooze', 'putrid', 'yeast', and—bizarrely for Indian yoghurt-lovers—'curd'. These all seem to incite feelings of queasiness in those who dislike or reject them.

There is, inevitably, a word in English for this kind of dislike for certain words: the feeling of aversion for specific words or terms is called 'logomisia'. A linguistics professor at the University of Pennsylvania, Mark Liberman defines logomisia as 'a feeling of intense, irrational distaste for the sound or sight of a particular word or phrase, not because its use is regarded as etymologically or logically or grammatically wrong, nor because it's felt to be over-used or redundant or trendy or non-standard, but simply because the word itself somehow feels unpleasant or even disgusting.'

Liberman adds: 'This demonstrates just how powerful language can be. Language has the ability to make us feel all types of positive emotions, including love and happiness. However… language also has the power to make us uncomfortable.' A moist wipe, anyone?

46

FORBIDDEN WORDS

There are some words in English that many newspapers won't print. They are considered 'bad' words, not fit for use in polite society. Popular euphemisms for using such 'dirty' words are 'cursing' and 'swearing'. Some scholars see such words as distinct linguistic forms, while others include them within a broader comprehension of 'taboo' language, including vulgar expressions, obscenity, or profanity. Cursing remains susceptible to religious restrictions, while swearing, specifically the use of expletives, is often deemed as 'indecent' language whose usage is forbidden, or taboo.

The term 'taboo' has its roots in Polynesian culture, originating from words like 'tabu' or 'tapu' in the Tongan language. It reached English during the eighteenth century via the explorer Captain Cook, in his account of his third global voyage, which included visits to Polynesia. During this journey, he observed various applications of the word 'taboo' in the context of diverse 'avoidance customs'. A taboo sometimes functions as a form of 'thought policing', dictating human conduct and also controlling thoughts. The initial Polynesian concept carried a distinct religious connotation. To use taboo words was offensive to God.

How do we grasp taboo words? Remarkably, there is a distinct lack of definitive understanding regarding the process by which a child learns them. Undoubtedly, no individual is inherently endowed with an innate awareness of these forbidden words. Rather, it is only as we reach a level of maturity that we become conscious of societal norms and become educated in the realm of taboo—often by learning of them through elders' disapproval, and sometimes because, in an act of rebellion, we want to shock or offend by employing a taboo term.

The utilization of 'taboo language' seems to be an age-old facet of human communication. In Shakespeare's play *The Tempest*, when Prospero asserts that Caliban had no knowledge of any recognizable language until Prospero educated and civilized him, Caliban's response serves as both an accusation and a form of linguistic defiance. Caliban retorts, 'You taught me language, and my profit on't/Is, I know how to curse/ The red plague rid you/ For learning me your language!' He employs the linguistic skills he has acquired to curse and thereby rebel against Prospero's oppression.

Employing 'swear words' and engaging in the use of 'taboo words' and expressions is a widespread practice. You come across them in books, cinema, rap music and in both private and public discourse, as well as in various forms of media. There's a vast lexicon of emotionally charged, offensive language—words and phrases that are generally deemed unsuitable in particular contexts but are resorted to when people seek to convey intense emotions, issue threats, or engage in unpleasant exchanges with others. While swear words and taboo expressions can heighten the impact of our words, they are also capable of eliciting shock or offence.

Of course, Caliban's actual words themselves do not possess inherent qualities of being 'taboo', 'indecent', or 'profane'. Many words now considered unsuitable for public discourse were, in earlier stages of the English language, neutral, conventional terms to describe objects or actions. Taboo words are also subject to change over time. Some of them may diminish ('damn' has lost its power to shock) or even vanish as language evolves, while others may transmute into euphemisms. People also engage in self-censorship, refusing to use words that others may disapprove of. Instead of using these words, individuals often employ euphemisms as more polite substitutes for the taboo terms. 'Gosh' and 'crikey!' evolved from needing to exclaim aloud without using the words 'God' or 'Christ'.

The categorization of language as 'taboo' is contingent upon cultural norms and not any inherent linguistic characteristics.

Linguists have adopted an impartial and descriptive approach when addressing taboo language, confining themselves to recording which words are avoided in particular contexts. In the context of modern Western culture, 'taboo' words are intrinsically linked with the principles of politeness, for social engagement revolves around conduct that is characterized by courtesy, respect, restraint, and taking utmost care not to offend.

'Bad' words are expected to be entirely avoided, or at least used sparingly in the presence of 'mixed company'. If at all you resort to them, be judicious—and use them only sparingly for special effect!

47

THE SIGNIFICANCE OF SLANG

All of us use slang, wittingly or unwittingly, though we use formal language more. Conventionally, most of what you'd read in a newspaper is the standard language, whereas a slang is a non-conventional or alternative way to express the same idea. The standard language usually denotes the 'correct', recognized, and controlled mode of expression in a society or linguistic group. Conversely, slang tends to be casual, challenges societal propriety and refuses to adhere to the rigid grammatical and usage standards associated with formal language. Though slang is a deviation from standard language, it frequently mirrors the ever-changing character of language and fulfils various social, cultural, and generational roles. With the passage of time, certain slang terms may achieve broad acceptance and integrate into the standard vocabulary. This occurs when particular slang terms become popular, widely recognized, and employed by a larger segment of the population.

Slang changes with time; a slang expression comes into vogue and often passes into obsolescence in a generation or two, while new terms come into existence. Schools are great incubators of slang. A century or so ago, a 'fruit' was a lenient teacher, and a 'heathen' was an unreasonable teacher. A 'blug' was one who was very stylish, 'chiselly' meant unpleasant. To 'jump' or 'bolt' meant to absent oneself from class. An 'ice wagon' was a slow student; an equivalent term now would be a 'doofus'. A 'grind' was someone who studied too much or too hard; today he'd be called a 'swot', 'geek', or 'nerd'.

Broader society invented slang too. 'Flim' meant to cheat; now, we would say 'scam'. Though such expressions are passé today, some slang words are here to stay. 'Bummer', which indicates an unpleasant experience, has managed to last several decades.

'Cool', meaning sophisticated, fashionable and up to date, which was first cited in 1918, has managed to remain slang for most of the twentieth century and into the twenty-first, even if GenZ prefers 'fire'. ('Hot' in the sense of attractive and desirable is of more recent vintage, dating to the 1960s). An eccentric person is 'bonkers', a weak one a 'wimp', an unpleasant one a 'jerk', for decades now. But 'groovy' (for 'with-it'; 'fashionable') dates you, since it is a relic of 1960s and '70s American hippie slang and only people of that vintage still use it.

Slang often originates within sub-cultures or from groups that are not part of the established power structures. It serves as a tool for these marginalized groups to critique the dominant mainstream culture, assert their unique identity, engage in linguistic innovation, stand out from the norm, form alternative language communities, and reject mainstream conventions. While doing so they may create meanings that may remain inaccessible to those within the mainstream. Slang is often a clever form of linguistic play. It has the power to elicit laughter and surprise by the choice of words, while expressing a sub-culture. The most famous example of this is Cockney rhyming slang, which originated in the East End of London, using phrases that rhymed with the formal words for an idea and then dropping the rhyming part of the phrase. Thus the phrase 'apples and pears' is used to mean 'stairs'; then 'and pears' is dropped, so a Cockney says 'I'm going up the apples' when he means 'I'm going up the stairs'. Sounds complicated, but it's hugely clever, and many of its expressions have passed into common language in working-class Britain. Beers are 'Britneys' because 'beers' rhymes with 'Britney Spears'. Get the idea?

You don't have to be a Londoner to use humorous slang: try 'brain burp' for a random thought, or 'beer goggles' for the phenomenon of perceiving someone as more attractive while drunk. The light-heartedness of slang vocabulary helps form a sense of community by conveying thoughts impertinently or irreverently. Of course it tends to be intentionally undignified, startling, or amusing, and occasionally both exaggerated and politically incorrect. Take, for instance, using the word 'raped' to mean 'defeated', which trivializes the serious crime of sexual assault. Less offensively, 'I'm wiped [out]' merely means I'm exhausted. 'I'm going to crash' is slang for 'going to bed'. Time for me to crash!

48

DYSPHEMISM

Dysphemism is the antithesis of euphemism, tracing its roots to the Greek words dys, meaning 'bad' or 'abnormal' and pheme, meaning 'utterance' or 'speech'. This rhetorical device, first documented in 1884, involves the deployment of derogatory or offensive language in place of inoffensive expressions, as well as the substitution of negative terms for positive ones. Instances of dysphemism include the colloquial use of 'shrink' to refer to a psychiatrist and 'loony bin' or 'nut house' to describe a mental hospital, and as these expressions suggest, are unpleasant words used to degrade or humiliate those referred to.

Some people habitually employ dysphemism as a way to express their frustration or annoyance when referring to individuals or objects. The use of derogatory terms and name-calling aimed at others is intended to insult, belittle, or hurt them. For instance, calling someone's extravagant mane a 'mop' is to reduce their hairstyle to something you would use to clean up a messy kitchen floor. Calling someone's statement a 'lie' or a 'falsehood' is a dysphemism; suggesting he has 'misrepresented the facts' is a euphemistic way of saying the same thing. (Winston Churchill once accused an opponent of 'terminological inexactitude'; by the time he realized he had been called a liar, the speaker had moved on.) Yet dysphemisms are commonly used in literature, political speeches, and everyday language.

Occasionally, a word may be considered a dysphemism in one cultural context but not in another. For instance, calling a gay person a 'fag' is typically viewed as a dysphemism in American culture. However, in British or Indian usage, 'fag' is merely a slang word for a cigarette, and the word would not carry the same negative connotation in those countries. The process of pejoration results in words that were once regarded as euphemisms transforming into dysphemisms. Frequently, a word that initially served both euphemistic and dysphemistic purposes becomes seen only as dysphemistic. The term 'retarded' was introduced as a more considerate alternative after the preceding terms like 'idiot' and 'moron' began to be regarded as dysphemistic; however, over time, 'retarded' itself has evolved into a dysphemism. Now you would be expected to use 'mentally challenged'. Similarly, 'handicapped' was a euphemism that became seen as a dysphemism, and was replaced by 'disabled'; but that too got regarded as dysphemistic, and was transformed via 'persons with disabilities' to 'differently-abled' instead.

In the cultural context of the United States, expressions such as 'coloured' and 'Negro' were formerly viewed as euphemisms but are now seen as dysphemisms, and have now been substituted with terms like 'Black' and 'African American'. Occasionally, minor modifications to dysphemistic terms can render them more acceptable. For instance, while 'coloured people' is perceived as dysphemistic, the phrase 'people of colour' is seen as avoiding the negative connotations associated with the former.

In Geoffrey Hughes' book, *An Encyclopedia of Swearing*, the author explores the various euphemisms associated with death, such as 'passed away', 'passed on', 'departed this life', and 'gone to meet his Maker'. Parallel dysphemisms would be 'snuffed it', 'croaked', 'he's six feet under', and 'he's pushing up the daisies', which vividly and harshly refer to the physical aspects of death and burial. Of course, context is all. Keith Allan and Kate Burridge, in the book *Euphemism and Dysphemism*, propose that addressing death humorously is considered dysphemistic only if the listener is likely to find it offensive. For example, if a physician were to inform a grieving family that their relative passed away using a colloquial expression like 'pegged out' or 'bit the dust' during the night, it would naturally be deemed dysphemistic. However, in an alternative context with a different set of people involved, the same expressions, when used by a friend, might be characterized as affectionately euphemistic.

While dysphemisms are frequently employed to shock or provoke, they can also function as markers of closeness. Referring to a child as a rat is undeniably a dysphemistic expression. However, when the term 'rug rat' is used to refer to children, it is usually accompanied by a sense of affection. But if you use it for someone else's toddler, their parents might consider it offensive. The basic rule of thumb remains: avoid dysphemism as much as possible. Politeness pays!

SECTION SEVEN

LITERARY TOOLS

This a multi-ethnic bilingual tongue-twisting limerick that I made up in my college days:

A young man, despite his garibi
Wished to marry his habibi, Phoebe
'But,' he said, 'I must see
What will the maulvi's fee be
Before Phoebe be Phoebe my Bibi!'

49

IT'S OK! (NOT OKAY)

If one were to meet someone who doesn't speak a word of English, then what is the one 'English' word that most of them probably do know? Almost certainly, it's *OK*.

The folks at the Merriam-Webster dictionaries speculate that 'OK' is 'very probably the most widely recognized word in the world'. It is certainly also one of the most versatile words in the world. It can be used as a noun: 'I got his OK on it'; as a verb: 'Did Mumbai Indians OK the deal with Hardik?'; as an adjective: 'I thought the actor did an OK job on the role'; as an adverb: 'My son seems to be getting along OK in the new job'; as humorous slang, such as 'I'm fine, just okey-dokey'; or as an interjection in two ways: to denote compliance ('OK, I'll do it before the end of the day') or to convey agreement ('OK, that is fine').

OK conveys subtle nuances too. As an adjective, OK really means 'adequate' ('The boss approved this draft, so it is OK to send out.'); or 'acceptable' as a contrast to 'bad' ('It's OK to accuse your opponent of dishonesty when he routinely misrepresents your record.'). It can also mean 'mediocre' when used in contrast with 'good'. ('The dosas were great, but the sambar was just OK.'). It fulfils a similar role as an adverb ('Not bad, you did OK for your first time speaking in public!'). OK, as an adjective, can express acknowledgement without approval. In spoken form, it can also be used with the appropriate voice tone to express doubt ('OK?'), to convey reassurance ('Everything will be OK'), to admonish and warn ('Don't tell anyone else about this, OK?'), to reflect cynicism ('He cheats shamelessly but thinks it's OK as long as no one finds out.'), or to seek confirmation ('Is that OK?'). OK is not just understood all over the world, even where English isn't spoken; the clincher is that it was even the first word spoken on the Moon.

But the funny thing—indeed the most astonishing thing of it all—is, as Merriam-Webster tells us, is that the etymology of the word 'OK' reveals that its origin is 'literally a joke'.

According to two people who have researched the word—yes, it took two scholars of eminence to study how this two-letter word came about—the term was invented in the United States (where else?) in an 1839 article in the *Boston Morning Post*. According to research by the historian Allen Walker Read, as reflected in the 2010 book *OK: The Improbable Story of America's Greatest Word*, by Allan Metcalf, the word's roots originate in a bit of jocular text—a suggestion by a Boston newspaper to their counterparts in Providence, Rhode Island, to sponsor 'a party for some boisterous Boston lads who might be stopping by'. This jokey text, borrowing from the prevailing fashion of deliberate misspellings (coupled with the newer fashion of abbreviating popular phrases to acronyms) rendered 'all correct' as 'oll korekt'—and summarized it as 'OK'.

Before you wonder how such a trivial joke caught on, it's important to understand that both the craze for abbreviations and for misspellings were the 1830s newspaper equivalents in those days of the trivialities that 'go viral' on social media nowadays. First, says Read, came the abbreviations of common expressions, including RTBS, 'remains to be seen', GTDHD, 'give The Devil his due', OFM, 'our first men' (a satirical description of Boston's leading citizens), and SP, 'small potatoes' (for something considered to be of little importance). Then came the deliberate misspellings (like 'kewl' and 'rite' so beloved of adolescents today) which also had their equivalents then, turning *no go* into *know go* and *no use* into *know yuse*—which when abbreviated, as the abbreviation fad required, made *no go* into '*K.G.*' and turned *know yuse* into 'KY'. '*Enough said*' became '*nuff ced*' and was abbreviated to 'NC'. In the same way, the expression *all right* was deliberately misspelled as *oll wright* and became O.W., as an abbreviation. And *all correct* became *oll korekt*—hence *o.k.!*

Here's where the plot thickens, according to Metcalf. *OK* did become one of the more commonly used expressions, but it's fair to point out that since all the other abbreviations cited above have passed into oblivion, how come OK survived and achieved global glory? The answer apparently lies in the US presidential election of 1840, when President Martin Van Buren was nicknamed 'Old Kinderhook' after his hometown of Kinderhook, New York. As a result, Van Buren fans organized themselves into 'OK Clubs' across the country, further popularizing the word. Merriam Webster tells us that as a result many wrongly attribute the origin of the word to 'Old Kinderhook', when it really should be credited to the jocular Bostonian editor who came up with 'oll korekt'. But the double-meaning that Van Buren was both 'OK' (by nickname) and *OK* (because he was right for the country) entrenched the term in the American consciousness, and from there it was not an enormous leap to its global spread.

Metcalf dismisses all the other 'origin stories', but details many of them, including alleged sources in various other languages, notably Latin, Greek, Scottish, French, Finnish, and Anglo-Saxon via Swedish, with two African languages, Mandingo and Wolof, also being credited. The list includes the following theories that OK originated: from the Choctaw-Chickasaw *okah* meaning 'it is indeed'; from a mishearing of the Scots *och aye*! (or perhaps Ulster Scots *Ough aye*!), 'yes, indeed!'; from West African languages like Mandingo (*O ke*, 'certainly') or Wolof (*waw kay*, 'yes indeed'); from Finnish *oikea*, 'correct, exact'; from French *au quais*, 'at the quay' (supposedly stencilled on Puerto Rican rum specially selected for export, or a place of assignation for French sailors in the Caribbean); or from French *Aux Cayes* (a port in Haiti famous for its superior rum). Other, perhaps more far-fetched, explanations suggest that OK comes from an abbreviation for: *Open Key*, popularized by early telegraphers; *Old Keokuk*, the name of a Native American Fox chief; the German ranks *Oberst Kommandant*, Colonel in Command, or *Ober Kommando*, High Command, because German army officers fought alongside the colonists in the American Revolution; the name of a freight agent, *Obadiah Kelly*, whose initials often appeared on bills of lading; or the initials of *Orrin Kendall* biscuits supplied to the Union Army during the Civil War.

The most creative and widely-believed story claimed it was one more thing that the white Americans looted from the Natives they had displaced in America. According to this theory, *OK* was a contraction of the Choctaw word *okeh*, which President Andrew Jackson allegedly stole (along with much of their land) from members of the Choctaw tribe. This theory was taken so seriously that President Woodrow Wilson, a former head of Princeton University before ascending to the nation's highest office, reportedly wrote *okeh* on papers he approved. When asked why he did not use *O.K.*, he replied, like the stern professor he used to be: 'Because it is wrong.'

Unfortunately for him, it was he who was wrong. *O.K.* was the real original. Which means that spelling *O.K.* as *okay* is also, strictly speaking, 'wrong,' though writing *OK* (without the old-fashioned full stops in between) and even choosing the lowercase *ok* are also acceptable, and indeed more popular. OK?

50

ACRONYMS

In the previous chapter I dwelled at length on one of the most common acronyms in use—OK. Time now to look at other acronyms that you are likely to encounter. Studying in Delhi University, I became acutely familiar with the local tendency to compress place names into acronyms—thus Connaught Place was 'CP', Kirori Mal College simply 'KM'—but working in government taught me the disease is far worse there. Everyone was reduced to an acronym. So the external affairs minister was EAM, his deputies, the ministers of state were MoS, and all the bureaucrats beneath them seemed to have no names, only letters to identify them, as FS, AS, JS, and so on. The last, joint secretaries, really ran the place, and their acronyms were compounded by their areas of competence—JSUN meant joint secretary United Nations, JSIO was joint secretary Indian Ocean. A young aide named Jacob, after meeting a series of such grandees, decided to introduce himself as 'J-A-C-O-B', which sounded authentic enough to send flunkies scurrying off to look up who was this new eminence with the title JSOB!

But acronyms which are obviously abbreviations of names or titles (like these above, or organisations like NATO or OPEC, or familiar terms like AM and PM) are not of much interest for a chapter on words. True, there are acronyms that have become indispensable in the language: in America, if you mail someone a letter, you need a ZIP code, a term that's an acronym of 'zone improvement plan'. (In India you need one too—it's called a PIN, for 'postal identification number', not to be confused with the PIN code you need at the bank's ATM machines, which stands for 'personal identification number'.) These are acronyms one uses all the time in daily life, along with FAQ, 'Frequently Asked Questions', BTW, 'By the Way', and MYOB, 'Mind Your Own Business'.

But they're still obviously contractions of longer terms. What's more fun are those acronyms we don't even realize are acronyms—words created from the initial letters of words in a term or phrase that have acquired currency of their own. These acronyms are pronounced like regular words and you really have to dig into their origins to realise they are actually acronyms.

Those of you who have gone scuba-diving are probably aware that the word 'scuba' is an acronym for 'self-contained underwater breathing apparatus', though I dare say most others are not. I hadn't realized, either, that 'radar' is an acronym: the term was coined in World War II by the United States Navy, as an acronym for 'Radio Detection and Ranging'. Similarly, 'sonar', which is based on the principle of reflection of high-frequency Ultrasonic sound waves, is an acronym for 'Sound Navigation and Ranging'.

Have you had, or contemplated, laser surgery? It's effective in making precision incisions and often used when operating on the eyes—and it's an acronym too, for 'Light Amplification by Stimulated Emission of Radiation'. When one reads of US law-enforcement subduing would-be troublemakers with a 'taser', one would be justified in thinking that, like laser, it's an acronym too. But there the resemblance ends: the acronym actually comes from 'Thomas A Swift Electric Rifle', after the inventor, Jack Cover, decided in 1974 to name it after his favourite children's book character, Tom Swift.

Other acronyms that have passed into common use in the English language as words in their own right include *Yuppie*: the Young Upwardly-mobile Professional, NIMBY: Not in My Back Yard, and DINKIE: Dual Income, No Kids. There are less familiar variants: YAPPIE*:* Young Affluent Parent, for instance, *SINK*: Single, Independent, No Kids, and OINK: One Income, No Kids. They're accompanied these days by some decidedly jokey ones: SITCOM: Single Income, Two Kids, Outrageous Mortgage, or SCUM: Self-centred Urban Male, or best of all, SINBAD, an acronym for Single Income, No Boyfriend, Absolutely Desperate.

Any SINBAD amongst you? It's the weekend, or as at least one newspaper prefers it, the WKND. (That's NOT an acronym but the name of their weekend supplement.) Well, if you're invited to attend a weekend party in America, you may be advised to BYOB, (Bring Your Own Bottle), though in Australia that same acronym stands for 'Bring Your Own Beer'. I am not sure whether it's students or office-goers who popularized TGIF, 'Thank God It's Friday'. AFAIK, 'As Far as I Know', it's the latter, but IMHO, 'In My Humble Opinion', it doesn't matter….

How often have you lately been sent the cryptic 'TL;DR'? I had no clue what it meant when I first saw it myself. 'TL;DR' means 'too long; didn't read,' and it functions in a variety of ways, whether apologetic (sorry, I didn't have the time to read the long piece you sent me), to accusatory (I asked you a question but what you sent was too long to read). But it's also increasingly being used to mean 'the gist' or 'the summary' of a long and complex idea, as in 'the TL;DR of this is', followed by a short explanation: 'the TL;DR of this is that global warming is real'. And it even serves as an adjective: 'I was trying to explain the concept to her but she shot off a TL;DR message and I gave up!'

Of course, as the frequency of the phrase's usage multiplies, 'TL;DR' also seems to be a contronym—a word whose usage incorporates two opposite meanings that contradict each other. After all, 'TL;DR' can be used both to introduce a brief summary of a topic, and to point to something as being too long to read!

Another increasingly popular acronym for today's young people is FOMO, for the 'Fear of Missing Out', which impels many into joining activities that otherwise they might have been inclined to skip. But the enforced home life of the Covid pandemic has led to a different set of habits, epitomized in the newly-popular expression 'goblin mode', where people prefer to remain curled up in bed, unshaven and in their pyjamas. This has led to the coining of 'JOMO', for the 'Joy of Missing Out'. The rest of you want to go and visit the latest club that's come up in town? Go ahead—I'm luxuriating in JOMO!

Everyone these days is familiar with NIMBY, or 'Not in my Backyard'—the attitude of all those who resist encroachments on their personal space, and more seriously organize protests against everything from nuclear plants to waste-processing units being located close to their homes. But now, at least in California, NIMBYs are giving way to their opposite, YIMBYs—folks who say 'Yes in My Backyard'. YIMBYs are quite willing to have projects built in their neighbourhoods, saying 'yes' to high-density development. The term arose because of a change in planning rules in California that will make it easier to build homes as well as offices and shops in the same areas. Hitherto, the NIMBYshad ensured strict zoning laws in California to separate living and working areas so that no one could build an office building next to their home, but now the YIMBYs have changed the rules—and as *The Economist* has observed, 'where California leads, the rest of the world tends to follow'. So you'd better get used to YIMBY!

All this must strike readers as very twenty-first century—it's a hallmark of our WhatsApp era that people prefer to say 'ROFL' to convey that they are 'Rolling on the Floor Laughing' or 'BRB' rather than taking the trouble to type the words 'be right back'. Of course, 'ASAP' for 'as soon as possible' and 'FYI' meaning 'For your Information' have been around for decades and can be called twentieth century terms, but 'G2G' for 'got to go' and 'TTYL' meaning 'talk to you later' are more recent and can be traced to the twenty-first century habit of sending short text messages.

But I was startled to discover that the early nineteenth century was just as bad. The Merriam-Webster Dictionary recently uncovered an 1839 New York newspaper report of a young woman remarking to her male friend 'O.K.K.B.W.P.' Apparently this cryptic acronym led to the young man rewarding her with a kiss. The newspaper explained that her acronym translates as 'one kind kiss before we part.' Or was that 'TMI'—'Too Much Information?' You decide! TTYL – BRB!

51

ALLITERATION

In the days when I was a regular writer of fiction, critics noted my fondness for alliteration—a literary device that repeats, in two or more nearby words, their initial consonant sounds. For alliteration to be an effective technique, alliterative words should flow in quick succession, and ideally catch the reader's or listener's attention. We all do this in everyday speech: expressions like 'big business', 'money matters', 'picture perfect', 'high heaven', 'tough talk', 'quick question', and 'no nonsense' are alliterations that are routine in conversation. And our daily life offers alliterations all around us: Coca-Cola, Dunkin' Donuts, hip-hop, Rainbow Room, Weight Watchers. You get the idea.

Literature abounds in alliteration, from Shakespeare's *Love's Labour's Lost* to Steinbeck's *East of Eden*. Shakespeare's play *As You Like It* has the lines 'And churlish chiding of the winter's wind/ Which, when it bites and blows upon my body'. Coleridge's poem *The Rime of the Ancient Mariner* uses alliteration too: 'The fair breeze blew, the white foam flew/ The furrow followed free'. Robert Frost's 'Acquainted with the Night' offers the memorable alliteration 'stood still and stopped the sound'. E. E. Cummings' poem *All in Green Went My Love Riding* includes the line 'Softer be they than slippered sleep the lean lithe deer the fleet flown deer.'

Children who read get used to alliteration pretty easily, because their stories are full of characters with alliterative names, which tend to be more enjoyable and memorable: Lois Lane, Peter Parker, Bugs Bunny, Peppa Pig, Mickey Mouse, Miss Muffet, Wonder Woman, and best of all (since it involves three alliterations) Wicked Witch of the West. In fact, Walt Disney was an ace at the game: he not only gave Mickey Mouse a sister named Minnie Mouse, but a whole string of alliterative ducks followed, in Donald Duck, Daisy Duck, Daffy Duck, and so on.

Alliterations can be fun to devise and even more fun to employ, but there are a couple of ground rules. It's not about repeating the consonant *letters* that begin words, but rather repeating the consonant *sounds*. So 'kissing cousins' is an alliteration, though the two words begin with different letters, but 'phony people' is not, even though both words begin with the same consonant, because the initial consonant sounds are different.

Second rule: have as many words as possible follow each other in quick succession. Two is everyday, even humdrum; three or more makes people sit up and take notice. And while the longer alliterative phrases may be forced to accommodate prepositions or articles beginning with other letters, you must keep them to a minimum; if there are too many non-alliterative words in between, then the literary device doesn't work.

Now that we have dispensed with the basics, here are some famous examples of alliteration, mostly not of my own devising:

- Slowly the slug started up the steep surface, stringing behind it scribble sparkling like silk.
- The chilling cold almost chopped him apart.
- The ship sailed smoothly but sadly sank like a submarine.
- Sam saw Susie sitting in a shoeshine shop.
- Nine nice night nurses nursing nicely.
- My counters and cupboards were completely cleared of carrot cake, cornbread, and crackers.
- Four fine fresh fish for you.
- Lesser leather never weathered wetter weather better.
- Claire, close your cluttered closet.
- The big bad bear bored the baby bunnies by the bushes.
- Go and gather the green leaves on the grass.
- Please put away your paints and practice the piano.
- The boy buzzed around as busy as a bee.
- Garry grumpily gathered the garbage.

- Lazy lizards are lying like lumps on the leaves.
- Paula planted the pretty pink poppies in the pepper-pot.
- Little Larry likes licking the sticky lollipop.

◆

Alliterative tongue-twisters are an extension of alliteration that I am especially fond of. 'She sells seashells by the seashore' is perhaps the most famous in the genre, but there are many more. 'Can you can a can as a canner can can a can?' is easier to say aloud than read on the page. Conversely, 'If a dog chews shoes, whose shoes does he choose?' looks deceptively easy in writing but is a challenge to enunciate.

English speakers take great pleasure in mastering tongue-twisters. They improve your speaking skills, train you to pronounce words clearly, and it's always fun, especially for the young, to play games in which you have to repeat a tongue-twister three times, fast.

Alliteration adds to the challenge of saying a tongue-twister out loud. (Try 'How many cookies could a good cook cook if a good cook could cook cookies?') So does the shift from single sounds to double sounds, such as from 's' to 'sh' (and back) in our first example. Changing the order of the sounds complicates this further because our tongue and brain develop 'muscle memory' that makes them return to the first way the words are said, and so trip up your tongue. ('If two witches were watching two watches, which witch would watch which watch?') Some tongue-twisters employ similar yet different sounds, such as a rhyme where only the first sound changes. ('I saw a kitten eating chicken in the kitchen.') Others use words that sound the same and are spelled differently, such as 'would' and 'wood'. A famous example of this technique: 'How much wood would a woodchuck chuck if a woodchuck could chuck wood? A woodchuck would chuck as much wood as he could chuck if a woodchuck could chuck wood.'

A tongue-twister that used most of these tricks, and which I learned in childhood many decades ago, ran like this: 'Betty Botter bought a bit of butter. But the butter Betty Botter bought was bitter, and Betty thought if she bought it for her batter, it would make her batter bitter. So Betty Botter bought a bit of better butter to make her bitter batter better.' I was never sure which was more difficult, this or the more famous 'Peter Piper picked a peck of pickled peppers. A peck of pickled peppers Peter Piper picked. If Peter Piper picked a peck of pickled peppers, where's the peck of pickled peppers Peter Piper picked?' Of course, the faster you say them, the greater the chance you'll trip up!

Though alliterative tongue-twisters are usually associated with children's games, they are in fact extremely useful for the adults reading this chapter too. They help in practising speaking the language out loud, improve pronunciation and clarity, and strengthen the speaker's fluency and articulation. Tongue-twisters are often used by actors, voice-over artistes, and public speakers (even politicians!) for their verbal vocal exercises. This one, for instance, would challenge many a top star: 'How much dew does a dewdrop drop, if dewdrops do drop dew? They do drop, they do, when due, as do dewdrops drop, if dewdrops do drop dew.'

While alliteration is essential to tongue-twisters, rhyme helps too, since it makes tongue-twisters easier to remember. One of my favourite tongue-twisters is actually a limerick, which makes it easier to say than most of our other examples:

> There was a fisherman named Fisher
> Who fished for some fish in a fissure.
> Till a fish with a grin,
> Pulled the fisherman in.
> Now they're fishing the fissure for Fisher.

This verse is another classic, and it's not as easy:

> A fly and flea flew into a flue,
> said the fly to the flea 'what shall we do?'
> 'Let us fly,' said the flea;

said the fly 'Shall we flee?';
so they flew through a flaw in the flue.

But for this audience it may be best to end with a multi-ethnic bilingual tongue-twisting limerick that I made up in my college days:

A young man, despite his garibi
Wished to marry his habibi, Phoebe
'But,' he said, 'I must see
What will the maulvi's fee be
Before Phoebe be Phoebe my Bibi!'

52

ANAGRAMS

Crossword addicts—cruciverbalists, as they are known—are, of course, familiar with anagrams. An anagram is a word created by rearranging the letters of another word: '*smart*', for instance, can be anagrammed as '*trams*' or '*marts*'. Cryptic crossword clues love this device.

But this isn't a chapter about solving crosswords. What I enjoy about anagrams is that they can be fun. Rearranging letters can often give you amusing results. The word '*anagram*' itself can be converted into '*nag a ram*'! '*The Morse Code*' anagrammed says '*here come dots*' (dashes, too, of course). Similarly '*Statue of Liberty*' is '*Built to stay free*'. Place names can be anagrammed too. If you fall sick in '*San Diego*', you need to be '*diagnose*'d'! And many a gambler '*salvages*' what he can in '*Las Vegas*'.

Names of celebrities are a favourite subject of amusing anagrams. *The Simpsons* animated television series had a character who created anagrams out of famous people's names that described them as well—thus '*Alec Guinness*' became '*genuine class*'. Not long ago in India, BJP supporters of the prime minister put it out that following this rule, '*Narendra Modi*' was '*a Rare Diamond*'. They were quickly corrected by language mavens who pointed out that the prime minister's name contained an extra N and the correct anagram would be '*Rare Diamond? Na*!' Political opponents of the PM leapt at the opportunity to come up with '*a modern drain*' and '*a modern nadir*'. The nastier ones, referring to his marital history, wrote, '*Married and No*!' The PM's fondness for the Indian diaspora ('Non-Resident Indians', or NRIs, many of whom are among this column's readers) led to suggestions of '*Narendra Modi*' being anagrammed as '*Adore Damn NRI*' and '*Dear Nomad NRI*'. Of course, his supporters also hit back with '*Dream and Iron*' as the qualities he represents to the nation.

Politics and history offer fertile grounds for anagrammers. Thus '*Adolf Hitler*' can become '*Hated for ill*'. Mao Zedong's historic Long March finds its echoes in the anagram of '*Chairman Mao*' as '*I am on a march*'. The nineteenth century British statesman Benjamin '*Disraeli*' can simply declare '*I lead, Sir*!' In his era, '*Flit on, cheering angel*' would be a suitable exhortation for '*Florence Nightingale*'. American liberals suggest that '*Ronald Reagan*' was '*a darn long era*'. Those who remember the bitter and long-lasting standoff between George W. Bush and Albert R. Gore in the US presidential elections of 2000 will not be surprised to realize that '*George Bush*' can be anagrammed as '*he bugs Gore*'! And '*Indira Gandhi*' can be made to say '*Hi, grand India*'!

Literature has often resorted to anagrams. Most famously, in Jonathan Swift's classic *Gulliver's Travels*, Gulliver visits '*Tribnia*', an anagram of '*Britain*'. And it turns out the place is also known as *Langden*, which of course is an anagram of '*England*'! Many will say that *The Da Vinci Code,* by Dan Brown, is not literature, but he employs a clever literary device in ensuring that the clues left by the museum curator who is murdered at the beginning of the novel are concealed in anagrams. Thus '*O, Draconian devil*' points to '*Leonardo da Vinci*'; '*Oh, lame saint*' aims at '*The Mona Lisa*'; and '*Madonna of the Rocks*' is rendered as '*So dark the con of man.*'

But the world of entertainment offers larger possibilities. Did you know that '*Britney Spears*' could become '*Presbyterians*'? '*Clint Eastwood*' stands appropriately for '*Old West action*' and '*Beyoncé Knowles*' becomes, less kindly, a '*cowboy's kennel*'. The Spanish actor '*Antonio Banderas*' is '*bandana sorter*'; the American actor '*Bill Murray*' is converted to something he decidedly is not, a '*burly mailer*'. Is '*Channing Tatum*' '*cunning at math*'?

These anagrams may seem irrelevant to the people whose names we're mangling, but three clever anagrams relating to the world of music seem more apt. '*Madonna Louise Ciccone*', that material girl, can be rendered as '*one cool dance musician*'. '*Justin Timberlake*' could be '*I am a jerk, but listen*'. And an anagram that, to the true believer, is also a tautology, is: *'Elvis' 'lives'!*

Which word lends itself to the most anagrams? '*Spear*' can be rearranged in thirteen different ways, including itself: *apers, apres, asper, pares, parse, pears, prase, presa, rapes, reaps, spare,* and *spera,* as well *asspear.* The possibilities are almost endless!

53

APTAGRAMS

After looking at anagrams, one might as well go one step further and examine aptagrams—anagrams that incorporate the meaning of a word. You can, for instance, convert the letters of the word 'astronomer' into 'moon starer'.

The word aptagram is a neologism, coined near the end of the twentieth century from a combination of the Latin word aptus, meaning connected, and the English word 'anagram'. Creating an aptagram is a fun way of fooling around with words, but there's surely a limit to how many meaningful coinages you can come up with that both make sense and retain the original sense of the word you are breaking up. The trick is to rearrange the letters of the word into another word or phrase that conveys a related idea or even, as with 'moon starer', define the word (in this case, 'astronomer') that you are turning into an aptagram. You have to use every letter in the one word to create the other for it to qualify as an aptagram. 'Tones' and 'notes' (in the musical sense) are aptagrams of each other. So are 'angered' and 'enraged'. One clever phrase I came across turns 'debit card' into 'bad credit'. Another transforms 'laptop machines' into 'Apple Macintosh'.

The most famously historic aptagram isn't in English, but in Latin. In a biblical passage, Pontius Pilate asks Jesus 'what is truth?'—or in Latin, 'quid est veritas?' Jesus responds with an aptagram of the question: 'estvir qui adest' meaning. 'It is the man who is here.' Brilliant, even if it didn't save him from the cross.

Some aptagrams can be pretty witty: converting 'dormitory' into 'dirty room' could only have been coined by a parent, and 'customers' as 'store scum' by an exhausted salesman! A conservative would convert 'a gentleman' to 'elegant man' and 'revolution' into 'love to ruin'. An irritated freelancer might have changed 'editor' to 'redo it', which editors often ask you to do, and 'irritated' itself becomes 'rat, I tried', which is guaranteed to offend most editors.

Some come close, but not quite: 'the evil eyes' can become 'vile, they see', but there's something artificial about the aptagram. The same, perhaps, with 'slot machines' rendered as 'cash lost in me'. Changing 'dictionary' to 'indicatory' isn't grammatically accurate enough to qualify, and 'laudatory' to 'adulatory' seems too obvious to elicit any applause. 'Lotus louts' might be anagrams for BJP-affiliated rowdies, but not aptagrams, since 'lotus' and 'louts' don't always connote the same thing!

Some aptagrams are clever but don't quite work: 'schoolmaster' doesn't really mean 'the classroom', though both use up the same set of letters. (On the other hand, if the schoolmaster gives an errant pupil 'nine thumps' in the classroom, that could be aptagrammed into 'punishment'!) To 'listen' is to be 'silent', whereas in 'conversation', you find 'voices rant on'.

The Harry Potter series has a character called Tom Marvolo Riddle whose name is an aptagram of 'I am Lord Voldemort', the series' villain. This 'inside joke' is a key part of one book's story line, but with the Harry Potter books being translated into sixty-eight languages, publishers around the world were forced to devise ingenious aptagrams that would mean the same thing. They found the solution in changing the name of the character to something that could be aptagrammed into 'I am Lord Voldemort' in their own language. (So in French, for instance, Tom Marvolo Riddle becomes Tom Elvis Jedusor, so that his name is still an aptagram of 'Je Suis Voldemort'). This worked in all the Romance languages, which changed the character's names into various aptagrams of the phrase 'I am Lord Voldemort' in their own languages—but when it came to Chinese, which uses characters and not letters, the translator was stumped. The publisher had to resort to a footnote to explain that English has something called aptagrams!

The cleverest aptagram of all, perhaps, is transforming 'eleven plus two' to 'twelve plus one', which apart from using all the letters, is also mathematically accurate. The more you try, however, the more contrived the exercise becomes ('brush' as 'shrub', for instance) which is why aptagrams haven't widely caught on. It could still work as a party game for bored English 'teachers', who could become 'cheaters' by using the internet to do their work for them!

54

ANAPHORA

As a public speaker, one of the classic bits of advice you're given is the simple dictum, 'Be bold. Be brief. Be gone.' You may not know it, but that's a great example of what this chapter is about, anaphora.

Anaphora sounds like some ancient Greek flask or vase, but it is in fact a rhetorical device in English. Anaphora features the repetition of a word or phrase, usually at the beginning of successive sentences or phrases, to emphasize and reinforce meaning and generate a stronger effect upon the reader or listener. Remember President John F. Kennedy's memorable line in his Inaugural Address, 'Ask not what your country can do for you—ask what you can do for your country'? That's anaphora. Patrick Henry's line during the American Revolution: 'Give me liberty or give me death.' Ditto.

Winston Churchill, a master of morale-booster rhetoric, used anaphora tellingly in his famous radio speeches during World War II: 'We shall fight in France, we shall fight on the seas and oceans, we shall fight with growing confidence and growing strength in the air, we shall defend our island, whatever the cost may be, we shall fight on the beaches, we shall fight on the landing grounds, we shall fight in the fields and in the streets, we shall fight in the hills.' The relentless repetition of 'we shall fight' drove home the message of determination and courage that inspired Britons listening to him. In his famous 'I Have a Dream' speech, the Black American civil rights leader Dr Martin Luther King used anaphora by repeating 'I have a dream' eight times throughout the speech to reinforce his visionary message.

Perhaps the most famous literary use of anaphora is in the opening paragraph of Charles Dickens' novel of the French Revolution, *A Tale of Two Cities*. 'It was the best of times, it was the worst of times, it was the age of wisdom, it was the age of foolishness, it was the epoch of belief, it was the epoch of incredulity, it was the season of Light, it was the season of Darkness....' The technique shows how anaphora works: repetition of the phrase 'it was' gives Dickens a chance to reinforce the impression that he is writing about a period of turbulent contradictions, and builds up an atmosphere in the reader's mind that sets the scene for the narrative to follow.

Of course, it doesn't take an entire para full of rhythmic phrases to achieve the same effect: pithy one-liners like Kennedy's can work just as well. Anaphora is an effective way of conveying a contradiction: 'You're damned if you do and you're damned if you don't.' It also helps make a banal thought sound more impressive: 'Stay safe. Stay well. Stay happy.' Wisdom can also be more effectively conveyed when packaged in anaphora: 'Fool me once, shame on you. Fool me twice, shame on me.'

Anaphora permits profundities to be communicated in a more accessible way. The Bible famously uses anaphora. Thus the Old Testament, Ecclesiastes 3:1–2, has the famous line: '...a time to be born, and a time to die; a time to plant, and a time to pluck up what is planted.' Such timeless thoughts persist into our times. Talking about the role of palliative care in terminal cancer patients, and how it eases pain without prolonging life, a doctor said, 'It's not the days in your life that matters, it's the life in your days.' The poet Rumi's famous lines about taking the rough with the smooth in life tellingly use anaphora: 'If you want the moon, do not hide from the night. / If you want a rose, do not run from the thorns. / If you want love, do not hide from yourself.'

Rumi's poetic words utilize anaphora to evoke emotion; Churchill's to exhort action. Anaphora helps reinforce understanding because its repetitions make it easier to remember. My favourite lines of T. S. Eliot stay in my head because of anaphora: 'Where is the Life we have lost in living? / Where is the wisdom we have lost in knowledge? / Where is the knowledge we have lost in information?' But when used poorly, anaphora can be off-putting by sounding simplistic or forced. If you use anaphora in your writing, remember to do so sparingly and tellingly, and always strike a balance between what is natural and what is worthy of literary effect.

55

BACRONYMS

In a previous chapter we looked at acronyms, words formed from contracting longer phrases, like laser and radar. But imaginative amateur linguists have reversed the process and created 'bacronyms'—taking words that aren't acronyms and inventing fictitious phrases that could have been abbreviated to form these terms. So rather than an acronym emerging from a longer set of words being compressed, a bacronym expands a word (or an acronym) to stand for something it was never meant to.

The term 'backronym' was the brainchild of Meredith G. Williams, who came up with it in a *Washington Post* competition in 1983. But bacronyms were already in existence well before the word was invented, as I recall from my childhood, when airline names (in most cases unwieldy acronyms to begin with) were hilariously reverse-expanded. The British Overseas Airways Corporation, as British Airways was then known, flew as BOAC, a term derisively bacronymed as '**B**etter **O**n **A** **C**amel'. The American Delta Airlines was said to stand for '**D**oesn't **E**ver **L**eave **t**he **A**irport'. Belgium's national airline Sabena (a name which was itself an acronym, derived from 'Société Anonyme Belge d'Exploitation de la Navigation Aérienne') was given the bacronym '**S**uch **a** **B**ad **E**xperience, **N**ever **A**gain'. My personal favourite bacronym savaged the Italian carrier Alitalia: '**A**rrived **L**ate **i**n **T**okyo **a**nd **L**uggage **i**n **A**msterdam'.

The aeroplane is not the only mode of transport to have been so favoured. The automobile manufacturer Ford would have been chagrined to find its founder's name bacronymed to 'Fix or Repair Daily'. Ships aren't exempt either: exhausted sailors say navy really means 'Never Again Volunteer Yourself'. And if you're on your feet wearing a particular brand of sneakers, Adidas, a contraction of the name of the company's founder Adolf '**Adi**' **Das**sler, has been bacronymed to 'All day, I dream about sports'.

Some words that are popularly assumed to have been acronyms actually aren't—they are bacronyms. I've lost count of the number of times that I've been earnestly told that the word 'posh', connoting luxury and expense, is an acronym of 'port out, starboard home'. On ships, the port is the left side, starboard the right, so ships sailing from Britain to India had their cooler, north-facing cabins on the port side heading to India and starboard back; thus, the more affluent or important passengers took the 'posh' cabins. Great story, but a myth.

Also a myth, alas, is the belief that the universal distress call, SOS, is an acronym for 'Save our Souls' (or at sea, 'Save Our Ship'.) In fact, SOS wasn't an acronym at all. The signal was chosen soon after the invention of Morse Code because it is easy to issue in an emergency—three dots, three dashes, three dots. The bacronym's a good one, though! More recent technology has also given us bacronyms: thus VHS tapes (the original acronym stood for 'vertical helical scan') were dismissed as 'virtually hopeless signal' and Microsoft's Bing, its big rival sneers, is no good 'Because It's Not Google'!

Sometimes a word you want to use is deliberately chosen because it lends itself to a bacronym. When the US was attacked on 9/11, it quickly passed the 'USA Patriot Act'—which used the evocative words 'USA' and 'patriot' but actually stood for 'Uniting and Strengthening America by Providing Appropriate Tools Required to Intercept and Obstruct Terrorism' Act.

My favourite set of bacronyms prick the pomposity of the exalted. Britain, a famously hierarchical society with titles, decorations, and orders of precedence attached to almost everyone and advertised with a string of letters after their names. Civil servants, for instance, are often made CBE, which officially stands for 'Commander of the Order of the British Empire', but is flung back at them by their underlings muttering 'Can't Be Everywhere'. Even grander are Britain's famed long-service awards which, in increasing order of seniority, are CMG, 'Companion of the Order of St Michael and St George', KCMG, 'Knight Commander of the Order of St Michael and St George', and GCMG, 'Knight Grand Cross of the Order of St Michael and St George'. These have been made into wonderful bacronyms for decades now by irreverent British civil servants: CMG, they say, means 'Call Me God', KCMG is 'Kindly Call me God'. And GCMG? 'God Calls me God'!

56

CONTRONYMS

A recent headline declared that the United States had sanctioned Iranian oil supplies. Many readers weren't sure what the newspaper meant, since 'sanction' is a contronym—a word that can also mean the opposite of itself, a feature more common in English than in any other language. In this instance, confusion was inevitable, because the headline could mean the President had *permitted* the oil supplies to flow, or that he had *prohibited* them. If you get a sanction from an authority to do something, it means the former; but if you impose sanctions on someone or something, it means the latter. The word 'sanction' can either refer to approval for a course of action or a penalty for disobeying an injunction. That's why it's a contronym, also sometimes known as a 'Janus word' (after the Roman god with two faces).

Confused? 'Sanction' is not the only case of a word that can be used to mean its own opposite. We use contronyms all the time without realizing it; the most common contronym might be the word 'off', since 'setting off' an alarm activates a warning bell, while 'switching off' the alarm deactivates it—and both use the same 'off'. If you find too many objects gathering dust at home, you can tell your maid that she needs to dust more so there is less dust (that's not a contradiction, just a contronym!) Similarly, strike can be used to mean to create (as in 'strike a deal') or to eliminate ('strike that line from the record').

When the United Nations created an in-house inspectorate and named the department the Office of Internal Oversight Services, I warned my colleagues, only half in jest, that every time the new office messed up, they could say, 'Hey, it was just an oversight.' Oversight is also a contronym: it can mean watchful supervision, but also an inadvertent error. Similarly, the word 'cleave' can mean both 'to cut apart' ('the warrior cleaved his enemy's head from his neck') or 'to bind together' ('the infant cleaved to his mother's breast'). So can 'clip' mean to cut something (as in a newspaper clipping) or to hold them together ('Can you clip those clippings together please?') A criminal might 'bolt' (meaning he runs away or 'exits quickly') but you can bolt the door shut (meaning fix it in place to immobilize it).

In one of the earlier chapters, we have discussed the amusing differences between British and American English that can often lead to misunderstandings. There are contronyms that demonstrate the truth of the adage that America and Britain are two countries divided by a common language. For example, 'table'—to table a bill means 'to put it up for debate' in Britain, while if you table a bill in the US Congress, it means 'to remove it from debate'. A 'moot' point is one that requires discussion and debate in Britain, whereas in America, if an issue is moot, it is dead and unnecessary to discuss.

American usage multiplies the range of contronyms. A 'hold-up', in the US, can either support or impede: wooden beams might hold up the ceiling, but a mugger might trap you in a hold-up at gunpoint (or traffic can create a hold-up on the road). Also in America, you can use bills to pay bills (what we call 'notes' are 'bills' in the US, so 'dollar bills' can be used to settle your restaurant bills!)

And if you say you have 'finished' something, is it completed or destroyed? (One wag on WhatsApp circulated an explanation of the difference between 'completed' and 'finished': 'When you marry the right woman, you are 'complete'. If you marry the wrong woman, you are 'finished'. And when the right woman catches you with the wrong woman, you are 'completely finished!')

'Give out' is our final example: a charity can give out aid to flood victims, or an exhausted victim fleeing the floods can collapse when his legs give out. My space has just given out, so I'll call it a day. That's perhaps the most common contronym of all—you usually call it a day when it's night!

57

EPONYMS

One of the fascinating quirks of any language is the way in which proper names insinuate themselves into our vocabulary, as eponyms—when a person's name becomes that of a place, a people, an era, or an institution, or even sometimes just a concept.

Eponym comes from the Greek eponymos, 'given as a name, giving one's name to something'. So the continents we know as North and South America are named for Italian explorer Amerigo Vespucci (1451–1512), who sailed four times—in 1497, 1499, 1501, and 1503—to the New World and whose name was placed on the map in recognition, even though Christopher Columbus had beaten him to it in 1492 (a feat the Spanish recognized by naming their major colony there Colombia). Similarly, the American capital, Washington DC, was never the residence of its eponymous first president, George Washington, but was named as a tribute to him. When you speak of the Victorian era, you are referring to the period of its eponymous monarch, Queen Victoria. The Modi government is headed by its eponymous prime minister, Narendra Modi; Obamacare is a health insurance scheme thus labelled for its eponymous president, Barack Obama; Thatcherism is an economic philosophy of laissez-faire capitalism named for its strident advocate, Prime Minister Margaret Thatcher. These are all eponyms.

Eponyms are not merely useful for referring to politics. A Tudor building refers to a style made popular during the rule of its eponymous British dynasty, and a Georgian square to the eponymous King George III. The diamond pattern known as argyle plaid, used on sweaters and socks, is named for the Duke of Argyle. 'Those Edwardian young men in spats' suggests the youth in question lived in the time of Britain's first post-

Victorian monarch King Edward VII. Bowler hats, then worn by those men in spats, were invented by the eponymous William Bowler. Queen Anne furniture alludes to the eponymous British monarch of the beginning of the eighteenth century.

Many words are so commonly used that we don't even realize that are eponyms. If you go berserk, you are living up to the name of a legendary Norse hero of the eighth century, Berserk, who fought with reckless fury. A skimpy women's swimsuit that came into fashion a year after the United States began testing atom bombs on the Bikini atoll of the Marshall Islands was called a 'bikini' for the explosive effect it supposedly had on men. 'Bogus' comes from mispronouncing the name of a crooked counterfeiter in the mid-nineteenth century US called Borghese, who circulated fake dollar bills. (At least that's the story I like; there is a pedantic alternative, which claims the word is derived from some eighteenth century apparatus to forging counterfeit coins.) And a child born through a caesarean section is reminding us of the first such case of birth through cutting the womb, that of Julius Caesar in 100 BCE.

Common household products also refer, often unknowingly, to their eponymous creators. 'I'll hoover it up' comes from the inventor of the vacuum cleaner that bore his name; 'I need to fill up some diesel' takes its name from the eponymous German, Rudolf Diesel, who invented that fuel; 'let's take the kids on the Ferris wheel' credits the eponymous engineer who first came up with that enormous contraption to whirl seated people around for pleasure. If you want to hop into the jacuzzi, you are tipping your hat (or doffing your clothes) to an eponymous pair of Italian brothers named, you guessed it, Jacuzzi. If you slip on some leotards, there's an eponymous French circus performer and trapeze artist extraordinaire Jules Léotard, you're memorializing. And if you eat a sandwich, you are paying tribute to the inveterate gambler the eponymous Earl of Sandwich, who had the snack invented for him so he didn't have to interrupt his card games for a meal. When I visited Sudan in the late 1970s, it was common to hear people saying 'I'll pick you up in my Tata,' without being conscious of the eponymous Indian vehicle manufacturer.

One 'boycotts' people throughout the English-speaking world without knowing a thing about the eponymous Captain Boycott, an English land agent in Ireland, who evicted poverty-stricken tenant farmers who could not pay their rent and who was ostracized by all his Irish neighbours and servants as a result.

I've often resisted the temptation to boycott the plethora of budding authors who ask for a 'blurb' for their book—a few lines of praise for its contents which, printed on the cover, might encourage prospective readers to buy their book. I usually oblige them if at all possible, mindful of the need to encourage talent. Few authors realize, however, that the term for this puffery is derived from a fictional character, Blinda Blurb, invented by a rather whimsical writer named Gelett Burgess (1866–1951) for one of his books. Burgess is best known for a piece of light verse: 'I *never saw a Purple Cow / never hope to see one; / But I can tell you anyhow, / I'd rather see than Be one'*—which was so extensively quoted that he disavowed it with another: '*Ah, yes I wrote the Purple* Cow */ I'm sorry now, I wrote it! / But I can tell you anyhow / I'll kill you if you quote it!*' (Many an author, coerced or seduced into giving a generous blurb to an undeserving volume, would echo those last sentiments).

If 'blurb' seemed an unlikely eponym, so too does '*candy*', which traditional linguists believe is derived from the Sanskrit word *kharidakah*. This is disputed, however, by those who trace the term instead to Prince Charles Phillipe de Conde, infant grandnephew of King Louis XIII of France in the late 1600s. The young royal was apparently excessively fond of sweets and ate nothing but sugary confections, prompting the royal chef to start glazing meat, vegetables, and fruit with sugar in the hope of getting the toddler prince to eat more nourishing food. The success of this experiment led to sweet snacks being called 'Conde' after him, rendered popularly as 'candy'. (Take this with a pinch of salt rather than sugar, in my view.)

Another unlikely eponym is '*hooligan*', which it turns out refers to an actual person, an obstreperous Irishman called Patrick Hooligan, who in the 1890s harassed, assaulted, and robbed the good citizens of Southwark, England. His rowdy behaviour ended up immortalizing his name, though the eponymous goon himself was sentenced to life and died in prison.

Similar lawlessness applies to another eponym, '*lynch*'—when a mob, claiming to act on behalf of public opinion, exacts vigilante retribution against an accused offender, often by hanging the victim. The word 'lynch', like 'boycott' and 'macadam', comes from the name of a person. In this case there are at least two possible claimants for this eponymous distinction. The expression derives from the American Lynch law of 1811, covering punishment without trial, named after either William Lynch (1742–1820) of Virginia, who in about 1780 led a vigilance committee to keep order in his home town of Pittsylvania during the American Revolution, or Charles Lynch (1736–96), a pro-revolutionary Virginia magistrate who fined and imprisoned British loyalists in his district without trial at about the same time, and got a law passed by the American government exonerating him for his actions.

Our final story is about '*nicotine*', that poisonous substance that comes from tobacco. It is named for French diplomat and scholar Jean Nicot (1530–1600), who was sent to Portugal in 1559 by King Francis II of France to arrange a child marriage (between the king's sister, Marguerite of Valois, six years old, and Don Sebastian, the king of Portugal, age five). Nicot's negotiations failed, and the proposed marriage fell through, but while in Portugal Nicot was given a gift of strange seeds by sailors who had recently come from America. From the seedlings, he grew tobacco leaves and sent some to Queen Mother Catherine de Medici, who crumbled the dry leaves and enjoyed sniffing them. Tobacco soon became fashionable, as others followed the queen's example. The French government realized the new commodity could be taxed and tobacco soon became a lucrative source of revenue, right to the present day. The scholarly Nicot had hoped to be remembered for his crowning achievement, a dictionary of the French language, but instead his name was immortalized for the toxin that comes from tobacco, nicotine—a word, ironically, that he had not included in his own dictionary!

58

HOMONYMS

Everyone knows what synonyms and antonyms are (and just in case you don't, *synonyms* are words that mean the same thing as another word, and *antonyms* are words that mean the opposite). But do you know what *homonyms* are?

If you don't, let me put you out of your misery: Homonyms are words that have the same sound or spelling as other words, but have different meanings. There are two kinds of homonyms, homophones, and homographs. Homophones—which comes from the Latin for 'same sounds'—are words like *aid* and *aide,* or *meat* and *meet*, that sound the same when they are spoken aloud the same but differ in meaning and often in spelling. Homographs are words that have the same spelling ('graph' means 'written') but differ in meaning and sometimes in pronunciation, such as the verb *bear* (to carry, suffer or endure) and the noun *bear* (the animal) or the verb *bail* (to clear water out of a boat) and the noun *bail* (releasing a prisoner).

Even if you didn't know the term, you're surely using homonyms all the time. You can *ring* a girl with the intention of one day slipping a *ring* on her finger. You can be on the *right* politically (and your views might even sometimes be *right*, or correct!) but you may not be standing on the *right* in a group photograph. Here, both *ring* and *right* are homophones, since they sound the same when spoken, but mean different things in those sentences. Or your *right*-wing friend might *write* a speech conveying his views, and 'right' and 'write' would be homophones too, though spelled differently. Just as you *might,* in mediaeval times, have earned your *mite* serving the local *baron* as a *knight*, though defending his *barren* lands at *night, might* be a challenge if you couldn't *see* invaders coming from the *sea*!

And then there are homographs. A Japanese executive might *bow* at a visitor wearing a *bow* tie or even carrying a *bow* and arrow. When a careless friend *tears* up the paper containing your homework, *tears* may flow from your eyes. When the *wind* blows fiercely, you may wish to *wind* a shawl around yourself. When the zoo attendant sees the *does* in the deer park aren't feeling well, she *does* get medicine for them. (But if she gives them the wrong *dose* of medicine, that wouldn't just be careless, it would also be a homophone.)

Spotting homonyms can be fun, but it's also important to be aware of them to avoid some common mistakes in English usage which come from the confusion that arises when two words of totally different meanings sound alike. People whose language skills are largely oral—acquired by hearing people speak—are particularly prone to errors like confusing '*write*' and '*right*', (or '*elicit*' (to derive something) and '*illicit*' (against the law). It would be rare to mix up the '*cell*' of a prison, or a battery, with needing to '*sell*' your phone because you need another; but it is not at all rare to see people writing 'can you please *male* me?' when they mean '*mail*'! Most common of all is people mixing up the homonyms '*there*', '*their*', and '*they're*'. '*There*' is an adverb used to indicate the location of something: 'please stand *there*'. '*Their*' is the possessive pronoun for the subject 'they': 'my friends are late because *their* taxi didn't show up on time'. And '*they're*' is a contraction that means '*they are*': 'I told you *they're* late, now what can I do?'

Lazy spellings—such as those used by advertisers—are also often guilty of causing confusion. 'Ladies' nite', posters will say, instead of 'Ladies' night', and 'Coke Lite' instead of 'Coke Light'. It's not a far stretch from commonly seeing such spelling errors around you to making them yourself, writing '*site*' for '*sight*' even though they are homophones that do not mean the same thing. You can say Dubai was the *site* of the expo, and you can add that it was a splendid *sight*—but you cannot write 'Dubai was the sight of the Expo'!

Feminists comfortable with homonyms might want to issue patriarchs a useful reminder: The *Son* is not the centre of the solar system; the *Sun* is!

59

OXYMORONS

A figure of speech that a politician like me needs to be familiar with is the oxymoron, a phrase in which seemingly contradictory terms appear in conjunction with each other. Take this sentence, for instance: '*Even as he swore his perpetual loyalty to his party leader, he was looking around to see if he could do better, but she was taken in by his falsely true manner.*' Oxymorons sound like idiots out of breath, gasping for air, but they're just phrases (like 'falsely true' in this example, or 'loving hate' in Shakespeare's *Romeo and Juliet*) that combine two words of opposite meaning to good effect. Of course, politics is full of people whose earnest professions are falsely true, but that's another subject altogether.

'Oxymoron' is derived from the Greek words *oksus*, meaning sharp or pointed, and *moros*, meaning dull or foolish. Of course, for an oxymoron to work, the combined expression has to make sense: there's no point saying 'black white' and expecting people to roar in appreciation, unless you are referring to an African gentleman named Mr White, in which case it's an oxymoron.

In fact, oxymorons are far more common than one might imagine. How often has someone, caught in a place where she shouldn't be, been told to 'act naturally'? You're either acting or you're natural—put them together and you have an oxymoron. How many seemingly knowledgeable people have confided in you an 'open secret'? How is it secret if it's open? How often has a clerk demanded an 'original copy'? Or, while negotiating a service, have you demanded an 'exact estimate'? These are all oxymorons, because if you look at each word, one seems to contradict the other, and yet their meaning is perfectly clear to all of us.

When I was assailed by politicians and media in India for my use of the expression 'cattle class', I was 'clearly misunderstood'—I had used the term, but it didn't mean what my critics thought it did. When roll-call was taken in a boarding school and a girl was 'found missing', that was an oxymoron as well as a major crisis for the school administration. (The girl was missing, she needed to be found!) Boys' boarding schools, of course, feature a lot of conversations about girls, and many of the superficial judgements passed involve oxymorons—'God, she's pretty ugly', 'she's awfully beautiful', 'that woman was barely dressed', and the like. Girls, being less superficial, are likely to describe the boys they know with other oxymorons: 'he's seriously funny', for instance, or 'he's terribly nice'.

By their very nature, oxymorons also lend themselves to low humour—when terms that are in fact not contradictory are placed together and described as oxymorons (even when they are not supposed to be), the joke is that you think the expression is a contradiction in terms. 'American culture', some Brits say, is an oxymoron. (When Washington was throwing its weight around the world, leading to the coining of the phrase 'the Ugly American', some commentators rudely suggested that 'American diplomacy' was an oxymoron too.) Many American diplomats, in turn, would consider 'United Nations' an oxymoron too, since nations are rarely united. Indeed, a common misprint, in the days before auto-correct, was 'Untied Nations'!

The armed forces are no stranger to oxymorons: think of 'friendly fire', which brings down your own soldiers. A few pseudo-intellectuals would go farther and list 'military intelligence' as an oxymoron, reinforcing the image of the bluff honest soldier without a thought in his head—since they sneer that only the unintelligent go off to risk their lives for the country in war. Or worse still, fight in another oxymoron, a 'civil war'—for what could be more uncivil than warfare? Of course, when they quit, many soldiers seek an 'active retirement'—another oxymoron.

The cynical public seem to think 'honest politician' is an oxymoron. So, the politicians retort, is 'business ethics'. Many would laugh at 'educational television' as a misnomer. And anti-romantics would claim 'Happily Married' is an oxymoron....

Ask frustrated computer-users to nominate an oxymoron from their daily experience, and many will suggest 'Microsoft Works'. Does it work for you?

SECTION EIGHT

LITERARY ACROBATICS

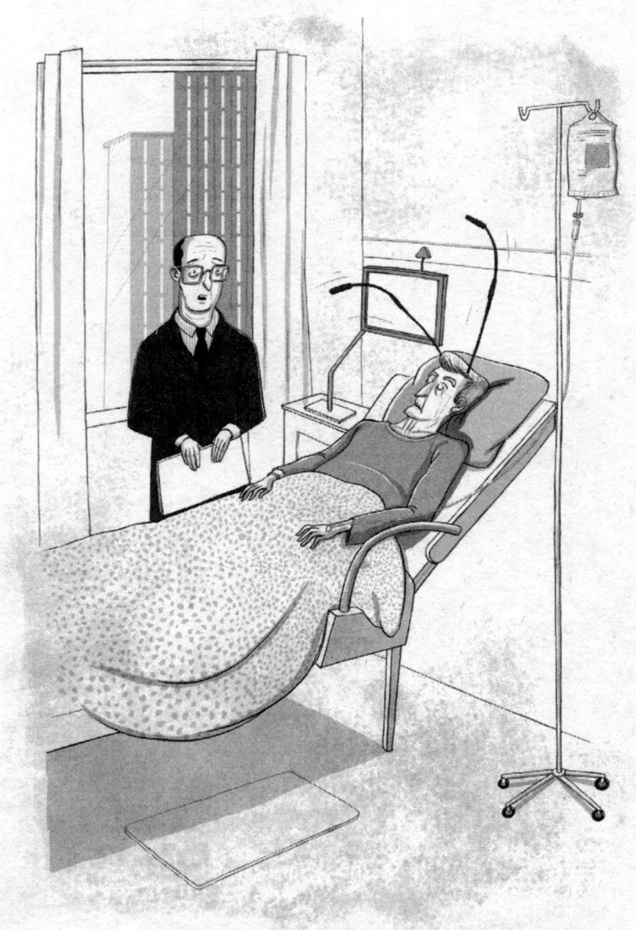

Archie Bunker's classic *All in the Family* series routinely uttered malapropisms: a dying man's 'last will and tentacle' (he meant testament), the adage 'patience is a virgin' (he should have said it's a virtue), and so on.

60

EGGCORNS

What, you may well ask, is an eggcorn? It comes from a mishearing of the word 'acorn', and has come to stand for any word or phrase that is mistakenly used in a seemingly plausible way for another word or phrase that it sounds like. We discussed malapropisms, which involve a slip of the tongue; eggcorns are sort of a slip of the ear. Take the expression '*Alzheimer's disease*'; someone mishears it as 'old-timers' disease', and writes it that way in print. That's an eggcorn.

Eggcorns are alarmingly common, even in the pages of newspapers. How often have you seen the eggcorn '*day-today* operations' (instead of *day-to-day*), an amateur philosopher ruminating that 'it's a *doggie-dog* world' (instead of '*dog-eat-dog*') or a witness to an accident quoted as saying 'It happened *all over sudden*' (instead of *all of a sudden*)? Common examples of eggcorns include 'curve your enthusiasm' (instead of 'curb'), 'escape goat' (instead of 'scapegoat'), and 'biting my time' (instead of 'biding').

Many clichés are misremembered as eggcorns: 'it was a *damp squid*' (instead of *damp squib*), 'I was on *tender hooks*' (instead of *on tenterhooks*), 'It was *nipped in the butt*' (instead of '*nipped in the bud*'), 'I can't make *heads or tales* of it' (instead of 'can't make *heads or tails* of it') and 'It's a *mute point*' (instead of moot point) are typical examples. The expression 'for all intents and purposes' is often rendered as 'for all *intensive* purposes'. And if I could have a rupee for each time I have seen the term *tow the line* (instead of *toe the line*), I'd be a very rich man indeed.

Normal, routine items lend themselves to eggcorns too. Many speak of 'cold slaw' when they mean 'coleslaw'. You want someone to get his 'just desserts' but think it's written 'just deserves'? Did you seek *free reign* (free rein) of your property or seek to put a *rot iron fence* (wrought iron fence) around it? Was it *nerve wrecking* (nerve-racking) to go through an interview and did you *pass mustard* (pass muster) after making a *last stitch effort* (last ditch effort)?

One acquaintance, writing about a relative who was allergic to milk, managed to create two eggcorns in one sentence: 'To be *pacific* (he meant *to be specific*),' he said, 'he is *lack toast and tolerant* (he meant *lactose intolerant*)'. Another talked about an Arab friend whose baby boy was '*circus-sized*' (the kid was actually normally proportioned, but had been circumcized). 'The UAE is full of *ex-patriots*,' wrote a correspondent (meaning *expatriates*).

As with those last two examples, many eggcorns are just one word, misheard and wrongly rendered. Others include *bonified* (for bona fide), *conscious* (conscience), *parody* (parity), *prospective* (perspective), *upmost* (utmost), *ringer* (wringer), and perhaps most forgivably, *expresso* for espresso. Somebody whom others dislike being around is a 'social leper' but an eggcorn calls him a 'social *leopard*'. Either way he might find it difficult to get a room at a local *bread and breakfast* (bed and breakfast), where he would want to *wet* his appetite (*whet* his appetite).

Two-word eggcorns are the most common, from *bare witness* (bear witness) and *bold-faced* (bald-faced) *lie,* to the classic assumption that some words must actually be brand names—like *Cadillac converter* (catalytic converter) and *Chester drawers* (chest of drawers). Many a woman has been found after a bad day, curled up in the *feeble position* (foetal position). My own favourite eggcorn renders *prima donna* as *pre-Madonna!* Such mistakes are just a hair's breadth away from being accurate, unless you wrote an eggcorn there too and assumed they were a *hare's breath* away.

But the longer phrases are the most fun: *don't get your dandruff up* (don't get your dander up) if I point out the *flaw in the ointment* (fly in the ointment), because it's an *old wise tale* (old wives' tale) that *peaked my interest* (piqued my interest), but it turned out to be *much to do about nothing* (much ado about nothing)!

As the world records increasing hearing loss and populations grow older and deafer, more and more eggcorns will be unwittingly invented. There'll be a lot of damp squids curled up in the feeble position. And none of this is a *pigment* (figment) of my imagination! It's time, clearly, to *give up the goat* (give up the ghost)!

61

MALAPROPISMS

English, like any language, lends itself to hilarious mistakes and confusion. One of the best-known of these is uttering a malapropism, a word misused or wrongly applied, usually with the intention of showing off one's erudition. The word comes from the name of a character in the Irish playwright Richard Brinsley Sheridan's play *The Rivals* (1775), Mrs Malaprop, noted for her ridiculous misuse of words (such as 'contagious countries' for 'contiguous' ones and 'allegories' on the banks of the Nile when she meant alligators). Her name is derived from the French for 'inappropriate' (*mal à propos,* literally 'poorly placed'), since in her pretentious attempts to sound refined and cultured by using sophisticated language, Mrs Malaprop invariably mixes up her words. 'You will promise to forget this fellow,' she haughtily tells a friend, 'to illiterate him, I say, from your memory.' She meant, of course, 'obliterate'! Unfortunately, she herself failed to live up to the advice she dispensed to another character 'that she might reprehend the true meaning of what she is saying'—she intended to say 'apprehend', not 'reprehend'.

Mrs Malaprop, of course, was merely a humorous fictional character in a piece of theatre, but malapropisms are far more common in real life than most people realize, since mixing up words one barely knows is a common human affliction. The American baseball player Yogi Berra famously spoke of Texas having a lot of 'electrical votes' when he meant 'electoral' ones. A television pundit solemnly spoke of 'entomology' for the study of word origins rather than 'etymology'. Many a would-be debunker of pedantry uses 'obtuse' (which means stupid or slow-witted) when meaning 'abstruse' (esoteric or difficult to understand). Others, trying to sound smart, render the expression 'for all intents and purposes' as 'for all intensive purposes'.

But to really qualify as a memorable malapropism, the misused word must be nonsensical or ludicrous in context, yet similar in sound to what was intended. One example is the person trying to pay a compliment—by describing another as 'the very pinnacle of politeness'—who instead praises him as 'the very pineapple of politeness'. A man excitably talking about a victim of snakebite rather spoiled the drama by explaining that a 'doctor administered the anecdote' when of course he meant the 'antidote'. A student boasting about his on-time attendance in school tells his parents, 'I have good punctuation—I'm never late!' Alas, he meant he was good at 'punctuality,' not 'punctuation'. The 2018 floods in Kerala had someone explain to me that 'The flood damage was so bad they had to evaporate the area.' (He meant 'evacuate', though evaporation of all the excess water might have helped too). My personal favourite: A prospective dinner guest emailed me that she couldn't eat crabs or any other 'crushed Asians' (she had clearly heard the word 'crustaceans' for shellfish but never seen it written). I was a pretty crushed Asian to receive that!

These are mistakes made by ordinary people, but malapropisms by the famous often make the news. Richard Daley, the former mayor of Chicago during that city's 1968 riots, notoriously declared: 'The police are not here to create disorder, they're here to preserve disorder.' His fellow mayor, Thomas Menino of Boston, described a deceased person as 'a man of great statue' when he meant 'stature'. Texas Speaker of the House Gib Lewis declared some event to be 'unparalyzed in the state's history' when he meant it was 'unparalleled'. An actor in the famous TV series *The Sopranos* spoke of 'creating a little dysentery among the ranks', when he meant 'dissension'. The character Archie Bunker in the now-classic *All in the Family* series routinely uttered malapropisms: a dying man's 'last will and tentacle' (he meant testament), the adage 'patience is a virgin' (he should have said it's a virtue), watching 'a menstrual show' (he'd heard a minstrel show), listening to a 'battery transvester radios' (it was, of course, a transistor radio), meeting someone suffering from 'very close veins' (her ailment involved varicose veins), 'the Women's Lubrication Movement' (for Liberation), and so on.

A famous comedian once declared that 'Having one wife is called monotony.' It's called monogamy, pal—but then maybe it wasn't a malapropism at all, and he said exactly what he meant!!

62

PARAPROSDOKIANS

Paraprosdokian comes from two Greek words, 'para' meaning 'against' and 'prosdokia', meaning 'expectation'. A paraprosdokian is a figure of speech in which the latter part of a sentence or phrase, or larger statement, is surprising or unexpected, in a way that prompts the reader or hearer to rethink the first part or understand it differently. My favourite paraprosdokian comes from the comedian Bob Monkhouse: 'I want to die peacefully in my sleep like my father, not screaming and terrified like his passengers.'

As that example suggests, paraprosdokians are frequently used for humorous or dramatic effect—'Today a man knocked on my door and asked for a small donation towards the local swimming pool, so I gave him a glass of water.' Groucho Marx loved using paraprosdokians for their anticlimaxes: 'I've had a perfectly wonderful evening, but this wasn't it.' I forget who said 'The last thing I want to do is hurt you, but it's still on the list.'

Paraprosdokians are particularly popular among stand-up comedians: 'When I was ten, I beat up the school bully. His arms were in casts. That's what gave me the courage.' Or 'I asked God for a bike, but I know God doesn't work that way, so I stole a bike and asked for forgiveness.' Marriage offers fertile ground: 'My wife and I were happy for twenty-five years; then we met.' And how about 'Always borrow money from a pessimist. He won't expect it back.'?!

Satirists can excel at paraprosdokians: what better way to skewer the pretensions of society? 'She got her good looks from her father; he's a plastic surgeon.' Or more notoriously: 'I can picture in my mind a world without war, a world without hate. And I can picture us attacking that world, because they'd never expect it.' These days people will observe: 'Artificial intelligence is no match for natural stupidity.' As cuttingly: 'When tempted to fight fire with fire, remember that the fire department usually uses water.' Most memorably: 'Going to a temple doesn't make you a Hindu any more than standing in a garage makes you a car.'

A good use of paraprosdokians is to send up the conventional wisdom people like to inflict on you. 'If at first you don't succeed, skydiving is not for you.' Or: 'If you can smile when things go wrong, you have someone in mind to blame.' Subverting clichés is best done with paraprosdokians: 'He who laughs last thinks slowest.' Or 'Hospitality is the art of making guests feel like they're at home, when you wish they were.' Another old favourite is: 'Change is inevitable, except from a vending machine.' A particularly clever one in this genre is: 'Take my advice; I'm not using it.' I'm still awed by the brilliance of 'Nostalgia isn't what it used to be.' Or the timeless 'To steal ideas from one person is plagiarism. To steal from many is research.'

Some paraprosdokians not only change the meaning of the first part of an observation, but also play on the meaning of a particular word: 'War does not determine who is right—only who is left.' Or 'I used to be indecisive. Now I'm not sure.' Better still: 'I was going to give him a nasty look, but he already had one.' That's why they say that 'the pun is the lowest form of humour—when you don't think of it first.'

Perhaps the greatest craftsman of paraprosdokians was the immortal P. G. Wodehouse. A mere sentence was not enough for him; his best examples built up slowly and at length. 'Myrtle Prosser was a woman of considerable but extremely severe beauty. She…suggested rather one of those engravings of the mistresses of Bourbon kings which make one feel that the monarchs who selected them must have been men of iron, impervious to fear—or else short-sighted.'

And that's probably enough paraprosdokians for one reading. I'm great at multi-tasking—I can waste time, be unproductive, and procrastinate all at once. But I must end this chapter now. After all, a bus station is where a bus stops. A train station is where a train stops. On my desk, I have a work station....

63

PUNS

The pun, it is often said, is the lowest form of humour, playing as it does on the double-meanings with which the English language is replete. 'No matter how much you push the envelope, it'll still be stationery,' is a clever example, conflating as it does the metaphorical meaning of the current expression 'push the envelope' with the two meanings of the identical sounding words 'stationary' and 'stationery'. Similarly, 'I changed my iPod's name to Titanic. It's syncing now' is an excellent pun, given the different meanings of 'syncing' and 'sinking'. Amongst the newer ones of our times, this one's fit to stand in their company: 'I've started telling everyone about the benefits of eating dried grapes. It's all about raisin awareness.'

A classic pun always looks for clever messaging, playing not just on double meanings but also conveying a larger point. 'I saw an ad for burial plots, **but that's the last thing I need**.' Or 'If you're bad at haggling, you'll end up paying the price.' Take the seemingly bland 'A thief who stole a calendar got twelve months.' Even cleverer is this one: 'Police were summoned to a day-care centre where a three-year-old was resisting a rest.'

Some are quite literal in their humour. 'I got some batteries that were given out free of charge.' Or, 'Prison is just one word to you, but for some people, it's a whole sentence.' And 'Why is 'dark' spelled with a k and not c? Because you can't see in the dark.' Even more simply, 'A dentist and a manicurist married. They fought tooth and nail.' And 'I lost my wife's audiobook, and now I'll never hear the end of it.' Or best of all: 'I did a menial job at a pizza parlour. I kneaded the dough.' Unless you prefer: 'I'm trying to organize a hide and seek tournament, but good players are really hard to find.'

Puns sometimes involve playing on place names: 'England

has no kidney bank, but it does have a Liverpool.' Or 'When the smog lifts in Los Angeles, UCLA' (if you don't get it, just say it aloud.). Puns also up-end clichés: 'Why is it unwise to share your secrets with a clock? Well, time will tell.'

Then there are the bilingual puns: 'French pancakes give me the crepes.' Or 'Did you hear about the pyromaniac yoga teacher who was convicted of asana?' There are also puns that stretch the literal meanings of English words: 'This girl today said she recognized me from the Vegetarians Club, but I'd swear I've never met herbivore.' Or 'When you get a bladder infection, urine trouble.' You can see this one coming: 'How much did the pirate pay to get his ears pierced? A buccaneer.'

Personally, I find some of the puns going around the internet to be a bit contrived, and their humour rather forced: 'Did you hear about the fellow whose entire left side was cut off? He's all right now.' By creating a premise that doesn't occur in real life, only for the purposes of a joke, I think the pun doesn't deserve more than a wry grimace. A very similar example: 'The guy who fell onto an upholstery machine last week is now fully recovered.' And 'What do you call a pig with laryngitis? Disgruntled.' One that seems funny till it isn't: 'I'm reading a book about anti-gravity. I just can't put it down.' Haha, but what on earth is 'anti-gravity'?

Some of the more amusing ones I've come across recently include: 'Did you hear about the crossed-eyed teacher who lost her job because she couldn't control her pupils?' And 'I stayed up all night to see where the sun went, and then it dawned on me.' Or 'Those who get too big for their pants will be totally exposed in the end.' How about this: 'When I told my contractor I didn't want carpeted steps, he gave me a blank stair.'

But the cleverest of all, in my view, is the double pun: 'When she saw her first strands of grey hair she thought she'd dye. But then it grew on her.' Punning is indeed a habit that grows on you!

◆

There is a particular genre of puns that has acquired a name of its own. A 'Tom Swifty' is a phrase in which a pun is used in reporting speech. The name comes from an American boys' fiction genre, the Tom Swift series of books, which were similar to the Hardy Boys series of children's adventure stories. The author went to great lengths to avoid the standard formula 'he said' or 'said Tom' when reporting something the characters uttered, tossing in an adverb to embellish the routine word 'said'. So instead of the typical '"We must find out who did this", said Tom', the author would write, '"We must find out who did this", Tom muttered desperately.'

Since adverbs were excessively attached to dialogue in the stories, to avoid repetition, impart colourful variety to the narrative and teach the books' young readers new words, this was widely noticed as a distinctive feature of the Tom Swift books. Jokes inevitably began to be made about this style, as in '"We must hurry", said Tom swiftly.' The adverb, in other words, contains the pun. 'Pass me the shellfish,' said Tom crabbily. 'We just struck oil!' Tom gushed. 'I'd like my money back, and then some,' said Tom with interest. 'The thermostat is set too high,' complained Tom heatedly. 'I love hot dogs,' exclaimed Tom with relish.

Get it? In the examples above, 'swiftly' relates to 'hurry', a crab is a shellfish, when you strike oil it gushes from the ground, a loan of money must usually be repaid with interest, thermostats regulate room temperature, and hot dogs taste better with relish. The adverbial pun makes a routine statement cleverer and therefore more amusing.

The more complicated the pun, the funnier the allusion is. Thus 'I forgot what I needed at the store,' Tom confessed listlessly. 'Get to the back of the ship!' Tom said sternly. Not having a shopping list when you arrive at the store is not the same as being listless, and to appreciate 'sternly' you need to know the word stern also means the back of a ship, as well as a person's strict manner. Such double meanings make the joke more enjoyable.

So 'I dropped my toothpaste,' a crestfallen Tom said is an allusion to Crest toothpaste, which would make no sense if you were not familiar with the brand. 'I enjoy painting,' Tom said easily requires you to know that painters' canvases rest on an easel. To smile at 'I decided to come back to the group' was Tom's rejoinder you need to understand that a rejoinder is a reply, but someone who exits a group and joins it again can be said to have re-joined. Synonyms are grist to the mill of Tom Swiftys: 'If you want me, I shall be in the attic,' Tom said, loftily. 'I need a towel,' said Tom dryly. 'Pass me another chip,' demanded Tom crisply. 'I can't find the apples,' said Tom fruitlessly.

Occasionally the pun benefits from using adverbs which sound the same as the word being alluded to but are spelled differently. 'Let's gather up the rope,' said Tom coyly. A 'coil' of rope has nothing to do with 'coyness', which is where the humour lies. 'I'd like to stop by the mausoleum,' Tom suggested cryptically. Mausoleums contains crypts, but being cryptic has no relation to the crypts you find in tombs. 'My windows were broken in the storm,' Tom wept, pained.' (Windows have panes, people have pain.)

Sometimes the puns are simple: 'Unlike you, I love dogs,' Tom barked. 'The eclipse is starting,' Tom observed darkly. 'Who was in the sauna with you while I was away?' she asked Tom hotly. Sometimes they require a little more figuring out: 'I lost my trousers,' said Tom expansively. (If he had no pants, he was ex-pants, therefore 'expansively'!) Even more complicated is 'I just rushed past my father,' Tom said transparently.

Even in the US, where they originated, Tom Swiftys appear to have fallen into disuse. It's time we revived them. Try and invent some of your own: 'They'll be a fun diversion,' Tom said distractedly.

To complete this chapter, I'm going to offer you several more in the genre, but without explanation. Read them to see if you get the joke.

First, a selection of simple Tom Swiftys: 'Watch out for that broken glass!' Tom exclaimed sharply. 'I need a pencil sharpener,' Tom demanded bluntly. 'This pencil tip is sharp,' she observed pointedly. 'Let's go watch the cricket match,' he said gamely. 'I like modern painting,' said Tom abstractedly. 'I don't like going to museums,' she responded artlessly. 'I never shed tears,' he observed dryly. 'It's not fair!' said Tom darkly. 'The vegetables are overcooked!' she steamed. 'The phone reception here is excellent,' he said clearly. 'I've gained ten kilos,' Tom confessed heavily.

Next, some that are a little cleverer: 'I really don't like being a gardener,' Tom said witheringly. 'I'm the butcher,' Tom claimed cuttingly. 'That's not how you draw a circle,' she criticized him roundly. 'Don't you dare shoot that rubber-band at me!' she snapped. 'Oops! There goes my hat!' said Tom off the top of his head. 'This must be an aerobics class,' Tom worked out. 'I only have diamonds, clubs, and spades,' said Tom heartlessly. 'Don't add too much water,' said Tom with great concentration. 'I'd like a number between seven and nine,' asked Tom considerately. 'My favourite number is two,' Tom said evenly. 'I hate mathematics,' he added.

In the same vein: 'She pulled the wool over my eyes,' Tom admitted sheepishly. 'I can't think of anything to write,' Tom confessed blankly. 'This is a masterpiece,' remarked Tom flawlessly. 'You are going to fail my class,' warned the teacher degradingly. 'The doctor amputated both my legs at the ankles,' mourned Tom defeatedly. 'What happened to the carpet on the steps?' asked Tom with a blank stare.

Then, some that require a little knowledge on your part to appreciate. 'I have read 93 of Wodehouse's 95 books,' Tom recounted. 'My favourite author is Hemingway,' she replied earnestly. 'I have no flowers,' Tom said lackadaisically. 'This tooth extraction could take forever,' commented Tom with infinite wisdom. 'Don't swing your fist near me,' said Tom, awestruck. 'I work as a freelancer', said Tom casually. 'I think I'll use a different font,' said Tom boldly. 'I manufacture tabletops for shops,' she said counterproductively. 'Name a unit of electric current,' said Tom amply. 'I'm on welfare,' she confessed dolefully. 'That doesn't add up,' said Tom nonplussed.

Sometimes the multiple meanings of a word-sound lend themselves to several Tom Swiftys: 'This boat leaks,' said Tom balefully. (Bailing water out of a boat). 'I'll get you out of prison in no time,' said Tom balefully. (Getting bail from a judge). 'There's no more room in the hay barn,' said Tom balefully. (Bales of hay.)

But these double-meanings are even better: 'Let's get married,' proposed Tom engagingly. 'Where's the cheese?' asked Tom gratingly. 'I'll try to dig up a couple of names,' said Tom gravely. 'It's my maid's day off,' said Tom helplessly. 'I keep banging against the furniture,' she complained bashfully. 'I knew the gun wasn't loaded,' Tom said blankly.' There's someone at the front door,' Tom chimed in.

Let's end with a miscellaneous collection combining several of these types: 'This lemon tastes bad,' Tom said sourly. 'I don't like Campari,' she said bitterly. 'This salad dressing has too much vinegar,' said Tom acidly. 'I love explosions,' Tom boomed. 'Happy Birthday,' Tom said presently. 'Walk this way,' Tom said stridently. 'I didn't see the steamroller coming,' said Tom flatly. 'This pizza place is great!' Tom exclaimed saucily. 'It's freezing,' Tom muttered icily. 'The desert is blazing!' Tom said hotly. 'Follow those ships!' Tom said fleetingly. 'Use your own hair brush', she bristled. 'Fire!' she yelled alarmingly.

Had enough? 'What a dull subject,' the editor commented bluntly. 'There's room for one more,' Tom admitted. 'My word is final!' she dictated.

64

HYPERBOLE

As a politician, I have become all too accustomed to hyperbole, a figure of speech in which extreme exaggeration is used for effect. Many of the best-known examples of hyperbole have become such clichés—like 'I'm so hungry I could eat a horse'—that it is always wise to avoid using them, because they have been drained of all meaning by overuse. The person using hyperbole does not intend to be taken literally, but rather to convey the intensity of his convictions or feelings about something—'if I'm wrong, I'll eat my hat' is a typical piece of hyperbole, often uttered by people who don't even possess a hat. The listener is also meant to understand that the statement merely conveys a feeling rather than embodying a promise.

Hyperbole is often used in casual speech as an intensifier, such as saying 'My poor boy! His schoolbag weighs a ton.' Hyperbole serves to make the point that the son of the speaker has an extremely heavy bag, although it obviously does not literally weigh a ton. Hyperbole can be used to convey or express humour, contempt, political views, and all sorts of emotions from excitement to distress, all intending to make an effect. The American humourist Will Rogers, for instance, once combined the first three of these purposes when he said of a particular politician that, if brains were gunpowder, he wouldn't have enough to blow the wax out of his ears.

Hyperbole is a favourite tool of political speech-making, but it's equally common in daily life: *'I've already told you a million times'* is a typical example. Or *'I'm buried under a mountain of paperwork.'* How many men, smitten by a lady whose *'mile-wide smile could melt anyone's heart'*, have assured women *'I'd go to the ends of the earth for you'?* (Three hyperboles there—and it would surely be wrong to actually expect a lover to fulfil that commitment.) Another favourite is a host assuring unexpected guests that his wife has *'cooked enough food for an army.'* And when someone tells you *'I'm so tired I could sleep for a million years'*, assume he or she is speaking hyperbolically, unless they are about to commit suicide.

It is also used a great deal in children's writing—fairy tales and legends need the overemphasis that hyperbole provides. Shakespeare used hyperbole quite brilliantly. Take Romeo's description of Juliet: *'The brightness of her cheek would shame those stars/As daylight doth a lamp.'*

Perhaps the best use of hyperbole in literature occurs in humorous prose, because it evokes a point and can be funny in its own right. Mark Twain wrote of a terrified boy that *'I could have hung my hat on my eyes, they stuck out so far.'* Paul Bunyan, the fictional character popular in American folklore, remarked: *'Well now, one winter it was so cold.... Late at night, it got so frigid that all spoken words froze solid afore they could be heard. People had to wait until sunup to find out what folks were talking about the night before.'*

Popular American humourist and columnist Dave Barry takes hyperbole to an extreme in describing men's ability to fool themselves: *'A man can have a belly you could house commercial aircraft in and a grand total of eight greasy strands of hair, which he grows real long and combs across the top of his head so that he looks, when viewed from above, like an egg in the grasp of a giant spider, plus this man can have B.O. to the point where he interferes with radio transmissions, and he will still be convinced that, in terms of attractiveness, he is borderline Don Johnson.'*

Obviously, no part of Barry's statement and none of his analogies and metaphors can be taken literally—but the combined effect of his hyperbole means he couldn't have made his point more clearly, or humorously.

Love, in particular, lends itself to hyperbole. But sometimes hyperbole is indeed meant to be taken seriously: *'I can't live without you'* is said with great seriousness by people who genuinely mean it when they say it. Of course, they don't necessarily continue to mean it—when the time for divorce comes, they always want to go on living.

Some argue that all this is just a simple overstatement. People exaggerate all the time; how can one elevate it to a literary figure of speech?

It's true that we all resort to overstatement commonly enough. 'Where were you? I called you a dozen times!' is often said by somebody who actually only dialled the offender, say, four or five times. Exaggerating the number is just overstatement, or exaggeration. 'My suitcase weighs a ton' or 'I'm so hungry I could eat a horse' are common examples of that kind of hyperbole.

But literature offers interesting examples of why hyperbole is much more than mere overstatement. When the eighteenth-century satirist Jonathan Swift, the author of *Gulliver's Travels*, decided to take on his own country's repressive policies in its Irish colony, his attack extended to making the seemingly ridiculous proposition that Britain may as well sell Irish children for their meat. 'I have been assured by a very knowing American of my acquaintance in London, that a young healthy child well nursed, is, at a year old, a most delicious nourishing and wholesome food, whether stewed, roasted, baked, or boiled; and I make no doubt that it will equally serve in a fricasie, or a ragoust,' he wrote in his savage tract *A Modest Proposal*. He did not intend, of course, for his idea to be taken literally: he was using the idea as hyperbole to draw his readers' attention to the plight of Irish children under British rule.

That's not a simple overstatement: it's not a difference of degree from the facts, it's a difference of kind. This is why hyperbole is much more than exaggeration: whereas overstatement often takes a fact and multiplies it for effect, hyperbole often may be in direct contradiction to the facts, as when your teenage daughter tells you, 'I literally *died*.' She is clearly alive when she says this—so she is merely using hyperbole.

Romance particularly lends itself to hyperbole: 'I'd do anything for you' surely ought to come with footnotes and caveats. 'I love you so much, it hurts' is an ardent declaration of feeling, but not an ailment for which any doctor can make a clinical diagnosis. (Similarly, 'I love you so much, my heart's pounding out of my chest'—sorry, that's not physiologically possible. 'You are brighter than the shiniest star'—sorry, not astronomically possible.) Separated lovers are the most prone to flights of fancy: 'I would walk 500 miles just to be with you' or 'I'd cross the universe if it meant seeing your smile just one more time' are typical examples of romantic hyperbole. Third parties are equally guilty. 'When they met, there were fireworks in their eyes' would, if it were not hyperbole, mean they could never see anything again, let alone each other!

Routine conversation is full of hyperbole. When someone says of a thin fashion model that 'she is skinny as a toothpick,' don't take her literally—unless you have never used a toothpick! 'She has a pea-sized brain' is another impossibility; so is 'she's dumber than a doorknob'. Your wife 'made enough food to feed an army' is something I've said often myself, usually as a grateful guest. And someone announcing on a visit to the desert that 'it's hotter than hell' is, let's face it, comparing Arabian sands with a place that he has never been to!

The advertising profession is a particular offender. Remember Gillette claiming to be 'The best a man can get'? (Literally? Poor man!) Or 'Red Bull gives you wings'? 'King of Beers' (Budweiser) and 'Breakfast of champions' (Wheaties) might be dismissed as mere overstatement, but the American cat food brand Meow Mix takes the hyperbolic prize for claiming its product 'tastes so good, cats ask for it by name'. A talking cat might express a contrary view, but there aren't any around, perish the thought!

My favourite humourist, P. G. Wodehouse, was famous for his brilliantly inventive use of language, which inevitably included hyperbole as well. 'She had more curves than a scenic railway' is one of his classics. And ending this chapter on that note would be, in his words, an idea 'handed to me on a silver platter with watercress around it....'

have said, 'Is it kisstomary to cuss the bride?' In these stories, Spooner renders a 'crushing blow' as a 'blushing crow', calls a well-oiled bicycle a 'well-boiled icicle' and describes a 'cosy little nook' as a 'nosey little cook.'

But, in fact, most of the famous Spoonerisms are apocryphal and cannot be convincingly attributed to him. *The Oxford Dictionary of Quotations* (3rd edition, 1979) lists only the 'weight of rages' as a substantiated Spoonerism. Most of us have uttered a Spoonerism unwittingly at some time—an error prompted by haste, carelessness, or fatigue. Only his are classics.

The Oxford provenance of most of these invented Spoonerisms is apparent in their content. Thus, the Reverend, wanting to find out 'Is the Dean busy?' asks 'Is the bean dizzy?' Wanting to accuse an undergraduate of lighting a fire in the college quadrangle, he says 'You were fighting a liar in the quadrangle.' Going to church and seeing his customary place in the pew taken, he complains to an usher: 'Someone is occupewing my pie. Please sew me to another sheet.' And the most brilliant of all has an indignant Spooner dismissing an errant undergrad from his presence with the words: 'You have hissed all my mystery lectures. You have tasted a whole worm. Please leave Oxford on the next town drain.' ('You have missed all my history lectures. You have wasted a whole term. Please leave Oxford on the next down train.')

The appeal of the Spoonerism is that it is a rich source of humour even when it has nothing to do with Oxford or the queer old dean himself. For example: 'I'd rather have a bottle in front of me than a frontal lobotomy.' There's something hilariously accurate about describing a bad 'grilled cheese' sandwich as a 'chilled grease sandwich'. The Washington DC political comedy sketch group Capitol Steps famously referred to President Reagan as 'Resident Pagan' and described US elections as 'Licking their Peaders' (picking their leaders).

That indispensable source of research material, the internet, tells me that in his poem 'Translation' Brian P. Cleary describes a boy who speaks in spoonerisms (like 'shook a tower' instead of 'took a shower'). Humorously, Cleary leaves the poem's final spoonerism up to the reader when he says,

> He once proclaimed, 'Hey, belly jeans'
> When he found a stash of jelly beans.
> But when he says he 'pepped in stew'
> We'll tell him he should wipe his shoe.

67

AMBIGUOUS SENTENCES

'Miners refuse to work after death', screamed the headline in a newspaper. So would I, one might well have thought, if I were dead! But the story sought to highlight a safety controversy at a mine: the intended meaning of the headline was that miners were refusing to work after a death there. But the ambiguous language of the headline invited ridicule rather than sympathy.

Ambiguous sentences occur far too often in newspaper headlines drafted carelessly by editors in a hurry to meet deadlines. 'Man Eating Piranha Mistakenly Sold as Pet Fish' could mean that a piranha that eats humans was mistakenly sold as a pet fish to someone, but it could also be read as saying that a man who was eating a piranha was mistakenly sold as a pet fish. The ambiguity arises from the fact that the phrase 'man eating' can be interpreted as describing either the piranha's behaviour or the man's action. The insertion of a hyphen in 'man-eating' could have made the meaning clearer. Similarly, 'Kids make nutritious snacks' suggests that children are actively involved in preparing healthy snacks, which is a positive statement. Alternatively, this sentence could be understood to mean that children, if eaten by those so inclined, are themselves nutritious snacks!

Ambiguity refers to the lack of a clear definition in a statement or phrase, leading to multiple credible interpretations. According to Merriam-Webster: 'Ambiguous has, like many words in English, more than one possible meaning; a quality some might refer to as ambiguous itself. This word may mean "doubtful or uncertain especially from obscurity or indistinctness", "capable of being understood in two or more possible senses or ways", and "inexplicable".' 'Russian man found wife using ChatGPT' was a recent ambiguous newspaper headline. It is unclear whether the

Russian came across his wife using ChatGPT or if he encountered his future wife by means of ChatGPT.

Verbal ambiguity is commonplace in conversation. While describing the events of a party the previous evening, if one were to say, 'Frank hugged his wife, and so did George', it's not entirely clear whether George also hugged Frank's wife or if George hugged his own wife. 'Abdul saw the mountains flying over Zurich', suggests that Abdul observed the mountains in motion, physically flying over the city of Zurich, though what the speaker intended to say was that Abdul saw the mountains while *he* was flying over Zurich. When someone tells you that 'visiting friends can be annoying', it could suggest that the act of visiting friends can be annoying, or that the friends who were visiting can be annoying. 'I was told to stop drinking at midnight' is another one—was he told at midnight to stop drinking altogether, or was midnight merely the deadline for that day's consumption?

Occasionally, individuals may not even realize they're employing ambiguous language. It's common to say 'the chicken is ready to eat'—what you mean is that you've cooked the chicken and it may be consumed now, but literally, the sentence could also mean that a hungry chicken is waiting for its own dinner. And there are examples where a sentence which, when expressed orally, may not be ambiguous at all, but can be ambiguous in writing: 'He fed her cat food' is an example. Did he give food to her cat, or did he feed her food meant for cats? When spoken, the phrase 'cat food' is clear; in writing, it is not. The most famous example of an ambiguous sentence is: 'Can you call me a taxi, please?' The speaker could be asking someone to call a taxi for him, meaning he wants someone to contact a taxi service on his behalf or hail him one. But the person could easily reply, 'OK, you're a taxi'! After all, you asked me to call you 'a taxi', so I did!

Another classic is: 'Groucho Marx said that he shot an elephant in his pyjamas.' What was the elephant doing in Groucho's pyjamas? Or the boast that 'brave men run in my family'? One could reply, 'There are many brave men in my family too, but they prefer to drive, rather than run.' Time for me to run, too!

68

MISNOMERS

How often have you heard of someone complain he's being treated as a guinea pig, a subject for other's experiments? It's reasonable for us to assume that the creature referred to is a pig from Guinea. But guinea pigs are neither pigs nor from Guinea; they're rodents that originated in the Andes. Even worse, they are not lab rats there, but an edible delicacy in Peru. Guinea pig is, in other words, a misnomer—a term which doesn't mean what the words themselves suggest it means.

English is full of misnomers—familiar terms or phrases that embody a misleading description of what they actually are. Black boxes on large jet aeroplanes are actually orange. Peanuts aren't peas or nuts; they're legumes. There is no butter in buttermilk. Tugboats don't tug or pull anything; in fact, they push bigger ships. There's nothing funny about hitting your funny bone; you're actually hitting your ulnar nerve, which can be extremely painful. Catgut has nothing to do with cats; it's made from sheep gut. Then why the name? One theory is that it might be derived from a corruption of kit, an old dialect word for a fiddle that was made of strings taken from animal guts.

Place names in particular lend themselves to misnomers. English muffins weren't invented in England but in America. Welsh rabbit is a cheese dish. Chinese checkers are not Chinese, but English; it's a game that descends from a nineteenth-century English game called halma. French poodles originated in Germany. French fries weren't invented in France but in Belgium. Danish pastries aren't from Denmark but Austria, and Great Danes come from Germany, not Denmark. The Norway rat originated in North China. Russian dressing was invented in the United States. Jordan almonds originated in Spain. The Dutch are blamed and credited for a lot of things they have nothing to do with: Dutch treats are not a habit in the Netherlands, people in Holland don't talk double Dutch, Dutch clocks originated in Germany, and Hollandaise sauce originated in France!

Sometimes the English misnomers are from other words garbled in translation from other languages. Jerusalem artichokes come from North America, not Palestine; the word 'Jerusalem' is most likely a mangling of the Italian word for 'sunflower', girasole! The English horn is neither English nor a horn. It is in fact an alto oboe from Poland, a woodwind instrument with an angled mouthpiece. The word English horn mistranslates the French word cor anglé, which means angled horn, which sounds similar to cor anglais (translated English Horn)! Bombay duck *is* from Bombay, but it's not a duck, it's a fish. The fish was sent up on the mail train from Bombay; mail is daak in Hindi. The Canary Islands weren't named after canary birds but after dogs, an extinct breed of large dogs (*Canis* in Latin) that once roamed there. The islands got the name before the bird did!

Sometimes misnomers come from simple mistakes of geographical attribution. Panama hats come from Ecuador. The Harlem Globetrotters began in Chicago. Although Venetian blinds were popular in Venice, they originated in Japan, where they were made of bamboo. The Isle of Dogs in central London isn't an island but a peninsula, but whoever named it had a better sense of euphony than accuracy. India ink is from China and Arabic numerals are from India. And while we're on the subject of numerals, and that too Indian ones, the famous Fibonacci sequence, in which each number is the sum of the previous two (1, 1, 2, 3, 5, 8, 13, 21...), was first discussed by Indian scholars several centuries before Fibonacci ever thought of it!

Numbers also lend themselves to English misnomers. The second hand on a watch is the third hand. There are 1,864 islands in the Thousand Islands archipelago. Napoleon's famous Hundred Days—the period between his return from exile on 20 March 1815 to the restoration of the French monarchy on 8 July 1815—lasted 111 days. The Thousand Days' War actually lasted 1,130 days. The Thirty Days' War was part of a series of larger battles that lasted 304 days. The Hundred Years' War in fact lasted 116 years—but the Eighty Years' War did indeed last eighty years!

SECTION NINE

BEER AND SKITTLES

A typical headline like 'Aggression: Why Even Small Children Bite and Hit' on the cover page of a magazine would not have been possible twenty-five years ago.

69

ENGLISH QUIRKS

When I began my United Nations career back in 1978 on the staff of the high commissioner for refugees, an American classmate from my graduate school sent me an intriguing Christmas card. Reacting to my newfound humanitarian career with a reference to my eating habits, he asked: 'If a vegetarian eats vegetables, what does a humanitarian eat?'

It was a clever question, because it got me thinking about the vagaries of the English language that make such observations possible. After all, vegetarians eat vegetables, but humanitarians don't eat humans. And that's not all: writers write, but grocers don't groce. For that matter, fingers don't fing, dangers don't dang, and hammers don't ham. You can say your teacher taught well, but you can't say the preacher praught well. If the plural of tooth is teeth, why isn't the plural of booth beeth? If one goose leads to two geese, why doesn't one moose multiply into two meese? Conversely, shouldn't cheese be the plural of choose?

Languages don't have to always be rational, but English probably wins the irrationality prize. If a delivery man delivers items and a bag man carries bags, why is a fireman someone who puts out fires rather than starts them? Why are goods sent by ship called 'cargo', and those sent by road on a truck or lorry called a 'shipment'? Why do we put cups in the 'dishwasher' and the dishes in the 'cupboard'? Why do people 'recite' (lines) at a play, and 'play' (music) at a recital? Why do you park on driveways and drive on parkways? Why do noses run and feet smell?

The names of things in English defy all logic too. There is no egg in 'eggplant' nor ham in 'hamburger'; neither apple nor pine in 'pineapple'. Sweetmeats are candies, while sweetbreads, which are neither sugared nor made in a bakery, are not sweet but meat. A 'guinea pig' is neither from Guinea nor is it a pig. English muffins were not invented in England nor French fries in France. When you skip work without seeking permission, the English call it 'French leave'; the French refer to an unauthorized or irregular departure (without a proper polite farewell) with the expression '*filer à l'anglaise*' (or Brexit, in short!) The Dutch have no idea what 'going Dutch' means, turkeys cannot be found in Turkey and 'Red Indians' were neither crimson-coloured nor from India.

English is full of popular expressions that involve their own idiosyncrasies. If 'money doesn't grow on trees', how do banks have 'branches'? Why do they call it a TV 'set' when there is only one? Why do airlines offer 'non-stop flights' when passengers have to get off somewhere? Why do people refer to 'rush hour' when traffic moves at its slowest then? Why do doctors 'practice' medicine and lawyers 'practice' law? If they are still practising, when will they ever be ready? How can the weather be 'hot as hell' in the summer and 'cold as hell' in the winter?

The truth is that paradoxes abound in English. A 'wise man' is a fount of wisdom who must be taken seriously, but a 'wise guy' is the opposite. 'Oversight' can mean watchful supervision, but also an inadvertent error. When a house burns up, it burns down. You fill in a form by filling it out, and an alarm clock goes off by going on. If you find too many objects gathering dust at home, you can tell your maid that she needs to dust more so there is less dust. When you sanction something, you can give it permission, or you can ban it using the same word. Words do often mean the direct opposite of what they seem: thus 'quicksand' actually works rather slowly, 'boxing rings' are square, and a 'slim chance' and 'a fat chance' actually mean the same thing: no chance!

But such quirks are part of the delight of working with or using the English language. Just don't look for logic in these English idiosyncrasies. After all, what can you say about a language in which the word 'funeral' starts with the word 'fun'? Or for that matter, when I 'wind up' my watch, I start it, but when I 'wind up' this chapter, I end it....

But I can't end this chapter just yet. One word both those examples had in common is arguably the most versatile in the English language—the word 'up'. It is, as far as I am aware, the only word in the English language that could be a noun, a verb, an adjective, an adverb, or a preposition. Its flexible usage goes far beyond the two examples with which I began this paragraph.

At its simplest, we all understand the word 'up' means 'at the top' or 'towards the sky', as in the simple exhortation to 'look up'. But 'look up' also means something quite different—to check a reference guide for a fact or a meaning. In fact, if you look up the word 'up' in a substantial dictionary, you will find it 'takes up' a large portion of the page. Some dictionaries provide as many as thirty definitions, depending on the usage of the word in context.

It gets more complicated than that, since 'up' features in multiple contexts that have nothing to do with an upward direction. When we awaken in the morning, we 'wake up'. We go to work because we have to, whether or not we 'feel up' to it. Then at a meeting a topic 'comes up', and if we think we have something to say about it, we 'speak up'. And then the note-taker or secretary must 'write up' a report on the discussion. If we disagree with her understanding of what was said, we 'call up' the secretary. Her apologetic smile might then 'brighten up' the office. If she is offended, we might have to 'make up' to her. And worse still, if she bursts into tears, it may smudge her 'make-up', and that would be all our fault!

When we get home, we find a lot of uses for 'up'—if we have 'worked up' an appetite, we 'warm up' our food, 'clean up' the kitchen, and 'lock up' the house. In our spare time we might 'polish up' the silver or 'fix up' the place. If we find the bathroom drains are 'blocked up', we get a plumber to 'open up' the drains. If we decide to go out, we 'dress up', 'line up' for tickets, and might finish our day with a late drink before the pub or restaurant 'closes up' for the night. And if you've stayed out too late in a bad neighbourhood, there's always a risk that you might fall victim to a 'hold-up' and be relieved of your wallet at knifepoint, or worse.

As a politician myself, I have many colleagues who are 'up for election'; some of them prevail easily, but in some cases, it is a 'toss up'. If they lose, they have to 'think up' excuses for their defeat. Perhaps some rival has 'stirred up' trouble for them? Mind you, it is never easy to get a politician to 'open up' about the real problems! And some of the things they say might 'crack you up'!

In short, there are plenty of reasons for us to get rather 'mixed up' about the many different uses if this simple two-letter word. If you are 'up to it', you might try 'building up' a list of the many ways you can use the word 'up'. Or maybe not, since it will 'take up' a lot of your time to do that, and you might be tempted to 'give up'. But if you persist, you may 'wind up' with a long list—'up to' thirty, as in this chapter, or many more. Of course, I can't oblige you to do this—it's 'up to you'!

One could go on and on, but I'll 'wrap it up' for now, since (on this subject) my 'time is up'....

70

KANGAROO WORDS

One of the delights of the English language is the unexpected discoveries it permits—and for me, 'kangaroo words' turned out to be just that. As every child knows, kangaroos carry their young, known as joeys, in a body pouch. The phrase *kangaroo word* therefore describes a word that contains all the letters of a synonym, called a joey word, within itself. One more catch: the synonym must also appear in a such a way within the kangaroo word so that the letters appear in the same order in both words. To take a simple example, the word *action* is a kangaroo word containing the joey word *act*. In a more complicated example, the word '*masculine*' contains its synonym '*male*', even though here, the letters of the joey word are separated within the kangaroo word, albeit in the right order. Similarly, the kangaroo word *chicken* contains the joey word *hen*.

Got it? Thus, the word *inflammable* contains the joey word '*flammable*', which means the same thing; *joviality* includes *joy* within itself; *regulate* includes *rule*, *indolent* contains *idle*, and *encourage* carries its joey, *urge*. Each, in other words, includes its own synonym. Similarly *pinioned* contains *pinned* and *rotund* includes *round*. There can also be a *twin kangaroo*—a kangaroo word that contains two joey words: *container,* for instance, includes both *tin* and *can; perambulate* contains both *ramble* and *amble!* The American writer and linguist Richard Lederer put it brilliantly: 'When you *deteriorate*, you *rot* and *die*. A *routine* is both *rote* and a *rut*. Brooding inside *loneliness* are both *loss* and *oneness*. A *chariot* is a *car* and a *cart*. A charitable *foundation* is both a *fund* and a *font*. Within the boundaries of a *municipality* reside *city* and *unity*, while a *community* includes *county* and *city*.'

Twin kangaroos are rewarding indeed—but even better, a *grand kangaroo* is a kangaroo word which has two joeys, one of which is in the pouch of the other. For instance, *alone* is a grand kangaroo since it contains the word *lone*, which itself includes its own synonym, *one*. *Complaisant* includes *compliant* and *pliant*; *expurgate* contains *purge* and *pure*, and *frangible* has both *fragile* and *frail*. Even grander still, the word '*feasted*' has triplet joeys, '*fed*', '*eat*', and '*ate*'. Then there can also be kangaroo phrases—a *malignant action* contains its synonym phrase, a *malign act*. But remember always the general rule: the synonym or *joey* within a kangaroo word should be the same part of speech as the kangaroo word, and its letters should appear in the same order.

It's amusing to sit down and think of such kangaroo words—for instance, '*curtail*' has the joey '*cut*', '*calumnies*' contains '*lies*', a '*devilish*' person is '*evil*, '*respite*' gives you '*rest*', '*splotch*' contains '*spot*', '*instructor*' carries '*tutor*', and '*destruction*' involves '*ruin*'. Cast your eyes down the alphabet and you'll find something for almost every letter: take P, Q, R, S, and you'll find after *observe (see)*, there's *plagiarist (liar)*, *quieten (quit)*, *rambunctious (raucous)*, and *supervisor (superior)*.

Kangaroo words were originally popularized as a word game by Ben O'Dell in a short article for the *American Magazine*, volume 151, published in 1956 and later reprinted in *Reader's Digest*. A kangaroo word is also called by some linguists as a *marsupial* or *swallow* word, but 'kangaroo word' sounds so much more amusing that these pretentious alternatives are not much in use.

It gets to be even more fun when you consider that there are also *anti-kangaroo* words—words that contain their opposites, or antonyms, while following the same rules. For example: *covert* includes *overt*, and *animosity* 'carries' the 'joey' of *amity!* The word *communicative* contains its antonym *mute*, *female*'s opposite is *male*, *pest* has *pet*, and *wonderful*'s antonym is *woeful*. When you *fabricate* something, you know it's not a *fact*, but the latter is a joey of the former. To *exacerbate* something is the opposite of taking steps to *abate* it. When you *feast* you don't *fast,* a true *friend* can't be a *fiend*, a *courteous* person is never *curt* and a *prurient* interest is never *pure*! But these are all anti-kangaroo words, which carry their antonyms within themselves.

Now that we have that brief refresher out of the way, I am sure you will have no difficulty reading the text that follows, which contains a long string of kangaroo words—and what's more, they're in alphabetical order!

When you get *accustomed* to something, you get *used* to it. If something tastes or smells *acrid*, it feels like *acid*. *Adroitness* is an *art*; to *affect* something you need to *act* on it; and when you *allocate* something, you *allot* it. An *amicable* person is usually *amiable*, and if he says something *apposite*, it's bound to be *apt*. An *arena* is a large *area*, *balsam* applies *balm*; a *barren* landscape is *bare*, whereas one with *blossoms* is in *bloom*. *Brackets* contain *braces*. *Gulliver's Travels* gave us the concept of *Brobdingnagian* for something truly *big*. The American brand *Budweiser* believes it's a synonym for *beer*. When something *bursts* it goes *bust,* a *capsule* is a *case* for medicaments, and a *catacomb* conceals a *tomb*. If you are left in *charge* of a baby, you have to *care* for her. If you take her to a *christening*, she undergoes a *rite*. A *closemouthed* person is often *mute*. A person who *complemented* his partner well has *completed* her, and their *conjunction* is a blessed *union* indeed. One must not *contaminate* it with the *taint* of negative thoughts. That would be *contradictory*—in other words, *contrary* to reality.

The *deceased*, sadly, are *dead*—and so are the *departed*: they are *dead*, too. A *deception* is a *con*. If you *deliberate* on something, you might *debate* it. A *department* of your organisation is an *arm* of it; its *destruction* would entail your *ruin*. It if *deteriorates*, it *rots*. You can *determine* to change things if you *deem* it necessary. When *disappointed*, you're *sad*. A *discourteous* person is *curt,* and he shows his *displeasure* by displaying *ire*. A *disputation* with him is a *spat* you don't want, so I'd *encourage (urge)* you to desist. If things are again *equitable*, they are *equal*. If not, you'd have to *evacuate*, i.e., *vacate* the place.

A *fabrication* is a piece of *fiction*, and if it's full of *falsities*, it contains *lies*. *Forbiddance* involves a *ban*, an *honourable* person is *noble* in his behaviour, an *illuminated* venue is *lit*. When you *impair* someone, you *mar* his prospects, though of course it may be his *incapability* (or his *inability*) that lays him low. This will be especially true if he's *indolent* or *idle* like the *inheritor* who is *heir* to a fortune and whose *joviality* expresses his *joy*. He may sport a *lighted* cigarette, which is *lit*, though if you *misinterpret* his tastes, you would *err*. If he's well *nourished*, he was probably *nursed* well. His *ornamented* mansion is *ornate*, and if you find him *outspoken*, that's because he's *open*. He might *prattle* on a bit, but this isn't just to *prate*; if you dismiss him *prematurely*, you'd be too *early* to do so, and he might *prosecute* (or *sue* you) rather than stay *quiescent* or *quiet*. Perhaps he might *recline* if he likes to *lie* down for a *respite* and a *rest*, though you may need to *restrain* him and *rein* him in to avoid a *retrogression* in which he might *regress*. You can *salvage* things and *save* him by acknowledging he's the *scion* you recognize as the *son* who succeeded. You can only *separate* from him if you *part*.

When you *sculpt* marble, you *cut* the stone. If its origins are *shadowy*, perhaps you cut a *shady* deal. Or if the sculptor was *stricken*, he was *sick* and however much he *strives* or *tries*, the product will be *substandard*, or simply *bad*. His *supervisor* is his *superior*, but if he's a white *supremacist*, he's *racist*, and that *transgression* is a *sin*. On that issue there's *unanimity*: we have *unity* on this.

This *variegated* list gives you an idea of how *varied* kangaroo words can be!

71

KENNINGS

Among the little-known terms of English grammar is the kenning, a stylistic device that involves a two-word compound phrase to describe something metaphorically. A kenning (the term comes from Old Norse poetry) employs figurative language to represent the object, such as using the phrase 'couch potato' for someone who is lazy and often parked in front of the TV, or referring to a crawling baby as an 'ankle-biter'. Neither may be very poetic, but each employs a metaphor that makes it more interesting than the simple regular word or term for the person or item you want to describe.

Thus 'arm candy' is a more expressive way of referring to a date who looks good and is brought to events to impress others; 'brown-noser' is more colourful than 'sycophant'. A car that consumes a lot of petrol is a 'gas-guzzler' (since the American term for vehicle fuel is 'gasoline'). 'Headhunters' are a common expression, no longer for cannibal tribes but for executives whose job is to search for and identify high-level recruits for companies. Television pundits are 'talking heads', and environmentalists are often called 'tree huggers', from a practice by the Chipko movement that tried to save trees in the Himalayan forests from being cut down by having protestors hug them when the loggers came. (Not to be confused with a 'tree swinger', who is merely a monkey.)

Whereas the literal term for each object or person being described is usually unremarkable, the 'kenning', by compressing a metaphorical expression, creates associations that make the speaker or writer sound more interesting. Describing a cigarette as a 'cancer-stick', an accountant as a 'bean-counter' and a bureaucrat as a 'pencil-pusher' conveys your disapproval of or disrespect for the item described, as well as being more vivid than the standard term. Something no one wants to touch is a 'hot potato'; someone who talks too much or too fast is a 'motor-mouth'; and a person who seems to know what you're thinking is a 'mind-reader'.

Kennings were important in the literature of the Norsemen, and so the classic examples refer to the terms that were important to them. For example, there are many different kennings for ships, like 'wave-swine' and 'sea-steed', since the Vikings were seafaring warriors. Kennings added a poetic dimension to the banal terms they needed to employ frequently, especially martial ones such as 'battle-metal' for weapons, 'battle-sweat' and 'slaughter-dew' for blood, or 'feeding the eagle' for killing enemies. The inhospitable frozen wastes that were home for the Vikings lent themselves to many kennings as well, from 'feather's fall' for snow and 'Northern kiss' (and 'winter's blade') for a cold wind, to 'Thor's laughter' for thunder and 'white death' for someone killed by an avalanche.

Most of these, of course, are not employed today. But kennings can be a useful metaphorical device in writing, helping an author make imaginative connections between otherwise unrelated ideas. Yet those modern authors who have tried to invent kennings of their own in works of literature have rarely produced phrases that stood the test of time. John Steinbeck in his 1950 novella *Burning Bright* created kennings such as 'wife-loss' and 'friend-right,' neither of which caught on.

Today's common kennings are more prosaic, but that's why they work. Some pass into the language; everyone knows that a bookworm is someone who reads a great deal or even excessively, but how many realize the term began as a kenning, 'book-worm', before being used so commonly that it shed its hyphen? Similarly, in discussing American politics, the term 'First Lady' is widely understood to mean the wife of the president—it too was a kenning, combining her gender (the assumption was the president was inevitably male) with her importance (she places above every other woman). The election of female governors and now a vice president has led to the creation of 'First Gentleman'. The US is fertile territory for kennings: there, a 'fender-bender' is a minor car accident, a 'rugrat' ('rug' is the preferred American word for a carpet) is a toddler or crawling baby, a dog is a 'postman-chaser', a 'show-stopper' is a performer receiving a standing ovation, a reliable work of reference is a 'myth-buster', and a lawyer ready to profit from accidents by filing lawsuits is an 'ambulance-chaser'. What does that make me? A dictionary-dissecter?

72

LIMERICKS

With so much serious material between the covers of this book, I thought it indispensable to offer at least one chapter of light entertainment, by writing about limericks. A limerick is a form of verse, usually humorous and frequently rude or even indecent, written in five-line, anapestic trimeter—strict rhyme scheme in which the first, second, and, fifth line rhyme and have the same meter, while the third and fourth lines are shorter and share a different rhyme.

Wherever it might have originated (presumably in reference to the City or County of Limerick in Ireland), and even though scholars have found a limerick in Shakespeare's *Othello*, the limerick form was popularized by Edward Lear in his *A Book of Nonsense* (1846) and later in *More Nonsense Pictures, Rhymes, Botany etc.* (1872). Lear wrote 212 limericks, not all of which, alas, have withstood the test of time. His best-known limerick was:

There was an Old Man with a beard,
Who said, 'It is just as I feared!
Two Owls and a Hen,
Four Larks and a Wren,
Have all built their nests in my beard.

Not terribly funny, I think you'll agree. The most successful limericks are both clever and witty, like this 1880 limerick, in a Canadian newspaper:

There was a young rustic named Mallory,
who drew but a very small salary.
When he went to the show,
his purse made him go
to a seat in the uppermost gallery.

Or this 1902 pun-laden classic by Danton Voorhees:

There once was a man from Nantucket
Who kept all his cash in a bucket.
But his daughter, named Nan,
Ran away with a man
And as for the bucket, Nantucket.

The limerick can embody knowledge as well, as in this by the British recreational mathematics expert Leigh Mercer:

A dozen, a gross, and a score
Plus three times the square root of four
Divided by seven
Plus five times eleven
Is nine squared and not a bit more.

Lewis Carroll of *Alice in Wonderland* fame wrote this (you have to read it aloud to get it):

There was a young lady of station,
'I love man' was her sole exclamation;
But when men cried, 'You flatter'
She replied, 'Oh! no matter!
Isle of man is the true explanation.'

The American humourist Ogden Nash was funnier in these two limericks:

There was a young lady called Harris
Whom nothing could ever embarrass
Till the bath salts, one day
In the tub where she lay
Turned out to be Plaster of Paris.

There was a young belle of old Natchez
Whose garments were always in patchez.
When comments arose

On the state of her clothes,
She replied, 'When Ah itchez, Ah scratchez.'

But high among my favourites is this limerick by the self-deprecating former British Prime Minister Clement Attlee (1883–1967) defending his own career:

Few thought he was even a starter.
There were many who thought themselves smarter.
But he finished PM,
A CH, an OM,
An Earl and a Knight of the Garter.

One of the particular joys of limericks is the form is simple enough to replicate. Why don't you try your hand at writing one today?

73

PALINDROMES

Those of us who speak Malayalam well know what a palindrome is, because we are constantly told that our language is the only one whose name is a palindrome—a word, phrase, or even number with characters in the same order forwards and backwards. We won't discuss numbers in this chapter (other than to reveal that all numerical palindromes with an even number of digits are divisible by eleven!), but words and phrases can be fun. Malayalam is a palindromic word, as are Anna, Hannah or Madam; kayak and race car are palindromic means of transport; civic, level, radar, and refer are ordinary everyday words that are also palindromes. Adaven, Nevada is a palindromic name for a palindromic US town. 'Madam, I'm Adam' (as the gentleman in the Garden of Eden introduced himself when Eve appeared) is a palindromic phrase; so are 'a Toyota', 'don't nod', and 'nurses run'.

If you're a cricket fan, you know the stats tell you about how many bowlers of both sexes get rotator cuff injuries; I could go on with their sagas, but it's a wise evitative tenet to avoid boring my readers. What's that sentence doing here? Well, it contains six palindromes!

Those are all fairly elementary palindromes, but they can get much more complicated. 'Was it Eliot's toilet I saw?' asks the English literature professor. 'Go hang a salami; I'm a lasagna hog!' says a greedy American. 'Desserts, I stressed,' he adds. 'Murder for a jar of red rum,' laments a cop. 'Red rum, sir, is murder.' These entire sentences read the same from left to right and right to left (ignoring punctuation, of course).

'Dennis and Edna sinned' says a disapproving preacher. 'Cain: A maniac,' he adds. 'Do geese see God?' the sinner replies. 'Evil I did dwell, lewd did I live,' he confesses. (One protests:

'Lived on decaf, faced no devil,' adding: 'We panic in a pew.' Another confesses: 'Reviled did I live, said I, as evil I did deliver.') Scandalously, 'T. Eliot nixes sex in toilet,' runs a headline. Another, wickedly: 'Tulsa night life: filth, gin, a slut.' Or how about 'A slut nixes sex in Tulsa' paired with 'Ah, Satan sees Natasha.' He did, eh? (Read that last query backwards now!)

The word 'palindrome' was coined by the seventeenth-century English dramatist Ben Jonson, but the person usually credited with inventing palindromes was Sotades of Maroneia (in ancient Greece), who lived 2,300 years ago and wrote palindromic poetry satirizing the Thracian government. The story has it that Ptolemy II was so infuriated by Sotades's palindromic attacks that he had him captured, sealed in a chest, and thrown into the sea.

Indeed, politics lends itself readily to palindromes. 'Drat Saddam, a mad dastard,' says an irritated American. (Or a variant: 'Mad dastard, a sad rat—Saddam.') 'Roy, am I mayor?' asks a confused candidate. 'No X in Nixon,' said Yanks cross with the disgraced American ex-president. 'A man, a plan, a canal, Panama!' exclaimed an admirer of President Theodore Roosevelt. 'Able was I ere I saw Elba,' reflected Napoleon regretfully. 'No, sir, a war is on.' Rise to vote, sir!

Such palindromic sentences get quite creative. 'Are we not drawn onward to new era?' or 'Draw putrid dirt upward' are thoughtful examples, as is 'Ogre, flog a golfer. Go!' 'Must sell at tallest sum,' screams an ad. '*E.T.* is opposite,' says a movie fan. 'Lew, Otto has a hot towel,' exclaims a man at a sauna. Also among my favourites: 'Niagara, O roar again.' 'Campus motto: Bottoms up, Mac!' 'Eva, can I stab bats in a cave?' 'Marge lets Norah see Sharon's telegram'. 'Norma is as selfless as I am, Ron.' 'A dog! A panic in a pagoda.' 'A Santa deified at NASA.'

'Never odd or even' is the title of a book on wordplay. But the longer the sentence, the greater the challenge for the palindrome creator. Among the very best: 'I saw desserts; I'd no lemons; alas, no melon. Distressed was I.' And: 'Doc note: I dissent. A fast never prevents a fatness. I diet on cod.' An exhausted visitor to the desert might gasp that it's 'Too hot to hoot'.

Two nuggets: While we mentioned the likes of Hannah and Anna, real people have palindromic names too, like the former Cambodian prime minister Lon Nol, the Japanese novelist Nisio Isin or the actor Robert Trebor. And the longest palindrome word in English? James Joyce is often credited with this for inventing the twelve-letter palindrome 'tattarrattat' in his 1922 novel *Ulysses* (to imitate the sound of a knock on the door).

Resuming with the classic ones where we left off, a man at a used-car showroom laments, 'Sad, no Hondas.' A football dispute is settled by the palindromic exhortation 'See referees'. A disillusioned Egyptologist laments, 'Sir, I soon saw Bob was no Osiris.' A moralistic government imposes 'Sex at noon taxes'. At a lawyer's office, 'some men interpret nine memos'. A mathematician observes, 'Sums are not set as a test on Erasmus.' An approving teacher surveys his class and exclaims, 'So many dynamos!'

You will notice that all these palindromes begin with the letter 's', since it is the easiest letter to begin and end palindromes with. It's more challenging to try with other letters. Thus, if you are told by an amateur palindromist that aged cats are 'senile felines', you could respond: 'Won't cat lovers revolt? Act now!'

All the palindromes involve words or phrases written and read left to right and right to left, and so rely on spelling, not pronunciation. But there are also the more challenging phonetic palindromes, where it's not the spelling that determines the palindrome, but its sound. In phonetic palindromes, a sound of speech is reversed yet identical, like 'crew work' and 'work crew'. The word 'easy' is a phonetic palindrome; so are 'new moon' or 'funny enough'. The trick is to say the word or phrase out aloud and you will see what I mean. 'Let Bob tell', for instance. Or 'Sorry, Ross'.

And then there are the word-unit palindromes, where it's not spelling or phonetics that can be read forwards or backwards, but each word. You can find such palindromes in works of literature: Alexandre Dumas's *The Three Musketeers* has the famous 'All for one and one for all.' Authors of books on language and wordplay have come up with the most complicated and memorable word-unit palindromes, like Martin Gardner's 'You can cage a swallow, can't you, but you can't swallow a cage, can you?' But it's very rare to find a sentence that works both as a regular palindrome (spelled the same way left to right and right to left) and as a word-unit palindrome (where the words can be read that way). One that works both ways: 'Was it a car or a cat I saw?'

Lovers of literature will be familiar with Scottish poet Alastair Reid's clever palindrome in *The Life of a Poet*: 'T. Eliot, top bard, notes putrid tang emanating, is sad. I'd assign it a name: gnat dirt upset on drab pot-toilet.' Auden is also credited with the simpler 'Norma is as selfless as I am, Ron.'

And the promised bonus? A palindromic poem, 'Doppelgänger', by James A. Lindon:

Entering the lonely house with my wife
I saw him for the first time
Peering furtively from behind a bush....

Blackness that moved,
A shape amid the shadows,
A momentary glimpse of gleaming eyes
Revealed in the ragged moon....

A closer look (he seemed to turn) might have
Revealed in the ragged moon
A momentary glimpse of gleaming eyes
A shape amid the shadows,
Blackness that moved.

Peering furtively from behind a bush,
I saw him, for the first time
Entering the lonely house with my wife.

What's special about this poem is that it is a verse palindrome; it reads the same from the first to the last line, as it does from the last line to the first line.

'Egad, an adage,' you might well say. I'd better stop or I might give you aibohphobia—another palindrome that means an irrational fear of palindromes! Evade me, Dave!

74

MIXED METAPHORS

When the *Times of India* ran a headline about rising inflation, declaring 'Tomato prices have become a hot potato', it may have had its tongue firmly in its cheek, but it was also indulging in a mischievous pleasure of the English language—the mixed metaphor.

A mixed metaphor, a common error in the use of the language by overenthusiastic speakers and writers, is a combination of two or more incompatible metaphors. Obviously, a tomato can't be a potato, so that's a mixed metaphor. Mixed metaphors often involve clichés; you might wish to call someone on your team 'a pillar of strength' and laud him for 'forging ahead', but if you declare that he is a pillar of strength who is forging ahead, you have mixed up your metaphors—a pillar can't move, let alone forge ahead anywhere.

Modern life offers plenty of examples of such mixed metaphors. Managers are particularly prone to fashionable sounding jargon culled from the latest gurus in order to sound both knowledgeable and decisive, but that can lead them to horribly mix their metaphors. 'We must iron out the remaining bottlenecks' is a famous example. Sometimes metaphors get mixed when the speaker accidentally confuses two well-known expressions. 'You hit the nail right on the head' and 'That's right on the nose' are both common expressions in English, especially in America. But if you say 'You hit the nail right on the nose', you've created a mixed metaphor.

Worse still are those examples of mixed metaphors which involve an error on top of the mixing—when someone inaccurately recalls one of the metaphors he's mixing and jumbles it with another. This has been dubbed a 'malaphor'—a blend of malapropism and metaphor, a term coined by Lawrence Harrison in 1976. One example is 'We'll burn that bridge when we come to it'—an erroneous conflation of two expressions, 'Don't burn your bridges' and 'We'll cross that bridge when we come to it'. Another hilarious image is conjured up by the malaphor 'She really stuck her neck out on a limb.' ('Stuck her neck out' and 'went out on a limb' both make sense, but imagine visualizing the combination…)! Or our favourite manager praising a valuable staffer: 'She is a pearl worth its weight in gold.'

I have collected a few examples of such mixed metaphors over the years. Among my favourites: 'The sacred cows have come home to roost with a vengeance'. 'He's burning the midnight oil from both ends'.

But the funniest mixed metaphors always involve avoidable mistakes from mis-remembering a cliché. 'Falling off a log' and 'a piece of cake' are both metaphors for something that's really easy, but if you say 'It's as easy as falling off a piece of cake', you've really made things difficult for yourself. 'Between a rock and a hard place' and 'between the devil and the deep blue sea' are both familiar metaphors, but don't announce that someone's 'between a rock and the deep blue sea'!

The incongruity of some metaphorical mixes is what makes them sound ludicrous. The woeful widower who lost his children's mother to illness wanted to elicit sympathy when he lamented that 'The hand that rocked the cradle has kicked the bucket', but even his parish priest had to suppress a chuckle. One of history's most famous examples of a recorded mixed metaphor is from a speech by Sir Boyle Roche (1736–1807) in the Irish Parliament: 'Mr Speaker, I smell a rat. I see him floating in the air. But mark me, sir, I will nip him in the bud.' The speaker was so familiar with the expressions 'smell a rat', 'floating in the air', and 'nip in the bud' that he got carried away and produced a classically absurd mixed metaphor from all three of them.

Are mixed metaphors just bad English, some readers have wanted to know. Not really, is my answer. They emerge from the carelessness, or more accurately thoughtlessness, of people who speak good English, are familiar with two or more expressions but fail to realize the incongruity of jumbling them up together.

This is because modern spoken (and indeed written) English is full of metaphors, several of which seem to mean related things—and yet they sound odd, or even funny, when put together. For instance, 'when things really get moving' can be made to sound more interesting and colourful if you say, instead, 'when the rubber hits the road' (that is, when you engage your car on a drive and the rubber tyres start moving on the road). And the act of taking tough or uncomfortable decisions lends itself to the military metaphor 'biting the bullet' (that is, releasing the cartridge from its pouch in order to shoot with it). But imagine you want to say, 'When things really get moving, you will have to take some tough or uncomfortable decisions.' That thought is clear enough, but if you try to express that thought by saying 'When the rubber hits the road, you'll have to bite the bullet,' it sounds silly—not because your meaning isn't clear, but because metaphors conjure up an image in the listener or reader's mind. And a metaphor that comes from driving a car sits oddly with another metaphor that implies firing a gun. That's why mixed metaphors must be avoided.

It can even get worse. An expression for delaying the taking of decisions, or postponing a difficult choice, is 'kicking the can down the road'. But imagine if the offending speaker above added that to the mix and said, 'So now what we are dealing with is the rubber meeting the road, and instead of biting the bullet on these issues, we just want to kick the can down the road.' A complete jumble of mixed metaphors! Additionally, let's say he wanted to characterize the issues in question as having unattractive aspects: a common expression for that is 'warts and all', warts being disfiguring growths on a person's face. Thus our speaker says: 'So now what we are dealing with is the rubber meeting the road, and instead of biting the bullet on these issues, whatever their warts may be, we just want to kick the can down the road.' Ridiculous? I am reliably informed that this very sentence was uttered by an American politician a few years ago!

Indeed, Americans tend to be habitual sinners when it comes to mixing metaphors. A Pentagon official once complained that efforts to reform the military were too timid: 'It's just ham-fisted salami-slicing by the bean counters.' A marketing man spoke of 'leaving a sour taste in the client's eye.' Or how about these two classic Americanisms, one from baseball and one from poker, in the same sentence: 'It's time to step up to the plate and lay your cards on the table.'

Before some of you say that I'm making these up, let me cite chapter and verse for a few classic mixed metaphors. The *Detroit News* actually printed this in 2012: 'I don't think we should wait until the other shoe drops. History has already shown what is likely to happen. The ball has been down this court before and I can see already the light at the end of the tunnel.' The then chairman of the US Federal Reserve, Ben Bernanke, broke all records for mixed metaphors when he told reporters that some economic data 'are guideposts that tell you how we're going to be shifting the mix of our tools as we try to land this ship in a smooth way onto the aircraft carrier.' (These were both quoted in the *New Yorker*, 26 November 2012).

Americans remain a rich source of such solecisms. 'Going to hell in a handbasket' is a commonplace expression, though rather devoid of meaning, but when somebody rants, as one politician did, that 'this country is going to hell in a handbag', he elicits laughter, not applause. So watch your tongue and don't leave your eyes in a handbasket!

A simple piece of advice to readers: Keep an eye on your words and an ear to the ground, with a finger on the pulse of your audience, to avoid putting your foot in your mouth!

To end this chapter, I'm going to provide a number of examples of mixed metaphors that various authors have culled from people's mistakes in a variety of publications. And believe it or not, none of these are made up!

The world of American politics seems to be particularly fertile territory for rib-tickling mixed metaphors, judging by this selection of on-the-record howlers:

- 'So now what we are dealing with is the rubber meeting the road, and instead of biting the bullet on these issues, we just want to punt.'
- '[T]he bill is mostly a stew of spending on existing programs, whatever their warts may be.'
- (Talking about the Democratic presidential candidates): 'This is awfully weak tea to have to hang your hat on.' (Hanging your hat on something is a popular ready-to-mix metaphor. From the other side politically, MSNBC, on 3 September 2009, declared that Republican arguments were 'awfully thin gruel for the right wing to hang their hats on.')
- 'The mayor often strips his gears by failing to engage the clutch when shifting what emanates from his brain to his mouth. The bullets he fires too often land in his own feet.'
- 'Top Bush hands are starting to get sweaty about where they left their fingerprints. Scapegoating the rotten apples at the bottom of the military's barrel may not be a slam-dunk escape route from accountability anymore.'

As a politician myself, albeit not an American one, let me point out that other professions are hardly exempt from mixing their metaphors. Journalism, for instance, gave us such gems as this one on the subways: 'The moment that you walk into the bowels of the armpit of the cesspool of crime, you immediately cringe.' Or, from the *London Evening Standard:* 'Her saucer-eyes narrow to a gimlet stare and she lets Mr Clarke have it with both barrels.' Then there's Robert D. Kaplan's 'I wanted a visual sense of the socioeconomic stew in which Al Qaeda flourished,' a sentence which has been described as a 'double mixed metaphor'.

No less an eminence than the *Washington Post*, the very paper that coined the term 'malaphor', wrote this spectacular jumble of metaphors in 1992: 'The committee was tired of stoking public outrage with fortnightly gobbets of scandal. It decided to publish everything it had left, warts and all. Now everyone is tarred with the same ugly brush, and the myth that forever simmers in the public consciousness—that the House shelters 435 parasitic, fat-cat deadbeat—has received another shot of adrenalin.'

American television, not to be outdone, produced these gems: a failed task 'left a sour taste in the client's eye.' A game-show contestant said his team were 'dancing around the bush'. A football coach rued that 'It's just apples versus oranges, and it's not a level playing field by any means.' The right-wing commentator Rush Limbaugh declared: 'I knew enough to realize that the alligators were in the swamp and that it was time to circle the wagons.'

We should conclude with this sage observation quoted by Willard R. Espy in his book *The Game of Words:* 'There is no man so low that he has in him no spark of manhood, which, if watered by the milk of human kindness, will not burst into flames.'

◆

Having discussed mixed metaphors, it's time to graduate to an advanced version of them—catachresis, another one of those terms only grammarians know. Catachresis is a figure of speech in which writers use mixed metaphors, sometimes intentionally, to create rhetorical effect (something Shakespeare was an expert at) but more often, inappropriately or awkwardly (the rest of us). The most common example of the latter is when people jumble up two common expressions that shouldn't go together (like 'he grabbed the bull by the horns of a dilemma'), or confuse two words that sound alike but don't mean the same thing (confusing 'mitigate' with 'militate', for instance, or mixing up 'reluctant' and 'reticent').

When it's used literally, catachresis can be an effective literary device, as Shakespeare repeatedly demonstrated. Scholars often quote this line from *Timon of Athens:* 'I fear 'tis deepest winter in Lord Timon's purse; that is, one may reach deep enough, and yet find little.' Depth, winter, and purse do not, at first glance, go together, but in Shakespeare's hands the catachresis is strikingly effective. Or his well-known phrase from *Hamlet*, 'to take arms against a sea of troubles.' How can any arms be effective against a raging sea? And yet the catachresis has entered the language as a familiar phrase. In his play *King John*, he gave us another memorable example of the genre, when the King says, 'I do not ask much: I beg cold comfort....' How can anything cold be comforting, you might well ask, but Shakespeare has given us an expression still in everyday use.

In Shakespeare's *The Tempest*, the character Gonzalo remarks of the Boatswain, 'His complexion is perfect gallows.' He is implying that the Boatswain looks like a criminal and must be hanged. The catachresis lies in the fact that someone's complexion and the hangman's gallows seemingly have nothing to do with each other, yet the mixed metaphor works.

But here's the catch: does it always? When Shakespeare's Hamlet says 'I will speak daggers to her', is he confusing the common expression 'to look daggers at someone', meaning to stare at someone in a very angry way, with the common phrase 'I will speak harshly to her'? Or are we to say that because it's Shakespeare, it's brilliant, but if you or I used the phrase 'I will speak daggers to her' we would be laughed at for mixing metaphors inappropriately?

Matters are made worse by the fact that the very origins of the term catachresis lie in the Greek words *katakhrēsis* or *katakhrēsthai* meaning 'misuse or abuse', and that the Latin name for catachresis is *abusio*. So if catachresis is an abuse or misuse of language, why are literary scholars celebrating it? The British newspaper *The Guardian*, famous for its misprints, once issued a correction noting, 'Attentive readers will have noticed a lamentable catachresis yesterday when we referred to some French gentlemen as Galls, rather than Gauls.' So the word 'catachresis' here serves as a synonym for 'error'. And indeed that is an acceptable usage, since the mix-up of two words by a speaker or writer mistaking one for the other is also called catachresis. Grammarians will include, in discussions of catachresis, such sentences as 'He looked at the price and his pockets ran dry'. Or 'His lie was the straw that broke the elephant's back'. Or even using words in the wrong sense, as in the angry wife expostulating, 'Can't you hear that? Are you blind?'

And yet, I am not prepared to leave Shakespeare stranded on the shores of abusio. Because other wonderful poets and writers have also resorted to catachresis to marvellous effect. When I was courting the lady who became my children's mother, a literature student herself, she introduced me to a poem by e. e. cummings (a poet who famously did not use capital letters, not even in his name!) which had the wonderful lines 'The voice of your eyes is deeper than all roses – / nobody, not even the rain, has such small hands.' I loved the lines since my lady love had small hands, but eyes don't have voices and rain has no hands. Catachresis at its best!

75

ZEUGMA

Every once in a while, English grammar throws up a term that doesn't even sound like English. Here's one: zeugma, from a Greek word meaning yoking or bonding, is a figure of speech in which a word, usually a verb or an adjective, applies to more than one noun, blending together grammatically and logically different ideas. For instance, in the sentence, 'Rana lost his raincoat and his temper,' the verb 'lost' applies to both the nouns 'raincoat' and 'temper'. Losing a raincoat and losing your temper are logically and grammatically different ideas, which are brought together in this sentence. That's zeugma.

English literature offers plenty of examples of zeugma. The poet Alexander Pope wrote of Queen Anne: 'Here Thou, great Anna! whom three Realms obey, / Dost sometimes Counsel take—and sometimes Tea.' Tennyson's zeugma is pitch-perfect: 'Waving, the moment and the vessel passed.' Mark Twain in *The Adventures of Tom Sawyer* talks of people who 'covered themselves with dust and glory'. Charles Dickens in *The Pickwick Papers* wrote of how 'Miss Bolo [...] went straight home, in a flood of tears and a sedan-chair.' In *Oliver Twist*, Dickens describes a character 'alternately cudgelling his brains and his donkey'. Henry David Thoreau wrote in *Walden*: 'I sometimes dream of a larger and more populous house...where the washing is not put out, nor the fire, nor the mistress.'

For a more recent example we have the bestselling American author Amy Tan's *The Hundred Secret Senses:* 'We were partners, not soul mates, two separate people who happened to be sharing a menu and a life.' And to be even more contemporary, here's a zeugma from *Star Trek: The Next Generation:* 'You are free to execute your laws, and your citizens, as you see fit.' The word 'execute' applies to both laws and citizens. The speaker could have said, 'You are free to execute your laws and execute your citizens as you see fit.' However, using the zeugma makes for a punchier sentence that has the power to shock.

Zeugma can make banal ideas more interesting, even entertaining: 'He fished for trout and compliments.' 'Every time he went out with her, he had to open his mind and his wallet.' 'She opened the door and her heart to the homeless child.' 'In quick succession, Shazia lost her job, her house and her mind.' 'By the end of the first day of their summer vacation, she had already exhausted her kids and her patience.' Or the classic: 'All over Ireland, the farmers grew potatoes, barley and bored.' Zeugma links unrelated terms—mental with moral, abstract with physical, high with low—and thus generates surprise and therefore effect.

As a literary device the zeugma serves the function of sharpening your style and making simple ideas more readable. For example, imagine you are writing of someone who invested his life savings in a boat, planning a lifetime of enjoyment on the water, took it out to sea on Day One, was hit by a storm and watched in dismay as the boat capsized and sank to the bottom. You could write, 'His boat sank in the storm. He could no longer fulfil his dreams.' Or you could resort to a zeugma and write, 'The storm sank his boat and his dreams.' Which do you think most readers would find more effective?

While we are being grammatical, let's also differentiate zeugma from syllepsis. Like zeugma, syllepsis also uses a single verb for more than one part in a sentence, but here that single verb applies grammatically and logically to only one. For example, in the Biblical sentence, Exodus 20:18, 'And all the people saw the thundering, and the lightning, and the noise of the trumpet, and the mountain smoking', the verb 'saw' is logically correct only for the lightning and the smoking—you can only *hear* thundering and trumpeting! That's syllepsis. So is Tennyson's line from Ulysses, 'He works his work, I mine', as the verb 'works' is grammatically correct with the first-person pronoun 'he,' but is incorrect with 'I'—you can't say 'I works mine'.

But unless you're a grammarian, the difference is trivial. As long as it works, it doesn't matter. Or to use a zeugma, let's drop our red pencils and our pretensions....

SECTION TEN

LEXICAL EVOLUTION

One of the signs of our times is how many words we routinely use that properly aren't words, but trademarks. A popular expression these days is to say 'someone has drunk the Kool-Aid', meaning he has swallowed propaganda and is regurgitating an official line.

76

FOOD FOR THOUGHT

One subject we might think doesn't need words, since it expresses a human need far more elemental than language, is food. After all, people are hungry before they need to (or even can) speak, so food has existed before language was even invented. Still, food has evolved a fancy vocabulary of its own, with unusual words for various ways of preparing it, and even more exotic terms to name or label each dish. And then there are words to describe you, the eater, depending on your food preferences.

In the old days when I was growing up, the world was divided into two kinds of people, vegetarians and non-vegetarians. Vegetarians didn't eat meat; the 'non-veg' folks did. In those less complicated times, the simple 'veg/non-veg' distinction was straightforward and clear, or so we thought. But with growing worldly sophistication, that's no longer enough. There are many more kinds of classifications of people by the food they eat, or don't. A vegan, for instance, doesn't eat animal products of any kind. Whereas a vegetarian only objects to consuming a creature that has been killed, and has no ideological problem with milk or eggs since the animal is not murdered for his meal, the vegan diet eliminates meat, fish, poultry, eggs, and dairy products, as well as other animal-derived products, such as honey. On this diet you also avoid rennet, gelatin, collagen, and other types of animal protein. Even soup made of animal stock or fats derived from animals are taboo.

Vegetarians themselves have become far more complex than just people who refuse to consume animal flesh products, whether fish, meat, or fowl. Now there are several sub-types of vegetarians. Most common are the *lacto-ovo* vegetarians, who won't eat meat, fish, and poultry but are happy to consume eggs and dairy products (I am one of those). Less common are the *ovo-vegetarians* who reject meat, fish, poultry, *and* dairy products but eat eggs. Next are the *pescatarians*, who in my book aren't vegetarians at all because though they abstain from eating all meat and animal flesh, they make an exception for fish. It's almost impossible to find a Bengali vegetarian, but if you do, the odds are that he is actually a pescatarian. Most Bengalis seem to think fish is a sea vegetable!

Recent years have seen the advent of *flexitarians*, who eat mostly vegetarian but are quite willing to lapse on occasion. When it suits them—they claim rarely—they do eat meat. Such people are also referred to as semi-vegetarians, though a simpler word for them might be hypocrites. On the opposite end of the flexibility scale are the devotees of *macrobiotic* food, a diet made popular by the Japanese. The macrobiotic diet isn't just about eating certain foods—mainly organically-grown whole grains, vegetables, legumes, and beans like tofu and tempeh—it's also about achieving balance in your life through food choices. Macrobiotic dieters are told they must eat regularly, chew their food thoughtfully, use their mind to listen to their bodies, be active and maintain a positive mental outlook. For all their prohibitions—strictly no dairy, eggs, poultry, red meat, refined sugars, tropical fruits, spices, alcohol, or coffee, nor anything refined, processed, or chemically-preserved—they do make an exception for fresh fish and seafood. No wonder it's a diet popular mainly among the Japanese!

These terms all relate to choices people make about food, but there are also food phobias—endured by people who suffer extreme anxiety when faced with some kinds of food they fear or have an aversion to, including panic attacks, irregular heartbeat, sweating, and nausea. You can enhance your vocabulary, though not your waistline, by being familiar with these fears and aversions: lachanophobia (fear of vegetables); carnophobia (meat); alektorophobia (chicken); mycophobia (mushrooms); alliumphobia (garlic); ichthyophobia (fish); and the even more specific ostraconophobia (fear of shellfish).

Some phobias, though, border on the extreme—acerophobia (fear of sourness), phagophobia (fear of swallowing), and geumophobia (fear of taste)—or the esoteric: consecotaleophobia (fear of chopsticks)! And some, frankly, are absurd, like arachibutyrophobia, the fear of peanut butter sticking to the roof of the mouth. Many may suffer from mageirocophobia (fear of cooking), but the worst of all would be cibophobiaorsitophobia, the fear of food and eating altogether. Such people would need tranquillizers before every meal. Even macrobiotic dieters would feel sorry for them....

77

COUNTRY NAMES

In case some of you missed the news, Turkey (the country) is no longer 'Turkey' in English. The country officially changed its name in 2022 to Türkiye, which the government felt better reflected its culture and traditions.

There were, of course, less exalted reasons for the change. As the Turkish news agency TRT World has pointed out, 'Turkey' is more commonly associated with a bird that features on Christmas menus or Thanksgiving dinners, and English dictionary searches for 'turkey' will also get results that include 'a stupid or silly person' or 'something that fails badly'. No wonder the Turks wanted the name changed.

While not a common practice, name changes by countries are not as rare as one might imagine. As far back as 1939, Siam changed its name to Thailand, since in the Thai language, the country's name is Prathet Thai, 'the country of free people'. Three decades later, Ceylon became Sri Lanka. Ceylon got its name from the Portuguese who landed there in 1505, and this continued to be used by the British who colonized the country. It took twenty years after independence in 1948 for the modern-day republic to revive its ancient name Sri Lanka. (This created some confusion abroad: I remember an American student at my graduate school, presenting a learned paper on the prospects for cartelization of tea, solemnly telling our class that his research showed that 'three countries dominate the world's tea production—India, Ceylon, and Sri Lanka'.)

Many other countries adopted new names immediately upon independence from colonial rule. The Netherlands East Indies became the Republic of Indonesia (a name coined from the Greek *indos*—for India or Indies—and *nesos*—for island). Dutch Guiana similarly became Suriname upon decolonization in 1975. The jointly administered Anglo-French condominium of the New Hebrides achieved independence in 1980 as Vanuatu, which means 'Our Land Forever' in many of the local Melanesian languages. German South-West Africa changed to Namibia when the country became independent in 1990 from South Africa, which had ruled it since Germany's defeat in World War I. In 1989, Burma's military government announced a change in name from Burma to Myanmar, but this was disputed by some within the country, and partly because of the junta's perceived illegitimacy, many still use the old name. Similarly, the Democratic Republic of the Congo became the Republic of Zaire in 1971 under President Mobutu, but reverted to its old name in 1997 after his ouster.

Some countries were given English names that seemed more like geographical descriptions than proper names, so they insisted upon standardizing these in names the local people preferred. Thus the Gold Coast became Ghana and the Ivory Coast was rebaptized Cote d'Ivoire (a French name) in English too. Similarly, in 2013, Cape Verde officially became the Republic of Cabo Verde, or simply Cabo Verde, which is what the Portuguese sailors who discovered the islands had called them since 1444. Upper Volta (named for the Volta River) was renamed 'Burkina Faso' to celebrate the twentieth anniversary of independence. The new name, in the local language, means 'country of incorruptible men.'

In 2016, the Czech Republic announced a change to Czechia, reasoning that a shorter name would be less unwieldy. Similarly, the Netherlands dropped Holland as an alternate name in 2019, saying having two names caused confusion and diluted the nation's branding. In 2018, Swaziland changed to Eswatini, both because that was the name in the national language (meaning 'land of the Swazis') but also because the old name was too often mistaken by foreigners for Switzerland!

Sometimes history and controversy lie behind name changes. When Yugoslavia broke up in the 1990s, Greece bitterly disputed the right of one of the successor republics, Macedonia, to use that name, claiming it threatened the sovereignty of the

Greek province of Macedonia. Under pressure from Athens, the new country had to carry the unwieldy name of the Former Yugoslav Republic of Macedonia, or FYROM for short. It took two decades of negotiations to finally arrive at a solution, and FYROM formally changed its name to the Republic of North Macedonia in February 2019. Of course, nothing changes for the inhabitants, who continue to call themselves 'Macedonians' and speak 'Macedonian'. But that's all Greek to the rest of us!

Reconciling irreconcilables is a great Indian virtue. When the Constituent Assembly was divided over whether to call our country 'India' or 'Bharat', our founding fathers and mothers found the perfect compromise in drafting the Republic's foundational document, referring to 'India, that is Bharat' and making both sides happy. The Preamble speaks of 'We, the People of India' in English, and '*Bharat ke log*' in Hindi. Article 52 declares, in English, that 'There shall be a President of India', and in Hindi calls the position '*Bharat ke Rashtrapati*'. A simple, uncomplicated practice followed from all this: In English, and therefore internationally, our country was referred to as India; in Hindi and other Indian languages, 'Bharat' was our country's name.

It worked, just as the country known in English as 'Germany' is Deutschland at home and to all who speak Deutsch (the language we refer to as 'German'). Nobody in that proud country, whose nationalism was at one time far more ferocious than ours, insisted that English speakers had to call them Deutschland too.

But what has worked for more than seven decades, and for a few millennia before that, is apparently not good enough for our government. The sudden unsettling decision to have the president of India issue formal invitations as 'the president of Bharat' and for the prime minister to sit behind a name plate at the G20 summit saying 'Bharat' in the Roman script, rather than 'India', has sparked off a controversy that is both pointless and totally unnecessary. Why tamper with an arrangement that was working perfectly satisfactorily? As the Americans like to say, 'If it ain't broke, why fix it?'

We know what the ruling party's defenders are saying: that 'India' is a colonial imposition and that reverting to an ancient, historically sanctified name is a way of rejecting the 'colonization of the mind' that the name India implies. They are wrong, and even if they were right, dropping 'India' would still be a bad idea.

Why are they wrong? Because the name India has nothing to do with British colonialism: it predates the British presence in India by nearly two millennia. The ancient Greeks and Persians used the term 'India' for the land beyond the river Sindhu, or 'Indus', well before the Christian era. The ancient historians Herodotus and Megasthenes wrote of India in the fifth and fourth centuries BCE. The term India existed in Old English (fifth century CE) and features in the King James Bible. And the word isn't just in English. The Dutch East India Company was established in 1602, at about the same time as the British one in 1599. Their colonization of the 'East Indies' gave Indonesia its name. As a name for our subcontinent, 'India' long precedes the British Raj.

But even if, for argument's sake, the natives were right that 'India' came with the British, it would still be wrong to dump it in favour of the desi 'Bharat'. It was Mohammed Ali Jinnah, the founder of Pakistan, who wanted our country named either Bharat or Hindustan, to deny it any right to claim the storied legacy of the name India, to which he felt his own state had equal claim. At the same time, our first prime minister, Jawaharlal Nehru, insisted on retaining the name 'India' for the newly independent country, in the face of resistance from nativists who wanted it renamed 'Bharat', in order to ensure that we were seen as the successor state to the India that had enjoyed membership of the United Nations and the League of Nations. By retaining India he ensured that Pakistan was just a seceding state, which had to apply afresh for international recognition.

There is also the undoubted fact that the name India has incalculable brand value built up over centuries. When a brand is mentioned, it carries with it a whole series of associations in the public mind, as well as expectations of how it will perform. A country isn't a soft drink or a cigarette, but its very name can conjure certain associations in the minds of others. This is why 'India' had value in the eyes of the world: it was a fabled and exotic land, much sought after by travellers and traders for centuries, the 'jewel in the crown' of Her Britannic Majesty Victoria, whose proudest title was that of 'Empress of India'. Nehru wanted people to understand that the India he was leading was heir to that precious heritage. He wanted, in other words, to hold on to the brand, though it was not a term he was likely to have employed.

This is why we should continue to use both words rather than relinquish our claim to a name redolent of history, a name that is recognized around the world. Of course, ultimately the only real guarantee of any brand's continued worth is the actual performance of the product or service it stands for. But why be so foolish as to relinquish all the benefits of the India brand globally when we can enjoy them without giving up the strength of 'Bharat' at home?

The final clincher: Since our neighbours the Arabs and the Persians pronounced 's' as 'h', it is also they who called the people across the Sindhu the 'Hindus'. So if the BJP rejects the name India, they will have to reject the name 'Hindu' by the same logic, since that is equally of foreign origin. No longer will they able to demand of us all, '*Garv se kaho ki hum Hindu hain.*' Etymologically that is just the same as declaiming '*Garv se kaho ki hum Indian hain!*' Which all of us have been for too long, really, to waste any more time debating this utterly fatuous and juvenile proposition.

78

LONG WORDS

Back in 2018, when my publishers, Aleph Book Company, asked me to announce the imminent release of my book *The Paradoxical Prime Minister*, I didn't want it to be just another book announcement. I was also conscious that a book on the prime minister by a writer who is also an Opposition MP would prompt some to assume right away that it was just a piece of political negativism, whereas I had made serious attempts to study the PM in depth. So to tackle both challenges, I tweeted: 'My new book, *The Paradoxical Prime Minister,* is more than just a 500-page exercise in floccinaucinihilipilification.'

The tweet had the desired effect—curiosity about the word, which means 'the act of estimating [something or someone] as worthless', spiked, and the tweet, if not the book, went on to acquire a wide readership. 'Floccinaucinihilipilification' caught on as a word to know, and for months afterwards I was subject to little kids being wheeled out by their parents to utter it aloud for my approbation.

A word as sesquipedalian as 'floccinaucinihilipilification' doesn't get used too often in everyday conversation, of course; it's memorable not because it's a word one employs every day, but precisely because of its rarity—and its length. When I first learned it, in my teens, I was wrongly told that it was the longest word in the English language, with twenty-nine letters. I later discovered there are many longer ones—but none that are quite as entertaining.

The 'official' longest word is actually one that no one uses, the full chemical name of the largest-known protein found in humans, titin, which contains 189,819 letters. If you disqualify that, the official longest word is 'pneumonoultramicroscopicsilicovolcanoconiosis'. According to the Merriam-Webster dictionary, this forty-five-letter monstrosity refers to an ailment 'caused by the inhalation of very fine silicate or quartz dust and occurring especially in miners'.

Ironically, however, language authorities—and doctors—tell us that it's not a term anyone actually employs to describe a real medical condition. The word was apparently made up for fun by the US National Puzzlers' League president, Everett K. Smith, in the 1930s, in an attempt to mimic medical terminology, but there really wasn't such an ailment at all, so not even doctors actually use it.

Interestingly enough, there is a real medical condition that, at thirty letters, comes pretty close: 'pseudopseudohypoparathyroidism', an inherited disorder that causes dwarfism (short stature) and a round face. It also pips 'floccinaucinihilipilification' to the longest real word post by one letter.

Till 'floccinaucinihilipilification' was invented by British undergrads with a fondness for Latin, the officially acknowledged longest word in the dictionary was 'antidisestablishmentarianism'. This was not an artificial coinage but referred to a real political stand in the UK, where people wanted to end the Church of England's status as the established church since the reign of Henry VIII, or dis-establish the Church—they were the disestablishmentarians. Those who opposed them, therefore, practised antidisestablishmentarianism. That particular controversy has long faded from the newspaper headlines, but the word persists in our dictionaries. That can't be said, however, for James Joyce, who in his novel *Finnegans Wake* famously invented words a hundred letters long. But since no one ever used any of them again, they never made it to the dictionaries!

Still, long words lend themselves to appreciation from various angles. For instance, what is the longest word in English without any letters repeated (these are known as 'isograms')? The answer is 'uncopyrightable', meaning a work that cannot be copyrighted. Or how about the longest word made up *only* of vowels? That's a term that comes from medieval music: 'euouae'. Somewhat less obscure, if not exactly overflowing with erudition, is the longest word that has *no* vowels—which, believe it or not, is 'tsktsk' an exclamation of disappointment or regret. To describe the kind of word 'tsktsk' is, however, you need a much longer word—for it's an onomatopoeia, a word that mimics a specific sound ('thud', for instance, or 'pitter-patter', are examples of onomatopoeia).

Of course, I have long objected to being described as someone who uses long words, a 'sesquipedalian'. Still, I do enjoy the fact that it's a word that contains six syllables and uses seven vowels. So it can't be all bad!

79

UNPAIRED WORDS

'I could see that, if not actually disgruntled, he was far from being gruntled.' So wrote the immortal humourist P. G. Wodehouse in his brilliant novel *The Code of the Woosters*. Wodehouse, as a stylist, revelled in breaking the canons of the English language, and in this sentence, he had done just that. He had poked fun at an unpaired word.

'Unpaired words' are those that, on the surface, appear to have a clear counterpart—an antonym—according to conventional English language patterns, and yet don't. What's peculiar about them is their prefixes and suffixes suggest the presence of a related opposite word, which, however, doesn't exist. Such words often emerge because the corresponding opposite term has become obsolete or might never have existed in the first place.

For instance, while you can describe someone as 'nonchalant', you can't call his opposite 'chalant', since that word doesn't exist—just as, when you're writing about someone who is 'dishevelled', it might seem logical that there should be a neat and well-groomed counterpart who is 'shevelled'—and there isn't. Similarly, you can be 'dismayed', but there's no counterpart of being 'mayed'. Something can be 'unwieldy', but it's opposite isn't 'wieldy'. These are unpaired words, of a specific type known as 'orphaned negatives'. An orphaned negative features a prefix or suffix, which gives the misleading impression that removing it would result in a word denoting the opposite.

Is it even possible to 'bunk' a rumour before debunking it? The short answer is 'no'. People can be reckless, but what exactly might it imply to be 'reck'? Interestingly, 'reck' existed once—as an archaic English term that denoted 'care' or 'thoughtfulness'. This word has its roots in Old English, where 'reccan' means 'to take care of' or 'to exhibit interest in'. Therefore, when someone is described as 'reckless', it implies they are acting without due regard for safety or caring about consequences.

'Unkempt' has its origins dating back to the fourteenth century, and 'kempt' appears to have arisen as a result of a process known as backformation, where the prefix 'un-'was removed to create its opposite meaning. An alternative account suggests that 'kempt' did exist but fell out of usage in the 1500s, only to re-emerge after a lapse of four centuries. So as a smartly-dressed person, you can be kempt, but not shevelled!

While we commonly declare we're 'overwhelmed' or (more recently) 'underwhelmed', it's rare to hear someone claim to be 'whelmed'. The term 'whelm', derived from the Old English word *hwielfan*, initially conveyed the idea of 'cover over', 'overthrow', or 'submerge completely', particularly in the context of ships facing rough waters. Consequently, 'whelm' formerly held a synonymous meaning to 'overwhelm', with 'over' serving as a redundant intensifier.

The term 'incorrigible' describes an individual who is resistant to correction and cannot, therefore, be changed or reformed. Consequently, 'corrigible' signifies something that is amenable to correction or improvement. Unlike its counterpart, 'corrigible' is typically applied to inanimate objects rather than individuals. Interestingly, 'corrigible' emerged in the fifteenth century, approximately a century after its opposite term, 'incorrigible'. The reason for its lack of popularity remains a mystery.

Of course you can emerge 'unscathed' from all this linguistic exegesis. The base word for 'unscathed' is 'scathe', which originates from an Old Norse word meaning to 'to cause harm' or 'inflict injury'. Consequently, an individual described as 'unscathed' remains untouched or uninjured. But a person who is hurt or injured is never referred to as 'scathed'. The base word survives in English usage only in the form of 'scathing', meaning 'very critical', as in a negative opinion or a 'scathing review'.

Back to P. G. Wodehouse, then: the master probably knew that his joke worked because 'gruntled' wasn't really an antonym of 'disgruntled'. But 'gruntle' was indeed a valid word, and interestingly, it meant to express discontent by grumbling or complaining, or the act of emitting small grunts. It's a unique case where the prefix 'dis-' serves as an intensifier, contrary to its more common role of negating or reversing the meaning of the word to which it is affixed. A disgruntled person is actually more intensely gruntled!

So when we employ unpaired words, let's mourn their dis(mayed) companions, languishing un(scathed) on the linguistic margins!

80

TALKING 'TURKEY'

We don't have too many turkeys around in either India or the UAE, but we have the word, if not the bird. The feathered creature called a 'turkey' is in fact native to North America. But *turkey* the word in English is named for the wrong country, not because its coiners didn't know their geography, but probably because Mamluk Turkish merchants in the fifteenth/sixteenth centuries sold wild fowl from Africa to European markets. This may have led English people to refer to the bird as 'turkey cock', which got contracted to 'turkey' for short. When, in due course, the British colonizers reached North America and settled in Massachusetts, they used the same term for the wildfowl they encountered in the New World—even though the American birds were a different species from the African ones!

Here's where the story becomes even more ironic: Turkey, the country, has no native turkeys. So no one there calls turkey *turkey—they call it a hindi!* The linguist Mark Forsyth theorizes that since the Turks knew the bird wasn't theirs, they 'made a completely different mistake and called it a hindi, because they thought the bird was probably Indian'. (Exotic creatures were, after all, associated with India.) The French made the same mistake—they originally called the North American bird poulet d'Inde (which translates to 'chicken from India'), and then abbreviated the cumbersome expression to dinde, which is how it is referred to in France even today. I am also informed that the turkey is named for India in a variety of languages, ranging from Catalan to Hebrew to Polish. To compound the irony, the bird might be hindi in Turkey, but in Hindi it's called ṭarki!

Indians may not be averse to getting the credit for the 'hindi' or the 'dinde', but Malayalis, of whom there are several reading this chapter, will no doubt be astonished to discover that the

Dutch language attributes the bird to them! The Dutch term for a turkey, kalkoen, is a contraction of Calicut-hoen, which literally means 'hen from Calicut' (today's Kozhikode). Some reverse labelling has occurred, though, thanks to Asian countries' experience of colonialism: Malaysians call the turkey ayam blander (Dutch chicken), while Cambodians term it moanbarang (French chicken). No one actually calls the turkey what it really is—American fowl!

It doesn't help, though, that the terms used by the Native Americans themselves for the bird are unpronounceable by the rest of us. The Aztec peoples are said to have domesticated the turkey a thousand years or more before the British colonists 'discovered' it, but they called the bird huehxolotl. Good luck popularizing that! The Native American tribes had their own words for the bird, of course; one I came across is the Blackfoot tribe's word omahksipi'kssii, which simply means 'big bird'. But it was white Americans who made the word 'turkey' stick—and in due course invented the expression 'talking turkey'.

The meaning of the phrase 'talking turkey' has evolved since it was invented in the early nineteenth century, from speaking agreeably or pleasantly, as people did over turkey at the Thanksgiving dinner table, to the contemporary meaning of blunt talk, frank speaking, or 'getting down to brass tacks'. To talk turkey is to discuss something frankly and in a practical rather than roundabout manner. When a businessman wants to get to the point and settle a business deal he might say to his potential partner, 'let's talk turkey'. This may well go back to the time when the English settlers needed to acquire turkeys from the Native Americans, who caught them in the wild and supplied them to the colonists. The story goes that the locals would ask, when they encountered a colonist, 'Have you come to talk turkey?'

The word 'turkey' also has a number of other meanings. While Americans enjoy their turkey, if they call you one, it is not a compliment—a 'turkey' is a stupid or inept person, rather like the bird. A show or a movie that is called a turkey is a flop. And then there's the expression 'to go cold turkey', meaning abruptly stopping a bad habit, such as consuming alcohol or taking an addictive drug. 'He used to drink half a bottle every day, but now he's gone cold turkey and won't touch the stuff.' Just don't go cold turkey on this book, though!

81

THE WATERGATE LEGACY

On a recent visit to Washington, I found the political chatterati all agog about the 50th anniversary of the break-in by Republican operatives at an office building in the United States capital named Watergate. The building on the Potomac riverside, still an iconic sight in Washington, also gave its name to the scandal that ensued, which led to the historic resignation of US president Richard Nixon. History knows the 1972 event and the resulting political drama by that name, Watergate.

But ever since the Watergate building lent its name to one of America's most memorable political scandals, '-gate' became the preferred suffix for all sorts of controversies, not just political ones. This was always a bit bizarre, since the Watergate scandal was neither about water, nor about a gate, but '-gate' still quickly devolved into the signifier of choice for scandals worldwide. This is why the world media was referring to former British prime minister Boris Johnson's indiscretions during the Covid pandemic—when, despite restrictions imposed on the general public, his staff and he were enjoying a tipple or three in the Downing Street garden—as 'Partygate'.

Indeed, that hardy source of not always reliable trivia, Wikipedia, tells us that over the past five decades there have been more than 200 -gate scandals. In the same year as President Nixon's resignation, 1974, the explosive news that French wine producers in the famed region of Bordeaux were adulterating their product was promptly dubbed 'Winegate'. When in 1975, the American multinational United Brands was exposed as having paid bribes to the president of Honduras to cut export taxes on fruit imported by United Brands from his country, the media breathlessly dubbed it 'Bananagate'. And the following year, when US congressmen were revealed to have accepted bribes from a lobbyist for South Korea, it was baptized 'Koreagate'. By then it was clear that the suffix had arrived, as a convenient shorthand for lazy headline-writers. Add '-gate' to anything and you had a catchy term in a crisis; 'gate' had become synonymous with 'scandal'.

The US media is particularly culpable, as are that country's politicians. In the 1990s, Republicans sought to get their own back after Watergate by trying to go after president Bill Clinton and his wife Hillary by tagging any accusation against them with the now-notorious suffix. The tactic didn't really work. It was tried at least a dozen times, as '-gate' was applied to one controversy after another by the Republicans to the Clintons, from 'Troopergate' and 'Travelgate' to 'Monicagate'—for Bill Clinton's affair with an intern, Monica Lewinsky. But they all failed to stick. And though Ms Lewinsky commanded oceans of media space, 'Monicagate' never really endured as a lasting term, with most references calling it 'the Lewinsky affair' or similar. Similarly, when American singer Janet Jackson, allegedly accidentally, bared her breast on live television during a concert, attempts to term it 'Nipplegate' failed since the excuse she gave—a 'wardrobe malfunction'—provided a far more memorable phrase than '-gate' did.

Still, the practice goes on, and Americans aren't the only guilty party when it comes to tagging every scandal with '-gate'. In Britain in 1992, the tabloid newspaper *The Sun* revealed salacious details from phone conversations between Britain's Princess Diana and her intimate friend James Gilbey, in the course of which the besotted lover affectionately called the Princess 'Squidgy'. The British media promptly seized on the nickname to dub Diana's scandal 'Squidgygate'. In India in 2014 we had 'Snoopgate', involving the Gujarat police tracking the whereabouts of a private citizen, allegedly at the behest of the powers-that-be in the state.

When the Democrats found themselves in opposition to then president Donald Trump, they persuaded the media to cover 'Russiagate', 'Ukrainegate', and more. But it's fair to say none of these '-gates' stayed open for long in our minds, perhaps because Mr Trump inflicted so many controversies on his nation that none retained a hold on the public imagination for long. Though Americans are once more riveted by a Trump scandal—the 6 January invasion of the Capitol by his supporters—the notorious suffix hasn't cropped up. Of course, 'January 6 gate' wouldn't work very well—it would be too hard to say.

Still, even fifty years after Watergate, no one should bet on the disappearance of the suffix when the next controversy arises. Some habits (both political and lexical) die hard!

82

WORDS FOR THINGS YOU COULDN'T NAME

The other day I acquired some notoriety (again!) by tweeting out a new 'Word of the Day'—*algospeak*, a noun, for words used on social media posts to avoid using other words that algorithms might identify as unsuitable or inappropriate and so filter. 'Algospeak' is a means of bypassing content moderation filters on social media platforms to avoid having your posts removed or down-ranked by content moderation systems. For instance, saying 'unalive' rather than 'dead'. Now you didn't know there was a word for that practice, did you?

Algospeak is a neologism—a new coinage invented for a recent need that didn't exist before—but English is full of very precise words for very common features we take for granted, words we didn't know even existed, and probably never felt the need for. For instance, *philtrum* is the vertical groove on your upper lip, below your nostrils. Bizarrely, seductive powers were once attributed to this common facial feature, so the Greek word for 'love potion'—philtrum—was used for it. Now when was the last time you went gaga over someone's philtrum?

Similarly, the smooth portion of the forehead between the eyebrows is called the *glabella*. Can you think of any time when you were so struck by someone's forehead that you rhapsodized over her glabella? Or examined his nails to baptize the crescent-shaped or half-moon whitish mark at the base of the fingernail a *lunule*? If you're besotted with someone's nails to the point that you need to name the marks on them, a ring might be more useful than a word!

Everyone ties shoelaces at some point or the other in their lives, but did you know there's a word for the tiny metal or hard plastic at the tip of both ends of a lace that reinforces it? It's called an *aglet*, a word that comes from the Latin acus, or needle—as does the word 'acute'. But the protective point or knob on the far end of an umbrella isn't called an aglet; it's a *ferrule* (which is also the term for the metal band at the end of a table leg).

I got these from the Merriam-Webster dictionary, a fertile source of such tales of word origins. Many, I would submit, are utterly useless for the non-specialist: I mean, who even needs to know that the indentation at the bottom of a moulded glass bottle is called a *punt*? Or that the strip separating the panes of glass in a window sash is called a *muntin*? All of us see window panes daily and notice the muntins, but have we ever felt the need to name them?

Then there are words that are essentially unnecessary because there are perfectly adequate alternatives to express the same thought. For example, we all know the infinity symbol, which looks like a figure 8 lying on its side. This figure-eight shaped curve has a name, the *lemniscate* symbol. But is there any reason why we can't just say 'infinity symbol'? The etymologists tell us that lemniscate comes from a Latin word that means 'with hanging ribbons'—an idea that's reflected in the symbol's graceful shape. But honestly, who cares? Or that little dot over the letters i or j is called a *tittle*. Why can't we just call it the dot? ('Tittle', by the way, does have other uses. If you want to express an idea of something utterly insignificant or minuscule you can use 'tittle'—'I don't care a tittle for what you think about the word lemniscate!')

Many years ago, the then US Defence Secretary Donald Rumsfeld famously uttered this gnomic wisdom: 'There are known knowns. These are things we know that we know. There are known unknowns. That is to say, there are things that we know we don't know. But there are also unknown unknowns. There are things we don't know we don't know.' I think it is quite safe to include most of these words in the last category—but to add, 'and there are things that it doesn't matter we don't know that we don't know!'

83

THE ANECDOCHE ANECDOTE

A college professor friend told me a fascinating story the other day. It seems that young impressionable female students sometimes convince themselves they are in love with their teachers, and usually teachers are able to gently disabuse them of such ideas by their own correct and professional demeanour. But one English teacher friend came up against an unusual challenge.

It started one day after class, when he received a WhatsApp message from one of his brightest students. 'I think I suffer from cingulomania when it comes to you,' it read. He was taken aback, first, because this was not a word he was familiar with in a long career of English teaching. Intrigued, he looked it up, and was even more taken aback. It meant 'an irresistible desire to hold someone in your arms'. There was even a hit song by that name, by Yoko Ono!

He replied calmly, telling her such messages were not appropriate. Swift came her reply: 'Sir, you suffer from myötähäpeä.' Now even more taken aback and forced to look it up, he discovered 'myötähäpeä: (n.) the feeling of shame or embarrassment you experience on the behalf of another person or a character when they do something stupid'. Now quite cross with her for her effrontery, he responded, 'And why am I supposed to feel any shame?' It's not just shame, she retorted, 'It's also embarrassment. And didn't you get embarrassed when I said I felt cingulomania for you?'

Defeated, the professor decided he would not encourage this exchange any further. But within a few minutes there popped up another message on his mobile phone: 'Sir, it's clear you're suffering from alexithymia, and I'm not.'

Intrigued despite himself—this was now the third word his student was using that he didn't know—the professor turned to his trusted dictionary once more. He learned that alexithymia was 'an inability to describe emotions in a verbal manner'. Offended, he replied stiffly: 'I have no difficulty expressing myself on any subject, thank you.'

He could almost hear her giggling as she messaged back: 'Not true, Prof! When it comes to me you're always struggling.' He took a deep breath. Soon enough this was followed by: 'I'm sorry about your alexithymia and myötähäpeä. Does't affect my affections in the least, though.'

'This has ceased to be funny,' he wrote in his most professorial manner. 'I really must ask you to stop this line of conversation forthwith. You are one of my best students. Don't spoil our relationship with this prattle.'

'Prof, I can't help myself,' the student replied. 'I'm really a nefelibata.' At this point the professor, more appalled by his own ignorance than the girl's forwardness, went online. 'The Portuguese word nefelibata literally translates as cloud walker,' he read. 'To be nefelibata means to think and live outside of preconceived boxes, to be true to your heart, and to follow your own path.'

The professor had never thought of the girl as anything but a brilliant young student, and so he thought the best way to defuse his mounting concern about this conversation was to pay her back in her own coin. 'You need to learn about the importance of tazenda,' he wrote. Tazenda referred to 'things better left unsaid; matters to be passed on in silence'.

But she was back soon enough: 'When I'm sitting in the front row of your class, I just want to wallow in opia.' The professor knew of 'myopia', but not of 'opia'. With a sigh, he looked it up too: 'Opia: the ambiguous intensity of looking someone in the eye, which can feel simultaneously invasive and vulnerable.' He started feeling uncomfortable, recalling her devoted gaze in his classroom, which he had thought was just a serious student paying attention. 'Please stop,' he wrote.

'Sir, why do suffer from mauerbauertraurigkeit?' She

asked. He turned wearily online. She was accusing him of 'the inexplicable urge to push people away, even close friends who you really like'.

This had to end. 'Stop, he said. There is no point participating in an anecdoche.' He believed she would get the message that this was 'a conversation in which everyone is talking, but nobody is listening.'

However, the matter did not end there. After a few days, the ensorcelled student responded: 'An anecdoche it may feel for you but not for me, for in my view tazenda rarely works. If it did, I would have skipped, not slipped, clues and cues to you through my messages, sitting on the first bench in the class, to overcome your callosity.'

Now the professor knew (because he had employed the term in the earlier exchange) that 'tazenda' referred to 'things better left unsaid; matters to be passed on in silence'. And 'callosity', like 'callousness', referred to the quality or state of being callous, usually marked by abnormal hardness and a lack of feeling or capacity for emotion. She was accusing him of being callous to her feelings by instructing her not to express them.

So far so comprehensible. But then the student went on: 'You must concede that you are deeply afflicted by philophobia with symptoms of atelophobia. I do feel like a shlimazel, I confess, as I wait for you to change your mind, with a feeling of desiderium that clings to the inner recesses of my soul. For instead of assuaging my thantophobia, you succumb to your own drapetomania.'

Defeated, the weary but curious professor turned to his dictionary. He didn't need to look up 'philophobia': he knew that meant the fear of love, since 'philo' always refers to the love of something (thus 'philosophy' is the love of knowledge) and 'phobia' is the fear of something (we have devoted an entire chapter in this book to phobias previously). But 'atelophobia' was a new one to him. He discovered that it meant 'an obsessive fear of imperfection'. Someone with this condition is usually terrified of making mistakes. So that was what the student thought his problem was!

But why did she feel like a 'shlimazel'? The word came from Yiddish and had entered the English language thanks to its use by American Jews. A shlimazel was a consistently unlucky person, afflicted by bad luck and misfortune. The professor began to feel bad for the girl. And her feeling of desiderium? That meant she was experiencing an ardent desire or longing, especially a feeling of grief for something lost. The professor began to feel distinctly uncomfortable.

She had wanted him to assuage her thantophobia: that meant she was suffering either fear of death (more commonly spelled thanatophobia), or the fear of losing someone she loved. But that was surely not his fault—it was her emotions that were inappropriate! And what was this 'drapetomania' she was accusing him of? He turned online: it meant 'an overwhelming urge to run away'. Yes, he conceded, in the face of her relentless linguistic onslaught, running away was indeed what he felt he needed to do.

He decided not to respond. But his silence did not end the conversation. Sure enough, an email came into his inbox a week later: 'My dear elusive professor, as you desperately weasel out of your gerascophobia, I must remain an eccedentesiast. For at the end of this clandestine correspondence, either you will end up with athazagoraphobia or I shall relinquish my anuptaphobia.'

He was offended to be accused of 'gerascophobia': he had no fear of ageing. But he felt amused that she called herself an eccedentesiast, one who fakes a smile. And she was saying that either he would end up forgetting her or she would give up her own fear of remaining unmarried or being married to the wrong person.

Suppressing a smile, he replied sternly: 'I have no time for such leucocholy!' That meant a preoccupation with trivial and insipid diversions. It was a rude reply, but this time he hoped that she would get the message.

84

TRADEMARKS IN LANGUAGE

One of the signs of our times is how many words we routinely use that properly aren't words, but trademarks. A popular expression these days is to say 'someone has drunk the Kool-Aid', meaning he has swallowed propaganda and is regurgitating an official line. But, of course, Kool-Aid is a commercial product, aiming to be a refreshing drink and not a substitute bromide for unpalatable views. When you describe someone as having drunk the Kool-Aid, you're actually running afoul of copyright law. And yet not being aware of the expression is worse, since it is used so often, accompanied by a knowing smirk.

Other such terms abound. If you cut your finger and ask for a Band-Aid, you're actually mentioning a specific company's trademark; strictly speaking, what you want is an 'adhesive bandage' or 'adhesive plaster'. There was a time when people would go to 'Xerox' something when they wanted to photocopy it. And today, of course, one is constantly Googling something when one is looking it up. (The process of using a word like this is known as anthimeria.)

Seeing your trademark becoming a commonly-used verb must be bliss for marketing people, but somewhat more worrying for their legal department. After all, too much success can hurt a trademark: the pharmaceutical company Bayer AG marketed acetylsalicylic acid under the trade name Aspirin, but taking 'aspirin' for a headache became such a common experience that courts ruled the name was now generic and could no longer be trademarked!

The same thing was in danger of happening to 'Polaroids'. This was the trade name for a special kind of camera: once you took a picture on it, the snapshots emerged from the apparatus and revealed themselves in minutes, even as you watched the images develop in front of your eyes. No one called these 'instant cameras', the generic name; they were simply Polaroids. Trademark protection might well have collapsed—except that the emergence of digital photography made the Polaroid experience much less magical. No one takes Polaroids any more.

That fate could still befall 'Rollerblade'—roller skates which have a single row of wheels down the middle of the skating shoe instead of two rows of wheels on the left and right of the skate. Kids who go rollerblading would never say they're wearing 'in-line skates', even if the wheels on their feet are made by another company. Rollerblade may soon find itself in the same position as aspirin—as a term so generically used that it can no longer enjoy trademark protection.

When you find yourself sniffing in public and in need of facial tissues, what do you ask for? If you're in America, the chances are you'd ask for a Kleenex, since that was the brand name that pioneered the facial tissue revolution and put an end to people sneezing ostentatiously into their pocket handkerchiefs. Elsewhere, of course, there are so many competing brands of facial tissues that 'Kleenex' doesn't have quite the same resonance as it enjoys in its original market in the US. Also in America, people in need of lip balm during the cold winters are quite likely to request a ChapStick—a product to counter chapped lips that has been around in the US since the late 1800s. It specifically refers to a brand of lip balm that is sold in a tube and applied like lipstick.

And then there are the ubiquitous 'Velcro' strips, the trademark of a company with that name which invented and patented hook and loop fasteners. The company made up the word 'Velcro' from combining two French words: velour (velvet) and crochet (hook). But we use the word indiscriminately even when the product we are using might have been manufactured by another company. Zipper, windbreaker, Scotch tape, escalator, hula hoop, yo-yo, and dumpster are other commonly used words that began life as trademarks, now long forgotten.

Many five-star hotels make it a point to include a Jacuzzi in their larger bathroom suites. But how many of us are aware that that, too, is a trademarked name? The concept of a hot tub was developed by an Italian company founded and run by seven Italian brothers in Northern Italy—named, of course, Jacuzzi.

For linguists, the process of a trademarked term becoming a generic term, such as Xerox being used to mean 'photocopy', is known as anthimeria. For the marketing folks, it's called genericization, generification, or even genericide (the last uses the suffix for 'murder'—thus 'fratricide' is the killing of a brother, and genericide refers to the 'killing' of a trademark through its becoming generic). Google, Xerox, Hoover, and B. F. Goodrich (who made zippers) have all fought genericide and either lost or are in the process of losing their struggles to protect their trademarks. (Google has a history of monitoring dictionaries ever since their name became a synonym for internet searching, arguing that generic use erodes the value of their brand. But they can't stop everyone who tells you to 'google it'!)

American life seems to lend itself readily to genericization. Aspirin, Band-Aid, ChapStick, cellophane, dumpster, escalator, granola, Jell-O, Jacuzzi, Kleenex, Laundromat, linoleum, pogo stick, Post-it, Q-tip, Rollerblade, Scotch tape, tarmac, thermos, Tupperware, TV dinner, Vaseline, Velcro, and yo-yo (in alphabetical order) all began life as trademarked brand names, but their copyright protection has long since collapsed in practice. This may perversely reflect the success of their marketing: they so entered public consciousness that people stopped thinking of any other term to represent the item or the function it performed. Let's face it: go through the list and practically no one would be inclined to replace those terms with their proper equivalents, which, in order, should be: headache remedy, sticking plaster, lip balm, transparent wrapping material, rubbish container, moving staircase, healthy breakfast cereal, edible jelly candy, whirlpool bath, facial tissue, wall-mounted automatic washing machine, synthetic floor covering, jumping toy pole with spring, sticky notes, cotton-tipped swab, in-line skates, clear adhesive tape, asphalt road surface, vacuum flask, plastic storage containers, frozen pre-prepared meal, petroleum jelly ointment, and a disc-shaped toy that moves up and down! So much easier to use the brand name as shorthand, isn't it?

But what surprised even me is the discovery of a number of commonly-used words that I didn't even know had ever been trademarks. 'Dry ice', for instance, was trademarked in 1925 by the Dry Ice Corporation, but the term 'dry ice' is now simply understood to mean solid CO_2. It lost its trademark in 1932. 'Heroin' is an even bigger surprise. The drug, derived from morphine, was named 'heroin', trademarked by Bayer in 1898 based on the German word *heroisch*, meaning 'heroic, strong'; but trademark protection was stripped from Bayer, a German company, during World War I in 1917. Similarly, the first modern 'trampoline' was built and trademarked in 1936, and comes from the Spanish for 'diving board'—*trampolin*. But no one uses any other word for a jumping board on which kids bounce up and down. The most astonishing is 'kerosene': it was registered as a trademark in 1854 by Abraham Gesner, who described 'kerosene' (derived from the Greek 'kerns' for wax) as a combustible hydrocarbon liquid. Only two companies were allowed to use the trademarked term, until eventually, and inevitably, kerosene became a victim of genericide.

A number of words are still trademarked, but they are so commonly used that they have passed into the language already. When you hear people talking of their 'adrenaline' pumping in moments of excitement or fear, they're using a trademark for epinephrine owned by Parke-Davis. Hockey and tennis fans are familiar with their sports being played on 'AstroTurf', an artificial ground-covering material trademarked by Monsanto. People mailing breakable items like to package them in 'Bubble Wrap', but if they call their inflated cushioning by that word, they are using the trademark of a company called Sealed Air.

When we heard of President Nixon promoting 'Ping Pong diplomacy' with China, we assumed that was merely the American expression for table tennis, just as they say 'soccer' for 'football', but it turns out to be a trademark owned by Parker Brothers. Even the generic name 'superhero' turns out to have been trademarked by DC Comics and Marvel Comics. If you don't believe me, google it!

85

CAN YOU UN-INVENT WORDS?

When I wrote the chapter about trademarks that have entered the English language and become so commonly used that their brand status is forgotten, I had overlooked the rare possibility of another problem—one that, I'm sure, affects many of my readers. What happens when a trademarked expression that has entered common use falls out of favour with its owners—and then decides to change?

That's exactly what has happened with X (formerly Twitter), the ubiquitous social media messaging app, which gained hundreds of millions of users around the world and entered into the language. Messages you sent on Twitter were called 'tweets', and when you sent them, you were 'tweeting'. Twitter became so popular in such a short span of time that in a few years from its appearance in 2006 it achieved what only a special short list of companies have accomplished: it entered the language.

As usual, news agencies were first off the mark. The Associated Press Stylebook adopted 'tweet' as an approved word in 2010. The following year, the top prize came Twitter's way, when the prestigious Oxford English Dictionary added 'tweet' as both noun ('I have issued a tweet,') and verb ('Will you tweet this story?') in 2011. America's equivalent, the Merriam-Webster dictionary, followed suit in 2013. The words twitter, tweet, tweeting, quote-tweet, and re-tweet were implanted into the lexicon of English speakers around the world.

Then, in less than a decade from that first breakthrough, came Elon Musk, who spent $44 billion to purchase Twitter. Within a year of his taking over he had decided to dispense with the name and familiar blue bird logo. 'Twitter, Inc.' is now 'X Corp'. The tweeting blue bird has been retired and replaced with a forbidding X against a black background. But what happens to words like twitter, tweet, tweeting, quote-tweet, and re-tweet? 'X' doesn't lend itself so easily to being transformed into a useful word—you can't say 'I have issued an X' or 'will you X this story?' or worst of all, refer to a recent post as 'my X' without sounding ridiculous.

Indeed, it's just as problematic the other way around. When someone speaking of a former partner or a divorced spouse refers to 'my ex', might they not be assumed to be referring to a post they've issued on Mr Musk's messaging platform?

The folks at X are still uncertain themselves. If they write you an email, your email in-box still shows you have a message from Twitter. If you try to do something on their site, you see evidence of their confusion: if you write a tweet, you still need to press a blue button to publish it, but it now says 'post' instead of 'tweet'. To re-post it, however, you still tap 'retweet'.

The Associated Press, which issued the famous Stylebook that first embraced 'tweet' as a word, analysed the problem by speaking to Nick Bilton, the author of a book on the phenomenon called *Hatching Twitter: A True Story of Money, Power, Friendship, and Betrayal*. His response: 'Language has always come from the people that use it on a day-to-day basis. And it can't be controlled, it can't be created, it can't be morphed. You don't get to decide it.' In other words, as long as people are speaking of tweeting and tweets, it doesn't matter what Musk wants or doesn't like, that will remain the term.

Interestingly enough, Twitter didn't start out as Twitter but as 'twttr'—without vowels, since it was inspired by SMS texting, which had severe limits on how many characters you could use. It changed to Twitter when the founders bought twitter.com from a bird fancier for $15,000, and the word took off. Initial uses even spoke of 'twittering' until 'tweeting' became the preferred word—until 2023, when Elon Musk decided to do away with it.

Imagine the irony: a billionaire spends $44 billion purchasing a brand-name that has entered popular usage and is an accepted part of the language, then decides he wants to change it, and people still continue to use it anyway! It seems there's one thing about language that money can't buy: you can't pay enough to un-invent words.

86

IDIOMS FROM GREAT STORIES

Have you sometimes wondered where some commonly used English idioms came from? I have, and many of them emerge from delightful stories. One of my favourites is 'turning a blind eye' to something, which means pretending not to notice it. This goes back to 1801, when the famed British Admiral Horatio Nelson, who had lost one eye, one arm, and one leg in battle (which in turn led to many Britons referring to the number 111 as a 'Nelson'), led a naval attack on the French under the overall command of Admiral Sir Hyde Parker in the Battle of Copenhagen. In those days instructions at sea were issued through flag signals from the commander's ship to his subordinates. With the battle going badly, Parker conveyed to Nelson, using flags, that he was ordered to disengage and retreat. Nelson, however, was not one for withdrawing; convinced that he could prevail if he pushed onward, he was disinclined to obey the command. Nelson is said to have viewed Parker's flags by holding the telescope to his blind eye, so he could truthfully claim not to have seen the signal—and sure enough, he went on to victory by pretending not to have received the order to retreat. Hence the expression 'turning a blind eye' was born.

Another British idiom is 'to read someone the riot act', meaning to order someone to stop what they're doing. This goes back a hundred years before Nelson, to the Riot Act passed by the British Parliament in 1714 to prevent unruly mobs from conducting lawless behaviour in the streets. At the time, the Hanoverian monarch of Britain, King George I, and his government were fearful of being overthrown by supporters of the Stuart dynasty he had replaced. The Riot Act forbade crowds of more than twelve persons from assembling; if they did so, the authorities would read them a portion of the Riot

Act, upon which they were obliged to immediately disperse and depart, or be arrested and imprisoned. The Riot Act has long fallen into disuse, but its legacy remains in the language: if someone is behaving in a manner that you find inappropriate, you can 'read them the riot act', meaning be tough with them in instructing them to cease and desist.

Even earlier in history lie the origins of the expression 'to spill the beans', or to reveal a secret. This comes from Europe's oldest democracy, ancient Greece, which decided important issues through a ballot of its citizens. Under the antique Greek voting process, citizens would vote by placing one of two coloured beans in a jar. White beans usually meant an affirmative 'yes' vote to a proposal, while black or brown beans meant a negative vote. Once the voting process was over, the beans in the jar would be counted and the result declared. But if somebody knocked the jar over accidentally and spilled the beans, the votes would be revealed prematurely, and the secret of how the election was going would be known before it was supposed to be announced. Hence, 'spilling the beans' became an expression for revealing confidential information, and the expression is used whenever anyone betrays a secret.

There's less history to two more common idioms, but good stories nonetheless. Have you told people you're feeling 'under the weather', without knowing where the term came from? The idiom is of nautical origin: when a sailor was feeling ill, especially in rough seas, he would go and rest beneath the front part of the boat, which would shield him from the worst effects of the conditions, since he would literally lie under the bad weather. That's why a sailor who was feeling sick would be described as being 'under the weather'—and the term began to be used by people who had never set foot on a boat!

And finally, if anyone accuses you of 'beating around the bush', they're using a phrase from British game-hunting. Bird-hunters used to literally beat bushes in order to draw out the pheasants hiding there—and only then did they get to the main purpose of the hunt: shooting the birds. So 'beating around the bush' means using a roundabout way to reach the real point. I'd better stop before I'm accused of the same thing!

87

NEWSPEAK OR GENOCIDE

In his famous 1946 essay 'Politics and the English Language', George Orwell wrote about how language was being corrupted in 'the defence of the indefensible'. When people were driven out of their homes, he wrote, it was euphemistically called 'transfer of population'; the killings of people eliminated by totalitarian regimes was described as 'elimination of unreliable elements'. Orwell developed this idea further two years later in his dystopian novel *1984*, when he wrote about how, in his fictional tyranny of the future, Oceania would have a new language called Newspeak, in which the 'Ministry of Love' was responsible for brainwashing the citizens, the 'Ministry of Truth' rewrote history to suit the Party, and the 'Thought Police' arrested those charged with 'thoughtcrime'. This brilliant and chilling novel gave the English language several new words, including 'doublethink'—simultaneous belief in two contradictory ideas, which, in *1984*, made critical thinking impossible for the citizens of Oceania.

Newspeak seems to be back with a vengeance in today's world. A piece in *The Economist* deplored Harvard students in October 2023 writing about the 'unfolding violence' in Israel without blaming Hamas's 7 October attack and the killings and kidnappings of Israelis. It was equally critical of those using the term 'collateral damage' for the innocent civilians, including large numbers of women and children, slaughtered in the Israeli bombing of Gaza. When Israeli soldiers actually shot some of their own citizens fleeing captivity, it was referred to as 'friendly fire'—is fire ever friendly to those at the receiving end of the firing?

The issue became even more complicated, however, when South Africa brought a case against Israel at the International

Court of Justice accusing Israel of committing a 'genocide' in Gaza. Israel vehemently denied committing genocide and accused Hamas of committing that very crime instead. So is this a case of misusing language? As with all geopolitical conflicts, it rather depends on which side you are on.

But first, to the basics: the UN Convention on the Prevention and Punishment of the Crime of Genocide defines it as acts intended 'to destroy, in whole or in part, a national, ethnical, racial or religious group'. The definition additionally amplifies the meaning of genocide as also including 'deliberately inflicting on the group conditions of life calculated to bring about its physical destruction, and inflicting 'serious bodily or mental harm', 'measures intended to prevent births', and 'forcibly transferring children of the group to another group'.

So which examples of recent history meet this definition? There is universal agreement on only two cases—the murder by Hitler's Nazis of 6 million Jews in the Holocaust, which led to the adoption of the Genocide Convention, and the wholesale massacre of perhaps a million ethnic Tutsis by Hutu militias in Rwanda in 1994. Indians and Bangladeshis describe the elimination of a million Bengalis by the Pakistani army in 1971 as a genocide (and Sheikh Mujibur Rahman used the marvellous neologism 'gonocide', since 'gono' means 'people' in his native Bangla), but few others concur. US President Trump described the Chinese oppression of its Muslim Uyghur minority as a genocide, but again found few supporters.

Opinion is similarly divided on whether the term 'genocide' can be applied to Israel's attacks on civilians in Gaza. Sympathizers of Israel argue that its actions do not meet the acid test: Israel does not 'intend' to destroy an ethnic group (the Palestinians), they say, but only the Hamas organization. Critics of Israel point to the words 'in whole or in part' and stress that Israelis are in fact exterminating all the Palestinian civilians in Gaza, which meets the definition. It would be hard for Israel to deny that it is 'deliberately inflicting on the group conditions of life calculated to bring about its physical destruction', and inflicting 'serious bodily or mental harm' on them—the conditions of life in Gaza are inhuman, and the continued bombing clearly does cause serious damage to both bodies and minds. But the International Court of Justice is clearly divided on whether what Israel is doing in Gaza meets the definition of genocide.

There is obviously no simple formula to apply. *The Economist* warned writers to avoid both 'the evasions of euphemism' and 'the temptations of exaggeration'. That is evidently easier said than done, especially in the era of social media, when strong language is unleashed more freely than in the days of responsible and carefully-edited publications. But the magazine was undoubtedly right to observe one thing: 'Crimes against language,' it observed, 'make it harder to describe crimes against humanity'. Whether you call what is happening a genocide or not hardly makes the suffering of non-combatants any more bearable.

88

PLASTIC WORDS

It turns out that no one is 'healthy' any more. The vernacular now contains words like 'cholesterol level' and 'blood pressure', 'pain threshold' and 'central nervous system', 'intestinal flora' and 'viral infection', 'inflammation of the upper respiratory passages' and 'antibiotics', 'side effects' and 'compromised breathing', 'heart failure' and 'kidney failure', 'potassium deficiency' and 'reduced resistance', and 'chronic illness' and 'acute illness'.' These terms were introduced into everyday language by disciplines such as health sciences, health economics, and health administration. As they transitioned into different contexts, their original technical definitions gave way to social interpretations in conversation.

In 1988, German linguist Uwe Pörksen introduced his groundbreaking work *Plastic Words: The Tyranny of a Modular Language*, detailing the rise and pervasive spread, particularly in the latter part of the twentieth century, of certain words that possess remarkable flexibility yet lack substantial meaning. These words are frequently exploited by those in positions of authority to sway opinions, making it imperative for us to remain alert when confronted with 'plastic words'.

One notable feature of plastic words is their integration into the global lexicon. Through their boundless universality, they create the illusion of bridging a void and meeting a requirement that was previously unfulfilled. Examples of such words in common usage include: development, welfare, resource, communication, progress, growth, information, strategy, process, exchange, planning, structure, value, and system. Although these words can't be easily defined, they wield a commanding presence that compels their acceptance and perceived indispensability. These words are often combined with one another or with supplementary terms to amplify their authority, as seen in phrases like 'resource development', 'information society', 'strategic relationship', 'problem-solving strategy', or 'communication process'. Certain words align themselves into sequences almost autonomously, forming a series of hollow but impressive-sounding terms. When 'problem' is paired with 'strategy' (a term from warfare), the phrase takes on lethal implications. One can see, therefore, how an almost-sentence such as 'problem-solving strategy' already is a fully stocked arsenal.

The transmission of words across boundaries is the most noticeable feature of our current use of language. Originating from the realms of science, technology, and mathematics, these terms carry an air of authority, often silencing alternative expressions. While they maintain precise and specific meanings within scientific or technological domains, their clarity diminishes upon widespread adoption. They colonize and reshape even the minute regions of daily living.

Words like 'innovation', 'integration', 'global', and 'security/safety' have become pivotal, versatile terms in the lexicon of the twenty-first century. Every day witnesses the emergence of new terminology aimed at conveying a sense of specialization. The 'good' and 'bad' gives way to the 'progressive' and the 'backward'. The 'modern', 'the current', 'the coming thing' replaces the 'old-fashioned', 'the anachronistic', the 'out-of-date', and 'ancient'. A word like 'communication' makes the alternatives—conversation, discussion and gossip—suddenly appear out of date.

But rather than being akin to a liberating tool, these words resemble a mechanism of domination. 'Both our public and our private use of language have thoroughly changed,' writes Pörksen. 'Aggression' didn't exist as a term of public discussion, and people felt no need of expert guidance in living their daily lives. A typical headline like 'Aggression: Why Even Small Children Bite and Hit' on the cover page of a magazine would not have been possible twenty-five years ago.

Plastic terminology has stealthily infiltrated our daily discourse, shaping our thought patterns. Pörksen's characterization of them as 'plastic' alludes to their malleability and susceptibility to misuse and manipulation. It's crucial to recognize the risks associated with using such terms, as they enable those in authority—be it corporations, governmental bodies, or other institutions—to manipulate their definitions. It colours the language of politics, of newspapers, and of public discussion.

And what is being left out? The phrase 'internet economy', for instance, should prompt us to ponder who is included in and excluded from this realm. In numerous countries worldwide, the elderly and economically disadvantaged face barriers to accessing the internet, a reality often overlooked in discussions about it. Are they in the 'internet economy' or out of it? When you stumble upon plastic words, don't just tiptoe around them: hack through the imprecision to challenge them with specific alternatives.

89

INKHORN TERMS

An inkhorn term is a word that is deemed to be unnecessary or overly pretentious. An inkhorn is an inkwell made of horn, and served as the container in which ink was stored. As such, it was an essential item for many scholars, and soon became symbolic of writers in general. The phrase 'inkhorn term' came into English in the sixteenth century, as a term of gentlemanly abuse, referring to words which were being used by scholarly or pedantic writers but which were unknown in ordinary speech.

The objection to inkhorn terms was a reaction against the sudden increase in English vocabulary derived from classical sources which was taking place at this time, with writers experimenting with language, inventing terms from Latin, Greek, and other languages to meet their needs, and thereby coming up with words that few understood. Though many of their creations and adaptations proved unsuccessful, being used once and soon forgotten—like 'illecebrous' to mean alluring or attractive—large numbers of others have survived into the present day. Words as common today as ingenious, capacity, mundane, celebrate, extol, dexterity, illustrate, superiority, fertile, contemplate, confidence, frivolous, and even verbosity were once denounced as 'inkhorn terms'.

Many of these so-called inkhorn terms, such as dismiss, celebrate, encyclopaedia, commit, capacity, and absurdity, stayed in the English language and are widely used today. Many other neologisms faded soon after they were first used; for example, 'expede' is now obsolete, although the synonym 'expedite' and the antonym 'impede' have survived. Why some new words survived while others faded or died out is a lexicological mystery to which there is no clear or satisfactory answer. Some were certainly awkward-sounding monstrosities that could never become anybody's regular usage; others merely provided rather highfalutin alternatives to existing words, like 'deruncinate', meaning 'to weed', though it was not clear why anybody weeding his garden would prefer to describe himself as 'deruncinating' instead! But there is real mystery to why some words survived and others did not: why, for instance, did 'commit' and 'transmit' become commonly used, but the shorter 'demit' be replaced by 'dismiss'? Why did 'impede' catch on but not 'expede'? Why did 'emacerate' get sidelined while 'emaciate' flourished? And if 'emacerate' sounded too pretentious, how did 'emancipate' survive?

Although the 'inkhorn controversy' was over by the end of the seventeenth century, the writers who disdained the use of Latinate words often could not avoid using other words loaned from non-English sources. In any case, many of the words coined in opposition to inkhorn terms did not remain in common use, while the supposedly pedantic words they sought to replace have lasted into the twenty-first century. A list of some of these words would prompt the modern English speaker to ask what the fuss was all about—why were these so objectionable? Here's a selection of words derided as 'inkhorn terms' that most of us use, or can and should use without pretension or embarrassment:

> Absurdity, adapt, agile, alienate, anachronism, anonymous, appropriate, assassinate, atmosphere, autograph, benefit, capsule, catastrophe, chaos, climax, conspicuous, contradictory, crisis, criterion, critic, disability, disrespect, emphasis, encyclopaedia, enthusiasm, epilepsy, eradicate, exact, excavate, excursion, exist, expectation, expensive, explain, external, extinguish, fact, habitual, halo, harass, idiosyncrasy, immaturity, impersonal, jocular, larynx, lexicon, lunar, monopoly, monosyllable, necessitate, obstruction, pancreas, parenthesis, pathetic, pneumonia, relaxation, relevant, scheme, skeleton, soda, species,

system, temperature, tendon, thermometer, transcribe, utopian, vacuum, virus.

In his 1623 eulogy to Shakespeare, playwright Ben Jonson praised the former's literary accomplishments despite his having 'small Latine, and less Greeke'. Jonson was writing when the 'inkhorn controversy' was raging, but he was right to praise Shakespeare's creativity in re-inventing the English language through linguistic innovations all his own. As the scholar, archivist, and cataloguer at the Folger Shakespeare Library in Washington DC, Sara Schliep points out, Shakespeare turned nouns into verbs (grace, season), created compounds (faire-play, pell-mell), and added prefixes and suffixes to make new words (courtship, dauntless, disgraceful). His works were the first in which such words as 'laughable', 'eventful', 'accommodation', and 'lacklustre' appeared. But as Schliep also notes, Shakespeare was far from alone in this lexical creativity. In fact, he was part of a trend in the fifteenth and sixteenth centuries that saw between 10,000 and 25,000 new words enter the English language. Inkhorns, in other words, were not just a bane for the language: they helped make it what it is today.

90

FOSSIL WORDS

I'm guilty, it seems, of using 'fossil words'. These are words deriving from older variations of the English language that have fallen out of common usage and have become largely obsolete, but which have nonetheless persisted in contemporary language. Fossil words occur in idioms or phrases where they have specific meanings, so their usage is restricted to that particular context. 'Turpitude', for instance, meaning depraved or wicked behaviour or character, is rarely employed in any other context than in the expression 'moral turpitude'. 'Turpitude' has essentially become fixed or fossilized alongside the term 'moral'. Hence it's a 'fossil word'.

Other examples abound. 'Fro' denotes a motion in the opposite or distancing direction; it's never employed, except within the idiom 'to and fro'. 'Yore' signifies a distant past, and it is not used except within the expression 'days of yore'. Other words like 'hither' (for here), 'amok' (describing violent, destructive, and unrestrained behaviour), 'ado', 'eke', 'beck', and 'knell' have become firmly embedded within various expressions, like 'come hither', 'run amok', 'much ado', 'beck and call', and 'death knell'—and are used nowhere else. Other fossil words include 'dint' (used only in 'by dint of'), 'fettle' ('in fine fettle'), 'kith' ('kith and kin'), and 'dudgeon', which only occurs in 'in high dudgeon', meaning 'very angry' or 'irate'. Slightly more complicated, 'wreak' is seldom used independently and is mostly associated with the expression 'wreak havoc'. In some medieval tales, individuals may occasionally 'wreak vengeance', yet the usage of 'wreak' today is predominantly linked with 'havoc'.

The noun 'pale', in its archaic sense, became ingrained in the English language during the eighteenth century through the expression 'beyond the pale'. The Pale referred to the area of

British colonial settlement in Ireland and had no correlation with the more familiar adjective indicating a lack of colour. The uncolonized Irish 'savages' lived 'beyond the pale', hence the expression, which over time, acquired a metaphorical meaning, signifying 'the boundaries within which one enjoys privilege, protection, or approval'. Consequently, being 'beyond the pale' implies being outside these protective boundaries.

'Kidnap' initially described the act during the 1600s and 1700s of abducting underprivileged children from cities in Great Britain and transporting them to British colonies in North America and the Caribbean, where they were sold into servitude. At the time 'napper' was slang for a 'thief'. By the twentieth century, 'nap' declined in usage, persisting solely in the term 'kidnap'. (The use of 'nap' to describe a brief daytime sleep is unrelated.) 'Bated' pertains to a decrease or weakening in strength. Therefore, 'bated breath' refers to a subdued and less forceful breathing, typically observed when influenced by emotions like awe or terror. Aside from the expression 'with bated breath' the word 'bate' had faded from common use by the late nineteenth century.

The term 'wend' traces its roots back to the thirteenth century and historically, just broadly signified 'to go'. But in contemporary English, the term 'wend' is only used in the phrase 'wend one's way' and would be archaic if used anywhere else. Similarly, the expression 'widow's weeds' once referred to a standardized outfit that widows were expected to wear in the eighteenth and nineteenth centuries, typically consisting of a black gown with wide white cuffs and, in public, a crepe veil, adhering to societal customs of that time. Historically, the word 'weeds' was commonly used alongside specific descriptors to denote the distinctive attire associated with a particular profession or social status: thus examples include terms like 'doctor's weed', 'shepherd's weeds', and 'monastic weeds'. In due course, the use of the term became limited to the attire known as widow's weeds. The use of 'weed' in the sense of 'garment' anywhere else has been uncommon since the nineteenth century!

Some fossils, known as 'born fossils', were formed from other languages. For instance, the word 'caboodle' isn't even English except for its use in the expression 'kit and caboodle', meaning 'everything available' or 'entirety'. That in turn evolved from 'kit and boodle', itself a fixed phrase borrowed as a unit from Dutch *kitte en boedel*. So like other fossils, 'fossil words' also require some digging up. Let's not disinter them from their resting places any more!

SECTION ELEVEN

LANGUAGE OF INCLUSION

Handbook on Combating Gender Stereotypes is a thirty-five-page document that details instances of misogynistic language used in Indian courts and describes how this hampers the impartial delivery of justice for women by perpetuating gender stereotypes. It unequivocally states that there is no place for regressive ideas about women in court rulings; judges must use alternate terminology to ensure their judgements are not only just, but gender-just.

91

EUPHEMISMS

One of the loveliest features of the English language is the prevalence of euphemisms, inoffensive words or phrases that substitute for words that might otherwise be seen as rude or insulting. The term has Greek origins: the noun *euphemismos* comes from the verb *euphemizein*, meaning 'to use auspicious words'.

The practice may have had religious origins. Since English was spoken in Christian countries where many took the commandment, 'Thou shalt not take the name of God in vain', literally, they felt using the word 'God' would be sacrilege. So they spoke instead of 'the Lord', 'the Creator', or 'the Almighty'—amongst the earliest known euphemisms. Those inclined to invoke 'God!' as an exclamatory term of surprise modified the word to 'golly' and 'gosh', while those who used 'Jesus!' similarly turned it to 'gee whiz', later reduced by Americans to just 'gee!' Saying 'damn' or 'hell' was also considered impolite for similar reasons, and the euphemisms 'darn' and 'heck' were born.

It's painful to speak of death or dying, so euphemisms abound for those words: 'pass away', 'depart', 'expire', 'decease', 'lost', 'gone', 'demise', 'met his Maker', 'is no more', 'is now in a better place', and 'resting in peace' are all ways of avoiding the direct mention of death. When official spokesmen during a war speak of 'collateral damage' instead of 'civilian casualties' you know that people have been killed who shouldn't have been. The use of figurative language through resorting to euphemisms softens the impact of an unpleasant subject. Thus a pet who is euthanized is 'put to sleep'. There are even jocular expressions like 'kick the bucket', 'six feet under', 'gave up the oxygen habit', 'sleeping with the fishes', and 'pushing up daisies', which may be used when you are talking about the death of someone you don't like or don't know, or joking about your own exit from the world.

How does euphemism differ from political correctness, which we have written about in previous chapters and which often vitiates the power and beauty of language? It does and it doesn't. Political correctness frequently relies on euphemisms: 'postal carrier' for 'postman', 'sanitation worker' for 'garbage collector', and 'person with disabilities' for 'handicapped person' are ways of avoiding the sexism or harshness of the older terms. It is always more humane to describe someone as 'developmentally challenged' rather than, as in the old days, as 'mentally retarded'. But political correctness goes beyond euphemism in avoiding, sometimes to a ridiculous extreme, expressions or actions that might be perceived as excluding, marginalizing, or insulting others, and in particular showing great sensitivity towards those who face discrimination or disadvantage because of who they are. Euphemism is usually more social and less convoluted.

Both euphemism and political correctness try to avoid words which might make others uncomfortable or be seen as harsh, impolite, or unpleasant. But whereas political correctness is always humourless in its grim determination to avoid all possible offence, euphemism is merely a way of softening the impact of what is said, usually for the sake of politeness, discretion, or social convention. Euphemisms are most often used to avoid embarrassment or awkwardness in speaking of subjects like death, sex, ageing, bodily functions, and getting fired from a job. Political correctness, as we have seen, is often embarrassing in its contrivances.

Among the euphemisms that commonly serve as polite surrogates for 'unmentionable' words previously used (here in brackets) are 'pre-owned' (for second-hand, or used); 'bun in the oven' (pregnancy); 'senior' (old); 'well-off' (rich); 'big-boned' (overweight); 'split' (divorce); 'enhanced interrogation' (torture); 'around the bend' (insane); 'thin on top' (bald); 'had one too many' (drunk); and 'water landing' (crashed into the sea). When you say someone is 'between jobs' rather than 'unemployed', or politely add, 'he was sent to a correctional facility' rather than that he was jailed, you are using euphemisms and being politically correct at the same time.

One final consolation: euphemism has room for humour. 'You're being economical with the truth' is a euphemistic way of telling a friend she's lying. 'May I be directed to the smallest room in the house?' avoids asking the way to the toilet. And 'sorry, my mind wandered' is better than confessing you weren't paying attention. Time for me to wander off!

92

WORDS YOU CAN'T USE AT STANFORD

America is where the entire notion of 'political correctness' was invented, so it comes as no surprise to learn that the distinguished private university in California, Stanford, has launched something called the 'Elimination of Harmful Language Initiative'. This is a multi-phase, multi-year project to address harmful language at Stanford, and respond to various requirements to express solidarity with victims of such language.

But what exactly is 'harmful language'? Slur words and insults—such as the notorious 'n' word about Black people—are of course known to everyone and for years have been unusable in polite company anywhere. But Stanford's project is considerably more far-reaching. 'The goal of the Elimination of Harmful Language Initiative,' says the Stanford announcement, 'is to eliminate many forms of harmful language, including racist, violent, and biased (e.g., disability bias, ethnic bias, ethnic slurs, gender bias, implicit bias, sexual bias) language in Stanford websites.'

It is necessary, Stanford says, to educate people about the possible impact of the words we use, even while it acknowledges that language affects different people in different ways. But it then proceeds to issue a thirteen-page list of words that should be avoided, and to suggest alternatives to them that it considers less offensive. It's impossible to do justice to the list in the space we have available, but here's a flavour of some of the terms you can't use at Stanford, along with an idea of what Stanford things you might say instead:

Instead of 'addict', for instance, you should consider using 'person with a substance use disorder'. 'Using person-first language,' Stanford helpfully explains, 'helps to not define people by just one of their characteristics.' Don't call a nervous person a 'basket case', since the expression 'originally referred to one who has lost all four limbs and therefore needed to be carried around in a basket'. Never call someone 'crazy', 'nuts', or 'insane', because that is 'ableist language that trivializes the experiences of people living with mental health conditions'.

Ableist? That term is defined too: 'Ableist language is language that is offensive to people who live with disabilities and/or devalues people who live with disabilities. The unintentional use of such terms furthers the belief that people who live with disabilities are abnormal.' Words like 'crippled', 'dumb', 'lame,' 'retarded', 'senile', or 'handicapped' are typical ableist terms, because they treat disabilities as deviations from the norm. They should be replaced by 'person with a disability'.

So far, so good. These are all words we use unthinkingly, in casual conversation, often for no other reason than that they are terms in widespread use and we employ them in unconscious imitation. None of us actually intends to speak offensively of people with actual disabilities when we use such terms as 'crazy' or 'nuts' not literally, but figuratively, to describe people whose conduct we think isn't acceptable or even normal. If you say someone had a 'lame' excuse you aren't actually trying to put down a person with a walking disability. But by using such words you are even unintentionally hurting people, Stanford feels, you must not do so. After all, political correctness must prevail.

Similarly with unconscious gender bias: some of us think 'chairman' is a position, like 'president', rather than a gendered term, and find 'chairperson' a clunky alternative, but we must use it to avoid excluding women chairpersons. Fair enough. Speaking of a mixed group as 'guys' is also wrong: the term 'reinforces male-dominated language'. And, of course, 'mankind' should be rendered 'humankind' if you want to include all human beings.

But some of Stanford's strictures seem far-fetched even to the most liberal and accommodative person. I often refer to someone who has completely missed the spirit of a conversation or an exchange as being 'tone deaf'—that is, that the person was completely insensible to the occasion in what he said or did. If I used that term in Stanford, it seems, I would fall afoul of the harmful language code, because of the same all-purpose objection: it's 'ableist language that trivializes the experiences of people living with disabilities'. I'm sorry, Stanford, but it's not: the speaker's intention surely has some relevance here?

It gets worse. Where Stanford goes really over the top is in its list of expressions that must be abandoned because they involve 'cultural appropriation'. Culturally appropriative language, the university explains, 'misuses terms that hold meaning to a particular culture' in a manner that 'often lacks respect or appreciation'. An example given is to 'bury the hatchet', an expression often used in English to describe a peace settlement, or just two people shaking hands to end a dispute. Stanford disapproves. 'Using this term is cultural appropriation of a centuries-old tradition among some North American Indigenous Peoples who buried their tools of war as a symbol of peace.' Excuse me, Stanford, but so what? All expressions in the language have come from somewhere—some from my culture, some from yours, and some from Native Americans (no one, rightly, calls them 'Red Indians' any more, thank God). Who on earth (or under it) is one offending by saying 'bury the hatchet'?

Many of us refer to a person, especially one slightly older or somewhat more senior in position, by the term 'chief'. It's semi-jocular, implying friendship, familiarity, and yet a degree of respect. Not at Stanford, apparently. Calling a non-Indigenous person 'chief' trivializes both the hereditary and elected chiefs in indigenous communities. Calling an indigenous person 'chief' is a slur. Excuse me while my eyes widen in disbelief.

You can't describe an enraged person as being 'on the warpath' at Stanford; you have to replace the expression with 'on the offensive'. Why? Because it's 'cultural appropriation of a term that referred to the route taken by indigenous people heading toward a battle with an enemy'. Even the colourful popular expression to describe a system without clear leadership—'too many chiefs, not enough Indians'—should be replaced, if Stanford has its way, by saying the establishment in question has 'a lack of clear direction' or 'too many competing ideas'. Why? Because it 'trivializes the structure of indigenous communities'. It does no such thing—it just uses an imaginative metaphor to depict an idea that might sound boringly banal otherwise.

This respect for cultures other than 'mainstream' American culture can border on the farcical. Stanford doesn't want anyone to refer to a junior official as the 'low man on the totem pole'. You guessed it: that 'trivializes something that is sacred to indigenous peoples'. But hold on, there's more: 'Also, in some First Nation communities, being low on the totem pole is actually a higher honour than being on top.' And then, almost as an afterthought: 'The term also reinforces male-dominated language.' Three strikes, and the low man on the totem pole is out!

Stanford won't even let me refer to someone as a guru—as in, 'on tech matters, he's my guru'. Tutu-tut, clucks Stanford: 'In the Buddhist and Hindu traditions, the word is a sign of respect. Using it casually negates its original value.' Oh, come on!

I genuinely believe that showing sensitivity to people in one's use of language is generally a good thing, and is often the decent thing to do. But where such attempts to eliminate harmful language go wrong is in denying the possibilities of language itself—its wonderful, eclectic habit of borrowing words, expressions, and images from around the world and incorporating them into everyday use, imparting freshness and colour to our conversations. If Stanford succeeds in getting us to watch our words to the point of self-censorship—and worse still, to incite a new kind of language policing on campus to object disapprovingly to every unintended slur—it will do real damage to the organic process by which languages are used and grow. And English itself will be all the poorer for it—at least at Stanford University.

93

THE OXFAM LANGUAGE RULES

No doubt prompted by Stanford University's 'Elimination of Harmful Language Initiative', under which the famous American university issued a list of words that people should avoid using because they are 'ableist', 'ageist', or show 'gender bias', a reader sent me a new Inclusive Language Guide issued by the British charitable agency Oxfam.

A glance at the guide suggests that the urge to get people to bite their tongues rather than use language which some may find 'politically incorrect' has now crossed all reasonable limits. Oxfam has urged its employees to avoid the terms 'mother' and 'father' and instead use 'parent'. It warns its staff to 'avoid assuming the adoption of gendered roles by transgender parents'. According to the guide: 'If trans parents have a preferred specified gender role, such as "mother" or "father", this should be respected. If unsure, it is more inclusive to use "parent".'

Including 'mother' and 'father' among its list of potentially offensive terms, however, defies simple common sense. These are among the most basic terms employed by the human race; there is no language on the planet that does not have words for 'mother' and 'father', depicting the primordial relationships a child encounters upon entering the world. Hilariously, Oxfam prefers the very words 'male' and 'female' to be replaced with AFAB and AMAB ('assigned female at birth' and 'assigned male at birth'). Isn't this taking political correctness too far?

Oxfam argues that 'the important principle here is to be inclusive in the broader sense by describing people as 'parents'. Of course, it also concedes that 'if individual parents have a preference for a role name, [staff may] respect their choice.' But it goes on to urge people to replace the term 'expectant mothers' with 'people who become pregnant'. How many such 'people' in the world would actually protest being called 'expectant mothers'?

I am not objecting to every point in the ninety-two-page Oxfam document, which is available online. It makes sense for a philanthropic body working around the world to guide staff to be sensitive to issues of race, gender justice, sexual diversity, and women's rights, disability, physical and mental health, migration, and the linguistic legacy of colonization, which left behind a number of terms whose unconscious use might indeed hurt people. Oxfam also warns employees to be conscious of words and phrases that might be considered 'discriminatory' or 'that have been used historically to oppress certain people or groups'. Thus it makes sense to say 'sex worker' instead of 'prostitute', or 'humankind' in place of 'mankind'.

But even innocent, commonplace everyday words are proscribed for reasons that seem absurd. For instance, Oxfam encourages its staff not to say 'attitudes' or 'behaviours' but to replace them with 'social norms, social beliefs, or collective beliefs'. Excuse me? Equally ridiculous is the exhortation not to use the word 'headquarters' because it 'implies a power dynamic that prioritizes one office over another. In the context in which we work the implication is very colonial, reinforcing hierarchical power issues.'

Oxfam's hyper-sensitivity to anything that might cause offence extends preferring the use of the terms 'menstrual products' in place of 'sanitary products' or 'feminine hygiene products' because such seemingly neutral terms imply 'that periods are in themselves unclean'. You can't say 'ethnic minority' because it 'places the emphasis on that ethnicity being a minority or having less power in a particular context'; instead, you must say 'minority ethnic person'. The guidebook also states that one should not speak of a 'migration crisis', only of 'migration as a complex phenomenon'. (Both these are examples of 'splitting hairs', except that perhaps that term itself would be outlawed as being offensive to bald people!)

Don't get me wrong: I agree with Oxfam that inclusive language is important. I accept Oxfam's justification that the guide intends to help employees 'communicate in a way that is respectful to the diverse range of people with whom we work. We…won't succeed in tackling poverty by excluding marginalized groups'. But the inclusion of silly prohibitions that can easily be caricatured risks undermining the more worthwhile ideas. It's important to know when you've gone too far. Stop!

94

THE LANGUAGE OF EQUITY

After my chapters about Stanford's and Oxfam's language guides, one more entrant in the fray is the environmentalist group Sierra Club's Equity Language Guide. This goes even farther, discouraging the use of the words 'stand' (since not everyone can stand), blind (insulting to those unable to see), and crazy (offensive to mentally challenged people). This is what's known as 'people-first language', under which 'everyone is first and foremost a person, not their disability or other identity'.

The guide is one more document that seeks to cleanse people's use of the English language, in order to eliminate suggestions of bias, racism, or exclusion. But the Sierra Club goes too far in dismissing 'urban', 'vibrant', and even 'hardworking' as reflecting subtle racism, and banning even 'empower' as condescending! Speaking of 'the poor' is classist (you have to say, apparently, 'people with limited financial resources'.) And what's wrong with 'migrant'? The club doesn't say, but it disapproves.

Equity-language guides are all the rage these days, and every university, non-profit institution, and civil society organization seems to be sprouting one. They all seem to be based on the same activist template but vary in their degrees of intolerance, each group seemingly striving to find something offensive that the others didn't think of. It seems to me unlikely that such hyper-sensitivity actually exists amongst ordinary people, even in 'woke' American society. How many people would follow the dictum of the San Francisco Board of Supervisors to replace 'felon' or 'accused criminal' with 'justice-involved person'? It is making a mockery of the language, and of common sense.

Interestingly enough, a backlash has begun. The general public reacted just as badly as we did in this space to Stanford's Elimination of Harmful Language Initiative, and the criticism of the university was so severe that it has scrapped the initiative altogether—not for being absurd and unnecessary, but, according to the university's announcement, for being 'broadly viewed as counter to inclusivity'.

But the truth is that the language of equity has already crept into the conversation and writing of most of us who pride ourselves on our linguistic common sense. In my childhood I was comfortable with the gender distinction between 'actor' and 'actress'; today applying the word 'actor' to a woman still jars my sexagenarian sensibilities, but I use it nonetheless, for fear of giving offence otherwise. Similarly, 'chairman' was seen as a gender-neutral term, but the clunky and non-sexist 'chairperson' now rules the roost.

Perhaps nothing is really lost in these changes, especially if something is gained in the self-respect felt by the beneficiaries—female actors and chairpersons, in these instances. But it worries me that over-sensitive experts have established a new orthodoxy in language without anyone really noticing. In America, some changes were politically needed: 'Negroes' became 'Blacks' and now is being overtaken by the more generic 'people of colour'. Of course, one must address people as they wish to be addressed, but the desire to avoid giving offence sometimes deprives language of the exactitude and colour that communicates most effectively. Would you prefer to learn that X was imprisoned, or that he was 'a person experiencing the criminal-justice system'? What on earth does that even mean?

The truth is that the path to 'equity language' is paved with good intentions but takes people to a place of euphemism, fuzziness, and disconnection from reality. Sometimes blunt and direct is better than inoffensive and circumlocutious. Vivid writing can sometimes hurt—to say 'that leader is blind to the problems of us ordinary people' or that 'he was crippled by indecision' or 'paralysed by fear' evokes a specific impact on the reader that more 'acceptable' alternatives to blind, crippled and paralysed would not. Intent matters: when it's obvious an expression is a figure of speech rather than a deliberate slur, it cannot be equated to someone deriding an entire community with a nasty term (like the 'n' word in America for black people or the 'P' word in Britain for brown ones).

Avoiding insults, taking care not to inadvertently slur whole communities, and treating others with dignity in your speech are all valuable practices in any decent society. But you don't have to destroy the power and beauty of your language to ensure that.

95

SEXIST LANGUAGE

A few months ago, India's Supreme Court took a step toward ridding court rulings of patriarchal language by issuing a *Handbook on Combating Gender Stereotypes*. The thirty-five-page document details instances of misogynistic language used in Indian courts and describes how this hampers the impartial delivery of justice for women by perpetuating gender stereotypes. It unequivocally states that there is no place for regressive ideas about women in court rulings; judges must use alternate terminology to ensure their judgements are not only just, but gender-just.

There's little doubt that the English language reflects an ingrained sexism. It is evidence of the cultural biases that have influenced people's attitudes over time, and it's important the court recognized its own role in perpetuating sexism through language. For instance, judgements in sexual assault cases have described a female victim as a 'woman of loose morals', 'a seductress', an 'adulteress', someone given to 'promiscuous' behaviour, or even as a 'slut'. But it's not negative language alone that the handbook decries. Even expressions like 'ladylike', or 'dutiful wife' (or 'good wife' or 'obedient wife') are described as 'incorrect' because of their 'patriarchal undertones'. Traditional gender roles for women in society are reflected in such language, implying that by using such phrases, the judge endorses the view that women are best suited to look after the home and care for the family and that deviations from this 'norm' are frowned upon.

The handbook warns of the larger impact of these societal stereotypes that entrench patriarchal roles for women. Judges have no business using language that seemingly compels women to conform to conventional roles, serve as chaste custodians of their family's honour, and 'dutifully' undertake household chores, child-rearing, and care for the elderly. The handbook says such language is not just anachronistic but 'unconstitutional', and should be avoided. Judgements should be impartially decided and written based on the law rather than on 'preconceived notions about men and women'. In many instances, the simple word 'wife' would be 'preferred'.

In his foreword to the handbook, the chief justice makes it clear that he hopes to remove patriarchal language from the court's legal parlance. A detailed glossary of terms lists regressive stereotypes for women, and offers alternative words that judges should use in their rulings. Misogyny is inherent in some judicial pronouncements, whereas the Supreme Court should foster an environment of 'gender equality' and work toward a 'gender-just environment'. Euphemisms like 'eve-teasing' should be dropped for the more accurate 'street sexual harassment'. References to a 'fallen woman' or to 'inherent characteristics' of women are nothing but stereotypes, the handbook argues. It differentiates between 'sex' and 'gender'; while the former is a biological attribute of an individual, the latter refers to socially constructed roles for girls and women (and for boys, and men for that matter), which should be eschewed. Gender stereotypes and traditional ways of 'harmful thinking', the handbook says, 'impact the impartiality and the intellectual rigour of judicial decisions'. Two years earlier, the then-attorney general K. K. Venugopal had told the Supreme Court that there is a need to educate judges on gender sensitisation, as language 'objectifying women is a gross trivialization of [their] distress'.

The handbook is an unprecedented initiative by the Supreme Court and should be welcomed. Though it is aimed at judges and the legal fraternity, the court expressed the hope that by taking on the issue of gendered language, it would set an example for society at large and be a 'catalyst for change'. 'Words influence society's attitudes' and 'inclusive terms will break traditional harmful thinking,' the handbook points out.

Three months after the handbook came out, India's Ministry

of Women and Child Development in turn issued a *Guide on Gender Inclusive Communication* for administrators and educational institutions. Though somewhat briefer—the guide has just over sixty words and phrases—it is sharply prescriptive in its desire to 'percolate a language which is more inclusive and just'. Amongst its recommendations are to use 'owner' instead of 'landlord or landlady', 'humankind' or 'humanity' instead of 'mankind', 'workforce' or 'workers' for 'manpower', and 'toughen up' instead of 'man up'. Releasing the guide, Minister Smriti Irani declared that 'the power of language has been embellished by empathy and equity because of this guide'. Let's hope more government institutions around the world follow suit.

SECTION TWELVE

MASTERS OF MIRTH

If you travel less than me and your tsundoku pile is on your bedside table, chances are that you are a *librocubicularist*—someone who likes to read in bed.

96

CAPTAIN HADDOCK'S EXPLETIVES

When my twin sons were little, and just beginning to discover the allure of strong language to let off steam, I managed to steer them away from the offensive terms they were hearing around them in the school playground by getting them to use more wholesome alternatives. My trick was simple: I had introduced them to my favourite series of comics by the Belgian cartoonist Hergé, *The Adventures of Tintin,* masterfully translated into English. Tintin is a boyish journalist in plus fours, with a quiff in his hair, and a white-furred dog, Snowy, trotting everywhere by his side. His mate in most of his adventures is a bluff, hard-drinking, pipe-smoking, and often coarsely cynical merchant mariner, Captain Archibald Haddock. And like most seafarers, the good captain, a short-tempered and emotional character frequently banging into objects, stubbing his toe and suffering other misfortunes, was given to venting his fury, frustration and rage frequently, in a string of expletives. A lesser cartoonist might render Captain Haddock's colourful curse words with a series of asterisks and punctuation marks—like this: *!**?!!—but Hergé was far too clever and original for such an uninspiring device. Where others needed such a technique to mask words too impolite (or too impolitic) to print, Captain Haddock's expletives were rendered by Hergé in full—but they involved neither profanity nor scatology, the usual resort of the angry, nor crude references to sexual activity. Instead, they stretched the vocabulary of Hergé's devoted young readers.

It is said that the idea occurred to Hergé in 1933, shortly after which the Four-Power Pact had been signed by France, Japan, the United Kingdom, and the United States, he had overheard a trader use the word 'four-power pact' as a curse. Hergé, who obviously could not use any swear words since his audience mainly consisted of children, was impressed by this use of an 'irrelevant insult'. He decided to try the same expedient for his colourful mariner. Why not, Hergé reasoned, have the cursing Captain Haddock resort to obscure or esoteric words that were not actually rude or crude, wouldn't offend his readers (or their parents), but could constitute a running joke? Haddock would be shown apoplectic with fury and venting his rage in expletives—but these would be innocent, irrelevant words projected as if they were very strong curses, whereas in fact they were perfectly harmless terms.

The device first appeared in the Tintin adventure comic *The Crab with the Golden Claws,* when Captain Haddock charges a party of Berber raiders in anger, yelling 'jellyfish', 'troglodyte', and 'ectoplasm'. Hergé's idea, of using 'irrelevant insults' as if they constituted colourful expletives, proved an instant success and he continued the practice in subsequent books, making these inoffensive exoticisms a defining characteristic of Haddock's outbursts. It is said that Hergé, much taken with his own idea, started collecting words for Haddock's use, searching dictionaries to unearth ever more useful ones.

Inspired by Hergé, I taught my little boys that these were the appropriate words to use when they were angry or annoyed with their friends, and that the words they were hearing hurled around the school playground were beneath them. Thus the United Nations International School in New York in the early 1990s was treated to the sight of two little Indian boys channelling their inner Captain Haddock in moments of anger and letting fly the most colourful expletives their friends had ever heard: 'bashi-bazouk', 'visigoths', 'kleptomaniac', 'sea gherkin', 'blundering Bazookas', 'ten thousand thundering typhoons!' and 'billions of bilious blue blistering barnacles!'

Hergé's Haddock had expanded my own vocabulary: while some of his words were hardly exotic ('pockmark', 'Fuzzy Wuzzy', 'bragger', 'coconut', 'miserable slugs', and 'parasites' failed to pass muster), and some really were insults ('maniacs', 'nincompoops', 'nitwits', 'scoundrels', 'pinheads', 'bandits', and 'ruffians' were actually rude and couldn't be used), others stretched the limits of my, and my sons', knowledge: 'anacoluthon', 'cercopithecuses', 'ectomorph', and 'pyrographer', for instance. Some were just clever: 'abominable snowman', 'miserable molecule of mildew', 'iconoclast', 'platypus', 'Popinjay', and 'orang-outangs' were effective zingers. Using 'logarithm' as an insult was devilish (in the pre-Google era, it didn't occur to Hergé or me to pair it with 'algorithm'!). Sometimes, though, Hergé and I had to part company: his Haddock used 'Polynesians', 'Aztec', and 'carpet sellers' as insults, which was simply racist, and even more bizarrely for me, thought 'vegetarians' worked as a negative epithet!

My sons, both writers, have refined vocabularies these days. I now have a six-year-old grandson. I hope one day I'll hear him uttering Haddockisms too!

97

WODEHOUSIAN WORDS

Those who follow my literary life are aware of my boundless admiration for P. G. Wodehouse (1881–1975), the great British comic novelist, playwright, and lyricist, whom I consider to be an absolutely unrivalled craftsman of English prose. But since this book is not about literature, I will refrain from sharing with you the many examples of Wodehousian style and technique that justify my judgement. Instead, since our subject is language, I will just confine myself to some of the words the master invented, or brought into circulation (a habit he shared with William Shakespeare, no less), to our endless delight. Of course, it's much more fun to encounter these words in his novels, but this is just to whet your appetite!

Wodehouse wrote ninety-five books, and authored more than thirty plays and musical comedies, and more than twenty film scripts. His impact on the English language was considerable. The Oxford English Dictionary, for example, contains 1,756 quotations from Wodehouse to explain word usage. It confirms he invented multiple common expressions, like the word '*cuppa*' (as in 'Come and have a cuppa', *Sam the Sudden*, 1925) and '*fifty-fifty*' ('Let's go fifty-fifty', *Little Nugget*, 1913). And his famous character Jeeves, the super-smart valet to the feckless Bertie Wooster, is entered in the dictionary as a generic noun. A 'Jeeves' means 'a valet or butler especially of model behaviour'.

The most-quoted Wodehouse invention must be *gruntled*. It's from his brilliant *The Code of the Woosters* (1938): 'He spoke with a certain what-is-it in his voice, and I could see that, if not actually disgruntled, he was far from being gruntled.' Now the word 'disgruntled' never had an antonym before, but here's a mock-serious adjective meaning 'satisfied' or 'contented'.

Wodehouse's upper-class idlers, members of the Drones Club,

were all steeped in alcohol, but the author did not describe them merely as inebriated. In his 1927 book *Meet Mr Mulliner*, Wodehouse had already anticipated new words for 'drunk': 'Intoxicated? The word did not express it by a mile. He was *oiled, boiled, fried…whiffled, sozzled, and blotto*.' His characters' lexicon for those who have consumed too much fire-liquid also included: *awash; lathered; illuminated; ossified; pie-eyed; polluted; primed; scrooched; stinko; squiffy; tanked;* and *woozled*.

And, as befits a master of comic-hall theatre, Wodehouse had a great ear for onomatopoeia. At the age of twenty-two, he published a story which used a new word for the sound of a cricket ball hitting a bat: 'There was a beautiful, musical *plonk*, and the ball soared to the very opposite quarter of the field.' (From *Tales of St. Austin's,* 1903)

The same talent is evident in this description from *Blandings Castle* (1935) of a pig eating: 'A sort of gulpy, gurgly, *plobby*, squishy, *wofflesome* sound, like a thousand eager men drinking soup in a foreign restaurant.' Neither 'plobby' nor 'wofflesome' will be found in your home dictionary, but they marvellously convey a greedy and ill-mannered creature tucking in. Apply it to some of your acquaintances at their next meal?

When someone speaks sharply, it's hard to think of a more original way of describing it than this, from the 1930 novel *Very Good, Jeeves*: 'When not pleased Aunt Dahlia, having spent most of her youth in the hunting-field, has a *crispish* way of expressing herself.' Also in *Very Good, Jeeves*, came a new way of saying things were 'all right' or 'fine': 'All you have to do,' I said, 'is to carry on here for a few weeks more, and everything will be *oojah-cum-spiff*.'

The Oxford English Dictionary includes at least one Wodehousian invention that didn't last: 'snooter', meaning to 'harass' or to 'snub', ('My Aunt Agatha wouldn't be on hand to snooter me for at least another six weeks', *Inimitable Jeeves,* 1923) never really caught on and is listed in OED with the parenthesis 'Only in P. G. Wodehouse'. But some Wodehousian words seem very contemporary. *Zing*, for instance, inserted to convey 'the sudden advent of a new situation or emotion', as the OED puts it, could work today but actually appeared in the 1919 book *Damsel in Distress*: 'The generous blood of the Belphers boiled over, and then—zing. They jerked him off to Vine Street [police station].'

Wodehouse's linguistic influences were varied. There was school slang: 'biff' for hitting someone ('he biffed the bounder') sounds like a word he might have picked up at school in Dulwich College. We all know longish words can be abbreviated, but some never were till Wodehouse took to them. Thus 'perspiration' took a new form in *The Inimitable Jeeves* (1923): 'The good old *persp* was bedewing my forehead in a pretty lavish manner.' Referring to an archbishop as 'archbish' may have come straight out of irreverent public school lingo. And unusual slang can be made respectable: the word 'potty', not for a child's toilet but for being slightly off one's rocker, became a noun in Wodehouse's hands: 'It was not primarily his *pottiness* that led him to steal [a pig called] the Empress.'

But beyond school, Wodehouse's early years in lower-middle-class suburbia may have helped influence his vocabulary. Writer and editor Robert McCrum theorizes that it was the atmosphere of suburban life, including commutes by Tube to the city, that prompted Wodehouse's use of '*giving someone the elbow*', in the sense of pushing someone aside, from his experience of taking a commuter train to the city. Suburban slang may also have prompted Wodehouse's use of '*chassis*' for the human body ('he had the chassis of a heavyweight'), and jocular descriptions of someone's beard as a '*fungus*' and moustaches as '*soup strainers*'.

The Edwardian era was when Wodehouse entered his twenties and came of age, and a lot of his words are redolent of that era: 'gave me the pip' (irritated me); 'restored the tissues' (had an alcoholic drink); 'off his onion' (unbalanced); and 'pure applesauce' (fanciful nonsense). Bertie Wooster and his fellow Drones used a lot of Edwardian slang—like 'cove' for a person, 'blighter' for someone you are referring to negatively, 'snifter' for a small drink, and 'pip pip' instead of goodbye. (Also, other equally Wodehousian words: 'In that case,' said Archie, relieved, 'cheerio, good luck, pip-pip, toodle-oo, and good-bye-ee!')

Then Wodehouse migrated to the United States and the prevalent terms infected his writing: zippiness, hotsy-totsy, ritzy, dude, lame-brain, zing, and rannygazoo all feature in his novels. But the most famous Wodehousian words are inimitably English: 'right ho', to express agreement or acquiesce ('She right-hoed like a lamb'); 'rummy' (not for a card game but as a synonym for 'odd' or 'strange', as in 'she has a rummy effect on me'); 'shimmy', to move lightly and swiftly ('Jeeves shimmied in'); 'bally', as a softer form of the mildly offensive 'bloody' ('the whole bally scheme has blown a fuse'); 'squiggle-eyed', to view askance ('There is a certain stage in the progress of a man's love when he feels like curling up in a ball and making little bleating noises if the object of his affections so much as looks squiggle-eyed at him'); or 'nosebag' for a meal (a British term for the canvas bag used for feeding animals by fastening it over their snouts, used to hilarious effect when describing aristocrats having a fancy meal).

The other Wodehouse technique was to convert perfectly ordinary words into unusual usages, often for comic effect: thus 'burglarious' for 'like a burglar', 'opprobrious' rather than saying 'deserving opprobrium', and 'unscramble' for restoring a situation to order. He may have put something of himself into his memorable character Psmith ('the P is silent as in psalm') since both love quoting from the classics (and occasionally deliberately misquoting them).

Wodehouse, like Psmith, was never lost for words—his own, or other people's. He had the uncanny gift of always coming up with the *mot juste*, an expression borrowed from the French (and meaning 'the right, appropriate word'): 'She legged it, and for a moment silence reigned. Then Bobbie said, 'Phew!' and I agreed that 'Phew!' was the *mot juste*.' (from *Jeeves in the*

Offing, 1960). And of course, if he didn't have the *mot juste* at hand, he simply invented it. For more, you must simply read the master yourself!

98

BOOKS AND READING

I've often been accused of *epeolatry,* the worship of words. I usually plead that I am not guilty as charged, since I adore words not for their own sake but because of the uses to which they can be put. True, I'm a *logophile*, a lover of words, but the best reason to know words is to read books—and the more books you read, the more words you'll know! So this chapter delves into words that are associated with books.

My favourite is a word that English has borrowed from Japanese, because there is no English word for this familiar sight. *Tsundoku* means the pile of unread books that every reader accumulates, for our greed for books is always greater than the time available to devour them. Whether on a crowded bedside table, an office desk or alongside an easy chair, inveterate readers have tsundokus of varying dimensions. Sometimes the books in it have been purchased with great enthusiasm and then not opened even once. 'What did you think of that book you bought last week?' well-meaning friends ask, and you guiltily reply: 'it's in my tsundoku pile'.

My hand-luggage on flights consists mainly of books, which makes me *book-bosomed,* a term invented by Sir Walter Scott to described people who cannot stay a moment without books. If you travel less than me and your tsundoku pile is on your bedside table, chances are that you are a *librocubicularist*—someone who likes to read in bed. There's something particularly relaxing about being horizontal with a book propped up in your hands, whether or not your health confines you to bed. And unlike the screen of a mobile phone, the book doesn't send blue light to your brain, waking you up and disturbing your sleep. It's the best way to manage a gentle transition from wakefulness to sleep.

Just before you fall asleep, if you are not a sensible soul who keeps a ready supply of bookmarks handy, you might fold over the corner of the page you were reading, so that you can find your place more easily when you return to the book. This is known as a *Dog's Ear*. Many a book-lover considers dog-earing a book to be a barbaric practice, though, and would consider you guilty of the sin of *bibliclasm*, the act of spoiling a book knowingly. So do go for the bookmark! If you have half-dozen half-read books lying around with dog's ears, though, then each is known as *ballycumber,* after an Irish town whose residents clearly enjoy *bibliosmia*, the smell of old books. (The smell of a newly purchased book, on the other hand, is known as *delitrium.*) This can happen when you begin reading a book and after some time decide you would rather resume another book you were reading, a condition known as *swapshame*. But if you don't stop at all, and read your book the whole night long, you are bound to feel a special kind of exhaustion the morning after, that is called *chaptigue*.

The problem with having too many dog-eared ballycumbers in your tsundoku is that you might end up returning so late to one of them that you forget what you had already read and have to start all over again, an affliction known as *mehnertia.* It's still preferable to *madgedy,* repeatedly reading a sad story in the vain hope that the end will be different next time, or feeling *bookklempt*—finishing the last volume of a series, realizing there is no more to come but being utterly unable to accept that reality.

Of course, readers like that might aspire to being *omnilegent*—reading or having read everything. I'd like to think that when I research my books, I read everything I can lay my hands on about the subject, so that with my encyclopaedic reading, no other writer on the same theme can be said to have been more omnilegent. Of course, this leads some friends to describe me as a *bibliobibuli*, someone who reads too much. Since I don't agree that there's anything like 'too much' when it comes to books, I prefer confessing to being a *bibliophagist*, a person who loves to read books (literally, one who devours books!). I hope that makes me, dear reader, your *scrollmate*—an author with whom you feel a deep connection….

SECTION THIRTEEN

BELLWETHERS

The world of business has contributed many words to recent English whose meanings have changed from their earlier uses. A haircut is not just a grooming treatment but an action involving the reduction in value of an asset, as in 'the bank took a haircut to settle a defaulting loan'. So, it seems, are fathers of a certain age, who are described as possessing dad bods, characterized by a thickening paunch and diminished muscularity, both allegedly typical of an average father.

99

WHEN MEANINGS CHANGE

English is famously a language that is constantly remaking itself, changing and adapting to new developments, absorbing words from a wide variety of sources. One of its interesting characteristics is how words that have seemingly settled meanings sometimes acquire additional, and often wholly different meanings.

Take a word as innocuous as *snowflake*. We all know the word, it falls from the sky—but now it is also used to mean 'someone regarded or treated as unique or special' and/or 'someone who is overly sensitive'. Similarly, aviation buffs are familiar with *tailwind* and *headwind*, but these words are now used figuratively as well in ways that have nothing to do with aircraft—a tailwind is a force or influence that helps one to succeed, while a headwind impedes or hinders progress. And every child knows the story of Goldilocks, who preferred her porridge to be neither too hot nor too cold—but few realize her fairy tale has been borrowed by astronomers to describe 'an area of planetary orbit in which temperatures are neither too hot nor too cold to support life.'

A particularly striking development in contemporary English has been the creation of new compound terms, made up of two or more ordinary and familiar words to now mean something that neither word by itself does. For instance, everyone knows the words 'page' and 'view', but *page view*, as a compound word, means something more, referring to a user viewing an individual page on a website. Similarly, with 'screen' and 'time', which has undergone not one but two compound mutations. At first, *screen time* referred to the amount of time someone appeared in front of a camera in a movie—'that promising actor didn't get enough screen time in this film'—but now it means the time an individual spends in front of the screen of his mobile phone or computer. ('You've had too much screen time, your eyes will start hurting.')

The world of computer technology has contributed its share of neologisms to our English. 'Deep' and 'fake' have obvious meanings, but a *deepfake* is an image or recording that has been deliberately altered and manipulated to misrepresent someone as doing or saying something they didn't actually do or say. You might find 'deepfakes' on the *dark web*, the sinister section of the internet whose web pages cannot be indexed by search engines, are not viewable through a standard web browser, require specialized software or a secret network configuration to access, and specifically attract criminal users by offering high levels of encryption and anonymity. It is also of interest to the *deep state*, a term originating in Turkey (but more used in recent years in relation to Pakistan) for a secret governmental network of military and security personnel operating beyond the control of the formal governmental apparatus (and also ignoring the bounds of the law).

The world of business has contributed many words to recent English whose meanings have changed from their earlier uses. A *haircut* is not just a grooming treatment but an action involving the reduction in value of an asset, as in 'the bank took a haircut to settle a defaulting loan'. *Vulture capitalism* is a form of venture capitalism that aggressively purchases a distressed business with the intention of stripping its assets and selling them off at a profit, with no commitment to reviving the business itself. The *gig economy* refers to the use of temporary or freelance workers to perform jobs instead of hiring regular employees, giving them salaries and benefits and attendant security. These '*gig workers*' are on their own, overworked and underpaid—and all the more vulnerable.

So, it seems, are fathers of a certain age, who are described as possessing *dad bods*, characterized by a thickening paunch and diminished muscularity, both allegedly typical of an average father. (We also tell *Dad jokes*, apparently, lame attempts at humour that are lost on our children's generation). Perhaps we will soon be victims of *cancel culture*, the habit of ostracizing someone as a way of expressing disapproval of his views and exerting social pressure to isolate him.

This is not a new phenomenon: words have changed their meaning throughout the history of the English language. *Awful*, for instance, along with '*awesome*', was synonymous with 'awe-inspiring', but evolved over the years to acquire a purely negative meaning—'that's an awful film'. Curiously enough, 'awesome' evolved the opposite way, and took on the connotation of 'extremely good'. In much the same way, '*fantastic*' used to mean only something from fantasy, an imaginary idea or story, but now is a word to convey praise and admiration. Similar progress was made by the word *naughty*. Originally a naughty person was one who had naught, or nothing. From that straightforward meaning, it came to imply one who was evil or amoral, devoid of any good qualities. Now it refers mainly to children who are badly behaved.

Naughty, these days, often goes with 'nice'. 'Nice' was originally a negative term for a stupid, ignorant, or foolish person, which is not surprising, since it is derived from the Latin *nescius,* meaning ignorant. Today you are unlikely to call an idiot nice. Meanwhile, *silly* went in the opposite direction: it first referred to people or actions that were worthy or blessed, gradually was used to refer to the weak and vulnerable, and now is only applied to those who are foolish, usually in a trivial way.

So given that words can change meaning over time, definitional changes are part of the historical evolution of the English language. This also means that historic events can have their own impact on the language. The coronavirus pandemic that has assailed the world in the last two years is no exception: it has given us words and expressions that didn't mean quite the same thing before 2020.

The best-known of the coronavirus-related terms that were added to our vocabulary was probably *social distancing*.

Before Covid-19, the term might have been used to refer to snobbish elites avoiding mixing with the hoi polloi, or racist colonials in the era of empire refusing to drink or dine at the club with the brown or black people they ruled. Since March 2020, however, 'social distancing' has been used to describe the practice of keeping physically apart from others to prevent the transmission of a virus—maintaining a greater than usual space between yourself and other people, and avoiding direct contact with them, especially in public places, in order to minimize exposure to contamination. What's interesting is not just that the meaning of the term has changed, but that it has acquired a narrower specificity it never possessed before the outbreak of a worldwide contagion necessitated measures that brought a new vocabulary with them.

A Covid-related term like '*self-isolation*' is obviously clear in meaning, but '*herd immunity*' is less so. One rather long and unwieldy definition of the term that I have come across runs as follows: 'a reduction in the risk of infection with a specific communicable disease that occurs when a significant proportion of the population has become immune to infection (as because of previous exposure or vaccination) so that susceptible individuals are much less likely to come in contact with infected individuals.' Again, specificity is key. You cannot use 'herd immunity' to describe, for example, the fact that a large mob or 'herd' that commits acts of mass violence like a riot cannot be prosecuted because of the legal difficulty of identifying individual law-breakers. That could be 'herd immunity' too, but it simply can't be used that way now!

Another term that Covid-19 brought into vogue is '*super-spreader*'—again we know what each of those two words mean, but now it applies very specifically to an event, an individual, or a place through which or whom a large number of people contract the same contagious disease. You can use 'super-spreader' as a noun ('my host on Christmas Eve was a super-spreader—every guest caught the virus') or as an adjective ('I wish I hadn't gone to that party—it turned out to be a real super-spreader event'). The term has turned out to be as communicable as the virus that promoted its use!

100

NEW WORDS FOR NEW YEARS

Each year brings its share of infusions into the English language, and various publications end each year with the customary genuflections to various 'Words of the Year' anointed by assorted dictionaries. Some go further, and refuse to let January pass without looking ahead to possible words we'd need to use in the New Year. After all, before the Covid pandemic, whoever thought we would become so rapidly familiar with terms like 'herd immunity', 'social distancing', 'flatten the curve', 'viral load', 'spike protein', and 'mRNA vaccines'? Why wouldn't the same thing happen to us in future years that broadened our vocabularies from 2020 to 2022?

That venerable custodian of Anglophile wisdom, *The Economist* (which despite being a weekly magazine, insists on calling itself a newspaper), in 2022 picked twenty-three terms it thought might catch on in the near future. Some of them are too technical, in this layman's opinion, to ever become the stuff of daily conversation—phrases like 'post-quantum cryptography' and 'cislunar', for instance. (The former would take too long to explain; the latter relates to the space between Earth and the orbit of the Moon). Some others are too culturally specific to be applicable to most of us, even if those in *The Economist*'s orbit disagree—a term like 'TWaT cities', for instance, which in the US relate to cities where the working week has been reduced to Tuesdays, Wednesday, and Thursdays, with people working for home on Mondays and Fridays. But some of the others on *The Economist* list might well be words we will all need to master before the New Year is out.

Take 'synfuels', for example. These are synthetic fuels, produced artificially rather than being made from oil—highly relevant in an era where governments are more determined than ever to turn away from fossil fuels and look for renewable sources of energy. Or 'green hydrogen', hydrogen made using renewable energy through techniques that use electrolysis to split water into hydrogen and oxygen. This is both cheaper and less polluting than conventional fuel, and Western countries are already promoting the use of 'green hydrogen' as the best form of renewable energy.

Indeed, climate change and environmental consciousness may continue to have as great an impact on our vocabulary in the proximate future as Covid has had. We'll need to understand about 'Scope 1, 2 and 3 emissions': respectively, those caused directly caused by a company's activities (Scope 1), indirect emissions (Scope 2) and all other emissions that arise from the activities of a company's suppliers and customers (Scope 3). These three kinds of emissions are going to be part of discussions about responsibility for global warming. Higher temperatures caused by climate change are leading to 'aridification', or the long-term drying of a region or an area—another neologism. Similarly, responses to increasing heatwaves will add to our vocabulary—cities like Los Angeles, Phoenix, and Tokyo are planning measures to reduce temperatures by introducing 'cool roofs' (covered with white paint or reflective materials) and 'cool pavements' (sidewalks treated with special coatings) to reflect sunlight away so that surfaces absorb less heat. Some may create 'resilience hubs'—buildings that provide air-conditioned oases of refuge with drinking water, internet access, and phone-charging facilities—within cities to combat heatwaves.

If climate change will add to our list of regularly-used neologisms, technology will continue to intrude as well. One term is already widely in use: 'eSIMs' have begun to supplant or replace SIM cards, the subscriber identity modules we've been inserting into our phones to connect to different networks. 'eSIMs' have begun to replace physical chips with digital codes that are part of the software on your phone.

Thanks to technology, 'reality' is already undergoing dizzying change. We already have 'virtual reality', when you wear a pair of goggles and a headset that immerse you in an alternative, computer-generated reality. Next there will be 'augmented reality', which will superimpose computer-generated elements onto your view of the real world. Watch out for 'mixed reality', which will go even farther by allowing real and virtual items to interact. What is real and what is digitally-generated will blend into each other in ways that may easily affect our vocabulary, our daily lives and one day, our sanity!

101

WORDS OF THE YEAR, 2021–23

The Covid pandemic in the years 2020 and 2021 inevitably contributed many words to the English language. Its principal custodian, the Oxford English Dictionary, regularly admits new words into the lexicon, and in 2021, the gurus of the OED chose as their 'word of the year'—yes, wait for it: *vax*! Yes, that short form for vaccination has swept the honours board. Words related to vaccines have spiked in frequency in 2021 due to Covid, they explain, and vax has been the preferred form, with *double-vaxxed*, *unvaxxed*, and *anti-vaxxer* all seeing significantly increased usage. OED senior editor Fiona McPherson says vax has made 'the most striking impact' that year, though its use 'goes back at least to the 1980s'. But this is the year it has finally come into its own, and like a struggling actor who finally lands a starring role and aces the part, *vax* walks away with the statuette. (The OED notes that *vax* and *vaxx* are both accepted spellings but the former, with one x, is more commonly used.)

Vax is nicely versatile. As a noun, it's just a vaccine or vaccination. As a verb, to vax means to vaccinate. If you're opposed to vaccination, you're anti-vax (an adjective), or an anti-vaxxer (another noun). If you've had two doses of a vaccine, you're double-vaxxed (another adjective). And if you point your phone at yourself during or immediately before or after a vaccination, especially one against Covid-19, and then share it on social media, you've taken a vaxxie—a vaccination selfie.

So you can see why the language mavens at the OED were enamoured of *vax*. Still, they could also have gone with *pandemic,* the use of which, they admit, has increased by more than 57,000 per cent this year. Oxford is not the only entity to announce a Word of the Year; their rivals at Collins do the same. The previous year the Collins Dictionary chose 'lockdown' as its word of the year 2020; Oxford Languages disagreed, instead choosing several joint winners from words associated with the year's events—including *lockdown, bushfires,* and *Covid-19* itself, as well as *Black Lives Matter* and even *WFH* [working from home]. In 2021, in *vax*, they found an undisputed winner.

Previous Words of the Year from Oxford have included 'selfie' in 2013, 'post-truth' in 2016, and 'climate emergency' in 2019. Collins, for its part, crowned 'geek' in 2013, 'photobomb' the year after, 'binge-watch' in 2015, and 'fake news' in 2017. Both sets of lexicologists are clearly watching the news closely in making their selections.

The 2021 Oxford-winning word, *vax*, was first recorded in English in 1799, while its derivatives *vaccinate* and *vaccination* both first appear in 1800. The words are rooted in the Latin *vacca*, or cow, since the English vaccination pioneer Edward Jenner used the virus of cowpox—a mild infection that occurs in cows—to inoculate people against smallpox in the late 1790s and early 1800s.

So vax is here to stay, with its Oxford Word of the Year imprimatur. What are some of the 'best supporting actor' awards for words in 2021 that OED saw fit to recognize as acceptable English for the first time? Again, many are anchored in the news reports: for instance, *anti-blackness*, a noun defined as 'prejudice, hostility, or antagonism towards, or discrimination against, black people.' Contemporary culture is also reflected in *body-shamer*, for 'a person who mocks, humiliates, or stigmatizes someone on the basis of supposed faults or imperfections in body shape, size, or appearance.' We can thank American politics for another term—*defunding*: 'The action or practice of withdrawing funding from an enterprise, institution, etc., either wholly or in part.' This word is the result of a passionate political movement in a number of American cities to 'defund' police departments that had mistreated black people. Minneapolis has already passed a defunding law. The rest of us have the word.

The OED, in the course of the year, also issues lists of words they have decided to include in their hallowed dictionary as having passed muster to be acceptable words in the English language. There are several dozens of these in 2021. I will give you a small selection of what made the cut last year past the Oxford gatekeepers of the English language.

Some are clearly reflective of the changes in our lives, and therefore in our linguistic usage, in the internet era:

> doxing, n.: The action or process of searching for and publishing private or identifying information about a particular individual on the internet.
>
> gig economy, n.: A labour market characterized by a prevalence of short-term contracts and freelance work, as distinct from permanent, full-time employment.
>
> livestreaming, n.: The action or process of broadcasting an event, etc., live over the internet.
>
> Some acknowledge the way in which alternative lifestyles have found mainstream acceptance in the English-speaking world:
>
> queerbaiting, n.: The harassment, abuse, or targeted provocation of LGBT people (esp., in early use, gay men). Cf. gay-baiting.
>
> transphobe, n.: A person who is hostile towards, prejudiced against, or fearful of transgender or transsexual people or of transgenderism; a transphobic person.

Some come from non-Anglophone roots and reflect the involvement of non-Western cultures in speaking English, with the inclusion of words from other mother-tongues:

> suhoor, n.: The meal eaten before sunrise during Ramadan, when fasting begins; the occasion or time of such a meal. Cf. Iftar.

ghoonghat, n.: The practice observed by some married (chiefly Hindu) women of wearing a covering over the head or face.

Many reflect terms that became politically important last year in the Western countries, whose usage of English remains dominant in the world:

virtue signalling, n.: The action or practice of expressing one's views or acting in a way thought to be motivated primarily by a wish to exhibit good character or social conscience.

visible minority, n.: An ethnic or racial group whose members are visibly distinguishable from those of the predominant ethnic or racial group in a society.

zoomer, n.: Originally and chiefly North American. Frequently with capital initial. A boomer who has now reached middle or retirement age.

Then there are familiar words which have acquired new meanings last year that I was unaware of but the OED has decided to recognize:

wine, v.: intransitive. Esp. of a woman: to dance with rhythmic gyratory movements of the hips and pelvis.

Some words are so widely used already that I was surprised that their official inclusion in the OED came so late. These include:

conflicted, adj.: Esp. of emotions or feelings: incompatible or at odds; confused, contradictory. Also (in later use) of a person: having, displaying, or characterized by such feelings.

chapstick, n.: A proprietary name for: a small stick or tub of ointment that is applied to the lips to prevent or soothe soreness, dryness, and cracking.

belly-dance, v.: intransitive. To perform or engage in a belly dance.

brown-nosing, n.: Excessive or insincere flattery, esp. with the aim of gaining favour or advancement; toadying.

foul-mouth, v.: transitive. To abuse (a person) verbally; to insult, disparage, or slander (someone).

ghostbuster, n.: A person who investigates or deals with supposed paranormal activity or phenomena; spec. (originally) a sceptic who exposes bogus claims of ghosts.

postpaid, adj.: Paid, or paid for, after a transaction has taken place or a service has been rendered. Now: spec. relating to a mobile phone or internet service....

And finally, some inclusions are frankly silly:

wagwan, int.: 'What's going on?' 'What's happening?' Frequently used as an informal greeting. (A sub-literate mangling of 'what's going on?' is not a word!)

womxn, n.: Women. Also occasionally as singular: a woman. (I'm as feminist as they come, but what's sexist about the letter 'e' that's improved by the letter 'x'?)

whoo-ee, int.: Used to attract attention, or to summon a person or animal. Also used to express various emotions or reactions, such as surprise, awe, excitement. (Is every sound we make worthy of inclusion in a dictionary?)

zom-com, n.: A comedy film featuring zombie characters. (No comment.)

Oxford Languages says its corpus, or language resource base, collects news content daily, regularly updates it and analyses it. Today the OED corpus contains over 14.5 billion words for lexicographers to search and study. Clearly a lot more neologisms will find their way into our language usage in future years!

When various dictionaries announce their Words of the Year, usually on the basis of those words that have been looked up or cited most frequently online on their sites, 2022 was indeed unusually interesting.

First off the blocks was the UK's Collins, with 'permacrisis'—a word describing the feeling of living through a period of war, inflation, and political instability—leading Collins's annual compilation of ten words or phrases. Language innovations serve as a mirror reflecting the major concerns of society, and 'permacrisis' reflected the uncertainties in British life caused by Brexit, the pandemic, severe weather, the war in Ukraine, political instability, the energy crisis and rising inflation. No wonder 'quiet quitting'—defined as 'the act of doing one's basic duties at work and no more, either by way of protest or to improve work/life balance'—also made the list.

Britain is also learning 'Carolean', the adjective relating to new King Charles III, soon after recovering from 'Partygate', the political scandal over parties held at 10 Downing Street in defiance of the public health restrictions that applied to everyone else.

Soon after Collins's announcement came the US Merriam-Webster's word of the year, 'gaslighting', meaning mind-manipulating, grossly misleading, or downright deceitful—which was looked up more often than any other neologism. Merriam-Webster's top definition for gaslighting is the psychological manipulation of a person, usually over a period of time, that 'causes the victim to question the validity of their own thoughts, perception of reality, or memories' and typically 'leads to loss of confidence and self-esteem, uncertainty of one's mental stability, and dependency on the perpetrator'.

Gaslighting happens in abusive relationships—between lovers, within a family unit, as a corporate tactic, among friends, and by politicians misleading the public. There's even 'medical gaslighting', when a doctor dismisses a patient's symptoms or illness by saying 'it's all in your mind'.

Next in the race to declare a Word of the Year was the Cambridge Dictionary, which surprised many by choosing 'homer' as the word most searched for in 2022. It was looked up more than 79,000 times this year, and an amazing 65,401 of those views happened on 5 May—when it was the answer for that day's popular Wordle quiz. Non-Americans who didn't know the word existed (it's short for a 'home run' in baseball) looked it up in droves, and it won the Cambridge distinction.

Cambridge explained its selection by arguing that the choice of 'homer' represented 'the challenges of learning English in an increasingly connected world'. The differences among national varieties of English, they said, 'can cause confusion in these international conversations—until we learn more about them!' In keeping with that, Macquarie Dictionary, in Australia, chimed in with 'bachelor's handbag'—a phrase used to describe a supermarket roast chicken carried home in a paper bag, 'so quintessentially Australian'.

Finally, and as usual garnering the most attention, came the Oxford Dictionary, which famously hit the headlines last year with 'vax' (and previously with 'post-truth' and 'selfie'). This time, for the first time in its history, the Oxford Word of the Year was decided by the public, 'the true arbiters of language', voting from a shortlist of three words—'metaverse', '#IStandWith', and the phrase 'goblin mode'. Metaverse, of course, refers to the virtual world where people can live, work, shop, eat, and make friends. #IStandWith is a hashtag recognizing 'the activism and division that has characterized this year,' according to Oxford University Press. But the winner, with an unexpectedly lopsided 93 per cent of the vote, was 'goblin mode', a new concept of rejecting societal expectations in favour of doing whatever one wants to. The term refers to 'a type of behaviour which is unapologetically self-indulgent, lazy, slovenly, or greedy, typically in a way that rejects social norms or expectations'. The hashtag #goblinmode is often used to challenge those telling you to be the 'best version of yourself'. It captures the prevailing mood of individuals rejecting the idea of returning to 'normal life' after the pandemic. As an American lexicographer observed: 'Goblin mode really does speak to the times, and it is certainly a 2022 expression.'

And what did 2023 give us? When dictionary-makers issued their choices for 'word of the year' 2023, they were clearly hoping to spark off an interest in the way the English language is responding to the challenges of modern life. All of them seemed inspired by AI-related concerns, as the immense popularity of artificial intelligence points to both its transformative impact and the threats it poses.

First off the blocks was the Cambridge Dictionary, with 'hallucinate'. The traditional meaning of the word is 'to seem to see, hear, feel, or smell something that does not exist, usually because of a health condition or because you have taken a drug'. Today it also refers to the production of false information by AI. As many students have learned to their chagrin from using ChatGPT and the like, AI programmes have an inconvenient habit of making up, or imagining facts to reply to your questions. This is known as hallucination—except that it's the AI, not the user, who's the one hallucinating. As Henry Shevlin, an AI ethicist at Cambridge University, observed, this may be because 'it's so easy to anthropomorphise these systems, treating them as if they had minds of their own'.

The Cambridge dictionary-makers explained that generative AI tools like ChatGPT, Bard, and Grok have all been guilty of hallucination. A US law firm's use of ChatGPT for legal research even led to fictitious cases being cited in court. A problem with AI programmes is that the more original you ask them to be, the greater the risk of hallucination.

The Collins Dictionary went one step ahead of Cambridge by choosing 'AI' itself as its word of the year for 2023. The dictionary defines AI as 'the modelling of human mental functions by computer programs'.

And Merriam-Webster was next to announce that its word of the year for 2023 is 'authentic', again an acknowledgement of the rise of artificial intelligence and the spread of misinformation on social media platforms. The search for something real and true that one can anchor oneself in is mirrored in a substantial increase in internet searches for the word 'authentic' in 2023, which the dictionary says was 'driven by stories and conversations about AI, celebrity culture, identity and social media.' Merriam-Webster said being 'authentic' is what influencers (another recent word!), celebrities, and brands all aspire to.

The risk of AI programmes providing misleading, fallacious, or simply false information is a phenomenon of our times, along with its capacity to produce 'deep fakes'—seemingly real photographs and videos of people wearing (or not wearing) clothes they have never actually donned, or depicted in situations they were never in. Disinformation (the deliberate manipulation of data for specific purposes) and misinformation (propagation of wrong or misleading information) can have far-reaching consequences in our lives, not least in wars, disasters, and elections.

These three Words of the Year, ranging from the realm of imagined hallucination to the increased need for authenticity, are not surprising. They acknowledge the way artificial intelligence has invaded our lives, our workspaces—and our vocabularies. So do others: 'prompt engineering', 'deepfake', 'large language model' ('LLM'), 'GPT' (an abbreviation of Generative Pre-trained Transformer), and 'GenAI' (generative AI) were among the several thousand words and definitions that these dictionaries also added in 2023.

Other options were, of course, also considered. The Collins Dictionary shortlisted many words before AI was selected—but many of those, too, bore the stamp of contemporary technology and the culture of the digital world. 'Influencer', in the context of social media, had already made it, as had other associated words like mega-influencer and micro-influencer, but Collins also shortlisted 'deinfluencing' for their word of the year 2023. 'Deinfluencing', according to the dictionary-makers, refers to when influencers use their power 'to warn followers to avoid certain commercial products, lifestyle choices, etc'. At the risk of quibbling, I think 'deinfluencing' is an unnecessary word, since influencing someone against something is essentially no different from influencing them in favour of it. Thumbs down, Collins!

One sidelight: for those of us who knew certain acronyms for years, we have new abbreviations to digest. 'AI' is no longer simply 'Air India', and 'LLM' is not just an advanced law degree!

Two others entered the fray with their words of the year along with Cambridge, Collins, and Merriam-Webster dictionaries.

The one that got the most attention worldwide was, of course, Oxford University Press, publishers of the venerable, and hugely revered, Oxford English Dictionary, which named 'rizz' as its word of the year. This selection marked a welcome departure from the artificial-intelligence-related themes of the three earlier choices, highlighting as it does the popularity of a term used by Generation Z. 'Rizz', apparently, describes someone's ability to attract or seduce another person, and is believed to come from the middle of the word 'charisma'. It can be used as a verb, as in to 'rizz up', or chat someone up, and as a noun, as in 'he's got rizz' (unless he's Tom Holland, who famously declared he didn't have any). I don't see myself using 'rizz', somehow, since 'charisma' is already in my vocabulary and I don't find it needs contraction—but to each his own, as we Baby Boomers find ourself frequently saying about members of Generation Z!

'It speaks to how younger generations create spaces—online or in person—where they own and define the language they use', the publisher explained. 'From activism to dating and wider culture, as Gen Z comes to have more impact on society, differences in perspectives and lifestyle play out in language, too.' (Interestingly, Merriam-Webster had included 'rizz' on its list of the year's top words too, but as discussed in this chapter, chose 'authentic' instead as its word of the year.)

Next, the highly-respected weekly magazine *The Economist*, which runs a column on language too, authored by the pseudonymous 'Johnson' (a tribute, no doubt, to Dr Samuel Johnson, who came up with the first-ever English dictionary), entered the lists. Wisely, given its global readership, *The Economist* chose several words to discuss. In Africa there have been two coups in 2023, so should 'coup' be the world of the year there? Or how about the Yoruba verb 'japa', used colloquially in Nigeria to describe making a quick escape from a precarious situation, or even to flee from misgoverned Nigeria itself? Why not the Sanksrit word 'vishwaguru', used frequently by Indian prime minister Modi and his admirers, meaning 'teacher to the world'? Modi has also been calling his country the 'voice of the global south', and *The Economist* wonders if 'global south', describing the countries that used to be called 'the third world', should be the word of the year.

From India it turns to China, and picks 'lanweilou', a Mandarin expression meaning 'rotten-tail building', reflecting the collapse of the country's property sector, with many partially complete building projects leaving their buyers in the lurch. Staying with economics (as befits its name!), *The Economist* turns closer to home, musing about the newly-in-vogue terms 'decoupling' and 'de-risking', which have come into use to describe Western economies' desire to reduce their dependence on China.

But then, perhaps inevitably, it too surrenders to the world of artificial intelligence, acknowledging yet again the way AI has invaded our lives, our workspaces—and our vocabularies. The words it discusses are the ones others picked too—'generative', 'large language models', and the like. But after discussing this long list, *The Economist* finally settles for 'ChatGPT' as its Word of the Year. As Johnson explains:

'Can a name be a word of the year? Is it even a word? Yes. Names are nouns. And Google searches for 'ChatGPT' are more than 90 times as frequent as those for 'generative AI' or 'large language model'. ChatGPT is the same in every language. Moreover, trade names have a long history of spreading into the collective parlance: aspirin, escalator, Hoover and Frisbee'. (We have discussed that phenomenon in an earlier chapter.)

So after going round the world, the weekly ends up where all the others bar Oxford did, in AI-land. Not surprising. As *TechCrunch* wrote, 'Few would disagree that 2023 was, in the world of technology at least, dominated by artificial intelligence.' I suppose one must concede the point: AI's got rizz!

CONCLUSION

THE LINGUISTIC LEGACY

When I was persuaded a couple of years ago to test my knowledge of Millennial English on a television show, I guessed my way past some of the answers and stumbled at the rest. One could guess the connotations of 'fleek', 'slay', and even 'adulting' from the way they sounded, but how was one to know that 'quiche' meant hotter than hot? The 'generation gap' is a cliché, but the use of language is the clearest evidence of its existence. That today's young have evolved a vocabulary that means nothing to their parents shouldn't surprise anyone, since the same charge has been levelled at every previous generation. But while most of us can understand why it's 'cool' to be seen with a 'hot' date, being told someone is a 'snacc' requires a cultural leap. After all, since when was a cheese toast or a sabudana-vada a symbol of attractiveness?

'Millennials' refers to the generation born between 1980 and 1994, and as a parent of two of that vintage (and uncle to four others), I am relieved that they have largely not chosen to address me in such language. They have already been succeeded by two more cohorts: 'Generation Z' (1995–2012, also known as 'iGen' or 'Zoomers', a reference to the video-chat app that so many of them used for school and work during the Covid-19 pandemic), and a generation born after 2010 (I call them kids; the scholar Jean Twenge dubs them 'Polars', since they live in polarized times but the broadly accepted term is Generation Alpha). The better-known millennial and Gen Z expressions are not new words but familiar English ones now assigned different meanings by the young—terms like 'woke' (nothing to do with your alarm clock, but meaning socially aware), 'lit' (connoting something that's amazing or fun), and 'thirsty' (meaning desperate for attention). Others have become part of the routine currency of everyday life in the twenty-first century—like 'meme', 'phishing', 'viral', and 'selfie'. Some others don't depart very far from their original meanings: 'low-key' on a millennial's tongue means not 'quiet', but 'subtle', 'fit' refers to a person's overall clothing ensemble (it's short for 'outfit'), and 'shook' means 'shaken'. And in the era of Netflix and other OTT platforms, everyone knows that to 'binge-watch' is to watch multiple episodes of a show (or indeed an entire series) in one sitting. Though I still have no idea why 'dope' means excellent, and 'sick' expresses admiration or high approval for something impressive or exciting.

Millennials are best known, however, for the tendency to abbreviate their emotions into acronyms that older people can only surmise the meanings of. This may no doubt be because millennials are also inveterate texters, a form of communication that encourages brevity. (They were the first generation to use mobile phones for texting rather than talking.) Thus FOMO, or 'fear of missing out', is a millennial creation that explains why many people rush to join others in a crowd, a party, or for that matter a mob, without fully understanding what they are up to. (Apparently, to add to the confusion, some millennials also use FOMO for 'fear of moving on', the reluctance to let go of a past relationship). Similarly, GYAT can mean either 'get your act together', or 'goddamn, you are thick', apparently an expression of approval for a person you find attractive (or for somebody with a substantial derriere). YOLO is another millennial acronym, for 'you only live once', an expression that justifies some of the more foolish decisions of the riskily adventurous. Other millennial and Gen Z terms include AFK (away from keyboard), BFF (best friend forever), ICYMI (in case you missed it), IMHO (in my humble opinion). JK (just kidding), NITM (not in the mood), ONM (on my way), SMH (shaking my head), TBH (to be honest), TMI (too much information), and TTYL (talk to you later).

Modern life and the internet have given us many millennial terms—emoji or emoticon, for the pictorial symbols people send instead of words to express simple emotions, for instance.

(People who texted LOL to indicate that they were 'laughing out loud' at something might now just send a picture of a laughing face instead, or post 'hearts'). Sometimes they send GIFs—little pictures or photos that bounce around repeatedly, made in the 'graphics interchange format,' hence the name GIF. 'Spam' used to be, for older generations, a kind of processed meat; today we all know the word in its application to unwanted emails. A 'troll' was a little Norwegian gnome; now it's an obnoxious person who deliberately provokes others online. And all of us who use X (formerly Twitter) are familiar with RT (for retweet), DM (for direct message), 'likes' and 'trending' (when a hashtag is repeated or RT-ed by a large number of internet users).

Most of these are examples of YABA, 'yet another bloody acronym'. But while many millennial expressions are indeed formed from acronyms, not all are. Thus BAE stands for 'before anyone else'—but it also refers to one's girlfriend, as a contraction of 'babe' (a word that would not have struck earlier generations as requiring any further contracting!). Another superfluous shortening is the millennial 'jelly', which merely means 'jealous'—and uses the same number of syllables, so why bother?

James Emery White's blog post entitled 'Understanding the Gen Z Vocabulary' makes it all amply clear.

> First, I want you to know it's totally lit to be writing this. Hope nothing that follows feels cringey. Sometimes I can get a little extra. And when we're not F2F, it's hard to tell. I'm just hoping it reads fleeky. But trust me, what follows is high-key. TBH, I just hope you don't throw any shade my way but, instead, will read and wig.

The only question that remains is, did any reader born before 1981 understand what he was trying to say?

I tend to pride myself on a fairly extensive vocabulary, but the opening paragraph of a recent article in an Indian newspaper left me completely flummoxed, with its use of words and expressions I found incomprehensible. The Valentine's Day feature article about romance, from the *New Indian Express*, began with this paragraph:

> Aastha Chowdhury, a 24-year-old budding lawyer from Dehradun, has had a rainbow dating trajectory over the past couple of years. Two years ago, emerging from a disastrous, emotionally abusive relationship,... she experienced a dating renaissance by downloading a plethora of dating apps for the first time. Keeping her mind open to possibilities, she began open-casting through a buffet of options; went on numerous first dates, and several secondary ones, and enjoyed memorable interactions...(dry dating helped her stick with her rule of ethical exploration). Having gained coronesty from her previous experience, however, she kept her guardrails up against potential emotional entanglements.... She also kept a check on her expenditure, aware of the rules of infla-dating as well as the fact that this phase of wanderlove wouldn't last forever.

That one para included eight expressions I hadn't encountered before, and though you could guess the meanings of some of them, others were genuinely puzzling. The ones that lent themselves to reasonable surmise were 'dating renaissance', since the latter word implies a 'revival' of dating, 'guardrails', and 'infla-dating', which seemed to combine inflation and dating. But puzzling over the rest, I began to realize the romantically inclined young of today had developed a vocabulary of their own that I had no clue about.

So I must confess, unashamedly, that I looked them all up. Where Google wasn't much help, I had to turn to ChatGPT. (Since my own intelligence wasn't up to the task, maybe artificial intelligence could explain it to me!) Here the new-fangled expressions are, in order of appearance:

- Rainbow dating: According to ChatGPT: 'The term 'rainbow dating' typically refers to a romantic relationship between individuals from different racial or ethnic backgrounds. The word 'rainbow' is often used to symbolize diversity, and in this context, it highlights the different colours of the racial and ethnic spectrum. Rainbow dating is a way of celebrating and embracing diversity, as well as breaking down cultural barriers and promoting inclusivity. The term can also be used to describe friendships or social interactions that cross racial or ethnic lines.'

- Dating renaissance: My guess was close enough. It means 'giving love another chance after failures'.
- Open-casting: The phrase exists in the world of movies: when a producer issues a call for 'open-casting', that means they're holding an open audition, so aspiring actors don't need an invitation but can instead drop by on the designated date and time (along with dozens of other hopefuls) for the chance of being selected for the cast. In the world of romance, however, it seems 'open-casting' translates to 'dating someone outside your type'. Go figure.
- Dry dating: This is the term for refusing to consume alcohol on a date. Staying sober, in other words, so that your judgement about your date isn't impaired.
- Coronesty: Now there's a word that sounds like a surgical procedure! But it apparently has nothing to do with either your coronary artery or an angioplasty. The word 'coronesty', says the UK website *Metro*, 'describes the increased desire for people to be honest with others—and crucially, themselves—about what they really want from a relationship.' Apparently both the word and the practice emerged from people's experiences during the coronavirus pandemic, hence the 'coron' part of the word.
- Kept her guardrails up: Daters who practise 'guardrailing' prioritize their own needs over those of their partner.
- Infla-dating: I wasn't wrong in guessing what this meant.

It relates to keeping a check on your expenditure on a date because you're conscious of rising inflation.

- Wanderlove: Suggested by the term 'wanderlust', which means an urge to travel, 'wanderlove' describes inter-city romances which require people to travel for a date.

Phew! I had no idea the young needed an entire new vocabulary for their love-life! And there's more, alas: potential daters who practise 'breadcrumbing' string you along, apparently, with no intention of actually dating you. And 'ghosting' is the practice of those who suddenly go silent towards a former romantic interest, conveying their loss of interest in maintaining a relationship by disappearing.

The announcement by an Indian girl in 2022 that she was going to marry herself introduced many to a new word—sologamy. Kshama Bindu, a twenty-four-year-old sociology graduate from Vadodara, announced she would be marrying herself. She felt ready for marriage but had no desire to marry a man, or indeed anyone else, so she decided to affirm her love for herself by conducting a marriage ceremony, complete with all the Hindu rituals. She has even found a priest willing to officiate, and has booked herself a two-week honeymoon afterwards—by herself!

While this may seem off the wall, and arguably is unprecedented in India, it is not only not unknown, but the practice even has a word for it, or even two. Just as monogamy is marriage to one person, bigamy to two, and polygamy to several at the same time, sologamy is the term for self-marriage. Some people even claim that individuals practising sologamy lead happier lives and are able to fulfil their own values and aspirations better. And yes, there is even an alternative term for sologamy: autogamy. Only one case, but two words for it in the English language! Go figure.

Of course, stand-up comics for years used to say that 'monogamy' was a synonym for 'monotony'. What would they say about sologamy, I wonder?

But if sologamy is a new word to most of us, a word we all assumed *is* new, turns out not to be. When Facebook gave people the chance to 'unfriend' others, many of us thought a neologism had been born. After all, what could be more twenty-first century than a term to abruptly stop sharing the most irrelevant details of your life with someone on social media? But apparently 'unfriend' has been around for an amazingly long time. Not, of course, in the sense of removing someone from your list of contacts on social media, a sense in which the usage only goes back to 2003, but just as a word in the English language. 'Unfriended' is at least as old as Shakespeare, but it was just used in the sense of 'friendless'. A person described as 'unfriended' was merely someone who had no friends. Whereas the contemporary word 'unfriend' is a verb, as in 'to unfriend' someone, ('I suggest you unfriend your ex', for instance), the noun 'unfriend' is recorded from the late thirteenth century, chiefly in Scottish, and was still in use in the nineteenth century. It actually meant 'enemy'—and calling someone an 'unfriend' was stronger than just saying 'he is not my friend'.

When American politics at the beginning of the century seemed full of people in high office who had a somewhat cavalier acquaintance with the truth—and asserted facts that sounded plausible but were in fact not true at all—the satirist Stephen Colbert came up in 2005 with a word even he thought he had invented, 'truthiness'. It seemed a clever way of saying somebody was lying or exaggerating excessively without insulting them directly—you could accuse them of 'truthiness', a term that seemed purpose-built for our brave new 'post-truth world'. But it turned out that the word 'truthiness' has been listed in the Oxford English Dictionary since 1824, not as a pejorative or even sarcastic term, but simply as an alternate word, or synonym, for 'truthfulness'. When Colbert was told that his neologism not only wasn't new but in fact meant something far more innocent than what he was trying to convey, his response was classic: 'You don't look up 'truthiness' in a dictionary, you look it up in your gut!'

Another word that we all assume to be of very recent coinage is 'influencer'—a term associated with social media, to refer to people with a large number of followers, who set the agenda, prompt trends, and influence opinions or purchases. Influencers are in great demand from social media marketers, who pay them to post favourable comments on their products on Instagram. But the word itself is not, in fact, new at all, and it wasn't created by social media. Apparently, the word 'influencer' dates back to the 1660s! 'Influencer' was used to refer to an influential person, fact, or circumstance that had an influence on people—for instance, 'Her mother's experience was the biggest influencer on her decision not to marry.' No one really uses it that way any more—unless, of course, you want to practise sologamy!

Generational differences and divides have always existed, but in the era of the internet, social media has taken them to a new level. I expect the language to undergo even more rapid change as a result. Gen Z has already introduced terms that millennials have had to embrace. Now the Alphas, all of ten years old or younger, have started inventing their own words. One of them, 'rizz', a contraction of 'charisma', was even named the Word of the Year 2023 by the Oxford English Dictionary, which defined it as 'style, charm or attractiveness'.

In November 2023, *New York Times* journalist Madison Malone Kircher interviewed half a dozen Alphas between eight and ten years of age about their vocabulary. Many of the children cited a catchy parody song making the rounds on TikTok to help her understand their popular usage. The lyrics, as quoted by Kircher:

Sticking out your gyat
For the rizzler
You're so skibidi
You're so Fanum tax
I just wanna be your sigma

'Having *rizz* is when you have good game,' one child explained. 'Being a *rizzler* is like when you're a pro at flirting with people.' Sticking out your *gyat* clearly refers to drawing attention to one's backside. Another child added that 'nobody really knows' the meaning of '*skibidi*'. It apparently entered the lexicon by way of the animated series 'Skibidi Toilet', a hugely popular dialogue-free series that depicts a conflict between singing human-headed toilets—the titular 'Skibidi Toilets'—and humanoids who just happen to have CCTV cameras, speakers, and televisions instead of heads. The show, according to Kircher, has racked up more than 700 million views on YouTube. '*Fanum tax*', it seems, refers to Fanum, a popular streamer on Twitch who regularly appears online and insists that people who are eating in his presence share their food with him. And *sigma,* Kircher tells us, has something to do with wolves. 'Everyone in my grade, at least, says it in a way where they're like the alpha of the pack,' one child told her. 'If you're trying to say you're dominant and you're the leader, you'll call yourself "sigma".'

So speaking the language that Alphas speak requires not just familiarity with offerings on the internet but a deep immersion in the prevalent social media culture in the United States (which by extension tends to influence the rest of the Anglophone world too). Just as, historically, classical languages like Sanskrit, Greek, Arabic, Latin, French, and German have all served as linguistic instruments for the transmission—or withholding—of important information in their regions of dominance, English has now become what scholars call 'the code of choice' for transmitting information in science and technology and for transacting economic and cultural exchanges across the world. It has no global challenger. In turn, the dominance of English has now become something of a self-reinforcing process in the age of internet and social media. This is partly because of the rapidly accelerating amount of information that the language encodes, which other languages would find extremely difficult to catch up with, and partly because of the speed at which it has been, and continues to be, adopted as the preferred medium of global communication. Perhaps sophisticated artificial-intelligence enabled translation tools will change this reality one day, but for now, the dominance of English makes it hugely attractive to potential learners from other linguistic streams.

'Potential participants in global communication have less and less incentive to make the effort to learn a language other than English,' observes the scholar Paul Bruthiaux. 'This is equally true both of speakers of English as a first language, who increasingly come to rely on others to do their language learning for them, and of speakers of English as a second language, who often take an instrumental, non-emotional view of a language they regard as serving their interests quite adequately and see no purpose in promoting another language of global communication. For these speakers, the effect of critical mass rules out any thought that a serious competitor to English as a global language may even exist.'

So the new words being coined by Generation Alpha even as this book is being written will infiltrate the entire planet before too long. One more example:

According to the website *hoomale.com*, 'Bruh', a versatile term originating from 'brother,' has evolved into a 'dynamic interjection' within Gen Alpha's lexicon. As the website explains:

> This succinct expression serves as a linguistic chameleon, capable of conveying a spectrum of emotions including exasperation, excitement, embarrassment, or surprise. Its adaptability transcends gender, making it a go-to exclamation for anyone navigating the unpredictable landscape of life. Use it when facepalming at a blunder, celebrating a triumph, or simply caught off guard by the unexpected, 'Bruh' is your linguistic sidekick.

Well, thanks, Bruh. Don't forget that Gen Alpha is still being born. It's clear we will need a whole new book soon.

ACKNOWLEDGEMENTS

This book is derived largely, but not wholly, from my 'World of Words' column in the Dubai newspaper the *Khaleej Times*, where much of this material originally appeared, though most of the pieces have been expanded and augmented since their original publication. I am grateful to the editors for commissioning the column and giving me a platform for my random musings on words and language, which have found a devoted readership in the Gulf, and now made this book possible for a wider audience.

I owe an enormous debt of gratitude, however, to an unsung friend who has single-handedly done the bulk of the research for my columns, Professor Sheeba Thattil. Her indefatigable efforts to identify interesting topics, to dredge up scholarly material about them and to supply me with an incessant stream of inputs, have sustained my columns amid a schedule so busy that I could not possibly have managed to write them—or this book—without her. To her, no word of thanks will ever be enough. This book is, in many ways, as much to her credit as to mine.

At Aleph Book Company, I would like to thank my publisher for over three decades, David Davidar, whose vision is visible in every one of my books; the diligent, meticulous, and thorough editor, Aienla Ozukum, who in her unobtrusive way leaves a mark of accuracy and precision on every volume that passes through her hands; and Vidisha Ghosh who helped in putting together the back matter of the book. Bena Sareen once again designed a stunning jacket. I would also like to thank Priya Kuriyan for her whimsical and charming illustrations, which feature in one of my books for the second time.

NOTES

vii **'The true alchemists do not change lead into gold':** William H. Gass, *A Temple of Texts*, New York: Alfred A. Knopf, 2006, p. 37.

vii **'I run after certain words... I catch them in mid-flight':** Pablo Neruda, *Memoirs*, Hardie St. Martin (tr.), London: Penguin Books, 1978, p. 53.

vii **'Raise your words, not your voice. It is rain that grows flowers':** 'Rumi (Jalal ad-Din Muhammad ar-Rumi)', Goodreads.com, available at www.goodreads.com/author/quotes/875661.Rumi_Jalal_ad_Din_Muhammad_ar_Rumi_.

INTRODUCTION: MY WORLD OF WORDS

xv **Incensed by a libellous TV programme about me, I had tweeted:** Shashi Tharoor (@ShashiTharoor), Post, X.com, 8 May 2017.

xvi **A clever meme-maker put my tweet**: KC Archana, 'Tintin's Captain Haddock Borrows Tharoor's "Exasperating Farrago Of Distortions" In Epic Meme', *India Times*, 6 Oct 2018.

xvi **While many of these were formulaic even if good-natured**: Ronnie Kuriakose, '"Farrago"-spurred Penguin adds 'Tharoorosaurus' to its flamboyant book mart!', *On Manorama*, 7 August 2020.

xvii **The earliest recorded usage of the word 'scrabble'**: *1537 Matthew's Bible*, John Rogers (tr.), [online facsimile], p. 407. Available at archive.org/details/1537-matthews-bible.

xvii **Almost four centuries later, in 1931, Alfred Mosher Butts**: Joe Sommerlad, 'Scrabble at 70: How an out-of-work architect devised the phenomenally popular word game', *Independent UK*, 13 December 2018.

xvii **The US dictionary's most recent update incorporated**: Justine McDaniel, 'From 'amirite' to 'zonkey,' new words join the Scrabble dictionary', *Washington Post*, 17 November 2022.

xviii **It has, however, removed over 200 words**: Scott Neuman, 'Scrabble Association Bans Racial, Ethnic Slurs from Its Official Word List', *NPR*, 8 July 2020.

xix **Wordle, invented by software engineer Josh Wardle:** Daniel Victor, 'Wordle Is a Love Story', *New York Times*, 3 January 2022.

xx **When a killjoy using the handle @wordlinator**: Mitchell Clark, 'Twitter suspends Wordle-ruining bot', TheVerge.com, 25 January 2022.

xx **I used to go to *https://www.devangthakkar.com/wordle_archive/***: Devang Thakkar, 'all good things must end', Devangthakkar.com, available at www.devangthakkar.com/wordle_archive.

xxi **This term was coined by the American essayist and critic**: Logan Pearsall Smith, *Reperusals and Recollections*, New York: Books for Libraries Press, 1968, p. 52.

xxii **As Barbara Chatton, professor of elementary education:** Barbara Chatton, *Using Poetry Across the Curriculum: Learning to Love Language*, 2nd edn., California: Libraries Unlimited, 2010, p. 8.

xxiv **The alarm bells have been sounded in a new scholarly article:** André Schüller-Zwierlein, Anne Mangen, Miha Kovač, and Adriaan van der Wee, 'Why higher-level reading is important', *First Monday*, Vol. 27, No. 5, available at firstmonday.org/ojs/index.php/fm/article/download/12770/10709.

xxv **The manifesto ends with Margaret Atwood's much quoted warning:** Margaret

Atwood, 'Why Wattpad Works', *The Guardian*, 6 July 2012.

xxvi **But he collected the names and addresses of as many directors:** Robert Pirosh, 'I Like Words', LettersOfNote.com, 13 March 2012, available at lettersofnote.com/2012/03/13/i-like-words.

SECTION ONE: BORROWED PLUMES

5 **American fighter planes in World War II used machine guns:** Claire Barrett, 'Can One Trace the Phrase 'The Whole Nine Yards' to WWII? Kind of…', Historynet.com, 7 August 2021, available at www.historynet.com/can-one-trace-the-phrase-the-whole-nine-yards-to-wwii-kind-of.

7 **If someone speaks of an 'iron-clad contract' or an agreement:** 'ironclad (adj.)', *Online Etymology Dictionary*, available at www.etymonline.com/word/ironclad.

8 **Heavy freight also travelled along the Mississippi in large barges:** Robert Hendrickson, *The Facts on File Encyclopedia of Word Origins: Definitions and Origins of More Than 15,000 Words and Expressions*, 4th edn., New York: Infobase Publishing, 2008, p. 61.

8 **Once in a while, of course, a boat would capsize:** Gary Martin, 'Over a Barrel', Phrases.org, available at www.phrases.org.uk/meanings/over-a-barrel.html.

9 **As a fascinating article in the *New York Times* describes it:** Damien Cave, 'The "Hard Yakka" of Defining Australian English's Many Quirks', *New York Times*, 19 June 2022.

10 **Former prime minister Scott Morrison described his rival:** Morrison's sledge against Albanese over wages', *Sydney Morning Herald*, 11 May 2022.

10 ***The Times* tells us that the first edition:** Cave, "The 'Hard Yakka" of Defining Australian English's Many Quirks'.

10 –11 **Might it include 'selfie' which the Oxford English Dictionary:** '"Selfie" named by Oxford Dictionaries as word of 2013', *BBC*, 19 November 2013.

12 **The most obvious evidence for Irish influence:** Una Mallaly, 'Up to 90: The best Irish words and phrases', *Irish Times*, 29 July 2017.

15 **In a tweet criticizing the media attacks on actor Shah Rukh Khan's:** Shashi Tharoor (@ShashiTharoor), Post, X.com, 4 October 2021.

16 **Realpolitik, which may gradually be falling into disuse in English:** Frank Bealey, *The Blackwell Dictionary of Political Science*, Oxford: Blackwell Publishers, 1999, p. 280.

18 **I was told by Catherine Henstridge of the *Oxford English Dictionary*:** John J. D. Trenor, *New York Times*, 7 December 1913.

18 **It didn't catch on much in the West, but the proceedings:** *Proceedings of the Thirty-ninth Indian Science Congress*, Calcutta: Indian Science Congress Association, 1952, p. 270.

32 **During World War I, the popular dish called sauerkraut:** Katherine Beck, 'Why people in the US once called sauerkraut liberty cabbage', *Tasting Table*, 27 September 2022.

33 **One Canadian café thought it was being clever:** 'Poutine: How Quebec's flagship dish is serving up controversy', *Malay Mail*, 9 March 2022.

34 **What, one might ask, is 'Finlandization':** Cora Engelbrecht, '"Finlandization" of Ukraine is part of the diplomatic discourse. But what does that mean?', *New York Times*, 8 February 2022.

35 **'Friend-shoring', also called 'ally-shoring', is an American term:** Atlantic Council, 'Transcript: US Treasury Secretary Janet Yellen on the next steps for Russia sanctions and 'friend-shoring' supply chains', *New Atlanticist*, 13 April 2022.

35 **The innocuous final letter of our alphabet has been transmuted:** Dipanita Nath, 'Why are Russians using the letter Z to show support for the war in Ukraine', *Indian Express*, 14 March.

37 **As the famous novelist Vladimir Nabokov explained it:** 'Vladimir Nabokov', Goodreads.com, available at www.goodreads.com/quotes/309633-toska---noun-t--sk---russian-word-roughly-translated-as.

37 **The Portuguese have a term that comes closer than any in English:** Jasmine Garsd, 'Saudade: An Untranslatable, Undeniably Potent Word', *NPR*, 8 January 2015.

38 **According to *Atlas Obscura*, 'Mamihlapinatapai' describes:** Zoe Baillargeon, 'How the Internet Changed the Meaning of 'Mamihlapinatapai', *Atlas Obscura*, 11 August 2017.

41 **The Supreme Court of India prides itself:** AIR (1952) SC 196

SECTION TWO: THE POINT OF PUNCTUATION

45 **One of the more delightful stories about the misuse of punctuation:** Lynne Truss, *Eats, Shoots and Leaves*, USA: Gotham Books, 2003.

46 **A similar story in Truss' book concerns an unpunctuated letter:** Ibid., pp. 9–10.

47 **But though it's a first for me, I wish to acknowledge my indebtedness:** The Cultural Tutor (@culturaltutor), Post, X.com, 8 November 2022.

52 **The closing of the Apostrophe Protection Society:** 'The pedants' pedant: why the Apostrophe Protection Society has closed in disgust', *The Guardian,* 2 December 2019.

52 **Derived from the late Latin *apostrophus* and the Greek *apostrophos:*** 'apostrophe (n.1)', *Online Etymology Dictionary,* 30 August 2023, available at www.etymonline.com/word/apostrophe.

53 **The *Oxford Style Guide* suggests spelling:** 'Apostrophe', in *University of Oxford Style Guide*, Oxford: Public Affairs Directorate, University of Oxford, 2014, p. 9.

53 **Lynne Truss argues for 'do's and don't's':** Truss, *Eats, Shoots and Leaves*, p. 45.

54 **The usefulness of the apostrophe was made clear:** 'Subeditor battled to save punctuation's endangered species', *Sydney Morning Herald*, 7 May 2021.

55 **This 'apostrophe apostasy' is not new:** 'George Bernard Shaw called them 'uncouth bacilli': 'The oul' apostrophe', *Irish Times*, 17 November 2008.

58 **According to linguist Angus Stevenson, there were 16,000 hyphenation changes:** Charles McGrath, 'Death-Knell. Or Death Knell', *New York Times*, 7 October 2007.

SECTION THREE: SPELLING BUGS

63 **Let's face it, English spelling is ridiculous:** Arika Orkent, 'Typos, tricks and misprints', Sally Davies (ed.), Aeon.com, 26 July 2021, available at aeon.co/essays/why-is-the-english-spelling-system-so-weird-and-inconsistent.

64 **But these aren't perfect either, as Karan Thapar wrote hilariously:** Karan Thapar, 'The mystery of the English language', *Hindustan Times*, 6 November 2021.

65 **I was reminded of this omission recently when a kerfuffle broke out:** Charles III, 'A message from The King to the Governor of Victoria regarding the ongoing flood emergency in Victoria', Royal.uk, 11 November 2022, available at www.royal.uk/message-his-majesty-king-governor-victoria-regarding-floods.

65 **One purist erupted in print. 'Realize?! I had to read the letter':** David Astle, 'To zee or not to zee? Why we're not amused about the King's English', *Sydney Morning Herald*, 7 December 2022.

66 ***Webster*, seeking to standardize spellings in American English:** 'Noah Webster's

Spelling Wins and Fails', *Merriam-Webster*, available at www.merriam-webster.com/grammar/noah-websters-spelling-wins-and-fails.

66 **Carnegie and his supporters argued that the only thing:** Paul Anthony Jones, 'When Theodore Roosevelt Tried to Reform the English Language', *Mental Floss*, 3 November 2016.

67 **When President Theodore Roosevelt endorsed:** Greg Daugherty, 'Teddy Roosevelt's Bold (But Doomed) Battle to Change American Spelling', History.com,4 September 2018.; Paul Anthony Jones, 'When Theodore Roosevelt Tried to Reform the English Language', *Mental Floss*, 3 November 2016.

69 **According to the author of *The Word Snoop*:** Ursula Dubosarky, *The Word Snoop: A Wild and Witty Tour of the English Language!*, USA: Dial Books, 2009, p. 25.

69 **Fans of the immortal English humourist P. G. Wodehouse:** P. G. Wodehouse, *Leave it to Psmith*, London: Penguin Books, 1923, p. 34.

72 **'The rogue knight doubted that the asthmatic knave':** Claire Nowak, 'The Real Reason Some English Words Have Silent Letters', Readers Digest, 19 July 2021.

74 **Because without our language, we have lost ourselves:** Melina Marchetta, *Finnikin of the Rock*, UK: Walker Books, p. 94.

77 **The best answer came from Marcus Geduld:** Marcus Geduld, 'Can you write a sentence without using a or e', Quora, available at www.quora.com/Can-you-write-a-sentence-without-using-a-or-e.

78 **In his introduction (which, not being part of the novel itself):** Ernest Vincent Wright, *Gadsby: A Story of Over 50,000 Words Without Using the Letter 'E'*, Los Angeles: Wetzel Publishing Co., 1939, p. 5.

SECTION FOUR: TYPOS, SUPERFLUITIES, MISPRINTS, AND OTHER ERRORS

84 **Even the famous *BBC News* is not exempt from such errors:** 'Knife crime: St John Ambulance to teach teens to help stab victims', BBC News, 7 May 2021.

84 **Thus the headline 'McDonald's Fries the Holy Grail for Potato Farmers':** 'McDonald's fries the holy grail for potato farmers', *Capital Press*, 24 September 2009.

86 **The second kind of misprint involves the omission of a letter:** Rachael Bletchly, 'The most hilarious typos, spelling mistakes and misprints - some even on a biblical scale', *Mirror*, 21 October 2015.

87 **But the prize for the most misprints undoubtedly goes to *The Guardian*:** Elisabeth Ribbans, 'Typo negative: the best and worst of Grauniad mistakes over 200 years', *The Guardian*, 12 May 2021.

89 **Language maven Richard Wydick, who objected to unnecessary legal jargon:** Richard Dydick, *Plain English for Lawyers*, 2nd edn., Durham: Carolina Academic Press, 1985, pp. 7–8.

93 **They were rendered respectable by no less an eminence:** William Shakespeare, *Julius Caesar*, [online facsimile], available at shakespeare.mit.edu/julius_caesar/julius_caesar.3.2.html.

95 **In short, as the grammarian Arthur Quinn explains in *Figures of Speech*:** Arthur Quinn, *Figures of Speech: 60 Ways to Turn a Phrase*, California: Hermagoras Press, 1993, p. 61.

96 **The term was coined by British philologist:** Walter Skeat, 'XIII.-FOURTEENTH ADDRESS OF THE PRESIDENT, TO THE PHILOLOGICAL SOCIETY, DELIVERED AT THE ANNIVERSARY MEETING, FRIDAY, 21ST MAY',

Transactions of the Philological Society, Vol 20, No. 1, November 1887, pp. 343–93.

96 The word 'phantomnation' appeared in the 1864 *Webster's Dictionary*: Homer, *Odyssey*, Alexander Pope (tr.), London: George Fell and Sons, 1906, p. 169.; Richard Paul Jodrell, *Philology of the English Language*, London: John Bohn, 1820.

96 *Webster's* have much to answer for in the ghost words department: '"Dord": A Ghost Word', *Merriam-Webster*, available at www.merriam-webster.com/wordplay/dord-a-ghost-word.

97 The 1755 *Johnson's Dictionary* defined the word 'foupe': Jack Lynch, 'Ghost Words and Mountweazels', *Lapham's Quarterly*, 23 February 2016.

97 Thus 'syllabus' is a transcription error of the word 'sittybas': John Ayto, *Word Origins: The Hidden Histories of English Words from A to Z*, 2nd edn., London: A&C Black Publishers, 2005, p. 493.

97 If you enjoy cherries, they come from the Old North French word 'cherise': 'How a Mistake Gave Us the Word Cherry', *Merriam-Webster*, available at www.merriam-webster.com/wordplay/cherry-history-origin.

96 –97 As did 'orange', which came from the Arabic 'naaranj': Annie Ewbank, 'How Orange (the fruit) inspired Orange (the colour', *Atlas Obscura*, 1 March 2018.

99 It's widely believed that that the word 'sandwich' was invented: Hendrickson, *The Facts on File Encyclopedia of Word and Phrase Origins*, p. 728.

99 The technical team documented this unusual incident in their logbook: National Geographic Society, 'Sep 9, 1947 CE: World's First Computer Bug', *National Geographic*, 19 October 2023.

100 The reality is that well before this event: 'Mr Edison and the Bacteria', *Pall Mall Gazette*, 11 March 1889.

100 –01 I'm rather fond of orange marmalade, complete with lots of peel: Elaine Lem, 'All About British Marmalade', *The Spruce Eats*, 29 August 2019.

SECTION FIVE: LINGUISTIC REGISTERS

108 It is said that Arabic has at least eleven words for love: Faraan Sayed, 'Surprising Facts about Arabic Language', British Council, 18 December 2015.

108 Although love is a powerful emotion, the word 'adore' is even more potent: Ayto, *Word Origins*, p. 359.

112 As far back as the 1940s, the author J. R. R. Tolkien: J. R. R. Tolkien, *On Fairy Stories*, [online facsimile], 8 March 1939, available at archive.org/details/on-fairy-stories_202110.

112 An intriguing pair, Heidi Quante and Alicia Escott: Richard Fisher, 'Why we need new words for life in the Anthropocene', *BBC*, 26 January 2023.

115 Countries like Argentina and Zimbabwe have, in the recent past: Farai Mutsaka, 'It's a nightmare: Zimbabwe struggles with hyperinflation', *AP News*, 10 October 2019.

115 Swiss chocolate addicts will recall when Toblerone in 2016: Beth Timmins, 'Toblerone: Swiss rules mean chocolate bar to drop Matterhorn from packaging', *BBC*, 6 March 2023.

117 Similar cultural prejudices are involved in the expression: Oliver Smith, 'French kiss, Chinese whispers, Dutch courage meanings: The origins of common geographic idioms', *Sydney Morning Herald*, 1 October 2018.

120 This too is pretty common: according to the American Psychiatry Association: 'Lethologica', Bionity.com, available at www.bionity.com/en/encyclopedia/

Lethologica.html.

120 **Lethologica is derived from the Ancient Greek word lethe, 'forgetfulness':** 'Lethologica: When a word's on the tip of your tongue', *BBC*, 8 February 2016.

123 **Again, the UAE, with perhaps as many as 89 per cent of its population:** 'Breakdown of expatriate population in the United Arab Emirates in 2018, by nationality', Statista.com, 12 September 2022, available at www.statista.com/statistics/984373/uae-expat-population-by-country-of-origin.

126 **They say that the Inuit dialect spoken in Canada's Nunavik:** David Robson, 'There are really 50 Eskimo words for "snow"', *Washington Post*, 14 January 2013.

128 **The German term 'blitzkrieg', meaning 'lightning war':** 'Blitzkrieg', History.com, 12 December 2022, available at www.history.com/topics/world-war-ii/blitzkrieg.

128 **'U-boat' was another term that found its way permanently into the English language:** Jay Hemmings, 'The German U-boats of WWII', War History Online, 12 February 2019, available at www.warhistoryonline.com/world-war-ii/the-german-u-boats-of-wwii.html.

129 **The colourful nicknames 'Moaning Minnie' and 'Howling Horace':** John Ayto, *Brewer's Dictionary of Phrase and Fable*, 17th edn., London: Weidenfeld and Nicholson, 2005, p. 916.

129 **The term 'quisling', for a traitor and collaborator:** Ibid., p. 1134.

130 **Similarly, a British propagandist on Radio Berlin:** Ibid., 649.

131 **The expression derives from nautical days of yore, where 'fathom':** Bill Beavis and Richard G. McCloskey, *Salty Dog Talk: The Nautical Origins of Everyday Expressions*, New York: Sheridan House, 1995, p. 32.

131 **Amusingly enough, the term is rooted in Old English:** Ayto, *Word Origins*, p. 212.

131 **'Keelhauling', a disciplinary measure once employed by the Dutch and English:** Kara Goldfarb, 'Keelhauling: Inside The Deranged Torture Method Used To Keep Sailors In Line', John Kuroski (ed.), *All That's Interesting*, 31 October 2022.

132 **Fresh water for immediate consumption on a sailing vessel:** Beavis and McCloskey, *Salty Dog* Talk, p. 72.

132 **Sailors onboard ships frequently found themselves occupied:** Ibid., p. 81–82.

134 **Derived from the French phrase 'm'aider':** Fred Sedgwick, *Where Words Come From: A Dictionary of Word Origins*, London: Continuum International Publishing Group, 2009, p. 15.; Rhik Kundu, 'How did Mayday come to be used as a distress call?', *Mint Lounge*, 26 July 2019.

134 **The term gained official international recognition:** *International Radio Telegraph Convention of Washington*, London: His Majesty's Stationery Office, 25 November 1927.

134 **The phrase derives from the mathematics of flight:** 'Ahead of the Curve', TheIdioms.com, available at www.theidioms.com/ahead-of-the-curve.

134 **This refers to the 'flight envelope':** Caroline Bologna, 'Here's Why We Say "Pushing The Envelope"', *Huffington Post*, 24 July 2018.

135 **It came into English from the German flak:** Hendrickson, *The Facts on File Encyclopedia of Word and Phrase Origins*, p. 307.

135 **The word 'gremlin' has come to mean a bug:** Ibid., p. 371.

135 **originated as 1950s US Air Force slang:** Ibid., p. 682.

137 **The word 'election' comes from the Latin:** Thomas Moore Delvin, '12 Political Word Origins That Can Help You Understand the Government', *Babel*, 28 October 2020.

137 **A 'campaign' seeks to place a candidate in office:** 'When Did 'Campaign' Become Political?', *Merriam-Webster*, available at www.merriam-webster.com/wordplay/

when-did-campaign-become-political.

137 Originally, 'manifesto' merely meant 'proof': 'The Vocabularist: Where did the word "manifesto" come from?', *BBC*, 16 April 2015.

137–38 The 'poll' in which one casts one's vote is derived from an old Germanic: 'poll (n.)', Online Etymology Dictionary, available at https://www.etymonline.com/word/poll.

138 The 'ballot' comes to us from the Italian word 'balotta': Ayto, *Brewer's Dictionary of Phrase and Fable*, p. 99.

138 Of course, you can always 'abstain' or refrain: 'abstain (n.)', Online Etymology Dictionary, available at www.etymonline.com/word/abstain.

138 The earliest recorded use of the noun 'recount' can be traced: 'recount (verb)', *Oxford English Dictionary*, available at www.oed.com/dictionary/recount.

139 Since language is an instrument of self-advancement: Charles E. Trevelyan, *On Education of the People of India*, Paternoster-Row: Longman, Orme, Brown, Green, & Longmans, p. 166.

139 Even the term 'native' carries a particular connotation: Ayto, *Word Origins*, p. 346.

140 The term 'safari', a Swahili word derived from Arabic: 'History of Safari: How It All Began', Eyes on Africa, available at www.eyesonafrica.net/Articles/safari-history.htm.

141 As Canadian freelance game and speculative fiction reviewer James Nicoll: James Nicoll, 'About the Purity of the English Language T-shirts', *James Nicoll Reviews*, 7 November 2014.

142 The earliest documented use of the term 'computer' goes as far back: R. B. Gent, *The Yong Man's Gleanings*, London: Iohn Beale, 1614, p. x.

142 Similar to many newly-coined words that gain wide recognition: Maureen Dowd, 'A.I.: Actually Insipid Until It's Actively Insidious', *New York Times*, 28 January 2023.

143 The term 'browser' is derived from the verb 'browse': Ayto, *Word Origins*, London: A&C Black Publishers, 2005, p. 78.

143 The unassuming computer 'mouse' began its journey from 1970: SRI International, '75 Years of Innovation: The computer mouse', *The Dish*, 7 May 2020.

143 –44 A computer 'file' is 'a compilation of data treated as a single unit': Ayto, *Word Origins*, p. 217.

151 As early as the twelfth century, 'Madras' referred to a type of handmade fabric: Nidhi Garg Allen, 'A Humble Origins & Fascinating Stories of the Fashionable Madras Checks', *Saar*, 24 September 2023.

152 The term 'paisley' came from the town of Paisley, in western Scotland: 'The History of the Paisley Symbol and Paisley Pattern', PaisleyPower.com, available at www.paisleypower.com/history-of-paisley.

152 'Seersucker', a lightweight linen material, derives its name: Hendrickson, *The Facts on File Encyclopedia of Word and Phrase Origins*, p. 740.

152 This remarkable luxury textile was termed 'chintz': Ibid., p. 175.

152 In a letter to her sister in 1851, the author George Eliot wrote: Joobin Bekhard,'The "Cutesy" Indian Fabric That Changed History', *The Print*, 30 April 2020.

153 'Calico' has its origins in Calicut: Hendrickson, *The Facts on File Encyclopedia of Word and Phrase Origins*, p. 146.

153 The Jacquard loom, an extraordinary innovation that revolutionized: 'Programming Patterns: The Story of the Jacquard Loom', MuseumOfScienceandIndustry.org.uk, 25 June 2019.

153 The roots of the term 'chambray' trace back to 1801: 'cambric', *Merriam-Webster*, available at www.merriam-webster.com/dictionary/cambric#word-history.

154 Chevron made its way into the English language: 'History of Chevron Fabric', *Cloth and Stitch*, 22 October 2021.

154 Moiré has its roots in the French language: Sarah Archer, 'This Throwback Fabric Is Back in Major Way', *Elle Décor*, 5 February 2022.; 'Moiré', Online Etymology Dictionary, available at www.etymonline.com/word/moire.

154 The origins of the 'poplin' fabric lie in the medieval French city: Hendrickson, *The Facts on File Encyclopedia of Word and Phrase Origins*, p. 667.

154 Tartan is believed to have its roots in the thirteenth century: 'tartan', Online Etymology Dictionary, available at www.etymonline.com/word/tartan.

155 Camouflage originates from the French word 'camoufler': 'camouflage', *Merriam-Webster*, available at www.merriam-webster.com/dictionary/camouflage#word-history.

155 Harlequin originating from the Commedia dell'arte: Ayto, *Word Origins*, p. 263.

155 'Argyle' rose to popularity: Hendrickson, *The Facts on File Encyclopedia of Word and Phrase Origins*, p. 37.

156 The 'herringbone' pattern has its roots in the Roman Empire: 'The History of Herringbone', *K and A*, 2 February 2017.

156 The term 'gingham' is believed to have its roots in the Dutch: 'Gingham History', *The Stiff Collar*, available https://www.thestiffcollar.com/blogs/the-collar-speaks/gingham-history.; 'Gingham', *Britannica*, available at www.britannica.com/topic/gingham.

156 'Batik', originating from Java, Indonesia: Anna Elise Anderson, 'Batik 101: Where It Comes From, How It's Made, and How to Use It in an Interior', *Architectural Digest*, 24 July 2023.

157 The term is derived from the Spanish 'brocado': Anna Elise Anderson, 'Brocade Fabric, Explained', *Architectural Digest*, 27 October 2023.

157 'Damask', derived from the ancient Syrian city of Damascus: Ayto, *Word Origins*, p. 149.

157 Historically, the fabric goes back to the Tang Dynasty in China: Ella Clarkes, 'History of Damask', *Schumacher*, 23 October 2022.

SECTION SIX: IN[APPROPRIATE] WORDS AND CARDINAL GUIDELINES

161–62 Akrasia comes from the Greek for 'lacking control of oneself: Sarah Stroud and Larisa Svirsky, 'Weakness of Will', *The Stanford Encyclopedia of Philosophy* (Winter 2021 Edition), Edward N. Zalta (ed.), available at plato.stanford.edu/archives/win2021/entries/weakness-will.

162 There's a word I can understand us not using much: Thomas Blount, *Glossographia, or, A dictionary interpreting all such hard words of whatsoever language now used in our refined English tongue with etymologies, definitions and historical observations on the same: also the terms of divinity, law, physick, mathematicks and other arts and sciences explicated*, 2nd edn., London: George Sawbridge, 1661, p. 54.

164 Shakespeare's *King Lear* has the most elaborate insult: Shakespeare, *King Lear*, [online facsimile], available at shakespeare.mit.edu/lear/full.html.

164 As early as 1652, the Scottish writer Thomas Urquhart: Charles Harrington Elster, *There's a Word for It: A Grandiloquent Guide to Life*, California: Gallery Books, 2005, p. 190.; 'quomodocunquizing', Oxford English Dictionary, available at www.oed.com/search/dictionary/?scope=Entries&q=quomodocunquizing; 'clusterfist', *Oxford English Dictionary*, available at www.oed.com/search/

dictionary/?scope=Entries&q=clusterfist.

164 **But the fading away of these fabulously insulting terms:** Emily Temple, 'A Selection of Virginia Woolf's Most Savage Insults', Literary Hub, 12 October 2017.

166 **'Gratiano speaks an infinite deal of nothing':** Shakespeare, *The Merchant of Venice*, [online facsimile], available at shakespeare.mit.edu/merchant/full.html.

166 **Charles Dickens wrote of a character, 'He would make a lovely corpse':** Charles Dickens, *Martin Chuzzlewit*, Oxford: Oxford University Press, 1998, p. 354.

166 **George Orwell dismissed another:** George Orwell, *The Lion and the Unicorn: Socialism and the English Genius*, London: Penguin Books, 1982, p. 56.

166 **An Ernest Hemingway character says:** Ernest Hemingway, *The Sun Also Rises*, USA: Scribner, 2021, p. 51.

166 **Agatha Christie is the politest of the lot:** Agatha Christie, *Murder on the Orient Express: A Hercule Poirot Mystery*, Leicester: Ulverscroft, 2010, p. 38.

166 **But the prize still goes to Shakespeare: 'I desire that we be better strangers.':** Shakespeare, *As You Like It*, [online facsimile], available at shakespeare.mit.edu/asyoulikeit/full.html.

167 **Bosh, it turns out, comes from *bos*:** Hendrickson, *The Facts on File Encyclopedia of Word and Phrase Origins*, p. 110.

167 **An even more dismissive term for nonsense was 'codswallop':** Ayto, *Brewer's Dictionary of Phrase and Fable*, p. 295.; 'Nooks and Crannies', *The Guardian*, available at www.theguardian.com/notesandqueries.

168 **A more straightforward etymology can be found for 'folderol':** Hendrickson, *The Facts on File Encyclopedia of Word and Phrase Origins*, p. 292.

168 **And the even more evocative 'poppycock' comes from a Dutch:** Sedgwick, *Where Words Come From*, p. 134.

168 **'Bunkum' came from American politics in 1820:** Ibid., p. 28.

168 **'Blatherskite', on the other hand, is of Scottish origin:** Ayto, *Brewer's Dictionary of Phrase and Fable*, p. 157.; 'blatherskite', *Merriam-Webster*, available at ww.merriam-webster.com/dictionary/blatherskite#word-history.

170 **There's an entire article you can google from the *Los Angeles Times*:** June Casagrande, 'A Word, Please: 'Moist' and other words people don't like', *Los Angeles Times*, 5 January 2023.

171 **I am clearly out of sync with the global mood:** 'Words Came In, Marked for Death', *New Yorker*, 23 April 2012.

171 **This was confirmed by another survey conducted:** 'Gross Beyond Words', CarpenterNYC.com, available at carpenternyc.com/thoughts/gross-beyond-words.

171 **A linguistics professor at the University of Pennsylvania, Mark Liberman:** Ibid.

173 **The term 'taboo' has its roots in Polynesian culture:** Ayto, *Brewer's Dictionary of Phrase and Fable*, p. 1351.

174 **In Shakespeare's play *The Tempest*, when Prospero asserts:** Shakespeare, *The Tempest*, [online facsimile], available at shakespeare.mit.edu/tempest/full.html.

179 **Dysphemism is the antithesis to euphemism:** 'dysphemism (noun)', *Merriam-Webster*, available at www.merriam-webster.com/dictionary/dysphemism#word-history.

179 **Winston Churchill once accused an opponent of 'terminological inexactitude':** 'Why are Members of Parliament not allowed to call each other liars in the House of Commons', *The Guardian*, 1 January 2011.

180 **Keith Allan and Kate Burridge, in the book *Euphemism and Dysphemism*:** Keith Allen and Kate Burridge, *Euphemism and Dysphemism: Language Used as*

Sheild and Weapon, New York: Oxford University Press, 1997, p. vii.

SECTION SEVEN: LITERARY TOOLS

185 **The folks at the *Merriam-Webster* dictionaries speculate:** 'The Hilarious History of OK', *Merriam-Webster*, available www.merriam-webster.com/wordplay/the-hilarious-history-of-ok-okay.

186 **According to two people who have researched the word:** Allan Metcalf, *OK: The Improbable Story of America's Greatest Word*, Oxford: Oxford University Press, 2011, p. x.

186 **Before you wonder how such a trivial joke caught on:** Ibid., p. 16.

187 **The answer apparently lies in the US presidential election of 1840:** Ibid., p. 41–2.

187 **Metcalf dismisses all the other 'origin stories', but details many of them:** Ibid., p. 6.

188 **The most creative and widely believed story claimed it was one more thing:** p. 86.

192 ***The Economist* has observed, 'where California leads':** Martin Adams, Aryn Braun, Joel Budd, Tom Standage and Vijay Vaitheeswaran, '23 items of vital vocabulary you'll need to know in 2023', *The Economist*, 14 November 2022.

193 **And churlish chiding of the winter's:** Shakespeare, *As You Like It*, [online facsimile], available at shakespeare.mit.edu/asyoulikeit/full.html.

193 **'The fair breeze blew, the white foam flew/ The furrow followed free':** Samuel Taylor Coleridge, *Rime of the Ancient Mariner*, Poets.org., available at poets.org/poem/rime-ancient-mariner.

193 **Robert Frost's 'Acquainted with the Night' offers:** Robert Frost, *Acquainted with the Night*, Poets.org., poets.org/poem/acquainted-night.

193 **E. E. Cummings's poem *All in Green Went My Love Riding*:** E. E. Cummings, *Songs (V)*, Poets.org, available at poets.org/poem/songs-v.

198 **Not long ago in India, BJP supporters of the prime minister:** 'Rearranging Narendra Modi Doesn't Give You Rare Diamond', SMHoaxSlayer.com, 1 June 2016.; 'Narendra Modi Anagrams', AnagramGenius.com, available at www.anagramgenius.com/archive/narendra-modi.htm.

201 **In a biblical passage, Pontius Pilate asks Jesus 'what is truth?':** 'John 18:38', BibleHub.com, available at biblehub.com/text/john/18-38.htm.

202 **The publisher had to resort to a footnote to explain:** 'Tom Marvolo Riddle', CVJLang.com, available at www.cjvlang.com/Hpotter/wordplay/riddle.html.

204 **Winston Churchill, a master of morale-booster rhetoric:** 'We Shall Fight on the Beaches', InternationalChurchillSociety.com, available at winstonchurchill.org/resources/speeches/1940-the-finest-hour/we-shall-fight-on-the-beaches.

205 **Thus the Old Testament, Ecclesiastes 3:1–2:** 'Ecclesiastes 3', BibleHub.com, available at biblehub.com/nkjv/ecclesiastes/3.htm.

205 **The poet Rumi's famous lines about taking the rough:** 'Rumi (Jalal ad-Din Muhammad ar-Rumi)', Goodreads.com, available at https://www.goodreads.com/quotes/9825163-if-you-want-the-moon-do-not-hide-from-the_.

205 **My favourite lines of T. S. Eliot stay in my head:** T. S. Eliot, *The Rock*, New York: Harcourt Brace, and Company, 1934, p.7.

208 **In fact, SOS wasn't an acronym at all:** Ethan Nelson, 'The History of Morse Code', DailyDabble.com, 1 October 2024.

210 **A recent headline declared that the United States had sanctioned:** 'US House easily passes bill to harden sanctions on Iranian oil', *Reuters*, 4 November 2023.

213 **A skimpy women's swimsuit that came into fashion a year:** Hendrickson, *The Facts on File Encyclopedia of Word and Phrase Origins*, p. 85.

213 **'Bogus' comes from mispronouncing the name:** Julia Cresswell (ed.), *Oxford*

Dictionary of Word Origins, 2nd edn., London: Oxford University Press, 2009, p. 54.

213 'I'll hoover it up' comes from the inventor of the vacuum cleaner: 'The Invention of the Vacuum-cleaner, from Horse-drawn to High-tech', ScienceMuseum.org, 3 April 2020, available at www.sciencemuseum.org.uk/objects-and-stories/everyday-wonders/invention-vacuum-cleaner.

213 'I need to fill up some diesel' takes its name: 'Rudolf Diesel', *Britannica*, available at www.britannica.com/biography/Rudolf-Diesel.

213 'let's take the kids on the Ferris wheel': Jamie Malanowski, 'The Brief History of the Ferris Wheel', *Smithsonian Magazine*, June 2015.

213 If you want to hop into the jacuzzi, you are tipping your hat: 'jacuzzi', Online Etymology Dictionary, 30 August 2023, available at www.etymonline.com/word/Jacuzzi.

213 If you slip on some leotards, there's an eponymous French circus performer: 'The History of the Dance Leotard', *Bloch World*, 15 October 2019.

214 One 'boycotts' people throughout the English-speaking world: Cresswell (ed.), *Oxford Dictionary of Word Origins*, p. 58.

214 Few authors realize, however, that the term for this puffery: Ibid., p. 58.

215 Another unlikely eponym is 'hooligan', which it turns out: Hendrickson, *The Facts on File Encyclopedia of Word and Phrase Origins*, p. 415.

215 Similar lawlessness applies to another eponym, 'lynch': Sedgwick, *Where Words Come From: A Dictionary of Word Origins*, p. 99.; Geoffrey Abott, 'Lynching', *Britannica*, 16 February 2024.

215 It is named for French diplomat and scholar Jean Nicot: Hendrickson, *The Facts on File Encyclopedia of Word and Phrase Origins*, p. 589.

220 'Oxymoron' is derived from the Greek words: Ayto, *Brewer's Dictionary of Phrase and Fable*, p. 1018.

SECTION EIGHT: LITERARY ACROBATICS

228 The word comes from the name of a character in the Irish playwright: Ayto, *Brewer's Dictionary of Phrase and Fable*, p. 856.; Richard Brinsley Sheridan, *The Rivals*, New York: Thomas Y. Cromwell & Co., 1905, pp. 17–20.

229 The American baseball player Yogi Berra famously spoke of Texas: 'Yogi Berra Quotes: Baseball legend's memorable saying', *BBC*, 23 September 2015.

229 Richard Daley, the former mayor of Chicago during that city's 1968 riots: 'Political Notes: Chairman Daley's Maxims', *TIME*, 18 July 1969.

229 Texas Speaker of the House Gib Lewis declared some event: Megan Jones, '16 of the Most Famous Malapropism Examples', *Readers Digest*, 9 May 2023.

229 An actor in the famous TV series *The Sopranos* spoke: Nathan Sharp, 'The Sopranos: The 10 Funniest Misquotes Of The Series, Ranked', ScreenRant.com, 10 August 2021.

229 The character Archie Bunker in the now-classic *All in the Family* series: Geof, 'The Best Archie Bunker Quotes Of All Time', 20 May 2020, available at www.archiefoundationhome.org.uk/money/archie-bunker-quotes.

231 My favourite paraprosdokian comes from the comedian Bob Monkhouse: 'Bob's Best Gags', *The Guardian*, 29 December 2023.

231 When I was ten, I beat up the school bully. His arms were in casts.': 'Emo Philips', AZQuotes.com, available at www.azquotes.com/quote/1178501.

231 Or 'I asked God for a bike, but I know God doesn't work that way': Emo Philips, 'The best God joke ever - and it's mine!', *The Guardian*, 29 September 2005.

231 My wife and I were happy for twenty-five years; then we met.': 'Rodney Dangerfield', Goodreads.com, available at www.goodreads.com/quotes/18223-my-wife-and-i-were-happy-for-twenty-years-then.

231 And how about 'Always borrow money from a pessimist.': 'Oscar Wilde', Goodreads.com, available at quoteinvestigator.com/2017/04/04/good-looks.

231 'She got her good looks from her father; he's a plastic surgeon.': 'Groucho Marx', Goodreads.com, available at www.goodreads.com/quotes/98968-she-got-her-looks-from-her-father-he-s-a-plastic.

231 'I can picture in my mind a world without war, a world without hate': Jack Handey, *Deep Thoughts: Inspiration for the Uninspired*, Berkley: Berkley Books, 1992.

232 'Artificial intelligence is no match for natural stupidity.': A. S. Panneerselvan, 'Is artificial intelligence fuelling natural stupidity?', *The Hindu*, 10 July 2017.

232 'If at first you don't succeed, skydiving is not for you.': 'Steven Wright', Goodreads.com, available at www.goodreads.com/quotes/141045-if-at-first-you-don-t-succeed-then-skydiving-definitely-isn-t.

232 Or: 'If you can smile when things go wrong': 'Ashleigh Brilliant', AZQuotes.com, available at www.azquotes.com/quote/1264801.

232 'He who laughs last, thinks slowest.': 'Daniel Lawrence Whitney (Larry the Cable Guy),' AZQuotes.com, available at www.azquotes.com/quote/855155.

232 'Change is inevitable, except from a vending machine.': 'Robert Gallagher', Goodreads.com, available at www.goodreads.com/quotes/78574-change-is-inevitable---except-from-a-vending-machine.

232 'Take my advice; I'm not using it.': 'David J. Henderhan', Goodreads.com, available at www.goodreads.com/quotes/441191-take-my-advice-i-m-not-using-it.

232 'Nostalgia isn't what it used to be.': Robert De Vries, *The Tents of Wickedness*, USA: Little Brown & Company, 1959, p. 6.

232 'Myrtle Prosser was a woman of considerable but extremely severe beauty': Wodehouse, *Ice in the Bedroom*, London: Pan Books Ltd., 1968, p. 15.

236 A 'Tom Swifty' is a phrase in which a pun is used in reporting speech: Ayto, *Brewer's Dictionary of Phrase and Fable*, p. 1397.

241 Mark Twain wrote of a terrified boy: Mark Twain, *Life on the Mississippi*, Boston: James R. Osgood and Company, 1883, p. 164.

241 Paul Bunyan, the fictional character popular in American folklore: *Babe and the Blue Ox*, retold by S. E. Schlosser, available at ww.americanfolklore.net/babe-the-blue-ox/.

241 'Popular American humourist and columnist Dave Barry': Dave Barry, 'Making Model Misconception', *The Washington Post*, 11 October 1986.

242 'I have been assured by a very knowing American of my acquaintance': Jonathan Swift, *A Modest Proposal and Other Works (Webster's Thesaurus Edition)*, USA: Icon Classics, p. 5.

243 'She had more curves than a scenic railway': 'P. G. Wodehouse', Goodreads.com, available at www.goodreads.com/quotes/142514-she-had-more-curves-than-a-scenic-railway.

244 'handed to me on a silver platter with watercress around it....': Wodehouse, *Leave it to PSmith*, London: Penguin Books, 1923, p. 146.

245 Red herring first appeared in the literal 'smoked fish' sense around 1420: Cresswell (ed.), *Oxford Dictionary of Word Origins*, p. 362.

252 Another classic is: 'Groucho Marx', Goodreads.com, available at www.goodreads.com/author/quotes/43244.Groucho_Marx.

254 Chinese checkers are not Chinese, but English: 'Halma', *Britannica*, available www.britannica.com/topic/Halma-game.

255 the word 'Jerusalem' is most likely a mangling: Shaffinalli, 'List of Folk Etymologies in English', *Lists of Everything*, 6 April 2011.

255 The word English horn mistranslates the French word: Nancy E. Clauter, 'Oboe and Music Theory', *Teaching Philosophy,* available at www.uky.edu/~oboenan/teach.htm.

255 Although Venetian blinds were popular in Venice: 'The History of the Blinds', Agostini Museum of the Window, available at www.museoagostini.com/en/blinds-history.

SECTION NINE: BEER AND SKITTLES

263 The American writer and linguist Richard Lederer put it: Richard Lederer, *The Word Circus: A Letter Perfect Book*, Massachusetts: Merriam-Webster, p. 129.

264 Kangaroo words were originally popularized as a word game: Ben O'Dell, 'Kangaroo Words' in *The American Magazine*, reprinted in *Reader's Digest*, 1956, p. 69.

265 *Gulliver's Travels* gave us the concept of *Brobdingnagian*: Jonathan Swift, *Gulliver's Travels into Several Remote Nations of the World*, 1997 [online facsimile], www.gutenberg.org/files/829/829-h/829-h.htm.

267 A kenning (the term comes from Old Norse poetry) employs: 'kenning', Britannica, available at www.britannica.com/art/kenning.

270 Wherever it might have originated: Cresswell (ed.*), Oxford Dictionary of Word Origins*, p. 252–53.

270 'There was an Old Man with a beard, Who said, 'It is just as I feared!': Edward Lear, *The Book of Nonsense*, London: F. Warne & Co., p.1.

270 There was a young rustic named Mallory: 'Wise and Otherwise', *Saint John Daily News*, 30 November 1880.

271 Or this 1902 pun-laden classic by Danton Voorhees: Danton Voorhees, 'There Was Once a Man from Nantucket', *Princeton Tiger*, 1902.

271 'A dozen, a gross, and a score': Leigh Mercer, *A Dozes, a Gross, and a Score*, YourDailyPoem.org, available at www.yourdailypoem.com/listpoem.jsp?poem_id=4294.

271 Lewis Carroll of *Alice in Wonderland* fame wrote this: Lewis Carroll, *To Miss Vera Beringer*, AllPoetry.com, available at allpoetry.com/poem/14327811-To-Miss-Vera-Beringer-by-Lewis-Carroll.

271 The American humourist Ogden Nash was funnier: Judson K. Cornelius, *Literary Humour*, 2nd edn., Bangalore: Better Yourself Books, 2005, p. 69.

272 Few thought he was even a starter: John Bew, *Citizen Clem: A Biography of Atlee*, London: Quercus Publishing, 2016, p. 535.

274 The word 'palindrome' was coined by the seventeenth-century English dramatist: Ayto, *Brewer's Dictionary of Phrase and Fable*, p. 1024.

275 James Joyce is often credited with this for inventing: James Joyce, *Ulysses*, Paris: Shakespeare and Company, 1922, p. 699.

275 –76 Alexandre Dumas's *The Three Musketeers* has the famous: Alexander Dumas, *The Three Musketeers*, 1998 [online facsimile], www.gutenberg.org/files/829/829-h/829-h.htm.

276 Authors of books on language and wordplay: Martin Gardner, 'A-Symmetry', *New York Review*, 3 December 1992.

276 Lovers of literature will be familiar with Scottish poet: *An Alastair Reid Reader:*

Selected Prose and Poetry, New England: Middlebury College Press, p. 1994, p. 175.

276 **A palindromic poem, 'Doppelgänger', by James A. Lindon:** Sona Simonian, 'Palindrome Poetry', *Writer's Block Magazine*, 5 November 2019.

278 **When the *Times of India* ran a headline about rising inflation:** Nida Sayed, 'Hitting Rs 140 per kg, tomatoes become budgetary hot potato', *Times of India*, 17 July 2023.

278 **This has been dubbed a 'malaphor':** Lawrence Harrison, 'Searching for Malaphors', *Washington Post*, 6 August 1976.

279 **One of history's most famous examples of a recorded mixed metaphor:** Elizabeth Knowles (ed.), *The Oxford Dictionary of Quotations*, 5th edn., Oxford: Oxford University Press, 1999, p. 630.

281 **The *Detroit News* actually printed this in 2012:** *Detroit News*, quoted in *New Yorker*, 26 November 2012.

281 **The then chairman of the US Federal Reserve, Ben Bernanke:** 'Transcript of Chairman Bernanke's Press Conference', 19 June 2013, available at www.federalreserve.gov/mediacenter/files/fomcpresconf20130619.pdf.

280 **But imagine if the offending speaker above added:** Geert Bronte, Kurt Fayaerts, and Tony Veale (eds.), *Cognitive Linguistics and Humour Research*, Vol. 26, Berlin: De Gruyter Mouton, 2015, p. 103.

282 **[T]he bill is mostly a stew of spending on existing programs:** David Leonhardt, 'A Stimulus With Merit, and Misses Too', *New York Times*, 27 January 2009.

280 **(Talking about the Democratic presidential candidates):** Bob Herbert, 'Behind the Curtain', *New York Times*, 27 November 2007.; Richard Nordist, 'Mixed Metaphor', *ThoughtCo.com*, 6 June 2019, available at www.thoughtco.com/what-is-a-mixed-metaphor-1691395.

282 **The mayor often strips his gears by failing to engage the clutch when shifting what emanates:** Nordist, 'Mixed Metaphor'.

282 **'The moment that you walk into the bowels of the armpit of the cesspool of crime':** 'Block That Metaphor!', *New Yorker*, 27 March 2000, p. 118.

282 **Or, from the *London Evening Standard*:** Nordist, 'Mixed Metaphor', available at www.thoughtco.com/what-is-a-mixed-metaphor-1691395.

283 **'The committee was tired of stoking public outrage':** Guy Gugliotta, 'Fallacious Full Disclosure', *Washington Post*, 16 April 1992.

283 **American television, not to be outdone, produced these gems:** Roz Laws, 'Funniest phrases from The Apprentice's Gary Poulton', *Birmingham Mail*, 26 November 2015.

283 **The right-wing commentator Rush Limbaugh declared:** Karen Sullivan, *Mixed Metaphors: Their Use and Abuse*, London: Bloomsbury Academic, 2018, p. 50.

283 **We should conclude with this sage observation quoted by Willard R. Espy:** Willard R. Epsy, *The Game of Words*, New York: Bramhall House, 1987, p. 163.

283 **–84 Scholars often quote this line from *Timon of Athens*:** Shakespeare, *Timon of Athens*, [online facsimile], available at shakespeare.mit.edu/timon/full.html.

284 **Or his well-known phrase from *Hamlet*, 'to take arms against':** Shakespeare, *Hamlet*, [online facsimile], available at shakespeare.mit.edu/hamlet/full.html.

284 **In his play *King John*, he gave us another memorable example:** Shakespeare, *King John*, [online facsimile], available at shakespeare.mit.edu/john/full.html.

284 **In Shakespeare's *The Tempest*, the character Gonzalo remarks:** Shakespeare, *The Tempest*, [online facsimile], available at shakespeare.mit.edu/tempest/full.html.

284 **When Shakespeare's Hamlet says 'I will speak daggers to her':** Shakespeare, *Hamlet*.

284 Matters are made worse by the fact: 'catachresis', *Merriam-Webster*, available at www.merriam-webster.com/dictionary/catachresis#word-history.

284 The British newspaper *The Guardian*, famous for its misprints: Sean Clark, 'The Wrapped: Re-united Nations', *The Guardian*, 9 June 2004.

285 'The voice of your eyes is deeper than all roses': E. E. Cummings, *somewhere I have never travelled, gladly beyond*, Poets.org, available at poets.org/poem/somewhere-i-have-never-travelledgladly-beyond.

286 The poet Alexander Pope wrote of Queen Anne: Alexander Pope, *The Rape of the Lock: Canto III*, available at www.poetryfoundation.org/poems/44908/the-rape-of-the-lock-canto-3.

286 Tennyson's zeugma is pitch-perfect: Alfred Tennyson, *Enoch Arden*, Farrinford.co.uk, available at farringford.co.uk/history/tennyson/poems/enoch-arden.

286 Mark Twain in *The Adventures of Tom Sawyer*: Mark Twain, *The Adventures of Tom Sawyer*, Chicago: The American Publishing Company, 1875, p. 24.

286 Charles Dickens in *The Pickwick Papers* wrote: Charles Dickens, *The Pickwick Papers*, London: Chapman and Co., 1900, p. 403.

286 In *Oliver Twist*, Dickens describes a character: Charles Dickens, *Works of Charles Dickens: Oliver Twist Vol. I*, New York: James G. & Gregory, 1861, p. 38.

286 Henry David Thoreau wrote in *Walden*: Henry D. Thoreau, *Walden: or, Life in the Woods*, Boston: Ticknor and Fields, 1854, p. 262.

286 For a more recent example: Amy Tan, *The Hundred Secret Senses*, London: Flamingo, 1995, p. 125.

287 For example, in the Biblical sentence, Exodus 20:18: 'Exodus 20', *New King James Bible*, [online facsimile], available at biblehub.com/nkjv/exodus/20.htm.

SECTION TEN: LEXICAL EVOLUTION

294 The country officially changed its name in 2022: 'Why Turkey is now 'Türkiye', and why that matters', *TRT World*, available at www.trtworld.com/magazine/why-turkey-is-now-t%C3%BCrkiye-and-why-that-matters-52602.

296 The sudden unsettling decision to have the president of India: 'G20 invite by President sparks Bharat/India row', *Hindustan Times*, 6 September 2023.

297 It was Mohammed Ali Jinnah, the founder of Pakistan: Shoaib Daniyal, 'Why Jinnah objected to the name "India"', *Scroll.in*, 19 June 2018.

299 So to tackle both challenges, I tweeted: Shashi Tharoor (@ShashiTharoor), Post, X.com, 10 October 2018.

300 Till 'floccinaucinihilipilification' was invented by British undergrads: Christina Sterbenz, 'The 6 English Words Longer Than Antidisestablishmentarianism', *Business India Insider*, 20 September 2013.

302 'I could see that, if not actually disgruntled, he was far from being gruntled': Wodehouse, *The Code of Woosters*, New York: Vintage Books, 1975, p. 8.

303 'Unkempt' has its origins dating back to the fourteenth century: Cresswell (ed.), *Oxford Dictionary of Word Origins*, p. 467.

303 The term 'whelm', derived from the Old English: Hendrickson, *The Facts on File Encyclopedia of Word and Phrase Origins*, p. 624.

303 Interestingly, 'corrigible' emerged in the fifteenth century: 'The Opposite of 'Incorrigible', *Merriam-Webster*, available at www.merriam-webster.com/wordplay/why-do-we-use-incorrigible-and-not-corrigible.

303 The base word for 'unscathed' is 'scathe': 'scathe', *Merriam-Webster*, available at www.merriam-webster.com/dictionary/scathe.

305 But *turkey* the word in English is named for the wrong country: Cresswell (ed.), *Oxford Dictionary of Word Origins*, p. 461.

305 The linguist Mark Forsyth theorizes: Mark Forsyth, *The Etymologicon: A circular stroll through the hidden connections of the English language*, Australia: Allen & Unwin, 2011, pp. 39–41.

311 The other day I acquired some notoriety (again!): Shashi Tharoor (@ShashiTharoor), Post, X.com, 20 July 2022.

311 Bizarrely, seductive powers were once attributed: 'Anatomy of the Philtrum', National Human Genome Research Institute, available at elementsofmorphology.nih.gov/anatomy-philtrum.shtml.

311 It's called an 'aglet', a word that comes from the Latin acus: 'aglet', *Merriam-Webster*, available at www.merriam-webster.com/dictionary/aglet#word-history.

312 Many years ago, the then US Defence Secretary Donald Rumsfeld: David A. Graham, 'Rumsfeld's Knowns and Unknowns: The Intellectual History of a Quip', *New York Times*, 27 March 2014.

318 The company made up the word 'Velcro' from combining two French words: 'How Velcro Brand Fasteners Were Invented', *Velcro Blog*, 22 June 2018.

320 The drug, derived from morphine, was named 'heroin': 'History of Heroin', United Nations Office on Drugs and Crime, available at www.unodc.org/unodc/en/data-and-analysis/bulletin/bulletin_1953-01-01_2_page004.html.

323 His response: 'Language has always come from the people': 'Elon Musk wants to turn tweets into 'X's,' but changing language is not so simple', *CBS News*, 27 July 2023.

325 This goes back to 1801, when the famed British Admiral: Ayto, *Brewer's Dictionary of Phrase and Fable*, p. 1418.

325 Another British idiom is 'to read someone the riot act': Ella Morton, 'What It Actually Means to 'Read the Riot Act' to Someone', *Atlas Obscura,* 23 July 2015.

326 Even earlier in history lie the origins of the expression: Marvin Teban, *Dictionary of Idioms*, New York: Scholastic, 1996, p. 179.

326 The idiom is of nautical origin: when a sailor was feeling ill: Beavis and McCloskey, *Salty Dog Talk*, p. 90.

328 In his famous 1946 essay 'Politics and the English Language': George Orwell, 'Politics and the English Language', OrwellFoundation.org, 1946 [online facsimile], available at www.orwellfoundation.com/the-orwell-foundation/orwell/essays-and-other-works/politics-and-the-english-language.

328 A piece in *The Economist* deplored Harvard students: 'American universities face a reckoning over antisemitism', *The Economist*, 12 December 2023.

329 But first, to the basics: 'Convention on the Prevention and Punishment of the Crime of Genocide', available at www.un.org/en/genocideprevention/documents/atrocity-crimes.

330 *The Economist* warned writers to avoid: 'Euphemism and exaggeration are both dangers to language', *The Economist*, 23 November 2023.

332 'Both our public and our private use of language have thoroughly changed': Uwe Pörksen, *Plastic Words: The Tyranny of a Modular Language*, Jutta Mason and David Cayley (trs.), Pennsylvania: Pennsylvania State University, 1995, p. 72.

336 In his 1623 eulogy to Shakespeare: Sara Schliep, 'Small Latin and Less Greek: A Look at the Inkhorn Controversy', *Folger Shakespeare Library,* 5 April 2019.

336 As the scholar, archivist, and cataloguer at the Folger Shakespeare Library: Ibid.

338 The uncolonized Irish 'savages' lived 'beyond the pale': Ken Jennings,

'What "Beyond the Pale" Actually Means', *Conde Nast Traveller*, 10 October 2016.

338 **'Kidnap' initially described the act during the 1600s and 1700s:** 'kidnap', *The American Heritage Dictionary of the English Language*', [online facsimile], available at ahdictionary.com/word/search.html?q=kidnapping.

SECTION ELEVEN: LANGUAGE OF INCLUSION

346 **The goal of the Elimination of Harmful Language Initiative:** 'Elimination of Harmful Language Initiative', Stanford University, available at wsj.net/public/resources/documents/stanfordlanguage.pdf.

350 **a reader sent me a new Inclusive Language Guide:** 'Inclusive Language Guide', Oxfam GB, available at policy-practice.oxfam.org/resources/inclusive-language-guide-621487.

353 **one more entrant in the fray is the environmentalist group the Sierra Club's Equity Language Guide:** 'Language Equity Guide', Seirra Club, available at www.sierraclub.org/sites/default/files/sce-authors/u12332/Equity%20Language%20Guide%20Sierra%20Club%202021.pdf.

356 **A few months ago, India's Supreme Court took a step:** 'Handbook on Combating Gender Stereotypes', Supreme Court of India, available at main.sci.gov.in/pdf/LU/04092023_070741.pdf.

357 **Two years earlier, the then-attorney general K. K. Venugopal:** Abraham Thomas, 'Judges need gender sensitisation, says Attorney general KK Venugopal', *Hindustan Times*, 3 November 2009.

358 **Releasing the guide, Minister Smriti Irani declared:** 'WCD Minister Smriti Irani launches guide on gender-neutral communication', *Deccan Herald*, 28 November 2023.

SECTION TWELVE: MASTERS OF MIRTH

364 **The *Oxford English Dictionary*, for example, contains 1,756 quotations:** Robert McCrum, 'P. G. Wodehouse in OED', OED.com, August 2012.; 'cuppa', OED.com, available at www.oed.com/dictionary/cuppa_n?tab=factsheet#7762575.; 'fifty-fifty', OED.com, available at www.oed.com/dictionary/fifty-fifty_adv?tab=factsheet#4437086.

365 **In his 1927 book *Meet Mr Mulliner*:** Wodehouse, *Meet Mr Mulliner*, London: Herbert Jenkins, p. 191.

365 **At the age of twenty-two, he published a story:** Wodehouse, *Tales of St. Austin's*, London: A&C Black Ltd., 1923, p. 9.

365 **The same talent is evident in this description from *Blandings Castle*:** 'P. G. Wodehouse, Blandings Castle, London: Arrow Books, 2008, p. 86.

365 **'My Aunt Agatha wouldn't be on hand to snooter':** Wodehouse, *The Inimitable Jeeves*, London: Arrow Books, 2008, p. 32.

366 **'The generous blood of the Belphers boiled over':** Wodehouse, *Damsel in Distress*, New York: A. L. Burt Company, 1919, p. 73.

366 **Thus 'perspiration' took a new form in *The Inimitable Jeeves:*** Wodehouse, *The Inimitable Jeeves*, London: Arrow Books, 2008, p. 26.

366 **Robert McCrum theorizes that it was the atmosphere:** Robert McCrum, 'P. G. Wodehouse in OED', OED.com, August 2012.

367 **He had the uncanny gift of always coming up with the *mot juste*:** Wodehouse, *Jeeves in the Offing*, London: Penguin Books, 1960, p. 47.

369 **My hand-luggage on flights consists mainly of books:** 'book-bosomed', OED.

com, available at www.oed.com/dictionary/book-bosomed_adj.

SECTION THIRTEEN: BELLWETHERS

375 **And every child knows the story of Goldilocks:** 'The Search for Life', Nasa Exoplanet Exploration, available at exoplanets.nasa.gov/search-for-life/habitable-zone.

377 **'Nice' was originally a negative term:** Cresswell (ed.), *Oxford Dictionary of Word Origins*, p. 291.

380 **That venerable custodian of Anglophile wisdom, *The Economist*:** Martin Adams, Aryn Braun, Joel Budd, et al., '23 items of vital vocabulary you'll need to know in 2023', *The Economist*, 14 November 2022.

383 **OED senior editor Fiona McPherson says vax:** 'Vax' is Oxford English Dictionary's 2021 word of the year', *The Statesman*, 16 November 2021.

383 **Still, they could also have gone with *pandemic*:** Alison Flood, 'Oxford Dictionaries: 2020 has too many Words of the Year to name just one', *The Guardian*, 23 November 2020.

384 **The 2021 Oxford-winning word, vax, was first recorded in English:** 'Vax declared Oxford English Dictionary's word of the year', *BBC*, 1 November 2021.

389 **It was looked up more than 79,000 times this year:** 'Cambridge Dictionary names 'homer' Word of the Year 2022', Cam.ac.uk., available at www.cam.ac.uk/research/news/cambridge-dictionary-names-homer-word-of-the-year-2022.

390 **As Henry Shevlin, an AI ethicist at Cambridge University:** Thom Carter, 'How AI Inspired Cambridge Dictionary's Word of the Year 2023', *DIGIT News*, 15 November 2023.

390 **A US law firm's use of ChatGPT for legal research:** Kamya Pandey, 'US Lawyer Uses ChatGPT For Case Research, Ends Up Citing Fake Cases In Legal Brief', *Medianama*, 30 May 2023.

393 **Wisely, given its global readership, *The Economist* chose several words:** 'Our word of the year for 2023', *The Economist*, 7 December 2023.

394 **As *TechCrunch* wrote, 'Few would disagree that 2023':** Devin Coldewey, 'AI invades 'word of the year' lists at Oxford, Cambridge and Merriam-Webster', *TechCrunch*, 5 December 2023.

395 **the scholar Jean Twenge dubs them 'Polars': Cassey** Schwartz, 'Jean Twenge is ready to make you defend your generation again', *Washington Post*, 20 April 2023.

397 **James Emery White's blog:** James Emery White, 'Understanding the Gen-Z Vocabulary', Crosswalk.com, 20 August 2018.

398 **The Valentine's Day feature article about romance:** Noor Anand Chawla, 'Love Talks 2.0: A guide to current lingo that defines dating, relationships in 2023', *New Indian Express*, 10 February 2023.

400 **Kshama Bindu, a twenty-four-year-old sociology graduate:** Parmita Uniyal, 'Kshama Bindu marries herself; relationship expert on pros and cons of sologamy', *Hindustan Times*, 9 June 2022.

401 **Whereas the contemporary word 'unfriend':** 'unfriend', *Dictionaries of the Scots Language*, available at www.dsl.ac.uk/entry/snd/unfriend.

401 **When American politics at the beginning of the century:** 'The Word Of The Year: "Truthiness"', *CBS News*, 9 December 2006.

402 **In November 2023, the *New York Times* journalist:** Madison Malone Kirchner, 'Gen Alpha Is Here. Can You Understand Their Slang?', *New York Times*, 8 November 2023.

404 **'Potential participants in global communication'**: Paul Bruthiax, 'Contexts and Trends for English as a Global Language', in Humphrey Tonkin and Timothy G. Reagan (eds.), *Language in the Twenty-first Century: Selected Papers of the Millennial Conferences of the Center for Research and Documentation on World Language Problems, Held at the University of Hartford and Yale University*, Amsterdam: J. Benjamins Publishing Company, 2011, p. 12.

BIBLIOGRAPHY

BOOKS

Agee, Jon, *Go Hang a Salami! I'm a Lasagna Hog! and Other Palindromes*, New York: Farrar, Straus and Giroux, 1991.

———*Palindromania!*, New York: Farrar, Straus and Giroux, 2002.

———*Who Ordered the Jumbo Shrimp? and Other Oxymorons*, New York: Farrar, Straus and Giroux, 2002.

Alexander, James, *The World's Funniest Puns*, UK: Crombie Jardine, 2006.

Algeo, John and Pyles, Thomas, *The Origins and Development of the English Language*, Boston: Thomson Wadsworth, 2004.

———*British or American English?: A Handbook of Word and Grammar Patterns*, Cambridge: Cambridge University Press, 2006.

Allan, Keith, and Burridge, Kate, *Forbidden Words: Taboo and the Censoring of Language*, Cambridge: Cambridge University Press, 2006.

———*Euphemism and Dysphemism: Language Used as Sheild and Weapon*, New York: Oxford University Press, 1997.

An Alastair Reid Reader: Selected Prose and Poetry, New England: Middlebury College Press.

Assouline, Pierre, *Herge: The Man Who Created Tintin*, New York: Oxford University Press, 2011.

Ayto, John, *Bloomsbury Dictionary of Euphemisms: Over 3000 Ways to Avoid Being Rude or Giving Offence*, London: Bloomsbury, 2000.

———*Brewer's Dictionary of Phrase and Fable*, 17th edn., London: Weidenfeld and Nicholson, 2005.

———*Dictionary of Word Origins: The Histories of More Than 8,000 English Language Words*, New York: Arcade Publishing, 1993.

———*From the Horse's Mouth: Oxford Dictionary of English Idioms*, New York: Oxford University Press, 2009.

———*Oxford Dictionary of Slang*, Oxford: Oxford University Press, 2003.

———*Word Origins: The Hidden Histories of English Words from A to Z*, 2nd edn., London: A&C Black Publishers, 2005.

Baker, Rosalie, *In a Word: 750 Words and Their Fascinating Stories and Origins*, Chicago: Cricket Books, 2004.

Barfield, Owen, *History in English Words*, London: Lindisfarne Books, 2002.

Bartlett, Christopher, *The Flying Dictionary: Fascinating Explanations for Journalists, Aviation Buffs and Concerned Flyers*, United Kingdom: Open Hatch Books, 2008.

Battistella, Edwin L., *Bad Language: Are Some Words Better Than Others?*, New York: Oxford University Press, 2007.

Bealey, Frank, *The Blackwell Dictionary of Political Science*, Oxford: Blackwell Publishers, 1999.

Beard, Adrian, *The Language of Politics*, New York: Routledge, 2000.

Beavis, Bill and McCloskey, Richard G., *Salty Dog Talk: The Nautical Origins of Everyday Expressions*, New York: Sheridan House, 1995.

Bergerson, Howard W., *Palindromes and Anagrams*, New York: Dover Publications, 1973.

Bew, John, *Citizen Clem: A Biography of Atlee*, London: Quercus Publishing, 2016.

Black, Donald Chain, *Spoonerisms, Sycophants and Sops: A Celebration of Fascinating Facts about Words*, New York: Harper & Row, 1988.

Blake, Barry J., *Playing with Words: Humour in the English Language*, London: Equinox, 2007.

Blount, Thomas, *Glossographia, or, A dictionary interpreting all such hard words of whatsoever language now used in our refined English tongue with etymologies, definitions and historical observations on the same: also the terms of divinity, law, physick, mathematicks and other arts and sciences explicated*, 2nd edn., London: George Sawbridge, 1661.

Blumenfeld, Warren, *Pretty Ugly: More Oxymorons and Other Illogical Expressions That Make Absolute Sense*, New York: Perigee Books, 1989.

Borgmann, Dmitri A., *Beyond Language: Adventures in Word and Thought*, New York: Scribner, 1967.

Bowler, Peter, *The Superior Person's Book of Words*, London: Bloomsbury, 2002.

———*The Superior Person's Second Book of Words*, London: Bloomsbury, 2003.

———*The Superior Person's Third Book of Words*, London: Bloomsbury, 2004.

Brandreth, Gyles Daubeney, *The Joy of Lex: An Amazing and Amusing Z to A and A to Z of Words*, New York: Morrow, 1982.

———*Word Play: A Cornucopia of Puns, Anagrams, and Other Curiosities of the English Language*, London: Coronet, 2015.

Brett, Simon, *Seriously Funny, and Other Oxymorons*, London: Robinson, 2018.

Briggs-Goode, Amanda, *Printed Textile Design*, London: Laurence King, 2013.

Bronte, Geert, Fayaerts, Kurt, and Veale, Tony (eds.), *Cognitive Linguistics and Humour Research*, Vol. 26, Berlin: De Gruyter Mouton, 2015.

Bryson, Bill, *Made in America: An Informal History of the English Language in the United States*, New York: William Morrow, 1994.

———*The Mother Tongue: English and How it Got that Way*, New York: William Morrow Paperbacks, 2015.

Burridge, Kate, *Weeds in the Garden of Words: Further Observations on the Tangled History of the English Language*, Cambridge: Cambridge University Press, 2005.

Butterfield, Jeremy, Fowler, Henry Watson, *Fowler's Dictionary of Modern English Usage*, Oxford: Oxford University Press, 2015.

Byrne, Robert, Heifetz, Josefa, *Mrs. Byrne's Dictionary of Unusual, Obscure and Preposterous Words*, New Jersey: Citadel, 1980.

Cassidy, Daniel, *How the Irish Invented Slang: The Secret Language of the Crossroads*, San Francisco: AK Press, 2007.

Chatton, Barbara, *Using Poetry Across the Curriculum: Learning to Love Language*, 2nd edn., California: Libraries Unlimited, 2010.

Christie, Agatha, *Murder on the Orient Express: A Hercule Poirot Mystery*, Leicester: Ulverscroft, 2010.

Claiborne, Robert, *Loose Cannons, Red Herrings, and Other Lost Metaphors*, London: W. W. Norton, 2001.

Claridge, Claudia, *Hyperbole in English: A Corpus-based Study of Exaggeration*, Cambridge: Cambridge University Press, 2011.

Cock-Starkey, Claire, *The Real McCoy: And 149 Other Eponyms*, Oxford: Bodleian Library, 2018.

Cornelius, Judson K., *Literary Humour*, 2nd edn., Bangalore: Better Yourself Books, 2005.

Cousineau, Phil, *The Painted Word: A Treasure Chest of Remarkable Words and Their Origins*, New Jersey: Viva Editions, 2012.

———*Wordcatcher: An Odyssey into the World of Weird and Wonderful Words*, New Jersey: Viva Editions, 2010.

Cresswell, Julia (ed.), *Oxford Dictionary of Word Origins*, 2nd edn., London: Oxford University Press, 2009.

Crystal, David, *Spell It Out: The Singular Story of English Spelling*, London: Profile Books, 2013.

———*The Fight for English: How Language Pundits Ate, Shot, and Left*, Oxford: Oxford University Press, 2006.

———*The Story of English in 100 Words*, UK: Profile Books, 2011.

———*Txting: The Gr8 Deb8*, Oxford: Oxford University Press, 2009.

———*Words, Words, Words*, New York: Oxford University Press, 2007.

Curzan, Anne, Emmons, Kimberly (eds.), *Studies in the History of the English Language II: Unfolding Conversations*, Berlin: Mouton de Gruyter, 2004.

Danziger, Danny, McCrum, Mark, *The Watchamacallit: Those Everyday Objects You Just Can't Name (And Things You Think You Know About, but Don't*, New York: Hyperion, 2009.

Davies, Christopher, *Divided by a Common Language: A Guide to British and American English*, Boston: Houghton Mifflin, 2007.

Delbridge, Arthur, *The Macquarie Dictionary*, Australia: Macquarie Library, 1982.

Dickens, Charles, *Martin Chuzzlewit* Oxford: Oxford University Press, 1998.

———*The Pickwick Papers*, London: Chapman and Co., 1900.

———*Works of Charles Dickens: Oliver Twist Vol. I*, New York: James G. & Gregory, 1861.

Dickson, Paul, *Authorisms: Words Wrought by Writers*, New York: Bloomsbury, 2014.

———*Dickson's Word Treasury*, New York: John Wiley & Sons, 1992.

———*War Slang: American Fighting Words and Phrases from the Civil War to the War in Iraq*, New York: Bristol Park Books, 2007.

———*Words from the White House: Words and Phrases Coined or Popularized by America's Presidents*, New York: Walker and Company, 2013.

Douglas, Auriel, *Webster's New World Dictionary of Eponyms: Common Words from Proper Names*, New York: Webster's New World, 1990.

Dubosarky, Ursula, *The Word Snoop: A Wild and Witty Tour of the English Language!*, USA: Dial Books, 2009.

Dumas, Alexander, *The Three Musketeers*, 1998, [online facsimile], www.gutenberg.org/files/829/829-h/829-h.htm.

Durkin, Philip P., *Borrowed Words: A History of Loanwords in English*, Oxford: Oxford University Press, 1st edn., 2014.

Dydick, Richard, *Plain English for Lawyers*, 2nd edn., Durham: Carolina Academic Press, 1985.

Eble, Connie, *Slang and Sociability*, Chapel Hill: University of North Carolina Press, 1996.

Editors of the American Heritage Dictionaries, *Dictionary of Computer and Internet words: an A to Z guide to hardware, software, and cyberspace*, Boston: Houghton Mifflin, 2001.

———*More Word Histories and Mysteries: From Aardvark to Zombie*, New York: Houghton Mifflin Harcourt, 2006.

———*The American Heritage Guide to Contemporary Usage and Style*, New York: Houghton Mifflin, 2005.

———*Word Histories and Mysteries: From Abracadabra to Zeus*, New York: Houghton Mifflin Harcourt, 2004.

Eliot, T. S., *The Rock*, New York: Harcourt Brace, and Company, 1934.Elster, Charles Harrington, *There's a Word for It: A Grandiloquent Guide to Life*, California: Gallery Books, 2005.

Elster, Charles Harrington, *There's a Word for It: A Grandiloquent Guide to Life*, California: Gallery Books, 2005.

Embree, Mary, *The Birds and Bees of Words: A Guide to the Most Common Errors in Usage, Spelling, and Grammar*, New York: Allworth, 2010.

Erard, Michael, *Um...: Slips, Stumbles, and Verbal Blunders, and What They Mean*, New York: Random House, 2008.

Ernst, Margaret S., *Words: English Roots and how they Grow*, New York: Knopf, 1954.

Espy, Willard R., *An Almanac of Words at Play*, New York: C. N. Potter, 1975.

———*The Game of Words*, New York: Bramhall House, 1987.

———*Words at play: Palindromes, Riddles, Malapropisms, and other Wonderful Word Games*, New York: Tess Press, 1972.

Evans, Rod L., *The Artful Nuance: A Refined Guide to Imperfectly Understood Words in the English Language*, New York: Perigee, 2009.

———*Thingamajigs and Whatchamacallits: Unfamiliar Terms for Familiar Things*, New York: Perigee, 2011.

———*Tyrannosaurus Lex: The Marvelous Book of Palindromes, Anagrams, and Other Delightful and Outrageous Wordplay*, New York: Penguin, 2012.

Farr, Michael, *Tintin: The Complete Companion*, London: John Murray Publishers, 2001.

Feldman, Gilda, Feldman, Phil, *Acronym Soup: A Stirring Guide to Our Newest Word Form*, New York: William Morrow, 1994.

Flavell, Linda, and Flavell, Roger, *Dictionary of Idioms and Their Origins*, London: Kyle Cathie Ltd. 2001.

Forsyth, Mark, *The Elements of Eloquence: How to Turn the Perfect English Phrase*, UK: Icon Books, 2013.

———*The Etymologicon: A circular stroll through the hidden connections of the English language*, Australia: Allen & Unwin, 2011.

———*The Horologicon: A Day's Jaunt Through the Lost Words of the English Language*, London: Icon Books, 2012.

Funk, Charles Earle, *2107 Curious Word Origins, Sayings and Expressions*, New York: Galahad Books, 1993.

Funk, Charles Earle, and Funk, Charles Earle Jr, *Horsefeathers & Other Curious Words*, New York: Quill, 2002.

Funk, Wilfred, *Word Origins and Their Romantic Stories*, New York: Bell Publishing, 1978.

Garrison, Webb, *What's In A Word?*, Tennessee: Rutledge Hill Press, 2000.

———*Why You Say It: The Fascinating Stories Behind Over 600 Everyday Words and Phrases*, Tennessee: Rutledge Hill Press, 1992.

———*Word Nerds Unite! : The Fascinating Stories Behind 200 Words and Phrases*, Tennessee: Thomas Nelson, 2023.

Gass, William H., *A Temple of Texts*, New York: Alfred A. Knopf, 2006.

Geary, James, *The World in a Phrase: A Brief History of the Aphorism*, New York: Bloomsbury, 2005.

Gent, R. B., *The Yong Man's Gleanings*, London: John Beale, 1614.
Gillard, Joe, *The Little Book of Lost Words*, UK: Allen & Unwin, 2019.
Gooden, Philip, and Lewis, Peter, *Idiomantics: The Weird and Wonderful World of Popular Phrases*, New York & London: Bloomsbury Academic, 2013.
Gooden, Philip, *May We Borrow Your Language?: How English Steals Words from All Over the World*, London: Head of Zeus, 2017.
Gookin, Dan, and Gookin, Sandra Hardin, *Illustrated Computer Dictionary For Dummies*, New Jersey: John Wiley and Sons, 1998.
Grothe, Mardy, *Oxymoronica: Paradoxical Wit and Wisdom from History's Greatest Wordsmiths*, New York: Harper Collins, 2015.
Handey, Jack, *Deep Thoughts: Inspiration for the Uninspired*, Berkley: Berkley Books, 1992.
Hargraves, Orin, (ed.), *Mighty Fine Words and Smashing Expressions*, Oxford: Oxford University Press, 2003.
Haspelmath, Martin, Tadmor, Uri, *Loanwords in the World's Languages: A Comparative Handbook*, Berlin, New York: De Gruyter Mouton, 2009.
Hauptman, Don, *Cruel and Unusual Puns*, New York: Dell, 1991.
Hellweg, Paul, *The Insomniac's Dictionary: The Last Word on the Odd Word*, New York: Ballantine Books, 1986.
———*The Wordsworth Book of Intriguing Words*, Hertfordshire: Cumberland Books, 1993.
Hemingway, Ernest, *The Sun Also Rises*, USA: Scribner, 2021.
Hendrickson, Robert, *Facts on File Encyclopedia of Word Origins: Definitions and Origins of More Than 15,000 Words and Expressions*, 4th edn., New York: Infobase Publishing, 2008.,
Hitchings, Henry, *The Secret Life of Words: How English Became English*, New York: Farrar, Straus and Giroux, 2008.
Hoad, T. F., *The Concise Oxford Dictionary of English Etymology*, Oxford: Oxford University Press, 2002.
Holder, R. W., *How Not To Say What You Mean: A Dictionary of Euphemisms*, New York: Oxford University Press, 2007.
Homer, *Odyssey*, Alexander Pope (tr.), London: George Fell and Sons, 1906.
Hook, J. N., *The Grand Panjandrum: And 1,999 Other Rare, Useful, and Delightful Words and Expressions*, New York: MacMillan Publishing, 1980.
Hughes, Geoffrey, *An Encyclopedia of Swearing: The Social History of Oaths, Profanity, Foul Language, And Ethnic Slurs in the English-speaking World*, London & New York: Routledge, 2006.
Hughes, Patrick, *More on Oxymoron*, London: Cape, 1984.
Hunter, Samuel C., *The Dictionary of Anagrams*, London: Routledge & Kegan Paul, 1986.
Jack, Albert, *Red Herrings and White Elephants: The Origins of the Phrases We Use Every Day*, New York: Harper Collins, 2004.
Jarvie, Gordon, *Bloomsbury Dictionary of Idioms*, UK: A & C Black, 2009.
Jeans, Peter D., *Seafaring Lore and Legend*, Maine: International Marine/Ragged Mountain Press, 2007.
Jodrell, Richard Paul *Philology of the English Language*, London: John Bohn, 1820.
Jones, Paul Anthony, *The Accidental Dictionary: The Remarkable Twists and Turns of English Words*, New York: Pegasus Books, 2017.
———*The Cabinet of Linguistic Curiosities: A Yearbook of Forgotten Words*, Chicago: University of Chicago Press, 2019.

Joyce, James, *Ulysses*, Paris: Shakespeare and Company, 1922.
Jurafsky, Dan, *The Language of Food: A Linguist Reads the Menu*, New York: W. W. Norton & Company, 2014.
Kacirk, Jeffrey, *Altered English: Surprising Meanings of Familiar Words*, San Francisco: Pomegranate Books, 2002.
Katamba, Francis, *English Words*, UK: Routledge, 1994.
Kemp, Peter, *The Oxford Companion to Ships and the Sea*, Oxford: Oxford University Press, 2005.
Kirkpatrick, Andy, *World Englishes: Implications for International Communication and English Language Teaching*, Cambridge: Cambridge University Press, 2007.
Knowles, Elizabeth (ed.), *The Oxford Dictionary of Quotations*, 5th edn., Oxford: Oxford University Press, 1999.
Lear, Edward, *The Book of Nonsense*, London: F. Warne & Co., p.1.
Lederer, Richard, *Crazy Fractured English: Two Bestselling Books in One*, New York: Pocket Books, 2009.
———*The Play of Words: Fun & Games for Language Lovers*, New York: Pocket Books, 2010.
———*The Word Circus: A Letter Perfect Book*, Massachusetts: Merriam-Webster, 1998.
Leeming, Joseph, *Riddles, Riddles, Riddles: Enigmas and Anagrams, Puns and Puzzles, Quizzes and Conundrums!*, New York: Dover Publications, 2014.
Lewis, C. S., *Studies in Words*, New York: Harper Collins, 2013.
Liberman, Anatoly, *Take My Word for It: A Dictionary of English Idioms*, Minnesota: University of Minnesota Press, 2023.
———*Word Origins and How We Know Them: Etymology for Everyone*, New York: Oxford University Press, 2005.
Loewen, Nancy, *Talking Turkey and Other Clichés We Say*, Minnesota: Picture Window Books, 2011.
Luntz, Frank, *Words That Work: It's Not What You Say, It's What People Hear*, UK: Hachette Books, 2007.
Marchetta, Melina, *Finnikin of the Rock*, UK: Walker Books.
Marr, Alexander, *Logodaedalus: Word Histories of Ingenuity In Early Modern Europe*, Pennsylvania: University Of Pittsburgh Press, 2018.
Maxwell, Kerry, *Brave New Words: a Language Lover's Guide to the 21st Century*, London: Macmillan, 2014.
McCrum, Robert, Cran, William and MacNeil, Robert, *The Story of English*, London: Faber and Faber, 1992.
McKean, Erin, *Totally Weird and Wonderful Words*, New York: Oxford University Press, 2006.
McPhee, Nancy, *The Complete Book of Insults*, UK: Book Club Associates, 1981.
McWhorter, John, *Words on the Move: Why English Won't—and Can't—Sit Still (Like, Literally)*, New York: Henry Holt and Company, 2016.
Meller, Susan, and Elffers, Joost, *Textile Designs: Two Hundred Years of European and American Patterns for Printed Fabrics Organized by Motif, Style, Color, Layout, and Period*, New York: Harry N. Abrams, 1991.
Metcalf, Allan, *OK: The Improbable Story of America's Greatest Word*, Oxford: Oxford University Press, 2011.
———*Predicting New Words: The Secrets of Their Success*, Boston: Houghton Mifflin Company, 2002.
Michaelsen, O. V., *The Word Play Almanac*, New York: Sterling, 2002.

Minkova, Donka, *Alliteration and Sound Change in Early English*, UK: Cambridge University Press, 2003.

Moore, Christopher J., *In Other Words: A Language Lover's Guide to the Most Intriguing Words around the World*, London: Bloomsbury Publishing, 2009.

Morice, Dave, *The Dictionary of Wordplay*, New York: Teachers and Writers Collaborative, 2001.

Morris, Evan, *The Word Detective*, Chapel Hill, NC: Algonquin Books, 2000.

Mossman, Jennifer, *Acronyms, Initialisms & Abbreviations Dictionary*, Detroit: Gale Research, 1993.

Mugglestone, Lynda, *Lost for Words: The Hidden History of the Oxford English Dictionary*, London: Yale University Press, 2005.

———*The Oxford History of English*, Oxford: Oxford University Press, 2013.

Neruda, Pablo, *Memoirs*, Hardie St. Martin (tr.), London: Penguin Books, 1978.

Newby, Peter, *The Mammoth Book of Word Games*, London: Robinson, 1995.

Norman, Philip, *Your Walrus Hurt the One You Love: Malapropisms, Mispronunciations, and Linguistic Cock-ups*, London: Elm Tree Books, 1985.

Ó Muirithe, Diarmaid, *The Last Word: More Words We Use (And Don't Use)*, Dublin: Gill & Macmillan, 2013.

Orwell, George, 'Politics and the English Language', [online facsimile], 1946, available at www.orwellfoundation.com/the-orwell-foundation/orwell/essays-and-other-works/politics-and-the-english-language.

———*The Lion and the Unicorn: Socialism and the English Genius*, London: Penguin Books, 1982.

Ostler, Nicholas, *Empires of the Word: A Language History of the World*, New York: Harper Collins, 2005.

Palin, Michael, *A Sackful of Limericks*, New York: Random House, 2016.

Parrott, E. O., *The Penguin Book of Limericks*, New York: Viking, 1986.

Payack, Paul J. J., *A Million Words and Counting: How Global English is Rewriting the World*, New York: Citadel Press, 2012.

Pei, Mario, *The Story of the English Language*, Philadelphia: Lippincott, 1967.

Peters, Pam, *The Cambridge Guide to English Usage*, Cambridge: Cambridge University Press, 2011.

Pörksen, Uwe, *Plastic Words: The Tyranny of a Modular Language*, Jutta Mason and David Cayley (trs.), Pennsylvania: Pennsylvania State University, 1995.

Pournelle, Jerry, McKean, Erin, *1001 Computer Words You Need to Know*, New York: Oxford University Press, 2004.

Proceedings of the Thirty-ninth Indian Science Congress, Calcutta: Indian Science Congress Association, 1952.

Quinn, Arthur, *Figures of Speech: 60 Ways to Turn a Phrase*, California: Hermagoras Press, 1993.

Rayevsky, Kim, Rayevsky, Robert, *Antonyms, Synonyms, Homonyms*, New York: Holiday House, 2006.

Rheingold, Howard, *They Have a Word for It: A Lighthearted Lexicon of Untranslatable Words and Phrases*, New York: Sarabande Books, 2000.

Rice, Christiano Marilyn, *Words and Their Stories*, US: VOA Special English, 2012.

Rogers. John, (tr.), *1537 Matthew's Bible*, [online facsimile], available at English (1537) Matthews Bible Text: Free Download, Borrow, and Streaming: Internet Archive.

Rubin, Robert Alden, *Going to Hell in a Hen Basket: An Illustrated Dictionary of Modern Malapropisms*, New York: Flatiron Books, 2015.

Salny, Abbie F., *The Mensa Book of Words, Word Games, Puzzles & Oddities*, New York: Harper Collins, 1988.

Schoeser, Mary, *World Textiles: A Concise History*, London: Thames & Hudson, 2003.

Scholastic Inc., *The Scholastic Dictionary of Synonyms, Antonyms and Homonyms*, New York: Scholastic Inc., 2001.

Sedgwick, Fred, *Where Words Come From: A Dictionary of Word Origins*, London: Continuum International Publishing Group, 2009.

Shakespeare, William, *As You Like It*, [online facsimile], available at shakespeare.mit.edu/asyoulikeit/full.html.

———*Hamlet*, [online facsimile], available at shakespeare.mit.edu/hamlet/full.html.

———*Julius Caesar*, [online facsimile], available at shakespeare.mit.edu/julius_caesar/julius_caesar.3.2.html.

———*King John*, [online facsimile], available at shakespeare.mit.edu/john/full.html.

———*King Lear*, [online facsimile], available at shakespeare.mit.edu/lear/full.html.

———*The Merchant of Venice*, [online facsimile], available at shakespeare.mit.edu/merchant/full.html.

———*The Tempest*, [online facsimile], available at shakespeare.mit.edu/tempest/full.html.

———*Timon of Athens*, [online facsimile], [online facsimile], available at shakespeare.mit.edu/timon/full.html.

Sheridan, Richard Brinsley, *The Rivals*, New York: Thomas Y. Cromwell & Co., 1905.

Sherk, Bill, *500 Years of New Words*, Toronto: The Dundurn Group, 2004.

Skeat, Walter W., *The Concise Dictionary of English Etymology*, UK: Wordsworth Editions, 1993.

Smith, Logan Pearsall, *Reperusals and Recollections*, New York: Books for Libraries Press, 1968.

Stamper, Kory, *Word by Word: The Secret Life of Dictionaries*, New York: Pantheon Books, 2017.

Steinmetz, Sol, *Semantic Antics: How and Why Words Change Meaning*, New York: Random House Reference, 2008.

———*There's a Word for It: the Explosion of the American Language Since 1900*, New York: Harmony Books, 2010.

Storti, Craig, *Speaking of India: Bridging the Communication Gap When Working With Indians*, Boston: Intercultural Press, 2007.

Strunk, William, White, E. B., *The Elements of Style*, 4th edn., Boston: Allyn & Bacon, 2002.

Sullivan, Karen, *Mixed Metaphors: Their Use and Abuse*, London: Bloomsbury Academic, 2018.

Swift, Jonathan, *A Modest Proposal and Other Works (Webster's Thesaurus Edition)*, USA: Icon Classics.

———*Gulliver's Travels into Several Remote Nations of the World*, 1997 [online facsimile], www.gutenberg.org/files/829/829-h/829-h.htm.

Symons, Mitchell, *The Weird World of Words: A Guided Tour*, San Francisco: Zest Books, 2015.

Tan, Amy, *The Hundred Secret Senses*, London: Flamingo, 1995.

Tannen, Deborah, *You Just Don't Understand: Women and Men in Conversation*, New York: William Morrow, 2007.

Teban, Marvin, *Dictionary of Idioms*, New York: Scholastic, 1996.

———*Guppies in Tuxedos: Funny Eponyms*, New York: Harper Collins, 2008.

Thompson, Harry, *Tintin: Hergé and His Creation*, London: John Murray Press, 2011.

Tonkin, Humphrey, and Reagan, Timothy, *Language in the Twenty-first Century: Selected papers of the millennial conferences of the Center for Research and Documentation on World Language Problems, held at the University of Hartford and Yale University*, Philadelphia: John Benjamin's Publishing Co., 2003.

Thoreau, Henry D., *Walden: or, Life in the Woods*, Boston: Ticknor and Fields, 1854.

Train, John, *Remarkable Words with Astonishing Origins*, New York: Clarkson N. Potter, 1980.

Trevelyan, Charles E., *On Education of the People of India*, Paternoster-Row: Longman, Orme, Brown, Green, & Longmans, 1838.

Truss, Lynne, *Eats, Shoots and Leaves*, USA: Gotham Books, 2003.

Twain, Mark, *Life on the Mississippi*, Boston: James R. Osgood and Company, 1883.

———*The Adventures of Tom Sawyer, Chicago: The American Publishing Company, 1875.*

Twenge, Jean M., *Generations: The Real Differences Between Gen Z, Millennials, Gen X, Boomers, and Silents–and What They Mean for America's Future*, New York: Atria Books, 2023.

Usborne, Richard, *Plum Sauce: a P.G. Wodehouse Companion*, New York: Overlook Press, 2003.

Vries, Robert De, *The Tents of Wickedness*, USA: Little Brown & Company, 1959.

Wallraff, Barbara, *Word Fugitives: In Pursuit of Wanted Words*, New York: Harper Collins, 2006.

Webster, Merriam, *Webster's English Usage Guide*, Massachusetts: Federal Street Press, 2006.

Williams, John D., *Word Nerd: Dispatches from the Games, Grammar, and Geek Underground*, New York: Liveright, 2015.

Wilton, David, Brunetti, Ivan, *Word Myths: Debunking Linguistic Urban Legends*, New York: Oxford University Press, 2004.

Winchester, Simon, *The Meaning of Everything: The Story of the Oxford English Dictionary*, Oxford: Oxford University Press, 2018.

Wines, J. A., *Mondegreens: A Book of Mishearings*, London: Michael O'Mara Books, 2007.

Wodehouse, P. G., *Blandings Castle*, London: Arrow Books, 2008.

———*Damsel in Distress*, New York: A. L. Burt Company, 1919.

———*Ice in the Bedroom*, London: Pan Books Ltd., 1968.

———*Jeeves in the Offing*, London: Penguin Books, 1960.

———*Leave it to Psmith*, London: Penguin Books, 1923.

———*Meet Mr Mulliner*, London: Herbert Jenkins, 1927.

———*Tales of St. Austin's*, London: A&C Black Ltd., 1923.

———*The Code of Woosters*, New York: Vintage Books, 1975.

———*The Inimitable Jeeves*, London: Arrow Books, 2008.

Wolfram, Walt, Natalie, Schilling-Estes, *American English: Dialects and Variation*, Massachusetts: Blackwell, 2006.

Wright, Ernest Vincent, *Gadsby: A Story of Over 50,000 Words Without Using the Letter 'E'*, Los Angeles: Wetzel Publishing Co., 1939.

ESSAYS, CHAPTERS IN BOOKS, AND JOURNALS

'Apostrophe', in *University of Oxford Style Guide*, Oxford: Public Affairs Directorate, University of Oxford, 2014, p. 9.

Bruthiax, Paul, 'Contexts and Trends for English as a Global Language', in *Language in the Twenty-first Century: Selected Papers of the Millennial Conferences of the Center for Research and Documentation on World Language Problems, Held at the University of Hartford and Yale University*, Humphrey Tonkin and Timothy G. Reagan (eds.), Amsterdam: J. Benjamins Publishing Company, 2011.

Schüller-Zwierlein, André, Mangen, Anne, Kovač, Miha, and Wee, Adriaan van der, 'Why higher-level reading is important', *First Monday*, Vol. 27, No. 9–5, available at firstmonday.org/ojs/index.php/fm/article/download/12770/10709.

Skeat, Walter, 'XIII.-FOURTEENTH ADDRESS OF THE PRESIDENT, TO THE PHILOLOGICAL SOCIETY, DELIVERED AT THE ANNIVERSARY MEETING, FRIDAY, 21ST MAY', *Transactions of the Philological Society*, Vol 20, No. 1, November 1887.

Tolkien, J. R. R., *On Fairy Stories*, [online facsimile], 8 March 1939, available at On Fairy-Stories: J. R. R. Tolkien: Free Download, Borrow, and Streaming: Internet Archive.

NEWSPAPER ARTICLES AND ONLINE RESOURCES

'"Selfie" named by Oxford Dictionaries as word of 2013', *BBC*, 19 November 2013.

'abstain (n.)', Online Etymology Dictionary, available at www.etymonline.com/word/abstain.

'aglet', *Merriam-Webster*, available at www.merriam-webster.com/dictionary/aglet#word-history.

'Ahead of the Curve', TheIdioms.com, available at www.theidioms.com/ahead-of-the-curve.

'American universities face a reckoning over antisemitism', *The Economist*, 12 December 2023.

'Anatomy of the Philtrum', National Human Genome Research Institute, available at elementsofmorphology.nih.gov/anatomy-philtrum.shtml.

'apostrophe (n.1)', Online Etymology Dictionary, 30 August 2023, available at www.etymonline.com/word/apostrophe.

'Ashleigh Brilliant', AZQuotes.com, available at www.azquotes.com/quote/1264801.

'Blitzkrieg', History.com, 12 December 2022, available at www.history.com/topics/world-war-ii/blitzkrieg.

'Block That Metaphor!', *New Yorker*, 27 March 2000.

'Bob's Best Gags', *The Guardian*, 29 December 2023.

'book-bosomed', *Oxford English Dictionary*, available at www.oed.com/dictionary/book-bosomed_adj.

'Breakdown of expatriate population in the United Arab Emirates in 2018, by nationality', Statista.com, 12 September 2022, available at www.statista.com/statistics/984373/uae-expat-population-by-country-of-origin.

'cambric', *Merriam-Webster*, available at www.merriam-webster.com/dictionary/cambric#word-history.

'Cambridge Dictionary names 'homer' Word of the Year 2022', Cam.ac.uk., available at www.cam.ac.uk/research/news/cambridge-dictionary-names-homer-word-of-the-year-2022.

'camouflage', *Merriam-Webster*, available at www.merriam-webster.com/dictionary/camouflage#word-history.

'catachresis', *Merriam-Webster*, available at www.merriam-webster.com/dictionary/catachresis#word-history.

'clusterfist', *Oxford English Dictionary*, available at www.oed.com/search/dictionary/?scope=Entries&q=clusterfist.

'Convention on the Prevention and Punishment of the Crime of Genocide', available at www.un.org/en/genocideprevention/documents/atrocity-crimes.

'cuppa', *Oxford English Dictionary*, available at www.oed.com/dictionary/cuppa_n?tab=factsheet#7762575.

'Daniel Lawrence Whitney (Larry the Cable Guy)', AZQuotes.com, available at www.azquotes.com/quote/855155.

'David J. Henderhan', Goodreads.com, available at www.goodreads.com/quotes/441191-take-my-advice-i-m-not-using-it.

'Devang Thakkar, 'all good things must end', Devangthakkar.com, available at www.devangthakkar.com/wordle_archive.

'Dord: A Ghost Word', *Merriam-Webster*, available at www.merriam-webster.com/wordplay/dord-a-ghost-word.

'dysphemism (noun)', *Merriam-Webster*, available at www.merriam-webster.com/dictionary/dysphemism#word-history.

'Ecclesiastes 3', BibleHub.com, available at biblehub.com/nkjv/ecclesiastes/3.htm.

'Elimination of Harmful Language Initiative', Stanford University, available at https://s.wsj.net/public/resources/documents/stanfordlanguage.pdf.

'Elon Musk wants to turn tweets into 'X's,' but changing language is not so simple', *CBS News*, 27 July 2023.

'Emo Philips', AZQuotes.com, available at www.azquotes.com/quote/1178501.

'Euphemism and exaggeration are both dangers to language', *The Economist*, 23 November 2023.

'Exodus 20', *New King James Bible*, [online facsimile], available at biblehub.com/nkjv/exodus/20.htm.

'fifty-fifty', *Oxford English Dictionary*, available at www.oed.com/dictionary/fifty-fifty_adv?tab=factsheet#4437086.

'G20 invite by President sparks Bharat/India row', *Hindustan Times*, 6 September 2023.

'George Bernard Shaw called them 'uncouth bacilli': "The oul" apostrophe', *Irish Times*, 17 November 2008.

'Gingham History', The Stiff Collar, available www.thestiffcollar.com/blogs/the-collar-speaks/gingham-history.

'Gingham', *Britannica*, available at www.britannica.com/topic/gingham.

'Gross Beyond Words', CarpenterNYC.com, available at carpenternyc.com/thoughts/gross-beyond-words.

'Groucho Marx', Goodreads.com, available at www.goodreads.com/quotes/98968-she-got-her-looks-from-her-father-he-s-a-plastic.

'Handbook on Combating Gender Stereotypes', Supreme Court of India, available at main.sci.gov.in/pdf/LU/04092023_070741.pdf.

'History of Chevron Fabric', Cloth and Stitch, 22 October 2021.

'History of Heroin', United Nations Office on Drugs and Crime, available at www.unodc.org/unodc/en/data-and-analysis/bulletin/bulletin_1953-01-01_2_page004.html.

'History of Safari: How It All Began', Eyes on Africa.net, available at www.eyesonafrica.net/Articles/safari-history.htm.

'How a Mistake Gave Us the Word Cherry', *Merriam-Webster*, available at www.merriam-webster.com/wordplay/cherry-history-origin.

'How Velcro Brand Fasteners Were Invented', *Velcro Blog*, 22 June 2018.

'Inclusive Language Guide', Oxfam.org, available at policy-practice.oxfam.org/

resources/inclusive-language-guide-621487.

'ironclad (adj.)', *Online Etymology Dictionary*, available at www.etymonline.com/word/ironclad.

'jacuzzi', Online Etymology Dictionary, 30 August 2023, available at www.etymonline.com/word/Jacuzzi.

'John 18:38', BibleHub.com, available at biblehub.com/text/john/18-38.htm.

'kenning', Britannica, available at www.britannica.com/art/kenning.

'kidnap', *The American Heritage Dictionary of the English Language*', available at https://ahdictionary.com/word/search.html?q=kidnapping.

'Knife crime: St John Ambulance to teach teens to help stab victims', BBC News, 7 May 2021.

'Language Equity Guide', Seirra Club, available at www.sierraclub.org/sites/default/files/sce-authors/u12332/Equity%20Language%20Guide%20Sierra%20Club%20 2021.pdf.

'Lethologica: When a word's on the tip of your tongue', *BBC*, 8 February 2016.

'Lethologica', Bionity.com, available at www.bionity.com/en/encyclopedia/Lethologica.html.

'McDonald's fries the holy grail for potato farmers', *Capital Press*, 24 September 2009.

'Moiré', Online Etymology Dictionary, available at www.etymonline.com/word/moire.

'Morrison's sledge against Albanese over wages', *Sydney Morning Herald*, 11 May 2022.

'Mr Edison and the Bacteria', *Pall Mall Gazette*, 11 March 1889.

'Narendra Modi Anagrams', AnagramGenius.com, available at www.anagramgenius.com/archive/narendra-modi.htm.

'Noah Webster's Spelling Wins and Fails', *Merriam-Webster*, available at www.merriam-webster.com/grammar/noah-websters-spelling-wins-and-fails.

'Nooks and Crannies', *The Guardian*, available at www.theguardian.com/notesandqueries.

'Oscar Wilde', Goodreads.com, available at quoteinvestigator.com/2017/04/04/good-looks.

'Our word of the year for 2023', *The Economist*, 7 December 2023.

'P. G. Wodehouse', Goodreads.com, available at www.goodreads.com/quotes/142514-she-had-more-curves-than-a-scenic-railway.

'Political Notes: Chairman Daley's Maxims', *TIME*, 18 July 1969.

'poll (n.)', Online Etymology Dictionary, available at https://www.etymonline.com/word/poll.

'Poutine: How Quebec's flagship dish is serving up controversy', *Malay Mail*, 9 March 2022.

'Programming Patterns: The Story of the Jacquard Loom', Museum of Science and Industry, 25 June 2019.

'quomodocunquizing', *Oxford English Dictionary*, available at www.oed.com/search/dictionary/?scope=Entries&q=quomodocunquizing.

'Rearranging Narendra Modi Doesn't Give You Rare Diamond', SMHoaxSlayer.com, 1 June 2016.

'recount (verb)', *Oxford English Dictionary*, available at www.oed.com/dictionary/recount.

'Robert Gallagher', Goodreads.com, available at www.goodreads.com/quotes/78574-change-is-inevitable———except-from-a-vending-machine

'Rodney Dangerfield', Goodreads.com, available at www.goodreads.com/quotes/18223-my-wife-and-i-were-happy-for-twenty-years-then.

'Rudolf Diesel', *Britannica*, available at www.britannica.com/biography/Rudolf-Diesel.

'Rumi (Jalal ad-Din Muhammad ar-Rumi)', Goodreads.com, available at www.goodreads.com/quotes/9825163-if-you-want-the-moon-do-not-hide-from-the_.

'Rumi (Jalal ad-Din Muhammad ar-Rumi)', Goodreads.com, available at www.goodreads.com/author/quotes/875661.Rumi_Jalal_ad_Din_Muhammad_ar_Rumi_.

'scathe', *Merriam-Webster*, available at www.merriam-webster.com/dictionary/scathe.

'Sep 9, 1947 CE: World's First Computer Bug', *National Geographic*, 19 October 2023.

'Steven Wright', Goodreads.com, available at www.goodreads.com/quotes/141045-if-at-first-you-don-t-succeed-then-skydiving-definitely-isn-t.

'Subeditor battled to save punctuation's endangered species', *Sydney Morning Herald*, 7 May 2021.

'The Hilarious History of OK', *Merriam-Webster*, available www.merriam-webster.com/wordplay/the-hilarious-history-of-ok-okay.

'The Hirstute History of Horror', *Merriam-Webster*, available at www.merriam-webster.com/wordplay/the-hirsute-history-of-horror.

'The History behind 8 Halloween Words', *Merriam-Webster*, available at www.merriam-webster.com/wordplay/the-history-behind-8-halloween-words/ghoul.

'The History of Herringbone', *K and A*, 2 February 2017.

'The History of the Blinds', Agostini Museum of the Window, available at www.museoagostini.com/en/blinds-history.

'The History of the Dance Leotard', *Bloch World*, 15 October 2019.

'The Invention of the Vaccum-cleaner, from Horse-drawn to High-tech', ScienceMuseum.org, 3 April 2020, available at www.sciencemuseum.org.uk/objects-and-stories/everyday-wonders/invention-vacuum-cleaner.

'The Opposite of 'Incorrigible', *Merriam-Webster*, available at www.merriam-webster.com/wordplay/why-do-we-use-incorrigible-and-not-corrigible.

'The pedants' pedant: why the Apostrophe Protection Society has closed in disgust', *The Guardian*, 2 December 2019.

'The Vocabularist: Where did the word 'manifesto' come from?', *BBC*, 16 April 2015.

'The Word of The Year: 'Truthiness', *CBS News*, 9 December 2006.

'Tom Marvolo Riddle', CVJLang.com, available at www.cjvlang.com/Hpotter/wordplay/riddle.html.

'Transcript of Chairman Bernanke's Press Conference', 19 June 2013, available at www.federalreserve.gov/mediacenter/files/fomcpresconf20130619.pdf.

'Transcript: US Treasury Secretary Janet Yellen on the next steps for Russia sanctions and 'friend-shoring' supply chains', *New Atlanticist*, 13 April 2022.

'unfriend', *Dictionaries of the Scots Language*, available at www.dsl.ac.uk/entry/snd/unfriend.

'US House easily passes bill to harden sanctions on Iranian oil', *Reuters*, 4 November 2023.

'Vax declared Oxford English Dictionary's word of the year', *BBC*, 1 November 2021.

'Vax' is Oxford English Dictionary's 2021 word of the year', *The Statesman*, 16 November 2021.

'Vladimir Nabokov', Goodreads.com, available at www.goodreads.com/quotes/309633-toska---noun-t--sk---russian-word-roughly-translated-as.

'WCD Minister Smriti Irani launches guide on gender-neutral communication', *Deccan Herald*, 28 November 2023.

'We Shall Fight on the Beaches', InternationalChurchillSociety.com, available at winstonchurchill.org/resources/speeches/1940-the-finest-hour/we-shall-fight-on-the-beaches.

'When Did 'Campaign' Become Political?', *Merriam-Webster*, available at www.merriam-webster.com/wordplay/when-did-campaign-become-political.

'Where does the word Dracula come from?', Dictionary.com, available at www.dictionary.com/e/dracula-fish.

'Why are Members of Parliament not allowed to call each other liars in the House of Commons', *The Guardian*, 1 January 2011.

'Why Turkey is now 'Türkiye', and why that matters', *TRT World*, available at www.trtworld.com/magazine/why-turkey-is-now-t%C3%BCrkiye-and-why-that-matters-52602.

'Wise and Otherwise', *Saint John Daily News*, 30 November 1880.

'Words Came In, Marked for Death', *New Yorker*, 23 April 2012.

'Yogi Berra Quotes: Baseball legend's memorable saying', *BBC*, 23 September 2015.

'zombie (n.)', *Online Etymology Dictionary*, available at www.etymonline.com/word/zombie.

Abott, Geoffrey, 'Lynching', *Britannica*, 16 February 2024.

Adams, Martin, Braun, Aryn, Budd, Joel, Standage, Tom, and Vaitheeswaran, Vijay, '23 items of vital vocabulary you'll need to know in 2023', *The Economist*, 14 November 2022.

Anderson, Anna Elise, 'Batik 101: Where It Comes From, How It's Made, and How to Use It in an Interior', *Architectural Digest*, 24 July 2023.

———'Brocade Fabric, Explained', *Architectural Digest*, 27 October 2023.

Archana, KC, 'Tintin's Captain Haddock Borrows Tharoor's 'Exasperating Farrago Of Distortions' In Epic Meme', *India Times*, 6 October 2018.

Archer, Sarah, 'This Throwback Fabric Is Back in Major Way', *Elle Décor*, 5 February 2022.

Astle, David, 'To zee or not to zee? Why we're not amused about the King's English', *Sydney Morning Herald*, 7 December 2022.

Atwood, Margaret, 'Why Wattpad Works', *The Guardian*, 6 July 2012.

Babe and the Blue Ox, retold by S. E. Schlosser, available at ww.americanfolklore.net/babe-the-blue-ox.

Baillargeon, Zoe, 'How the Internet Changed the Meaning of 'Mamihlapinatapai', *Atlas Obscura*, 11 August 2017.

Barrett, Claire, 'Can One Trace the Phrase 'The Whole Nine Yards' to WWII? Kind of…', Historynet.com, 7 August 2021, available at www.historynet.com/can-one-trace-the-phrase-the-whole-nine-yards-to-wwii-kind-of.

Barry, Dave, 'Making Model Misconception', *The Washington Post*, 11 October 1986.

Beck, Katherine, 'Why people in the US once called sauerkraut liberty cabbage', *Tasting Table*, 27 September 2022, available at www.tastingtable.com/1027647/why-people-in-the-us-once-called-sauerkraut-liberty-cabbage.

Bekhard, Joobin, 'The "Cutesy" Indian Fabric That Changed History', The Print, 30 April 2020.

Bletchly, Rachael, 'The most hilarious typos, spelling mistakes and misprints - some even on a biblical scale', *Mirror*, 21 October 2015.

Bologna, Caroline, 'Here's Why We Say "Pushing The Envelope"', Huffington Post, 24 July 2018.

Carroll, Lewis, *To Miss Vera Beringer*, AllPoetry.com, available at allpoetry.com/poem/14327811-To-Miss-Vera-Beringer-by-Lewis-Carroll.

Carter, Thom, 'How AI Inspired Cambridge Dictionary's Word of the Year 2023',

DIGIT News, 15 November 2023.
Casagrande, June, 'A Word, Please: 'Moist' and other words people don't like', *Los Angeles Times*, 5 January 2023.
Cave, Damien, 'The 'Hard Yakka' of Defining Australian English's Many Quirks', *New York Times*, 19 June 2022.
Charles III, 'A message from The King to the Governor of Victoria regarding the ongoing flood emergency in Victoria', Royal.uk, 11 November 2022, available at www.royal.uk/message-his-majesty-king-governor-victoria-regarding-floods.
Chawla, Noor Anand, 'Love Talks 2.0: A guide to current lingo that defines dating, relationships in 2023', *New Indian Express*, 10 February 2023.
Clark, Mitchell, 'Twitter suspends Wordle-ruining bot', TheVerge.com, 25 January 2022.
Clark, Sean, 'The Wrapped: Re-united Nations', *The Guardian*, 9 June 2004.
Clarkes, Ella, 'History of Damask', Schumacher, 23 October 2022.
Clauter, Nancy E., 'Oboe and Music Theory', Teaching Philosophy, available at www.uky.edu/~oboenan/teach.htm.
Coldewey, Devin, 'AI invades 'word of the year' lists at Oxford, Cambridge and Merriam-Webster', *TechCrunch*, 5 December 2023.
Coleridge, Samuel Taylor, *Rime of the Ancient Mariner*, Poets.org., available at poets.org/poem/rime-ancient-mariner.
Cummings, E. E., *somewhere I have never travelled, gladly beyond*, Poets.org, available at poets.org/poem/somewhere-i-have-never-travelledgladly-beyond.
Daniyal, Shoaib, 'Why Jinnah objected to the name "India"', *Scroll.in*, 19 June 2018.
Daugherty, Greg, 'Teddy Roosevelt's Bold (But Doomed) Battle to Change American Spelling', History.com,4 September 2018.
Delvin, Thomas Moore, '12 Political Word Origins That Can Help You Understand the Government', *Babel*, 28 October 2020.
Dowd, Maureen, 'A.I.: Actually Insipid Until It's Actively Insidious', *New York Times*, 28 January 2023.
Engelbrecht, Cora '"Finlandization" of Ukraine is part of the diplomatic discourse. But what does that mean?', *New York Times*, 8 February 2022.
Ewbank, Annie, 'How Orange (the fruit) inspired Orange the colour', *Atlas Obscura*, 1 March 2018.
Fisher, Richard, 'Why we need new words for life in the Anthropocene', *BBC*, 26 January 2023.
Flood, Alison, 'Oxford Dictionaries: 2020 has too many Words of the Year to name just one', *The Guardian*, 23 November 2020.
Frost, Robert, *Acquainted with the Night*, Poets.org., poets.org/poem/acquainted-night.
Gardner, Martin, 'A-Symmetry', *New York Review*, 3 December 1992.
Garsd, Jasmine, 'Saudade: An Untranslatable, Undeniably Potent Word', *NPR*, 8 January 2015.
Geduld, Marcus, 'Can you write a sentence without using a or e', Quora, available at www.quora.com/Can-you-write-a-sentence-without-using-a-or-e.
Geof, 'The Best Archie Bunker Quotes Of All Time', 20 May 2020, available at www.archiefoundationhome.org.uk/money/archie-bunker-quotes.
Goldfarb, Kara, 'Keelhauling: Inside The Deranged Torture Method Used To Keep Sailors In Line', John Kuroski (ed.), All That's Interesting, 31 October 2022.
Graham, David A., 'Rumsfeld's Knowns and Unknowns: The Intellectual History of a Quip', *New York Times*, 27 March 2014.
Gugliotta, Guy, 'Fallacious Full Disclosure', *Washington Post*, 16 April 1992.
Harrison, Lawrence, 'Searching for Malaphors', *Washington Post*, 6 August 1976.

Hemmings, Jay, 'The German U-boats of WWII', War History Online, 12 February 2019, available at www.warhistoryonline.com/world-war-ii/the-german-u-boats-of-wwii.html.

Herbert, Bob, 'Behind the Curtain', *New York Times*, 27 November 2007.

Jennings, Ken, 'What "Beyond the Pale" Actually Means', *Conde Nast Traveller*, 10 October 2016.

Jones, Megan, '16 of the Most Famous Malapropism Examples', *Readers Digest*, 9 May 2023.

Jones, Paul Anthony, 'When Theodore Roosevelt Tried to Reform the English Language', *Mental Floss*, 3 November 2016.

Kirchner, Madison Malone, 'Gen Alpha Is Here. Can You Understand Their Slang?', *New York Times*, 8 November 2023.

Kundu, Rhik, 'How did Mayday come to be used as a distress call?', *Mint Lounge*, 26 July 2019.

Kuriakose, Ronnie, '"Farrago"-spurred Penguin adds "Tharoorosaurus" to its flamboyant book mart!', *On Manorama*, 7 August 2020.

Laws, Roz, 'Funniest phrases from The Apprentice's Gary Poulton', *Birmingham Mail*, 26 November 2015.

Lem, Elaine, 'All About British Marmalade', *The Spruce Eats*, 29 August 2019.

Leonhardt, David, 'A Stimulus With Merit, and Misses Too', *New York Times*, 27 January 2009.

Lynch, Jack, 'Ghost Words and Mountweazels', *Lapham's Quarterly*, 23 February 2016.

Malanowski, Jamie, 'The Brief History of the Ferris Wheel', *Smithsonian Magazine*, June 2015.

Mallaly, Una 'Up to 90: The best Irish words and phrases', *Irish Times*, 29 July 2017.

Martin, Gary, 'Over a Barrel', Phrases.org, available at www.phrases.org.uk/meanings/over-a-barrel.html.

McCrum, Robert, 'P. G. Wodehouse in OED', *Oxford English Dictionary*, August 2012, available at www.oed.com/discover/pg-wodehouse-in-the-oed.

McDaniel, Justine, 'From 'amirite' to 'zonkey,' new words join the Scrabble dictionary', *Washington Post*, 17 November 2022.

McGrath, Charles, 'Death-Knell. Or Death Knell', *New York Times*, 7 October 2007.

Mercer, Leigh, *A Dozes, a Gross, and a Score*, YourDailyPoem.org, available at www.yourdailypoem.com/listpoem.jsp?poem_id=4294.

Morton, Ella, 'What It Actually Means to 'Read the Riot Act' to Someone', *Atlas Obscura,* 23 July 2015.

Mutsaka, Farai, 'It's a nightmare: Zimbabwe struggles with hyperinflation', *AP News*, 10 October 2019.

Nath, Dipanita, 'Why are Russians using the letter Z to show support for the war in Ukraine', *Indian Express*, 14 March.

Nelson, Ethan, 'The History of Morse Code', DailyDabble.com, 1 October 2024.

Neuman, Scot, 'Scrabble Association Bans Racial, Ethnic Slurs From Its Official Word List', *NPR*, 8 July 2020.

Nicoll, James, 'About the Purity of the English Language T-shirts', *James Nicoll Reviews*, 7 November 2014.

Nordist, Richard, 'Mixed Metaphor', ThoughtCo.com, 6 June 2019, available at www.thoughtco.com/what-is-a-mixed-metaphor-1691395.

Nowak, Claire, 'The Real Reason Some English Words Have Silent Letters', Readers Digest, 19 July 2021.

O'Dell, Ben, 'Kangaroo Words' in *The American Magazine*, reprinted in *Reader's Digest*, 1956.

Orkent, Arika, 'Typos, tricks and misprints', Sally Davies (ed.), Aeon.com, 26 July 2021, available at aeon.co/essays/why-is-the-english-spelling-system-so-weird-and-inconsistent.

Pandey, Kamya, 'US Lawyer Uses ChatGPT For Case Research, Ends Up Citing Fake Cases In Legal Brief', *Medianama*, 30 May 2023.

Panneerselvan, A. S., 'Is artificial intelligence fuelling natural stupidity?', *The Hindu*, 10 July 2017.

Philips, Emo, 'The best God joke ever - and it's mine!', *The Guardian*, 29 September 2005.

Pirosh, Robert, 'I Like Words', LettersOfNote.com, 13 March 2012, available at lettersofnote.com/2012/03/13/i-like-words.

Pope, Alexander, *The Rape of the Lock: Canto III*, available at www.poetryfoundation.org/poems/44908/the-rape-of-the-lock-canto-3.

Ribbans, Elisabeth, 'Typo negative: the best and worst of Grauniad mistakes over 200 years', *The Guardian*, 12 May 2021.

Robson, David, 'There are really 50 Eskimo words for "snow"', *Washington Post*, 14 January 2013.

Sayed, Faraan, 'Surprising Facts about Arabic Language', British Council, 18 December 2015.

Sayed, Nida, 'Hitting Rs 140 per kg, tomatoes become budgetary hot potato', *Times of India*, 17 July 2023.

Schliep, Sara, 'Small Latin and Less Greek: A Look at the Inkhorn Controversy', *Folger Shakespeare Library*, 5 April 2019.

Schwartz, Cassey, 'Jean Twenge is ready to make you defend your generation again', *Washington Post*, 20 April 2023.

Shaffinalli, 'List of Folk Etymologies in English', *Lists of Everything*, 6 April 2011.

Sharp, Nathan, 'The Sopranos: The 10 Funniest Misquotes Of The Series, Ranked', ScreenRant.com, 10 August 2021.

Simonian, Sona, 'Palindrome Poetry', *Writer's Block Magazine*, 5 November 2019.

Smith, Olive, 'French kiss, Chinese whispers, Dutch courage meanings: The origins of common geographic idioms', *Sydney Morning Herald*, 1 October 2018.

Sommerlad, Joe, 'Scrabble at 70: How an out-of-work architect devised the phenomenally popular word game', *Independent UK*, 13 December 2018.

———*Songs (V)*, Poets.org, available at poets.org/poem/songs-v.

SRI International, '75 Years of Innovation: The computer mouse', *The Dish*, 7 May 2020.

Sterbenz, Christina, 'The 6 English Words Longer Than Antidisestablishmentarianism', *Business India Insider*, 20 September 2013.

Stroud, Sarah and Svirsky, Larisa, 'Weakness of Will', *The Stanford Encyclopedia of Philosophy* (Winter 2021 Edition), Edward N. Zalta (ed.), available at plato.stanford.edu/archives/win2021/entries/weakness-will.

Temple, Emily, 'A Selection of Virginia Woolf's Most Savage Insults', *Literary Hub*, 12 October 2017.

Tennyson, Alfred, *Enoch Arden*, Farrinford.co.uk, available at farringford.co.uk/history/tennyson/poems/enoch-arden.

Thapar, Karan, 'The mystery of the English language', *Hindustan Times*, 6 November 2021.

Tharoor, Shashi (@ShashiTharoor), Post, X.com, 10 October 2018.

———Post, X.com, 20 July 2022.
———Post, X.com, 4 October 2021.
———Post, X.com, 8 May 2017.
The Cultural Tutor (@culturaltutor), Post, X.com, 8 November 2022.
Thomas, Abraham, 'Judges need gender sensitisation, says Attorney general KK Venugopal', *Hindustan Times*, 3 November 2009.
Timmins, Beth, 'Toblerone: Swiss rules mean chocolate bar to drop Matterhorn from packaging', *BBC*, 6 March 2023.
Trenor, John J. D., *New York Times*, 7 December 1913.
Uniyal, Parmita, 'Kshama Bindu marries herself; relationship expert on pros and cons of sologamy', *Hindustan Times*, 9 June 2022.
Victor, Daniel, 'Wordle Is a Love Story', *New York Times*, 3 January 2022.
Voorhees, Danton, 'There Was Once a Man from Nantucket', *Princeton Tiger*, 1902.
White, James Emery, 'Understanding the Gen-Z Vocabulary', Crosswalk.com, 20 August 2018.

LEGAL CITATIONS

State of Madras vs V.G. Row. Union Of India & State, AIR (1952) SC 196.